T0363642

Praise for Racha

'Johns draws readers in with her richly complex characters.' —*Daily Telegraph* on *Just One Wish*

'Polished writing, and great dialogue drive this story forward. The perfectly structured plot holds plenty of surprises, but it's the beautifully crafted characters that are the glue in this wonderful novel ... Utterly delightful.' —*Better Reading* on *Just One Wish*

'If you like your chick-lit with a dash of intelligent social commentary, *Just One Wish* is the perfect summer read ... sparklingly funny, quirky and totally of this moment' —*Herald Sun*

'Johns knows how to weave the experiences of different generations of women together, with nuance and sensitivity, understanding how competing contexts shape women's choices ... *Just One Wish* will make you look at the women in your own life and wonder what stories they haven't told.' —*Mamamia*

'Heart-warming and compassionate ... Any book lover interested in life's emotional complexities and in the events that define and alter us will be engrossed in *Lost Without You*.' —*Better Reading*

'Full of heartache and joy with a twist that keeps the pages turning ... *The Greatest Gift* will appeal to fans of Jojo Moyes and Monica McInerney.' —*Australian Books + Publishing*

'Heartbreaking and heartwarming in equal parts, Rachael Johns' *The Greatest Gift* takes readers on a rollercoaster ride

of emotions. My advice? Make sure you have tissues handy!'
—Lisa Ireland, author of *The Shape Of Us*

'Rachael Johns has done it again, writing a book that you want to devour in one sitting, and then turn back to the first page to savour it all over again. I loved the characters of Harper and Jasper; their stories made me laugh and cry, and ache and cheer and ultimately reflect on all the many facets of that extraordinary journey called motherhood.' —Natasha Lester, author of *A Kiss From Mr Fitzgerald*, on *The Greatest Gift*

'A beautiful story of love and loss, heartbreak and hope—this is Rachael Johns at her very finest. With achingly endearing characters and a storyline that packs a punch, *The Greatest Gift* will make your heart swell as you reach for the tissues and leave you smiling when you turn the final pages. Told with warmth, empathy and wisdom, it's a book that will appeal to everyone who has laid plans for their life and discovered that life is something that can't be controlled and that even if you think you have it all worked out, you never know what's around the corner. My favourite Rachael Johns by a country mile.' —Tess Woods, author of *Love At First Flight*

'Fans of emotional, issue driven women's fiction will welcome Johns' US women's fiction debut.' —*Booklist* on *The Art of Keeping Secrets*

'... a compelling and poignant story of dark secrets and turbulent relationships ... I fell completely in love with the well-drawn characters of Flick, Emma and Neve. They were funny and flawed and filled with the kind of raw vulnerability that makes your heart ache for them.' —Nicola Moriarty, bestselling author of *The Fifth Letter*, on *The Art of Keeping Secrets*

'Written with compassion and real insight, *The Art Of Keeping Secrets* peeks inside the lives of three ordinary women and the surprising secrets they live with. Utterly absorbing and wonderfully written, Johns explores what secrets can do to a relationship, and pulls apart the notion that some secrets are best kept. It is that gripping novel that, once started, will not allow you to do anything else until the final secret has been revealed.' —Sally Hepworth, bestselling author of *The Secrets Of Midwives*

'A fascinating and deeply moving tale of friendship, family and of course—secrets. These characters will latch onto your heart and refuse to let it go.' —*USA Today* bestselling author Kelly Rimmer on *The Art of Keeping Secrets*

'Rachael Johns writes with warmth and heart, her easy, fluent style revealing an emotional intelligence and firm embrace of the things in life that matter, like female friendship.' —*The Age* on *Lost Without You*

Rachael Johns is an English teacher by trade, a mum 24/7, a Diet Coke addict, a cat lover and chronic arachnophobe. She is also the bestselling, ABIA-winning author of *The Patterson Girls* and a number of other romance and women's fiction books including *The Art of Keeping Secrets*, *The Greatest Gift*, *Lost Without You*, *Just One Wish*, *Something to Talk About* and *Flying the Nest*. Rachael rarely sleeps, never irons and loves nothing more than sitting in bed with her laptop and imagining her own stories. She is currently Australia's leading writer of contemporary relationship stories around women's issues, a genre she has coined 'life-lit'.

Rachael lives in the Swan Valley with her hyperactive husband, three mostly gorgeous heroes-in-training, two ravenous cats, a cantankerous bird and a very badly behaved dog.

Rachael loves to hear from readers and can be contacted via her website rachaeljohns.com. She is also on Facebook and Instagram.

Also by Rachael Johns:

Man Drought
Talk of the Town

The Hope Junction novels
Jilted
The Road to Hope

The Bunyip Bay novels
Outback Dreams
Outback Blaze
Outback Ghost
Outback Sisters

The Kissing Season (e-novella)
The Next Season (e-novella)

Secret Confessions Down and Dusty: Casey (e-novella)

The Patterson Girls
The Art of Keeping Secrets
The Greatest Gift
Lost Without You
Just One Wish
Flying The Nest
How To Mend A Broken Heart

SOMETHING
TO TALK
About

RACHAEL
JOHNS

mira

First Published 2020
Second Australian Paperback Edition 2021
ISBN 9781867225386

SOMETHING TO TALK ABOUT
© 2020 by Rachael Johns
Australian Copyright 2020
New Zealand Copyright 2020

This is a work of fiction. Names, characters, places, and incidents are either the product of the author's imagination or are used fictitiously, and any resemblance to actual persons, living or dead, business establishments, events, or locales is entirely coincidental.

Published by
Mira
An imprint of Harlequin Enterprises (Australia) Pty Limited (ABN 47 001 180 918), a subsidiary of HarperCollins Publishers Australia Pty Limited (ABN 36 009 913 517)
Level 13, 201 Elizabeth St
SYDNEY NSW 2000
AUSTRALIA

® and TM (apart from those relating to FSC®) are trademarks of Harlequin Enterprises (Australia) Pty Limited or its corporate affiliates. Trademarks indicated with ® are registered in Australia, New Zealand and in other countries.

A catalogue record for this book is available from the National Library of Australia
www.librariesaustralia.nla.gov.au

Printed and bound in Australia by McPherson's Printing Group

MIX
Paper from responsible sources
FSC® C001695

For Lorreen—one of the best bosses I've ever had and a real-life, one-armed heroine! If the character of Tabitha is even half the woman you are, I've done my job as a writer.
And to Peta—who was my very first reader for my first book, Jilted, *and gave me the idea for this book! Keep 'em coming. xx*

The nice part about living in a small town is that when you don't know what you are doing ... someone else does!

—Anon

Chapter One

Welcome to Walsh ~ Population 1381

As Fergus McWilliams drove into his new life he wondered if his arrival meant the population was now 1382. He turned to look at the cat sitting resentfully in her carry box on the passenger seat.

'Does that include animals, do you think?'

Mrs Norris gave him a look of disdain and then turned around so he was looking at her fluffy tortoiseshell butt.

'I guess not. The animals down here probably outnumber the people a hundred to one if the cows in the paddock we just passed are anything to go by. And what happens when someone is born or dies? How often do you think that sign gets updated?'

Judging by the faded colour and the way the paint flaked at the edges, probably not that often.

He shook his head as he realised that not only was he talking to a cat, but also asking her the kinds of questions the kids in his classes would ask. That's what happened when you spent the majority of your time with children: you started thinking like them. Then again, that was probably a good thing—kids, he'd decided, were far better humans than their adult counterparts.

1

The advertisement for a Year 3 and 4 teacher at the small primary school in the dairy farming community of Walsh, three hours south of Perth, couldn't have appeared at a better time. Ferg needed a fresh start—away from the gossip and pitying glances of his colleagues, neighbours and so-called friends—almost as much as the small school needed a teacher. Their current principal, Carline Saunders, had been recently diagnosed with cancer and while she was on sick leave, their usual Year 3/4 teacher was stepping up into the role.

Fergus slowed the car as the lush winter-green paddocks that bordered the main road through town made way for houses and then a row of shops on either side. It was like he'd driven out of Perth and back in time forty years—he spied a post-office, a café called 'A Country Kitchen' (that according to its sign out the front promised you the best coffee in the south-west), a hardware store, an IGA supermarket, a pub, an agricultural supplier, a vet and a yarn store. The latter seemed surprisingly busy for a Saturday morning, with dozens of people milling about outside.

Ferg guessed there wasn't much to do in the country but knit, not that he planned on taking it up as a hobby. Glancing at the time and seeing there were still twenty minutes until he had to be at the school to meet Joanne Warburton, the acting principal, he decided he wouldn't mind stopping and testing that coffee promise. Unlikely the coffee would be up to the standards of the local café he'd left behind in Perth but he'd need somewhere to get his morning caffeine hit on the way to school. Not even the best of teachers could be expected to face a class of thirty without at least one coffee in their system, not that there'd *be* thirty kids in his new class. Small class sizes were one of the benefits of country teaching.

Late September, the temperature was mild, so Mrs Norris would be fine in the car for a few minutes with the windows ajar. She wouldn't like it any more than she'd liked being cooped in a box on the three-hour journey, or the fact he was now her primary caregiver, but ... she'd live.

However, within minutes of trying to find a parking spot, Ferg realised it wasn't only the yarn store that was busy but the whole damn town. Vacant parking spots were non-existent. It felt like each and every one of the 1381 people were in town this morning, all of them wearing identical red and white scarves and beanies, making it like a page in a *Where's Wally* book. Wasn't this supposed to be a small, sleepy rural community?

Long ago, he, his mum and his twin sister had driven through Walsh on one of those very rare family holidays they'd taken when he was a kid, and he remembered it as a blink-and-you'd-miss-it town with next to no life. The perfect place to hibernate for a few months while he planned his next move. Today, Walsh appeared anything but quiet. In addition to all the Wallys and Wandas, every shop had red and white balloons and streamers littering its front windows and the queue to the café was out the door. There had to be some kind of game happening. He'd heard country towns went rabid for sport.

Mourning the loss of the coffee that never was, he continued down the main street and soon came upon the school. He turned into the empty car park and took in the old buildings, which looked like something out of *Seven Little Australians*. In the playground there was one of those big, modern, climbing web things, but also some monkey bars, an actual roundabout and the kind of tall steel slide with no sides that could burn a hole in your pants on a hot day. The type of equipment that had been banished years ago in the city.

Ferg put the windows down a bit for Mrs Norris and climbed out of his wagon to look around while he waited for Joanne. He'd barely made it past the front gate when a silver four-wheel drive, followed by a dirty, once-white ute, entered the car park.

'Hello.' A middle-aged woman with wavy shoulder-length dark hair and a ridiculously large smile leapt from the four-wheel drive. A red and white striped scarf flapped in the air as she waved her arms excitedly and hurried towards him. 'You must be Fergus?'

'Yes,' he replied as a younger woman burst from the ute and jogged to keep up with the other. She too wore red, white and chirpiness.

The older woman landed beside him and thrust out her hand. 'I'm Joanne. So lovely to meet you.'

'You too.' He nodded and accepted her hand.

'And this is Beck, our school receptionist. Although she's much more than just a receptionist. We'd all flounder without our dear Rebecca.'

'Good to meet you both.' He smiled as he shook her hand as well, noticing that in addition to the scarves, both women were wearing T-shirts with the words 'Walsh Wanderers' and a matching logo stamped on their chest pockets.

'You must excuse us for being slightly late,' Beck said. 'We've been down at the oval helping in the canteen, getting ready for the big game.'

'First time the Wanderers have been in the footy grand final for thirty-seven years,' Joanne said as if he was supposed to know who these Wanderers were. 'And their last final win was thirty-nine years ago.'

Beck nodded. 'This is monumental. A lot's riding on today. My hubby's on the team and is beside himself with nerves and excitement.'

'Do you play footy?' Joanne gave him a once-over as if she was eyeing up his potential.

'Nope. Fraid not.'

Joanne showed momentary disappointment, then shrugged. 'Never mind, season's practically over anyway. But you should come along and watch the game. It'll give you a chance to meet the locals. We haven't had a male teacher in years. You're going to give all the mums something to talk about, that's for sure.'

'Especially the single ones.'

As Joanne and Beck exchanged an amused glance, Ferg shifted from foot to foot; were they *trying* to make him feel uncomfortable?

'Plus, there's always a good feed,' added Beck, as if this would twist his arm.

'Well …' He cleared his throat. 'Thanks for the offer, but I think I'd rather get settled in this afternoon. I'm sure there'll be time to meet everyone when school starts.'

'Oh, you won't have to wait that long,' said Joanne. 'Now, do you want to check out your classroom or just head straight to the farm?'

'Farm?'

Beck chuckled. 'Didn't Jo tell you? Don't worry, the land is leased by the two farms on either side and the cottage is very homely.'

'It's Mrs Lord's house. She's only recently had to move into the nursing home but has lived in that place since she got married at twenty-two. Lucky for you or you might have had to sleep on my couch or take a room at the hotel.'

Beck made a face. 'They had a bedbug infestation recently— not surprising really, they haven't replaced the beds since the nineteen-fifties.'

Ferg knew the house of the principal wasn't available as she was still living there with her husband, and there wasn't any other education department accommodation available in town, but he'd assumed he'd be staying *in* town. Never mind, as long as he wasn't expected to milk any cows, he didn't care where they put him. 'Since you two are busy with the football, maybe you could just leave me the key to the cottage and give me directions?'

'Oh no, we wouldn't do that,' said Jo. 'Beck and I will show you out to your new home. We've got an hour or so till the game starts.'

'Thanks.' Ferg hoped he didn't sound too unappreciative and tried to maintain an acceptable level of friendliness as the two women gave him the school tour, but he really just wanted to be alone again. For a place with only four classrooms, a big room that housed the library, music and art areas, and a small office/staffroom, it took longer than he'd have hoped due to the local history Joanne and Beck provided and the numerous questions they asked. If they ever lost interest in their current jobs, both of them could have promising careers in investigative journalism. It was only when he remembered Mrs Norris in the car they finally hit the road.

After about ten minutes following Joanne's four-wheel drive down roads in dire need of some TLC, they turned on to a gravel track. Fat black and white cows in the paddocks eyed the cars suspiciously as they drove past and then the track widened and a little cottage appeared in front of them. With its tin roof, faded blue weatherboard exterior, wooden rocking chair on the verandah and established fruit trees out the front, he guessed it was built sometime in the early 1900s. Jools would have been in heaven in a place like this.

But he didn't want to think about Jools.

He parked alongside Joanne, then went around to the passenger door to retrieve the cat box.

'Aw, isn't she the sweetest thing,' Joanne cooed as she peered into the box under his arm. 'Is she friendly?'

'Not at all.' The only person Mrs Norris liked was his ex. Pity said ex had decided she liked somebody else better than the both of them. Just as well misery loved company.

'What type of cat is she?' Beck asked.

'A Maine Coon,' he said as Mrs Norris's paw swiped at him through the bars. 'I should probably get her inside before she claws me to death.'

The women chuckled and started up the rocky garden path to the cottage. Joanne opened the door without using a key.

'It's not locked?' he asked, the scuffed floorboards creaking as he followed the others inside.

'Nobody bothers locking up out on farms, most of the crims round here are too lazy to come this far. Mrs Lord couldn't even tell us where the keys were.'

Placing the cat box on the floor but not releasing its occupant, Ferg looked around. He imagined this was what his grandmother's house might have looked like … if he'd ever had a grandmother. A crochet rug hung over the back of a floral sofa that looked as if it had been bought mid last century. The walls were covered in black-and-white photos and watercolour paintings in tarnished gold frames. A glass cabinet filled with trinkets stood along one side of the living room and a bookshelf overflowed with hardbacks. And likely dust.

The décor wasn't exactly to his taste, but his contract was only for six months.

'This will do nicely,' he said.

'Feel free to move or box anything up,' said Joanne. 'Mrs Lord won't be coming home sadly—she has Alzheimer's and she doesn't have any family. She and the late Mr Lord were never blessed with children. Make yourself at home.'

Ferg didn't know where he was supposed to put any of the stuff if he did clear it out, but decided not to ask in case it prolonged the conversation. He was working out how to politely send the women on their merry way when Joanne glanced at her watch.

'Look, we hate to dump you and run, but the game will be starting soon and we don't want to miss the bounce. Sure you don't want to come?'

'No, I'd rather get settled in, but thanks. It was kind of you to escort me out here.'

'No worries.' Beck smiled. 'It's easy to get lost when you don't know the roads.'

'Well then,' Joanne said, 'you get settled and Trev and I will have you round to dinner in a few days. I'll invite Beck and the rest of our staff so you can get to know everyone before school starts.'

'Thank you.'

He waved them off and, as the four-wheel drive grew smaller, let out a long slow breath. Aside from the occasional murmur from the cows in the paddock close to the house, there was absolute silence. He'd gotten used to quiet (except when at school) over the last few weeks and told himself it was better than meaningless chatter, or worse, pretence. And the air felt so fresh! Maybe he'd like living in the country after all.

Heading back inside, he approached Mrs Norris's box as if she were a lion.

'Hey there, gorgeous girl.' Although she might be pretty on the outside, there was nothing beautiful about her on the inside, but Ferg attempted sweet talk anyway.

Holding his breath, he released the latches to open the door of the cage and stepped back. Mrs Norris glared at him as she slowly reached one paw out of the box and took a tentative step towards freedom. She hissed at him and then ran straight under the coffee table.

'Trust me,' he told her, 'life hasn't exactly gone according to my plans either, but we just gotta make the best of a shitty situation.'

Then, leaving her to sulk in solitude, he went into the kitchen to make a coffee.

Chapter Two

'Oh my God! They won!'

As the siren sounded, the townfolk erupted in cheers and screams, her sister-in-law Meg jumped up and down like a kid on Red Bull, and Tabitha Cooper-Jones stifled a yawn. It wasn't that she wasn't excited about the local team's first grand final win in thirty-nine years—she loved football as much as the next person and had even played until she'd lost her arm—but it had already been a long day.

That morning, she and Meg had been working at their tea rooms in nearby Rose Hill, where Tabitha now lived. It had been one of their busy mornings, with the supporters from the other footy team stopping by for a drink, scone and/or ice-cream on their way to Walsh. Things had died off just after the lunch rush due to everyone being at the game and so they'd decided to close early. Tab had sent Meg off so she wouldn't miss the starting siren and cleaned up the day's mess herself. Afterwards she'd been sorely tempted to sneak upstairs for a nap, but she'd never hear the end of it if she didn't at least make an appearance at the oval.

'Aunty Tab, Aunty Tab! Did you see Dad kick that goal? We won because of him.'

She chuckled as her almost ten-year-old nephew threw his arms around her waist. 'I most certainly did. You must have been giving him some pointers.'

Ned laughed. But while he had a talent for footy and was better than most his age, Tab attributed her brother's performance to something else entirely. He'd been an awesome single dad to Ned since the death of his first wife, Leah, and had maintained his passion for dairy farming, but in every other aspect of life he'd operated almost on autopilot. His best mate Funky had voiced his fears to Tab that Lawson was in danger of becoming a recluse, but neither of them had had a clue what to do about it.

And then Meg had driven into Rose Hill.

Her moving into a haunted house in what had practically been a ghost town had been the talk of the town for a while and, when local busybody Adeline Walsh dug up dirt on Meg, it had been quite the scandal.

But Lawson had been smitten in spite of her not-so-glowing past.

It made Tab's heart sing to see how good he and Meg were together, and she loved the tight-knit team of three they'd formed with Ned. Tab was pretty sure that even Leah couldn't have picked a better stand-in mother for her son. Tab had been well and truly relegated to the position of aunty, and while she loved the role and the opportunities it brought to spoil her nephew, her brother's happily-ever-after had made her re-evaluate her own spinster status.

'Come on, let's go see Dad.' Ned tugged her and Meg towards the team who were now shaking hands with the opposition.

'I'm not sure we'll even be able to get near him,' Tab replied, but let him drag her nonetheless. Adeline was already there taking photos for the *Walsh Whisperer* and the rest of the town were crowding in around their heroes.

Music had just kicked off from the loudspeakers—the Wanderers theme song on repeat—and someone nearby cracked a bottle of bubbly. The atmosphere held the promise of a party and Tab guessed it would be a late night for the players and their supporters, which accounted for pretty much everyone who lived in Walsh. Many past residents had even returned for the big day. The oval was packed; there wasn't space for one more ute around its perimeter and the recently refurbished recreation centre was already filling with people trying to be first in line at the bar.

Ned let go of their hands to weave through the hordes and while Meg hurried after him, Tab chose to hang back. The sweaty stink of all the players was already wafting towards her, making her nauseous.

'Can you believe it?' Tennille Wellington came up beside her, her usual sunny smile on her face. She was pushing a baby in a pram and wrangling a squirming toddler on her hip—with six kids, she and her husband Boots were halfway to creating a team of their own. 'They won!'

Tab tried to summon a smile. 'It's fantastic.'

'Are you okay?' Tennille's forehead scrunched up in concern.

'Yes. Of course. I think I just need something to eat.'

'Come on then.' Tennille nodded towards the building. 'Let's go grab a plate before the kids scoff it all.'

The club already buzzed with people and Tennille was quickly distracted trying to stop her kids from stealing too much chocolate cake off the long trestle table, heavy-laden with baked goods from the CWA.

Tab took a moment, leaning back against a wall and trying to catch a few moments of open-eyed sleep while she waited for Lawson, Meg and Ned to make it inside. She'd give her big bro a congratulatory hug and then offer to take Ned home, so he and Meg could make a night of it.

'How's the form, mucker?'

The voice of Ethan, their high-spirited but conscientious farm worker, interrupted her vertical nap. In the few years he'd been in their employ, he'd taught Tab a fair share of Irish slang, so she knew 'mucker' was actually a term of endearment.

'Did ya see me fine form out there? Not bad play for a boy from Galway.'

'Not bad at all. Guess you and Lawson will be in for a big night.'

'You betcha. Ya seen Kimmy?'

'Sorry.' She shook her head. Ethan had fallen head over heels for Kimmy, the new vet, when she'd come out to the farm to help with a difficult birth. Luckily the feeling was mutual. Not that Tab would admit it to anyone, but she'd been surprised by their hook-up as she'd suspected Ethan had a thing for her. But he just saw her as a good mate, like every other bloke in town.

'Never mind, she'll be somewhere round here. Now, what can I get you to drink?'

'I'm right at the moment. You go find Kimmy.'

It wasn't long before the rest of the team poured into the building and Tab offered up congratulations to Funky and a number of other guys she'd grown up with before Lawson accosted her. He swung her round, making both Meg and Ned giggle.

'We did it, sis,' he said as he hugged her.

'Well done.' Tab tried not to recoil at the smell of sweat that permeated her brother's skin. There were showers in the change rooms that the team could avail themselves of, but she guessed that would waste valuable drinking time … and when they had a grand final win to celebrate, time was precious.

'Dad, can I go see my friends?'

Lawson released Tab and nodded. 'Sure, mate, but come check in with one of us every half an hour or so.'

Tab knew that once the food had been devoured, the kids would escape outside and get up to who knows what mischief on the playground next to the oval. With all the excitement going on, it looked unlikely she'd be able to use Ned as an excuse to leave early. He wouldn't want to go home and miss out on all the action with his little mates. Maybe she could feign a headache.

'Right, I'm getting drinks,' Lawson exclaimed as Ned disappeared. He looked to Meg. 'Do you want a lemon lime and bitters?' When she nodded, he turned to Tab. 'And what does my other fave lady want? Champers, wine or beer?'

She hesitated a moment. 'Bubbles, please.'

As Lawson headed for the bar, Tab and Meg mingled with the crowd, everyone reliving the high points of the game.

'I can't believe it was so close.'

'We were four points down,' said Terrence, a middle-aged farmer who'd been on the team the last time they won. He spoke as if he was the only one who'd seen the game. 'Then Lawson took a mark just before the siren.'

'He'd never have lived it down if he missed that goal,' said someone else.

They all laughed and Meg said, 'But he made it.'

'He sure did,' Terrence agreed, raising his beer in the air. 'And now he'll go down as a local footy legend.'

It was a good twenty minutes before said legend returned with the drinks.

'Attention, everyone!' Coach Macca, also a local councillor, stood on a milk crate in the corner of the room and shouted at the crowd. The din died down and all eyes turned to him as he sang the praises of his team, made individual references to particular players and then raised a toast to the men who'd broken Walsh's winning drought. 'To the Wanderers. A bunch of men who train hard, play hard and win! You all deserve a drink. Or ten.'

The crowd raised their glasses in agreement.

'Why aren't you drinking?' Adeline accused Tabitha, as if not doing so was a cardinal sin. Of course the town's eagle eye wouldn't miss a thing.

Tab ignored her, hoping nobody else had heard. But no such luck.

Funky leaned around Adeline. 'Yeah, Tabs, why aren't you toasting our win?'

'I'm driving,' she replied.

Adeline snorted. 'That's never stopped you before. And I don't know if you noticed, but Walsh just *won* the grand final—it would be mean-spirited of you not to toast them.'

'I'm not feeling well,' she hissed, hating that she felt compelled to say anything. It wasn't Adeline's or anyone else's business what she did or didn't put into her mouth.

'You're not pregnant, are you?' Adeline laughed as if she'd just made a huge joke.

Tab waited a second too long to laugh it off and felt her cheeks heat to boiling; no doubt they were now the colour of the Wanderers' red. 'I'm ...' She meant to say *of course not*, but she'd never been a good liar and instead found herself saying, 'Yes, actually I am.'

Meg gasped, Adeline's mouth fell open, Lawson frowned, and all other eyes in their little group bulged. Her friends and family were silent from shock a few long moments and Tab's heart beat so loudly she swore she could hear it.

This was not how she'd planned on announcing her news. The idea had been to wait until her twelve-week scan in just over a week and then if all was well, tell her family the news first. Beyond that she'd only given brief thought to. Well, that was something she wouldn't have to worry about anymore. Now Adeline had this bit of juicy gossip, it'd be round the building faster than an epidemic of chicken pox.

'Tabitha.' Lawson glanced at his near empty glass as if maybe he'd had more to drink than he remembered. 'Did you just say you're *pregnant*?'

'Yes,' she confirmed. 'I am. Eleven weeks to be precise. I'm sorry, Law, I was going to tell you guys when I got to twelve weeks. I didn't want to jinx anything.'

'It's alright, I just …' Lawson struggled to finish the sentence.

'We're surprised, is all,' Meg continued. 'But congratulations. Are you happy?'

Tab felt her shoulders loosening and even the nausea easing a little. 'Yes.' She put her untouched champagne glass down on a nearby table and smiled genuinely for the first time that afternoon—she felt better now it was out in the open. 'I've never been happier in my life. I can't wait to be a mum.'

'Who's the father?' Adeline asked the question everyone wanted to know. 'I didn't know you were seeing anyone.'

She probably couldn't imagine anyone would want to sleep with Tabitha unless they were off their face, and she'd probably be right. Tab had known most of the blokes her age her whole life and they regarded her as just one of the guys, had done even before her cancer. She'd long ago resigned herself to the fact she wasn't destined to find Mr Right and settle down, but that didn't stop her craving a baby. And, being a modern, independent, self-sufficient woman, she'd decided to take control of her own destiny.

'Maybe Tabitha would rather not discuss that here,' Meg said.

'No, it's fine,' she found herself saying. She'd decided to be completely honest about her baby's origins, hoping that by the time he or she was old enough to understand, any negative gossip would have passed. She took a quick breath. 'I don't know exactly who the father is; I conceived in a clinic using donor sperm.'

If people had been stunned with the news that she was pregnant, this announcement took their shock to a whole other level. They all stared as if horns had just sprouted from her head.

Funky was the first to speak. 'Why didn't you ask me if you needed sperm? I'd have been happy to have a baby with you.'

'Yeah.' Ethan nodded, a rare frown creasing his brow. 'I'd wank in a jar for you any day, Tabs.'

No one laughed and Kimmy elbowed him in the side.

'Thanks, guys,' Tab said. They almost sounded hurt that she hadn't asked them, and to be honest, she'd given the possibility a great deal of thought, but in the end, she wanted this to be entirely her baby. Sure, one day when the kid was old enough they could get the name of the donor from the register but Tab hadn't wanted to complicate the situation by raising a baby that was biologically also part of someone she knew. And she hadn't wanted her friends to feel *obliged*. This way she'd avoided any awkward conversations and wouldn't have to answer to anyone else about decisions regarding her baby.

'I appreciate that, I really do, but it was just easier this way.'

'What happens if you meet someone? You're still young, and ...' Kimmy smiled mushily at Ethan, 'you never know when love is just around the corner.'

Tab almost laughed. It had been ten years since she'd had an actual boyfriend; she was realistic enough to know when to admit defeat. And she'd always wanted to be a mum, but lately the urge had grown stronger. Now that Lawson, Meg and Ned had formed a little family of their own, she sometimes felt a bit excluded and craved a family of her own. 'Well, if that happens, then whoever the lucky guy is will just have to understand I'm a package deal. At least I won't have an annoying ex still lingering like many single mums.'

'That's true,' Funky said with a chuckle. 'Remember when I dated that single mum from Harvey? Her ex tried to run me off the road.'

'Wanker,' Ethan said. 'He should have treated her better if he didn't want anyone else to have her.'

'Anyway.' Adeline cleared her throat. 'How much thought did you give this exactly? I'm surprised the doctors allowed someone with your physical disability to attempt such a thing without a partner. How are you going to look after this poor baby with only one arm? How do you plan on changing a nappy? What if you drop it?'

Tab's hackles rose. Adeline had always been a pain in the arse, but ever since she'd lost Lawson to Meg (at least that's how she saw it), she'd been unbearable.

'I've probably changed more nappies than you,' Tab snapped, her blood boiling, even though Adeline was merely voicing what many others were probably thinking.

But it wasn't like Tab had made this decision on a whim—the clinic where she'd undergone artificial insemination wouldn't have allowed it. In accordance with their guidelines, she'd had extensive counselling sessions, including ones about how she would manage parenting with her disability, about the support she'd have and what would happen to her baby if she died. Even without asking, she'd known that Lawson and Meg would step in if that ever happened, just as she would with Ned. She'd even undergone genetic counselling and testing to ensure she wasn't carrying a faulty gene that might account for her cancer and be passed on to her child. Thankfully, all had come up clear.

Still, Adeline's intrusive questions unnerved her. 'Name one thing you can do that I can't do better? Go on,' she demanded.

Adeline stepped back as if she thought Tab might be about to punch her. 'I ... I ...'

Lawson stepped between the two of them. 'Shut up, Adeline. No one cares for your opinion. Tab will make a fantastic mum and she'll have me and Meg for support, just like she's there for us with Ned. So maybe it's time you start minding your own business.'

'Here, here,' said a voice from behind.

Tab wasn't sure who it belonged to but she appreciated the sentiment. She was pretty sure that after the shock wore off, she'd have the backing of everyone else in town. And she didn't care for Adeline's interference in her child's life anyway.

'Fine. I have photos to take.' Adeline lifted her camera and flounced off in a huff.

'Good riddance,' Funky said, then turned to Tab and gave her a hug. 'I'm stoked for you. So stoked I'm off to get another beer.'

'Thanks.' Tab laughed as he pulled away and then accepted more congratulations from the rest of the small crowd that had gathered around them.

Finally, she looked to her brother and Meg. 'I'm sorry, Law, I wanted to tell you guys first in private and I certainly didn't mean to take away the glory from your impressive footy win.'

'I don't give a damn about that and you know it.' Lawson put his arm around her. 'All I care about is that this is right for you. I wish you'd talked about it with us first though, we could have been there to support you through the whole process.'

'I know. But this is something I had to do for myself.' Tab didn't tell them she'd been scared they might have tried to talk her out of it, tried to convince her to give fate a few more years to find her a partner to parent with. She knew how hard being a single parent could be, but her circumstances were different to what Lawson's had been—she was going into the adventure with her eyes wide open.

'I understand,' he said.

'Me too,' Meg added, 'but tomorrow you're coming over for dinner and you're going to tell us everything. I want to know all the details.'

'Deal. Although here's hoping I can have a little nap after the lunch rush, otherwise I'm liable to fall asleep on my plate.'

'So that's why you've been so tired lately?' Meg mused. 'Maybe we should talk about hiring some more casuals to help us out at the tea rooms. We'll need some extra help when the baby arrives anyway.'

'That's a good plan,' Lawson agreed. 'But right now, we'd better find Ned and tell him he's going to be a cousin before he hears it on the grapevine.'

'Good idea,' Tab said.

And then, flanked by her brother and Meg, she went outside to look for her nephew, thinking how lucky she and her baby were to have such a wonderful family. She didn't need anyone else.

Chapter Three

Taking her hand off the steering wheel for a moment, Tab jabbed her car radio off as the latest hit by country singer Ryder O'Connell came on. She didn't begrudge her first (and only real) boyfriend's success, she just wished she didn't have to hear his voice so often. Especially not today, when her stomach was already in knots about the questions she might have to face in the next few hours.

Since leaving the football celebrations early, she'd laid low, only venturing out of Rose Hill to have dinner at the farm on Sunday night and visit her grandmother at the nursing home that same afternoon. Granny had been delighted by the news she was going to be a great-grandmother again, although she took a while to get her head around the fact Tabitha didn't know the father. And, as the tea rooms were only open Friday through Sunday and no one from Walsh had ventured in for tea and scones on Sunday, she hadn't yet run into anyone who wanted to talk about her 'announcement'. Going to knitting circle, as she did every second Wednesday, would be like being a corrupt politician and walking into a press conference.

Tab wasn't sure she had the mental energy for that right now. Even after three days doing practically nothing, she hadn't been able to shake this pregnancy fatigue. But if she didn't go, people would only talk behind her back. She and Meg didn't call knitting circle Stitch'n'Bitch for nothing, but attending the group always made Tab feel closer to her mum. It was the one outing she had each week when Tab was little and for as long as she could remember, she'd begged her mum to teach her to knit so she could go as well. When she'd lost her arm, knitting—among many other things—had been a struggle, but one she'd persevered with until she'd taught herself all over again.

To Tab's utmost surprise, no one even turned their head as she entered. They were all ensconced in conversation.

A few of the women looked up briefly and offered a 'hi' as she took the vacant seat next to Meg.

'Hey.' She smiled back warily, then dug her knitting out of her mum's faithful old craft bag and whispered to Meg, 'What's going on?'

'Kathy's been telling us about the new teacher in town.'

'Ah, I see.' Tabitha began to knit, wedging one needle under her armpit and holding the other in her hand. No wonder the women were so animated—there was nothing these old dears liked better than matchmaking; no new teacher or nurse was safe! Those reality TV dating shows had nothing on these country matriarchs. The number of newcomers they'd tried to set Lawson up with before he met Meg had been mind-boggling.

'Is he married?' asked Eileen Bennett. She had three unmarried daughters in their early twenties. All still lived in Walsh—two of them working with their father on the farm and one the local hairdresser—and the fact they were all single caused their mother much distress. Every time Tab heard her speak, a vision of the *other* Mrs Bennett from *Pride and Prejudice* landed in her head.

Hang on? Her thoughts caught up with the conversation and she looked up from her knitting. The new teacher was *male*? This really was a turn-up for the books.

'Joanne doesn't think so,' said Kathy, who was Joanne's mother-in-law. 'There was no mention of a partner in their early communications, and he hasn't brought anyone with him ...'

'Except for a cat,' interrupted Eileen; she'd obviously done her research.

'And,' Kathy continued, 'Joanne said he wasn't wearing a ring.'

Tab was about to say that didn't necessarily mean he didn't have a partner—he could be in a long-term relationship, hell, maybe he was gay—but it was impossible to get a word in over the excitement. No wonder the news had trumped the scandal of her getting pregnant to a turkey baster; she couldn't remember the last time there'd been a man teaching at Walsh Primary School.

'I saw him yesterday morning when I drove past the school,' said Beth in her very posh voice. She'd come out from England seventy years ago to marry a farmer she'd met through a pen-pal scheme and had never lost her accent. At almost ninety, she was the oldest member of knitting circle and also one of Tab's favourites. 'He was carrying a box from his car.'

'Ooh, what does he look like?' Adeline asked.

Tab was surprised she hadn't already engineered a meeting herself.

'Well, if my old eyes weren't deceiving me, he's very tall and has muscles in all the right places. His sleeves were pushed up and I couldn't help notice he had very tanned skin too. He was wearing a cap but I think I saw dark hair curling at his neckline.'

Tab was impressed—if anyone ever needed a witness to a crime, Beth would be perfect.

The elderly woman visibly blushed. 'Let's just say if I was sixty years younger ...'

'If you were sixty years younger,' interrupted Doris Weatherby, 'I'd be sixty years younger too and you'd have competition.'

Everyone laughed, but Tab saw Adeline's eyes sparkle like a tiger who'd just spotted a gazelle grazing not too far away. There was new blood in town; of course she'd be on the scent.

'I wonder why he was able to come at such short notice,' mused Chloe Wellington. 'I know when Carline was diagnosed she was very anxious they wouldn't be able to find a replacement and there'd be too much pressure on Joanne.'

'Could be some kind of scandal,' said Suzie McDonald, a mischievous glint in her eyes. 'Maybe he had an affair with one of the mums and was *encouraged* to leave. My sister works at a school in Albany and that's what happened with their principal.'

'Or maybe he had a thing with one of the students.' Doris looked horrified at her own suggestion. 'I'm always reading in the paper about male teachers taking advantage of teenage girls.'

'Don't be ridiculous,' Chloe snapped. 'The man's a primary school teacher—and anyway, the police would be after him if that were the case. Wouldn't they?'

The circle went quiet for a moment as the mums and grandmothers pondered this possibility. Tab felt compelled to stand up for the poor man and stop this line of thought before it got out of hand. Lord knew how easily rumours started in small towns, but this one was particularly nasty and she could just imagine what would happen if it took hold. A vision of all the locals charging the school with pitchforks came into her head.

'Of course he wouldn't still be teaching if he was involved in anything like that,' she reassured everyone. 'We should be grateful that whatever his reasons, he's been able to take up the position at such short notice. And it'll be great for the kids to have a guy at school for a change.'

'Yes, indeed.' For once Adeline agreed with her, but the wolfish smile on her face reminded Tab that it wasn't only vicious rumours the new guy needed to be wary of.

'What's his name?' she asked the circle.

'*Fergus McWilliams,*' Adeline announced, swooning.

Fergus sounded like someone her dad's age, but Tab assumed he had to be a lot younger to be making all these women so hot under the collar.

'I wonder if he'd like a puppy? I have a litter due any day and, if he *is* alone, it'd be good company for him.'

Adeline thought her fluffy white dogs were the answer to everything. She'd tried to use them to get into Lawson's pants too, but that had backfired and now it irritated her something chronic that Meg owned one of her Maremmas.

'The cat might have something to say about that,' Meg said.

'And what would the poor puppy do all day while he's at school?' Eileen asked with a roll of her eyes. She clearly didn't want Adeline getting an in with Fergus before she could introduce him to her daughters.

Tab stifled a giggle as Adeline and Eileen eyed each other off. Whatever Fergus McWilliams' story, she hoped he knew how to handle a pack of piranhas. Adeline and the Bennett girls weren't the only single women in Walsh and they wouldn't take any prisoners in their mission to score a man.

'He could take the dog to school with him. Maremmas are great with kids,' Adeline spat.

'What about the kids that are allergic?' said Kathy.

Getting bored with this conversation, Tab focused on her knitting and made a mental note to thank the poor man when she met him for taking the limelight off her.

'How you feeling?' Meg whispered, leaning in close to her.

'Still so tired I could sleep for a year, but the nausea might be settling a little bit, thank God. I actually managed to keep down my toast this morning.'

Meg smiled. 'Ned's so excited. When you left on Sunday night, he started making a list of possible baby names. So far Harry and Hermione are top contenders, and I should warn you, he seems to think it's his privilege as cousin to pick the name.'

'There are worse names than Harry.' Tab was almost as much a fan of the Harry Potter books as Ned was.

'Ooh, are you talking baby names?' Chloe Wellington smiled from across the circle. 'I heard your news, Tab, and I wanted to say massive congratulations. I think it's wonderful what you're doing. Lord knows if there'd been that option in my day, I might have taken it. Men are way more hassle than they're worth.'

'Thanks.' Tab smiled.

A few of the older women wanted her to explain exactly how she'd managed to conceive on her own, but there were surprisingly few judgemental comments.

'You'll make a fine mother,' Beth said, patting her hand. 'When's the baby due?'

'Mid April.' She couldn't help grinning at the thought and resisted the urge to place her hand on her stomach; it seemed silly when there was nothing to see yet. Often when she was alone, she found her hand drifting down to her still flat belly. It was hard to believe there was anything in there, but she'd heard its heartbeat during her dating ultrasound and she already loved the life within her more than she'd ever loved anything.

'April's a lovely time,' Chloe said. 'Not too cold yet, but not too hot either.'

'Once I've finished this jumper for my brother-in-law in England—' Beth held up the bright yellow knitting in her hands, '—I'll start on a special blanket for your baby.'

'Will you stay in Rose Hill when the baby's born?' asked Kathy.

'Yes, I think so. There's plenty of room to decorate a nursery and we need someone on site in case of power cuts.' If no one was there to start the generator, they were liable to lose a lot of ice-cream.

'It's quite far from Walsh if there's any sort of emergency with the child,' Adeline said, a scowl on her face once again.

'Not really,' Tab replied. 'Besides with the B&B next door now, there's often someone around. And I do have internet and a phone line out there now, you know.'

The women chuckled, but Adeline was not to be deterred.

'And when you've been up all night with the baby, are you going to get up and provide breakfast for your guests?'

'We appreciate your concern, Adeline,' Meg said, before Tabitha could reply, 'but Tab isn't running a one-man show out there—it's actually *my* business as well and we'll work out the logistics as a family.'

'And I'll be happy to help with the guests or the baby anytime,' Chloe said, and although her offer was followed by many others, Tabitha suddenly wondered if she was crazy to have thought this was a good idea.

Yes, she wanted a baby more than anything and yes, she already loved it with everything she had, but *was* her decision a selfish one?

Lawson, Meg, her dad and stepmother had been very support-ive when she'd finally discussed her pregnancy with them, but her father and stepmum didn't live close enough to be of practical assistance, and Lawson and Meg had their hands full on the farm. The business she and Meg operated from Rose Hill had grown from Meg's original vision of tea rooms and a craft shop to some-thing much bigger. It now also included Tab's ice-creamery, an art gallery, and a bed and breakfast in the building next door, and was a good supplemental income to the farm and a fulltime job for Tabitha.

When Meg and Lawson got engaged, Meg and Tabitha had in essence swapped places, with Meg moving to the farm and Tabitha to Rose Hill. The tea rooms, and everything that went with it, had become a tourist destination much quicker than any of them had ever hoped or dreamed and now they had a number of casual staff, but Tab worked harder than anyone. And she loved it, but wasn't stupid enough to think she'd be able to continue at such a rate once the baby arrived. It was already becoming a struggle.

As if sensing her anxiety, Meg reached out and squeezed her knee. 'Want to get a cuppa?'

'Good idea,' said Beth next to Tabitha. 'I think my fingers have done their dash for the day. Must be time for afternoon tea.'

Murmurs of agreement echoed around the circle and one by one the women packed up their knitting and went into the kitchen to organise the feast. Tab nibbled on a couple of scones, fielded more questions about her baby plans, listened to the older women as they reminisced about pregnancy cravings and then announced she was heading home for a nap.

'Don't forget your plate of leftovers,' Beth insisted as Tab went to retrieve her bag.

'Thanks,' she said, going back to put a few slices and a couple of scones on a plate. She kissed Meg on the cheek, told her she'd see her tomorrow and then waved goodbye to the rest as she went to her car.

As she was driving out of Walsh, Tab caught a flicker of movement in the corner of her eye. She turned her head to see a man she didn't know painting the brick wall at the front of the school—shirtless—and almost drove off the road.

He had muscles in all the right places.

As Beth's words repeated themselves in her head, there was no question in Tab's mind that this was the new teacher. What he was doing painting, she had no idea, but, with a quick glance at the plate on the passenger seat beside her, she found herself turning into the school car park. Surely all that manual labour would be making him hungry and it would be a shame for all this food to go to waste; she had enough for herself at the tea rooms.

With that thought, she parked her van alongside the wagon she guessed belonged to him. Loud rock music sounded from a portable stereo a metre or so from where he was painting, which meant he didn't hear her approach until her shadow fell over him. He spun around and her mouth went dry as she took in the sight before her. She didn't usually get all that excited over bare male skin. Perhaps it was pregnancy hormones or maybe it had just been so long since she'd seen any, but as her gaze skimmed the contours of his perfect six-pack, covered in tawny-brown skin that glistened from the exertion, Tab forgot to breathe a moment.

No wonder Beth had blushed when speaking about him.

'Can I help you?' he asked as he dumped his paint roller in a tray on the ground. Dark sunglasses covered his eyes so she couldn't read his expression, but his tone and stance told her he didn't appreciate being ogled.

Whoops.

Tab found her voice. 'No. I was just driving by and thought I'd introduce myself. I'm guessing you're the new teacher? Fergus?'

He nodded.

'I'm Tabitha Cooper-Jones. My nephew Ned's in your class.'

Then, forgetting about the plate she was holding, she shot out her hand to offer it to him and ended up somehow throwing scones and hedgehog slice at him instead. Dammit, why hadn't she taken the time to cover them with cling-wrap?

'Oh my God, I'm so sorry.' Almost dropping the plate in her efforts to put it down, she rushed forward and tried to wipe the cream off his impressive six-pack.

Fergus quickly stepped back, wiped his chest with the heel of his hand and then wiped his hand against his faded jeans, which sat very snugly on his hips.

Realising she was once again staring quite inappropriately, Tab dragged her eyes back up to his face, only to find him looking at her in an equally disconcerting way. For one ridiculous second she imagined he was checking her out as well and then realised it was her arm, or rather lack thereof, that had stolen his attention. Most of the time she forgot she only had one functioning arm—after almost a decade without it, she simply didn't notice the loss any-more—but whenever she met someone new she was reminded. People always stared when they first saw her 'little arm' and gen-erally it didn't bother her. Mostly they didn't mean offence, they were simply shocked, and gawked before their brain kicked in to remind them that staring was rude.

Usually she'd break the ice by telling them the story of how she lost it—let's face it, that's what *everyone* wanted to know—but today the words died on her tongue.

'Well, now you'll have to take my word that these goodies were indeed delicious,' she said as she dropped to her haunches to collect the scattered cakes.

He stooped down beside her to help. As he snatched up the plate and took control, picking up the now useless cakes and put-ting them into a nearby bin, Tab quickly realised it wasn't so much that he was being gentlemanly but that he didn't think her capable of doing it with only one arm.

'Would you like me to take this back to your car?' he asked.

'No thanks. I can manage.' She graciously thanked him as she took the plate again and held it close to her body.

For the first time in a long while she was acutely aware of her little arm hanging awkwardly beside her. A voice in her head told her to walk away, but she'd never been good at following instructions.

'So why are you painting the wall?' she asked in an attempt to defeat the awkwardness. 'Isn't that a job for maintenance?'

'I thought it needed it.'

'Right. Fair enough.' So he wasn't a chatty one.

'Anyway, I better get back to it. Thanks for … ah, the gesture.'

At this, she decided maybe he was shy rather than rude or maybe he was simply better at interacting with children than he was with adults. Her judging him on this would be almost as bad as him making assumptions about her because of her little arm. And, if he was shy and awkward, how on earth would he handle the onslaught of single women who were about to unleash themselves on him?

'You're welcome. I wanted to welcome you to town, and … I should also probably give you a warning.'

'Oh?' One of his dark eyebrows crept skywards.

'I've just come from the town hall—we have a fortnightly knitting session where we make things for charities, local fundraisers and stuff like that … Anyway, you should know that you're the first male teacher this town, hell, this region has seen in at least thirty years and that makes you very interesting.'

'I'm flattered.'

'Have you lived in the country before?' she found herself asking.

'Nope.'

'Well, there's kind of this thing about new teachers. Especially if they're good ones. The town wants to keep them so they try to marry them off to single farmers—only usually the teachers are women and the local guys are happy to go with the flow and see what happens. Not so some of the single women around here—they're voracious so you're fair game. Just thought I'd warn you what was coming.'

Fergus pushed his sunglasses atop his thick black curls. 'Are you single?'

Tab blinked. *OMG*, those eyes—the whites were so bright compared to the warm caramel of his pupils. 'Well ... yes.' Something fizzed inside her—was this cute guy about to make a move? How ironic would that be?

'So what makes you any different to these women you're telling me about?' He glanced around as if the fact single girls didn't jump out from behind the bushes called her out as a liar.

She opened and closed her mouth—speechless for the first time in as long as she could remember. Speechless and stupid. As if someone like *him* would look twice at someone like *her*.

'How do I know your attempt to bring me food isn't a ploy to get to my ...' He paused and she flushed even more. 'Heart?'

'What?' she blurted, stunned at his cockiness.

He merely cocked his head to one side.

'I can assure you,' Tab said, resisting the urge to throw the plate at him again, 'that is not the case. I'm quite happily single. So happy that even if you were good-looking, charming, rich *and* the last man on earth, I wouldn't be interested. I was simply trying to be nice!'

'That's good then,' he said with a smirk. 'Because I too am happily single and have no interest whatsoever in dating you or anyone else in this town. Now, if you don't mind, I'd like to get back to my painting.'

Mind? Tab couldn't stand to be in his insufferable presence a moment longer and couldn't get out of the car park, out of the *town*, fast enough!

Chapter Four

Fergus made a face at the bathroom mirror as he tried to do up his tie. He'd never perfected the art of tying them. The rare times he'd needed one growing up, he'd managed to con his sister into helping and the last few years Jools had been his chief tie-doer. It was something the three of them often joked about.

Annoyed, he yanked at the knot and tugged the tie right off. This was a barbecue in a country town not a formal dinner with the queen.

With a quick run of his fingers through his still damp hair, he went out to give Mrs Norris her dinner. She glared at him as he opened the tin and he glared right back as he crinkled his nose at the smell. He couldn't help being a little envious of the cat. Not of her fishy feast, but of the fact she had a night of solitude ahead. He'd kill for a beer and a TV dinner.

'You don't know how lucky you are,' he told her as he scratched her head. She rewarded him with a hiss and he held up his hand in surrender. 'Personal space. I get it.'

He wondered if any of the single women that girl yesterday—what was her name?—had spoken about would be at Joanne's house or if, as he suspected, that had simply been a ploy to start a conversation with him.

As he scooped his keys and wallet off the hall table, he heard a car approaching. The cottage was a good kilometre from the road and he hadn't heard any traffic since he'd arrived. Assuming it must be the farmer who leased the land, he stepped outside and was surprised to see a pristine white four-wheel drive pulling up alongside his wagon. It had to be the first clean car he'd seen since leaving the city four days ago.

He frowned as a tall, incredibly thin woman with straight blonde hair hanging down to her waist got out of the car. She didn't look like a farmer.

'Hi.' The woman waved as a massive white dog jumped out of the driver's side behind her and ran over to him. As the dog sniffed at his groin, the woman giggled in a way that grated on his nerves, but didn't call the animal off. 'Sorry, she's not much of a lady.'

He smiled through his teeth and ruffled the dog's fur. He had to admit, it was a good-looking animal and very friendly. 'May I help you?'

'Oh, excuse my manners. I'm Adeline Walsh,' she said, thrusting her hand at him. He shook it reluctantly. 'I've come to welcome you to town.'

'Walsh? As in the town?'

'That's right.' She beamed. 'My descendants were the town's first settlers and we've been here ever since. I'm not just a Walsh either, but also related to the Elverds, who were—'

'That's great,' Ferg cut her off. He didn't have the time for a local history lesson or he'd be late to Joanne's.

'Shall we have a drink?' Adeline asked.

He suddenly realised she had a bottle of champagne in her free hand. Who turned up unexpectedly on a stranger's doorstep with alcohol? These country women were weird.

'Thanks, but I'm heading out.'

'Oh.' She honest-to-God pouted. There may even have been a flutter of eyelashes. 'But I was so looking forward to getting to know you. Where are you off to?'

Her direct question surprised him so much that he answered her before realising it was none of her business. 'To the Warburton farm. Joanne's having a barbecue.'

'Really?' Adeline looked put out that she hadn't been invited.

'So I can meet the other teaching and school support staff,' he said, squeezing his fist around his keys.

'Well, that's a pity, but maybe we can take a raincheck. We'll need to organise a time so I can interview you for the *Whisperer* anyway.'

'The what?'

'The local paper. I'm the editor-in-chief. Purely a voluntary position but still very demanding. I like to do my bit for my community.'

'Ah, right.' Ferg couldn't imagine what a town this size could have to put in a newspaper.

'All new teachers have an interview in the paper. What are you doing tomorrow night?'

'Um …' Shit, he needed to think quick—an interview was one thing, but this sounded more like a date. 'I might be heading back to Perth to collect a few more things.'

'Oh, okay. Well, I'm sure we'll work something out. I also wanted to talk to you about my dogs.'

'Your dogs?' He looked down at the beast between them. She had more than one of these things?

'Yes.' She touched his arm and he couldn't help noticing her long red talons, which didn't seem to gel in this rural setting. Adeline Walsh looked as if she'd stepped right off a Hollywood film set. 'My other bitch, Bella, has recently had puppies and I thought maybe you'd like one. They'll be ready in two weeks. I usually charge two thousand dollars a pup, but I'm sure we could come to some arrangement. With you being all alone out here, maybe you could use the company?'

'Thanks for the offer,' he said, stepping back to put distance between them, 'but I've got a cat and she can't stand dogs.'

Adeline frowned, her nose curling upwards a little. 'Oh, that is a shame.'

'Now, I'm really sorry, but I don't want to be late. Nice to meet you.'

He was pulling open his car door when she called out, 'What about Friday night?'

'Sorry. Can't. Busy.' With those three words he escaped into his car and without a backward glance started down the long drive a little too fast.

Joanne's farm was only five minutes away and he was almost at his destination when a massive kangaroo hopped out in front of his car. He swore and slammed his foot on the brakes, letting out a sigh of relief when the roo continued on across the road without even a glance towards him. As Fergus's heart rate returned to normal, he decided he was well and truly in the country now but would prefer to deal with kangaroos over women any day.

Everyone was already there when Joanne welcomed him into her house and he apologised for his delay. 'I got held up by an unexpected visitor.'

'No worries. Come on through and meet the team,' she said, linking her arm through his as she led him down a long wide hallway in the direction of loud chatter.

'Lovely house,' Ferg said. It was triple the size of the place he and Jools had rented in Perth, and with lovely high ceilings boasting ornamental floral mouldings, he guessed this home was built sometime around the turn of the twentieth century.

'Oh thanks, but don't look too closely. It's in dire need of renovation. Sadly, my husband doesn't agree; making stuff look pretty is the last thing farmers want to spend money on.'

They emerged into a massive country-style kitchen that opened up onto a large back verandah and Ferg counted about twelve people all sipping beer or wine. They turned to scrutinise him.

'Everyone, I'd like you to meet Fergus McWilliams, our new teacher. Now, can I get you a beer?'

He nodded. 'Thanks, that'd be great.'

'You already know Beck.' Joanne gestured to the woman with black frizzy hair sitting at one end of the table. Beck lifted her hand in a wave. 'But I'll let everyone else introduce themselves.'

While she went to fetch his beer, the other guests rushed forward to say hello and shake hands.

Maria, a grey-haired, slightly overweight but very smiley woman, taught art, library, sport, Italian and 'whatever else the Ed department decides we need to squeeze into the curriculum'. She'd been at the school on and off for forty years, only stopping to have kids. Next was Haylee, who taught the kindy and pre-primary classes and didn't look to be much older than her students. She wore bright pink glasses and two big silver hoops in her ears. Vanessa, the Years 1 and 2 teacher, fell somewhere in the middle in terms of age and had long, wavy red hair that hung right down to her butt, a hippy-type skirt that dragged along the floor and a bright-multicoloured macaroni necklace around her neck. Another young woman, Taya, took Years 5 and 6 and told Ferg she was glad not to be the town's newest teacher anymore. The final woman, Judy, was a teacher's assistant who only worked part-time because she babysat her grandkids two days a week. A pair of spectacles hung round her neck on one of those chain things and she wore very bright orange lipstick.

'Sadly, Molly, our other TA, couldn't make it tonight as she's on her honeymoon, but she's fantastic as well.' Joanne smiled at the women—this was clearly a tight-knit team.

The husbands introduced themselves next and Fergus began to wish they were wearing name badges. He was good at remembering kids' names, but for some reason he'd never been so good with adults. But as he shook hands with the men, he felt a little of the tension he'd brought into the house ease. Granted, he'd only been to the hardware store, the supermarket and the café so far, but he'd been beginning to think Walsh was populated only with women. Mostly crazy, desperate, single ones, if his interactions so far were anything to go by.

At least all his colleagues appeared happily married, so he didn't have to worry about being accosted near the photocopier.

Joanne's husband Trevor announced the meat was done and as he delivered it to the table, Joanne and Beck brought out bowls of salad from the fridge to go with the fresh home-baked rolls and local butter already there. Fergus couldn't imagine them even putting a dent in this mountain of food.

'So, how's your first few days in Walsh been?' asked Maria (or was she Molly?).

'Good. I've been busy getting my classroom ready and painting the wall.'

'Oh, Joanne mentioned your idea to have the kids help paint a mural on it,' said Haylee. 'That's very sweet of you.'

Fergus smiled, uncomfortable with praise.

'We'll take some photos for Carline while the kids are painting. We're trying to keep her in the loop,' Joanne explained to Fergus.

'Poor Carline.' Maria shook her head sadly. 'She's the last person who deserves anything like this.'

'Nobody deserves cancer,' Joanne said, 'but in my experience it seems to pick only the best people to prey on.'

'Yes,' Maria agreed. 'This town has lost a fair few good people to the Big C.'

'Not only people,' Judy said. 'Tabby Cooper-Jones lost her arm. And only a few years after losing her mother. Poor girl.'

Fergus's ears pricked up. They had to be talking about the woman he'd met yesterday. How many people with only one arm could a town the size of Walsh have? He felt like a bit of a tool for the way he'd stared at her stump, but it had taken him by surprise.

'The Cooper-Jones sure seem to have their fair share of bad luck,' said one of the husbands—Fergus had forgotten his name. 'Hopefully times are a-changing though. Meg seems a good sort.'

Ferg had no idea who Meg was and wondered what other bad luck they were talking about.

'Yes, she is.' A smile split Beck's face. 'And did you guys hear Tabitha's pregnant?'

'Yes.' Even the blokes grinned and nodded at this news.

'What?' Ferg almost choked on the sip of beer he'd just taken. But hadn't she said she was single?

'Sorry,' Joanne said. 'We shouldn't talk about people you don't know. Although you'll probably meet Tab soon—her nephew's in your class.'

Ferg was about to say he didn't mind, but a shout-out from the front of the house interrupted the conversation.

'Yoo-hoo? Is anyone home?'

'Who on earth could that be?' Joanne shook her head as she pushed back her chair.

Trevor held up his hand as he too stood. 'It's alright, love, I'll go.'

'Thanks. Would anyone like another drink?' Joanne asked as he headed to the front door.

'No thanks.' One beer was enough—Ferg didn't want to let down his guard around his new colleagues.

'Yes, please,' came the chorus from almost everyone else.

As Joanne refilled the wineglasses, Trevor appeared with a plump, middle-aged woman wearing pearls around her neck and a fancy blouse as if she was heading to church or something.

'Eileen said she's seen some cows on the main road she thinks might belong to us,' Trev said to Joanne.

'Really?' Joanne's eyebrows rose slowly.

The woman nodded. 'I'm so sorry to interrupt your soiree, but just doing my neighbourly duty.'

'Neighbourly?' The youngest bloke—Haylee's husband—snorted, and when she elbowed him in the side, he tried to hide it by taking a mouthful of beer.

'A phone call would have sufficed, Eileen,' Joanne said, 'but thanks for your concern. Trevor will go check now.'

'On my way.' He was already starting back in the direction of the front door.

'I'll come with you,' said another man; Ferg thought he belonged to Judy and that his name might have been Pete.

'You can see Eileen out on your way.'

But Eileen seemed in no hurry to leave. 'You must be Mr McWilliams,' she said, coming around the table towards Fergus.

'Hello.' He felt obliged to stand and offer his hand.

She beamed as they shook hands—surely Eileen wasn't one of the single women on the prowl? She was old enough to be his mother.

'It's so lovely to have a male teacher in town. I don't have any children there myself anymore but I've been a big supporter of the school—I was P&C president for almost eleven years and I hope to have grandchildren there one day. My husband and I would love to have you round for dinner one night, or maybe Sunday lunch? I cook a very good roast lamb, even if I do say so myself.'

If Ferg wasn't stuffed full of barbecue, his mouth might have watered a little at the mention of roast lamb, and she'd spoken of a husband, so it was probably safe to assume she wasn't a cougar.

Beck clicked her fingers. 'What a pity we're having a staff meeting on Sunday.'

'On the weekend?' Eileen frowned.

'Yes,' Joanne confirmed. 'And Fergus just told us he's vegan, so your roast won't suit him. Never mind.'

Vegan? Ferg thought as Joanne stood and started ushering Eileen towards the front door. 'Thanks for telling us about the cows.'

As the two women disappeared down the hallway, the others erupted into giggles.

'You owe me one for that,' Beck said.

'What?' he asked. 'She seemed like a nice lady.'

'With three single daughters she wants married off asap,' Maria told him with a wink. 'I'd bet money they'd all be at lunch on Sunday if you'd said yes and Eileen wouldn't let you escape without agreeing to take at least one of them on a date!'

Surely this was some kind of joke. These country folks had to be a having a laugh at his expense.

Haylee's husband—Brad, that was it!—leaned back in his seat and laughed loudly. 'Hasn't anybody warned you that new teachers to town are fair game? I snapped Hayles up the moment she arrived.'

'Actually, someone did, but I didn't know they were serious.'

Ferg's thoughts turned to Tabitha. He found himself wondering who the father of her baby was and wishing Eileen hadn't interrupted that conversation.

Was her pregnancy the result of a one-night stand or had she broken up with the father? If so, it couldn't have happened that long ago as she wasn't showing yet. Perhaps she was fresh out of a bad break-up, meaning she probably meant it when she'd said she wasn't interested in him. His face suddenly felt impossibly hot as he recalled their exchange. Maybe he owed her an apology.

'It's alright, we'll look out for you,' Beck said. 'We'll let you know who to steer clear of.'

'Thanks.' Ferg shook his head. 'But I'm here to teach and that's it. I'm focused on the kids; I'm not looking for a relationship.'

'Have you got someone special already back in Perth?' Haylee asked.

It crossed his mind that maybe he should invent a girlfriend (or boyfriend) but then everyone would probably pester him, wondering when she (or he) was coming down to visit.

'No. It's just me.'

'Interested in hooking up with anyone?' Brad asked with a chuckle.

He shook his head. 'I just came out of a long-term relationship and I'm not ready to date again just yet.'

'Aw.' The women around the table looked at him like he'd just announced his cat had died.

'It is what it is.'

'Do you play sport?' Judy asked, and Ferg was glad of the change of topic.

'A little.'

'What about cricket?'

'Yeah, played a bit in my time.'

'I was wondering if you'd be interested in helping coach junior cricket for the kids? Terry Saunders, Carline's husband, has been running it for years but he's reluctantly withdrawn this year because he's going to be too busy driving Carline to and from chemo over the next couple of months. I've asked around but, heading into harvest, most of the dads say they'll turn up when they can but can't commit.'

'Sure. I'll do it.' Ferg didn't have to think twice. He was rapidly coming to understand that everyone pitched in where they could in a country town and this way he'd tick that community-spirit box and be helping kids at the same time.

'Fantastic!' Judy applauded him and the others also smiled their approval. 'Training has always been Thursday afternoons, and they start next week.'

'What's all the excitement?' asked Trevor as he and Judy's husband trundled back into the room.

'Fergus has agreed to help coach junior cricket,' Beck said.

'That's wonderful news.'

'Let me guess … there were no cows on the road?' Joanne asked Trevor.

'Not even one,' he replied.

Chapter Five

'It's about time we had a male teacher in Walsh. Of course I want Carline to get better, but it'd be wonderful if we could somehow get the new man to stay too. It would be so good for the kids to have a good male role model, especially the boys.'

'But did you hear he's a vegan?'

'No! Surely not. How did you find that out?'

Tab cleared her throat as she hovered beside a table where two women who had been friends with her mum sat wearing tennis uniforms. She couldn't care less what Fergus McWilliams chose to put in his mouth but she wished people would stop talking about him as if he were royalty come to town.

'Good afternoon, Mrs Brown, Mrs Walker, what can I get you today? Meg has made some delicious blueberry and lemon scones, or are you after something cold on this warm afternoon? I can recommend our choc-orange ice-cream cookie sandwich.'

'Oh, hello, Tabby.' Mrs Walker smiled up at her. 'They both sound delicious. How ever are we supposed to choose?'

'Why don't we get both and we can share?' suggested Mrs Brown. 'We have, after all, just burned off a number of calories playing tennis.'

'Good idea.' Tab nodded. 'And can I get you something to drink?'

They ordered a pot of herbal tea for two and just as Tab stepped away, Mrs Walker said, 'And congratulations on your lovely news, dear. Your mother would have been so proud of your independence and the way you've overcome so many hurdles in your life.'

'Thanks.' Tab smiled. 'I'm very excited.'

'We were just talking about the new teacher. Of course there's a few years till your little one will be at school,' mused Mrs Brown. 'Perhaps Ned will be in his class?'

'I guess so,' Tab said dryly. 'Now, I'd love to stay and chat but we're short-staffed in the kitchen today, so …' She turned away and rolled her eyes as she went to start on the order.

She huffed loudly as she grabbed a plate and two cookies from the cabinet, went back into the café to scoop the ice-cream from the display fridge and then returned to work her magic with the trimmings. Desserts had become their speciality at Eliza's Tea Rooms and they took great pride in presentation.

'Are you okay?' Meg asked, as she pulled a fresh batch of scones out of the oven.

'Yes, but if I hear one more word about the new teacher … I might throttle someone. '

'Mr McWilliams?' Meg looked confused. 'You know him?'

'I met him on Wednesday afternoon and I don't wish to know him any more than that. He's an arrogant arse. We can only hope Carline has a miraculous recovery and he goes back to the city before he can infect our kids.'

Meg held up a hand. 'Whoa … rewind a little. What happened?'

The bell on the counter dinged, signalling another customer.

Meg groaned. 'Do you want to get that and I'll take this order out? Then you better tell me everything.'

'Sure.' Tab put the final touch of candy floss on top of the sandwich and then went outside to greet their new customer. Thankfully it wasn't anyone from Walsh. 'Hi, what can I get for you?'

'Can I have two takeaway flat whites and three chocolate milk-shakes?' asked the man, glancing around. 'This place is fantastic. How long have you been open?'

'Just over a year.'

He nodded. 'We haven't driven through Rose Hill in a couple of years. Last time we were here it was a ghost town so my wife and I are pleasantly surprised to see the change.'

'It's still pretty quiet, but since we opened the tea rooms, it's getting a little more traffic. There's talk of reviving the park across the road as well. We're a nice distance between Perth and Marga-ret River for those wanting to take the scenic route.'

The man grinned. 'That's why we come this way and it's so good to see a bit of life again—it breaks my heart when small towns die.' He pointed into the small gallery off the main café. 'Is the artwork all local?'

'Ah huh. We have plenty of talent in the region,' she said as she started on the coffees. 'Everything is local, from the jams we use on the scones to the ice-cream.'

His gaze went to the glass display fridge that housed all her current flavours. 'The ice-cream is local?'

Tab nodded proudly. 'Yes, it's mine actually. We source the milk from my family's dairy farm and make the ice-cream right here on the premises. Would you like a taste-test while you wait for your drinks?'

'Yes, please.'

Tab gave him a spoonful of her latest creation—crunchy cara-mel donut—and glowed inside at the expression on his face as he tasted it.

'That's out of this world. Who'd have thought of putting donuts into ice-cream? We'll definitely drop in for desserts with the kids on our way home. Catch ya.'

After the happy camper left with his drinks and a couple of chocolate brownies to go, there was a late afternoon rush, so Meg didn't get the chance to grill Tab until they were closing up.

'I'm dying to hear about Mr McWilliams,' she said as she flipped the sign on the door to closed, pulled out the nearest chair and flopped into it. 'Where did you meet him?'

Tab took a weight off her feet in the seat opposite. 'At the school. I saw him painting out the front on my way home the other day and thought I'd go welcome him and offer him my left-overs from Stitch'n'Bitch.'

'That was a nice idea.'

'I thought so, but it was a debacle. When I tried to shake his hand, I ended up throwing the whole plate of food at him.'

'What?' Meg's eyes widened.

Tab nodded and filled her in on how he'd gaped in disgust at her arm and then when she'd tried to give him a friendly warning, insinuated she had ulterior motives for bringing him food. Meg seemed to find great amusement in the story.

'The man's got tickets on himself.'

Meg smirked. 'Sounds like he's got under your skin.'

'He most definitely has not!'

'Okay, okay, I believe you, but maybe you got him on a bad day, or maybe there's a good reason why he was a little standoffish and unpleasant.'

'A *little*?'

Meg chuckled. 'Don't let him get to you. As we've all told Ned, a person's bad behaviour is a reflection on them, not you. I think people probably thought I was standoffish when I first came to town, but as you know, I had my reasons.'

Meg's reasons were major indeed and had almost kept her and Lawson apart.

'I don't think you were ever rude exactly.'

Still, Meg's comment did make Tab think. Although she didn't believe there was ever any excuse for being rude to another human being, could there be more to Fergus's story than met the eye?

Chapter Six

Ferg took a sip of his coffee and glanced around his classroom. He'd been up since the crack of dawn and had arrived at school a good hour before any of the other staff.

'You all ready?' At the question, he looked up to see Joanne standing in the open doorway. 'Carline usually greets everyone at the gate on the first day back, but I thought I'd check if you wanted me here to introduce you to the class instead.'

He shook his head. 'Nah, I'll be fine. I can't wait to meet the kids.'

'They're a great bunch. As I said, there are a few boys who can be difficult and like to push boundaries, but if you show them who's boss right away, you'll be fine.'

It was the difficult, troubled kids Fergus was looking forward to the most—he'd been one himself thanks to his messed-up childhood and knew first-hand how a great teacher could turn a person's life around. He'd chosen to become a teacher because he wanted to make that kind of difference in kids' lives, to help them believe in themselves, whatever life threw at them.

But before he could reply, his phone buzzed with a text message.

Joanne nodded. 'Do you need to answer that?'

'Nah, it's probably just the dentist or someone.' He took a final sip of his coffee then threw the disposable cup in the bin.

'Okay then, well, I'll be off. Break a leg.' She laughed a little. 'I'll pop in sometime this morning to see how you're going.'

'Thanks.' As Joanne left, Fergus glanced down at the message.

Good luck on your first day. Would love to hear all about it. Miss you. E.

Despite the unfamiliar number, it didn't take a genius to know who 'E' was. He'd blocked her (and Jools), but she must have borrowed someone else's phone to message him.

Why couldn't they just leave him alone?

They were obviously feeling guilty and wanted his forgiveness, but that would only make *them* feel better—it wouldn't change the situation, and it sure as hell wouldn't make *him* feel better. What did they expect? That he'd give them his blessing and they could go back to playing happy families? He shook his head and made a mental note to call Telstra and get himself a new number. Maybe then they'd get the message that he didn't want them in his life anymore.

At the sound of footsteps, Fergus looked up to see two little boys shuffling into the room. He shoved his phone in the desk drawer and went over to greet them.

'Hi guys.' He stooped down to their level and they looked up at him warily. 'I'm Mr McWilliams, your new teacher. It's a pleasure to meet you.'

'I'm Levi and this is Tate.' The one on the left pointed to the other boy—it was impossible to tell them apart.

'You must be the Walsh twins.' Fergus remembered seeing that surname on his class list and wondering if they were any relation to Adeline and the founding Walshes.

'Good morning. I'm Sally and these ratbags belong to me.'

He glanced up to see a pretty but harried-looking woman standing behind them—he'd not even noticed her come in.

'Hi.' He smiled at the mother and ruffled each twin's hair. 'They don't look like ratbags at all.'

The woman snorted. 'Looks can be deceiving.' Then she stooped down and kissed them both goodbye. 'Don't forget you're getting the bus to the farm this afternoon.' As the twins wandered off, Sally explained, 'The boys' father and I are divorced. They're with my ex-husband this week, but please call me if there are any issues.'

Fergus nodded and as Sally left there was an influx of kids.

'I came on the bus,' said one little girl, who introduced herself as Lisl, then glanced around the classroom and noticed the new desk arrangement and theme.

'Harry Potter,' she mused, and he wasn't sure if she was impressed or not with the set-up.

'That's right. Have you seen the movies?'

'I've read the books *and* seen the movies.'

'Even better,' he replied. 'I can tell you and I are going to get on like a house on fire.'

Lisl raised her eyebrows. He guessed this little girl might take a little bit of winning over, but that was okay. Ferg liked a challenge. Lisl went off to unpack her bag and he introduced himself to the rest of the first load of bus kids.

'Are you really a teacher?' asked a little boy with a thick mop of black hair that fell across his eyes.

Ferg nodded. 'Sure am. Did four years at university and have a certificate to prove it. What's your name?'

'Jimmy.' The boy frowned. 'But I thought only women could be teachers.'

Another boy backed him up. 'Mum says girls can be doctors, boys can be nurses and men can be teachers but we've never seen one before.' His tone said he'd believed the male teacher was a myth, up there with Santa Claus, the Easter bunny and the tooth fairy.

'Just because we've never had a male teacher,' Lisl interjected with an obvious roll of her eyes, 'doesn't mean they don't exist. Women can be anything they want to be and I guess that means so can men.'

Ferg fought a smile. 'That's right, Lisl. In Perth, I know lots of male teachers.'

Before anyone in the small crowd could say anything else, two more little girls and a tall slim woman with a wide-brimmed straw hat entered the classroom.

The woman strode across the room and held out her hand. 'Good morning, Mr McWilliams,' she said with a wide grin. 'I'm Tennille Wellington, and these two delights are my eldest kids, Victoria, Year 4, and Amelia, Year 3.'

'Although everyone calls me Milly,' announced the shorter of the two girls.

'I've got to rush 'cause my other three are outside on the play-ground and lord knows what strife they're getting up to, but I just wanted to say hi and welcome to town. You've chosen a good time to land. We're gearing up for the annual agricultural show and it's an anniversary year, so it's going to be bigger and better than usual. I'm not sure if Joanne's told you yet—she probably didn't want to bombard you—but we like to get as many kids entering our competitions as possible, get the younger generations excited about the show. So many other small shows are dying and we don't want that to happen to ours. Anyway, it'd be good if you could allocate a couple of afternoons to this for the kids who don't have the encouragement at home. I'm happy to come in and help—I'll drop my young ones off at occasional care. Just let me know.'

Tennille plopped a kiss on each of her girls' heads, then wag-gled her fingers at him as she left the classroom. 'We'll talk soon.'

Ferg had never known anyone to talk so much, so quickly, without expecting so much as a word in reply.

Rachael Johns

'I won the junior art prize at the show last year,' Lisl told him.

He looked down at her. 'I'll bet you did.'

He barely had time to recover from the whirlwind that was Tennille before another two parents arrived. He tried to focus on the kids, but after a quick hello, they ran off to see their friends.

The parents introduced themselves but their names went in one ear and out the other.

The woman thrust a Tupperware container at him. 'White chocolate and raspberry muffins,' she announced. 'They're my speciality. You can send the container home with Eli when you're done.'

'Thanks.' Why was it that almost every woman in this town seemed intent on feeding him? And mostly sugary stuff. He'd have diabetes before his contract was up.

'Have you lived in a small town before?' asked the bloke.

Ferg shook his head. 'This is my first.'

The woman chuckled. 'It takes some getting used to. I've lived here twelve years and I'm still not considered a local but I don't think I could live anywhere else now. No small community is perfect, but Walsh is very welcoming and everyone mucks in and does their bit to keep the community spirit alive.'

The man nodded. 'I'm with the volunteer firies and we're always looking for an extra pair of hands if you're interested. Won't be long before we're in the midst of bushfire season again.'

'You get many fires down here?' Ferg asked.

'You'd be surprised. We've got a meeting tomorrow night if you want to come along. There's always a bit of a laugh and a few beers at the end of it.'

'I'll see if I can make it,' he promised, 'although I'm only here a couple of months and I want to focus on the kids while I am.'

'Fair enough.' The man shrugged. 'But the offer's open to come along and meet the guys—'

'And women,' the woman interrupted.

'And women,' he conceded. 'We have a few of them now. Look, if you're at a loose end tomorrow night, come say hi. No pressure.'

'Okay.' Ferg glanced surreptitiously at his watch. It was one minute past nine—why hadn't Joanne rung the bell yet? He suddenly remembered she'd said it was his class's responsibility to ring the bell and that the kids usually took turns.

'Excuse me,' he said to the parents, then called, 'Lisl!' So far hers was the only name he was a hundred per cent certain of.

'Yes, Mr McWilliams?'

'Can you go ring the bell for me?'

Her face lit up with the first genuine smile he'd seen as the other kids all groaned their disappointment. As she grabbed the bell from his desk and rushed outside, Ferg made his apologies to the remaining parents. 'Nice to meet you both, and thanks for the muffins.'

'No worries. See you round. Maybe tomorrow night.' After a quick wave to his daughter, who was ensconced in a board game on the floor with some other students, the man left.

'Well, I guess I'd better be off too,' said the woman, leaning a little too close for Ferg's liking. 'I hope you like the muffins and …' She hesitated a moment. 'We live on the outskirts of town in the old roadhouse; I'm an artist and sadly Eli's father died a couple of years ago. I know it gets lonely without adult conversation, so if the firies aren't your thing but you're bored of an evening or weekend, feel free to drop by our place.'

'Ah, thanks.' Ferg couldn't quite tell if Eli's mum was just being friendly or hitting on him—he would have assumed the first if Tabitha's warning wasn't still fresh in his mind. But either way, even if he was going to be here longer and even if he was looking for a relationship, he didn't get involved with parents.

At the sound of the bell, the students scrambled to their desks, all apparently eager to please the new teacher. Lisl had just returned to the classroom when one more boy and his dad hurried into the room.

The man nodded and gave a sheepish smile. 'Sorry Ned's a little late. We had an issue with our milking machine and he missed the bus.'

Now that was an excuse Ferg had never heard in the city. 'No worries.' He grinned at the kid and thrust out his hand. 'Nice to meet you, Ned.'

'You too.' Ned beamed up at him then went to take a seat.

'I'm Lawson Cooper-Jones.' Ned's dad also offered his hand. 'Promise we won't make a habit of this, but my wife and my sister had to go to Bunbury early this morning and I had to fix the problem before organising Ned.'

'It's really fine,' Ferg said, all the while wondering *Cooper-Jones?* Was that Tabitha's surname? He'd been hoping to run into her so he could apologise but so far, despite the miniscule size of the town, their paths hadn't crossed again.

'I've been meaning to stop by your place and say hi, but things have been a little hectic,' Lawson said as if he could read Ferg's mind. 'We're on the farm next door and actually lease some land off Mrs Lord, so if you ever need anything, just holler! And feel free to pop round for a drink one night.'

'Thanks.'

'Anyway.' Lawson cleared his throat, his friendly smile still filling his face. 'Hope the first day is a ripper.'

As he left, Ferg shut the door and then turned to all the eager little faces staring back from their desks. 'Good morning, everyone.'

'Good morning, Mr McWilliams,' they chanted like they were in some kind of trance.

'No, no, no, no, no!' He held up a hand and shook his head at them. 'That won't do at all. I want you guys to sound alive when you greet me. Let's try it again. This time I want the cows in the next town to hear you.'

Delighted by this challenge, the kids all opened up their lungs and almost burst his eardrums as they gave him a very different good morning. Even Lisl looked like she enjoyed it.

'That's better. Now, before we get to know each other, I'm going to read you the first chapter of my very favourite book.'

Although some of the class had already read *Harry Potter and the Philosopher's Stone* and many more had seen the movies, no one complained about hearing it again. Once he'd finished, he handed each child a letter, which was a version of the letter to Hogwarts that Harry Potter had received, and watched their eyes widen with glee as he explained that this term their school was going to be Hogwarts. 'We're even going to learn to play quiddich!'

There were squeals of excitement at this news and he waited for the noise to die down before he said, 'But first, I want to get to know you all. We're going to take it in turns telling each other three facts about ourselves. Who wants to go first?'

Unsurprisingly, Lisl's hand shot up into the air. She sat up even straighter and cleared her throat as someone five times her age might do. 'I'm Lisl Diamond. I have a pony called Veronica Jane and we came first in Showjumping and Dressage at the last club trials. I *don't* like bananas.'

'Thanks, Lisl.' Ferg smothered a smirk. 'I'll remember that.'

Jimmy went next, proud as punch to tell the class that his family were Noongar people and had been in this region longer than anyone else in the class's families. The twins joyfully explained what Adeline had also told him, that their family, the Walshes, had been the first after the Aboriginal people. It seemed about seventy per cent of the kids were from farming families, others had parents who owned locals businesses, some worked for the shire, and then there was Eli's mum who was an artist.

As the kids spoke, Ferg tried to listen eagerly to each and every one of them but his gaze kept drifting to Ned, scrutinising the poor boy to see if he bore any resemblance to Tabitha. Whereas he had white-blond, slightly wavy hair that brushed the collar of his school polo shirt, Tabitha's hair was almost jet-black and hung in a short, jagged chin-length bob.

He shook his head—why couldn't he get her out of his head?

Probably because he'd acted like such an arse towards her. It was one thing not wanting to get involved with anyone, but that didn't mean he had to be rude. The mess that was his life wasn't Tabitha's fault and he shouldn't take his anger out on her just because the perpetrators weren't around to take it themselves. Not that he wanted them around—they were the sole reason he'd fled the city.

'Ned? Do you want to go next?'

The blond kid's eyes widened as he nodded enthusiastically. 'I'm Ned Cooper-Jones. I live on a dairy farm and my aunty makes the best ice-cream in the world. And she lives in a haunted house!'

'Wow.' There was a lot to unpack there but Ferg resisted the urge to ask further questions.

The last few kids took their turns—one was obsessed with Pokémon cards, even though in the city that craze had died years ago; another said she was reading the *Guinness Book of Records* and wanted to get her name in there one day; and the last told Ferg he was going to be an international soccer star. There was one in every class.

'Right,' he clapped his hands together, 'now we're going to write holiday recounts.'

'Hang on,' Lisl's hand shot into the air as the others started to stand. '*You* haven't given us your three things yet?'

'Ooh yes, we want to know about you,' said *Guinness Book of Records* girl.

'Fair enough.' He addressed the eager crowd at his feet. 'Well, number one, I'm actually named after a duck.'

Half the kids burst into giggles and he explained to them who Fergus McDuck was—most of them probably didn't even know who Donald was.

'Number two, I play the piano accordion.' Again, most of the kids obviously had no idea what that was.

'It's like a mini piano,' Lisl explained in that smug tone Fergus wasn't sure whether to be amused or irritated by, 'and you carry it in your arms to play. I think it belongs to the wind instrument family. Do you have it with you?'

'I do.'

'Can you play it for us?' begged Milly.

'Of course, but first our recounts.'

'But you've only given us two things,' said Victoria.

These country kids were on the ball.

'Number three, I only like black jelly beans.'

The kids giggled.

'Do you have a wife?' Lisl asked.

'No.'

She nodded and then Ned fired another question. 'Do you have any pets?'

Geez, these kids were as nosy as their parents. 'A cat. Her name is Mrs Norris, like the caretaker's cat in *Harry Potter*.'

'You really like *Harry Potter*, don't you?' said Lisl.

'What's not to like? Now—'

But before he could get the kids back on track, Victoria interrupted, 'What about brothers or sisters? I have four, do you have any?'

He hesitated a moment, not wanting to lie to his class but wanting to nip this conversation in the bud. 'No, I don't. Now,' he spoke firmly this time, 'no further questions until we've done some work.'

The rest of the day went well. Ferg had fun with the kids and got used to their constant barrage of questions. He kicked the footy with some of the boys at lunch, read some more *Philosopher's Stone* and introduced them to his accordion in the afternoon. He didn't even realise it was almost home time until parents started lining up outside.

'Alright, every one, time to go home. See you tomorrow.' He stood by the door, saying goodbye to each child by name as they filed out the room.

'Ned!' He heard someone call and looked up to see two women waving. One had long mahogany-coloured hair halfway down her back and the other one was … Tabitha Cooper-Jones.

Chapter Seven

'Thanks for coming with me today,' Tab said as Meg drove them out of Bunbury, pop music from the local radio station softly filling the car.

'Are you kidding? Thank you for letting me come with you and share this big moment. I still can't believe you're having a baby, so actually seeing it on the screen and hearing the heartbeat was magical, yet also made it real.'

'I know.' Tab gazed down at the black and white image of her baby. The first time she'd seen him or her on the screen, she'd been eight weeks pregnant and although she'd heard the heartbeat nice and strong, the image on the screen had been more like a jellybean than a person. But today … today she'd cried as she watched her baby wriggle around, its limbs all clearly visible. Meg had assumed they were tears of joy and perhaps some of them were, but she suspected some might have been oh-hell-what-on-earth-have-I-done tears of fear. 'Am I totally insane? This isn't like going to see a movie on my own.'

'What?' Meg took her eyes off the road and glanced at Tab. 'No, of course you're not. And stop saying you're on your own.

You've got me, Lawson, hell, a whole town behind you, but even if you didn't, you could do this with your eyes closed. You, Tabitha Cooper-Jones, are single-handedly—no pun intended— the most capable person I know. This little baby is going to be the luckiest kid on the planet.'

Tab laughed and relaxed a little at Meg's words. She did want this more than anything, she was just scared that going ahead with it was a selfish decision. 'And it's also going to be the best-dressed kid on the planet if you have anything to do with it!'

Meg smiled sheepishly. 'Hey, I can't help being excited, and who in their right mind can resist all those tiny clothes?'

'I have no idea,' Tab agreed.

After the ultrasound, the two of them had enjoyed a lovely brunch by the beach and then shopped until they'd pillaged prac- tically every store that sold anything baby-related in town. Tab dared not check her bank account. 'This pregnancy is going to send us both broke, but at least I'll have plenty of hand-me-downs when you and Lawson have a baby.'

'If.' Meg's one word was filled with sadness.

Tab had assumed her brother and sister-in-law were simply enjoying a few years of married life before they added to their family, but suddenly wondered if that was not the case. 'Have you guys been trying?'

'Yep,' Meg whispered. 'Almost twelve months.'

'Oh Meg.' Tab's heart squeezed. 'Why didn't you say some- thing? Have you seen a doctor about it?'

'I don't need to. I know what's wrong. All my years of drug abuse have affected my fertility. Thank God Lawson already has Ned, but we both would have liked a child together.'

Tab understood that—she couldn't deny that she herself would have liked an actual present father for her child that was also a part- ner in all things for her, but life wasn't perfect. Meg and Lawson had the great love affair, she was going to have a baby—no one ever got it all. 'Have you guys considered IVF?'

'We've just started talking about it, but … never mind.' Meg sniffed and shook her head. 'Sorry. I didn't mean to take away from your excitement.' She reached across, turned up the radio and started bopping in her seat. 'I love this song!'

Tab didn't know it—she rarely listened to the radio as more often than not, one of her ex-boyfriend's songs would come on and although she would never admit it, she couldn't bear listening to his lyrics about true love. It was almost a decade since they'd broken up but she thought about him far too often. She even dreamt about him, and although the dreams were wonderful, she always woke up irritated at herself. People say you never get over your first love and maybe that was the problem, or maybe it was that the world wouldn't let her forget. Ryder's handsome face often appeared on the cover of the glossy magazines that sat at the front of the checkouts at IGA and, as his extended family were locals, people tended to keep her up to date, however much she tried to shut down such conversations.

Perhaps if she'd had other boyfriends he wouldn't be the only one to occupy her thoughts, but he was the first and only notch on her bedpost.

The current song faded away and a chirpy sounding woman came onto the airwaves to read the two o'clock news, which consisted of a shark sighting off the coast of Augusta, a school bus that had crashed on the freeway—thankfully, no fatalities—and then, just before a weather update, she mentioned Ryder O'Connell. Tab's heart slammed into her chest and Meg rushed to change the station, but Tab stopped her. If there was news about Ryder getting engaged or anything like that, she wanted to hear it. It was best to be prepared for the inevitable gossip and questions people would throw at her.

But it wasn't a warm-fuzzy announcement.

'The ARIA Award winner, former golden boy from the west, has been fighting rumours of wild partying ways, and it seems there may be some truth to this gossip. Sydney police arrested the country music singer last night and have charged him with drink driving after being caught at more than double the legal limit. He allegedly tried to evade a police random breath test by doing a U-turn and was eventually caught and taken into custody. O'Connell himself is yet to comment on the charge.'

'Holy shit.' Ever since dumping her and soaring to success in a solo career, it had been one triumph after another. Tab reckoned he probably thought himself invincible and immune to the law, and, although not proud of it, couldn't help the little kick of delight inside her at this news.

'Well,' Meg said, 'that'll damage his reputation a bit. All those mums won't be quite so happy about their kids looking up to him and idolising him now.' Then she coloured slightly. 'Not that I can talk. And who knows, maybe something bad happened that upset him and this was a one-off?'

Tab nodded; Meg was probably right and really, it had nothing to do with her anymore anyway. Another song began and their conversation turned to the upcoming show and how much extra ice-cream they were going to have to make. Tab's business had started from the farm and she used to go to all the local shows selling her gourmet delights, but since they'd opened the tea rooms, most of her business had been done there. She didn't have time for traipsing about anymore, but they were making an exception for the Walsh Ag Show, as everyone had begged her to be there.

'Do you mind if we stop by the school and collect Ned?' Meg asked as they slowed on the outskirts of Walsh. 'It's quite hot and he'll get home quicker than if he has to take the bus. It feels cruel to subject him to that when we're in town anyway.'

'Of course not,' Tab replied. She'd left her car at the farm this morning and although she was tired, getting Ned wouldn't add more than another hour to her day.

'Thanks. I can't wait to hear how his first day with the new teacher was.'

'Yeah.' Tab tried not to frown at the mention of Fergus McGrumpy. As long as he was kind to Ned, it didn't matter what he thought of her, or she him.

When Meg parked in the school car park a few minutes later, she practically leapt from the car. 'Aren't you coming? Ned will be so excited if you're here to collect him.'

If not for this last statement, Tab would have remained firmly glued to the passenger seat, but she loved her nephew and didn't want to let his teacher stop her from being a doting aunt.

'Yes,' she said, unclicking her seatbelt and climbing out.

There were a number of mums already waiting outside the class and of course all of them wanted to ask Tab's opinion on Ryder's delinquency. As if her opinion actually mattered. Why did everyone have such long memories in the country? And why did her only serious boyfriend, her very first and only love, have to be so bloody famous?

Thankfully, it wasn't long before Jimmy Long ran outside and rang the bell and kids started spilling out of the classrooms, putting an end to the conversation. Tab hung back, letting Meg go forward to get Ned. As the crowd started to disperse, she got her first glimpse of Fergus McWilliams since their awkward introduction.

And good grief, he was far hotter than her memory had given him credit for.

Standing in the doorway watching his class depart, he was wearing navy blue smart trousers and a shirt of a lighter blue, the sleeves pushed up to his elbows and the top button open in a casual way. He could have been a model in a fashion catalogue.

Although he was fully clothed this time, Tab's mind flashed with an image of him shirtless and her cheeks immediately burned. *So he's hot? So what?* Ryder had been handsome too—in a different, more boy-next-door kinda way—so Tab knew well enough that looks did not a person make.

Still, she couldn't look away. She watched, almost touched by the sweet way he farewelled each kid individually.

'Bye, Ned,' he said, grinning down at her nephew.

'See ya, Mr McDuck.'

McDuck?

Ned waved as he laughed and threw himself into Meg's arms. She must have whispered something to him, because he looked up and screamed, 'Aunty Tab!'

It was her turn for a hug and as Ned gripped her hard and launched immediately into his awesome day, Meg hung back to introduce herself to Fergus. A safe few metres away, Tab couldn't hear what they were saying, so was shocked when Meg started to walk towards them and Fergus followed.

His hands shoved in his pockets, giving him an almost boyish charm, he nodded at her. 'Afternoon, Tabitha. I was wondering if we could have a quick word?'

'What?' She blinked, surprised he even remembered her name. 'You want to talk to *me*?'

'Yes. It won't take long.'

Meg looked between them and grinned. 'Ned and I will wait in the car.' She practically dragged the boy off by the scruff of his collar.

Tab had no idea what he wanted but she could guarantee it wasn't anything like Meg was obviously thinking. Or wishing. Her sister-in-law was a hopeless romantic.

'Do you want to come inside?'

Tab swallowed at the thought of being alone in the classroom with him. 'I don't think that's a good idea.'

He looked confused, probably thinking she didn't trust her hormones alone with him. She rolled her eyes — he wasn't *that* hot.

'I don't have a child in your class.' She gestured to the few parents who were still lingering and lowered her voice. 'People in small towns jump to conclusions quickly.'

'Ah, right, okay. Sorry, I'm still getting used to how things work.'

She nearly smiled at that; his uncertainty was almost sweet, but then she remembered what a wanker he'd been and levelled with him instead. 'What was it you wanted to talk to me about?'

He glanced quickly at the ground and then back up to meet her gaze. A tinge of red spread in his cheeks. 'I … I just wanted to apologise.'

Wow. Tab didn't know what she'd been expecting but it was not this—in her experience men rarely went out of their way to admit they were wrong. 'For?' she prodded.

There were a number of possibilities—for his rude behaviour when she'd tried to welcome him, for gawking at her arm as though she were an alien *or* for assuming she was cracking onto him when she was just trying to be nice.

'For my ungraciousness when you came to say hi and for my embarrassing assumption that you were coming onto me. I heard about your pregnancy.' He nodded towards her still-flat stomach. 'Congratulations.'

Her hand drifted instinctively to said stomach and she couldn't help smiling. 'Apology accepted.' She'd never been good at holding grudges and felt her dislike towards Fergus wavering a little.

'You were right about the women,' he added. 'It sounded so ludicrous and far-fetched, but …'

She raised her eyebrows and couldn't help a little smirk even though she normally wasn't one to gloat. 'You've had some interest?'

'You could say that.' He grimaced and she felt a little tingle of something dance down her spine at the combination of amusement and horror in his eyes. 'I've never had so many invitations to dinner in my life. But it's not just that; I even had the offer of—'

'Let me guess,' she interrupted. 'A puppy?'

'Yes.' His caramel eyes widened. 'How'd you know?'

'Not to make you feel any less special, but you're not the first guy Adeline Walsh has tried to lure with one of her adorable Maremmas. I *did* try to warn you.'

He had the good sense to look abashed. 'Yes, you did.'

'Of course, you could always take the puppy and run?'

Fergus chuckled. 'Tempting, but my cat already hates me enough.'

He was handsome even when he scowled, but the smile that lifted his lips now made him cute in a less polished kind of way, and she tried to ignore the way her breath quickened at his deep throaty laugh. 'Your cat hates you?'

He nodded. 'It's a long, boring story.'

Tab found she actually wanted to hear it but Meg and Ned were waiting in the car. 'Right, well, I'd better be going. Hope your first day at school was good. I'll probably see you around.'

'Sure. Sorry again. And, I promise I'm not always such a wanker.'

'I'll reserve my judgement on that,' she said, resisting the urge to ask him why he'd acted like one.

As she turned to go, he said, 'One more thing?'

'Yes?'

'I know you don't owe me any help, but … Adeline keeps pestering me for an interview for the local paper. Is that legit or …?'

Tab laughed—a week in Walsh had made him paranoid. 'It is. Adeline is the editor of the *Walsh Whisperer*. The way she talks you'd think it was the *New York Times*, but locals do love it and they will all be curious about you, so an interview is a good idea because it means less chance of a grilling when you're in IGA trying to buy milk.'

'Right. Thanks.' He ran a hand through his hair as if exhausted by all of this. 'I guess I'll do the interview then. Is there anything else I should know?'

And because she was in a good mood from seeing her healthy baby on the screen, she decided to give him one more piece of advice. 'Well, something to keep in mind is that pretty much everyone is related to everyone else in one way or another, so be careful what you say about anyone because it might come back to bite you on the bum.'

'Got it. Appreciate the tip.'

'You're welcome, and good luck.'

There was a swing in Tab's step as she walked out of the school-yard and across to Meg's four-wheel drive.

'You look happy,' her sister-in-law declared the moment Tab opened the passenger door and slid into her seat.

'It's been a great day.' She turned to Ned in the back seat. 'Do you wanna see a picture of your cousin?'

His eyes widened. 'For real?'

She nodded, dug the ultrasound photos out of her bag and handed them to him. 'Be careful.'

'Wow.' His expression was full of awe. 'How does the camera see through all your skin? Is that the baby's arm or leg? Is it a boy or a girl?'

Both Tab and Meg laughed at his barrage of questions and Tab answered them all patiently. 'So how was your first day of school?' she asked, as Meg turned off the main road in the direction of their farm.

'Awesome. Mr McDuck is the coolest teacher ever.'

'Why do you call him Mr McDuck?'

'He's named after a duck,' Ned explained. 'Apparently his mum loved Donald Duck but didn't love the name Donald so called him after one of the other ducks.'

Meg and Tab exchanged a look of horror. 'No duck names for your baby, okay?'

'Deal,' Tab said.

The moment Meg stopped the car, Ned leapt out and rushed off to find Lawson to tell him all about his day. As their dogs stopped him briefly in his tracks to welcome him, Tab put her hand on the door.

'Not so fast,' Meg said. 'I see what you mean about Mr McDuck. Until he spoke, I thought McDreamy was a more suitable title, but he definitely didn't give off a friendly vibe when I introduced myself. He barely met my eye and made it very clear he'd rather be doing anything but talking to me.'

'Really?' Tab hadn't got that impression at all this time.

'Ah huh. Ned obviously thinks he's the cat's pyjamas though.'

'Maybe he's just one of those people who has difficulty talking to adults?'

Meg raised an eyebrow. 'You've changed your tune. What did he want with you anyway?'

'Oh, just to apologise for the way he acted the other day.'

'Wow, that is noble,' Meg conceded with a slight pout. 'Now I'm not sure whether I'm supposed to like him or not.'

Tab laughed. 'Well, since Ned likes him and he tried to make amends with me, I think we should give him the benefit of the doubt. We'll assume he's just shy and a little awkward, unless proven otherwise.'

'Good plan. I have to say it would be a struggle to dislike someone that looks like him.'

'Hey, looks aren't everything, and you're a married woman! Married to my brother, in case you need the reminder.'

It was Meg's turn to laugh. 'Being married doesn't make you blind.' She paused a moment. 'But in case you need the reminder, you're *not* married. And now McDuck doesn't think you're coming onto him like most of the other single women in town, perhaps you have an advantage.'

Tab scoffed. 'Oh yeah, being pregnant, suffering extreme tiredness and the odd bout of morning sickness is a massive advantage. Soon I'll probably have swollen ankles as well. What guy in their right mind could resist that?'

A serious expression came across Meg's face. She opened her mouth but Tab jumped in before she could say whatever it was she wanted to say.

'Anyway, I'm not looking for a partner.'

'I just want you to be happy,' Meg whispered.

'I am. I know you and Lawson are so darn in love with each other that it's hard to believe anyone could be truly happy without the same, but I've got a wonderful life, a great family, a thriving business, and a lot to look forward to.'

'What about a bit of fun then?'

Tab shook her head. 'You're incorrigible, you know that?'

But despite her declaration of un-intent to her sister-in-law, she *was* only human and there was a tiny little something inside her that buzzed at the prospect of getting to know Fergus McWilliams a little better.

Chapter Eight

On Thursday afternoon when Ferg arrived at the sporting complex for cricket training, there were already a few cars parked around the edges of the oval. He was looking forward to coaching the kids cricket—the evenings were long down here, so at least it would keep him busy a little longer before he headed home to an empty house. Well, empty bar Mrs Norris, who he was still no closer to winning over.

He chuckled as he envisaged how the session might run—Lisl bossing him about and telling him how to do everything while Levi and Tate ran amok and tried to lure the rest of the young cricketers into mischief.

'Hey, Mr McDuck!'

As Ferg climbed out of his car, the few kids that had been careening around on the oval ran over to him. He was already regretting telling them the origins of his name.

'Hi Jimmy, Hi Victoria, Hi Milly, Hi Max. You guys want to help me set up?'

'Yes,' they cheered in unison. This was what he loved most about teaching the middle primary years—they were still all so enthusiastic and eager to please; life hadn't soured them yet.

He gave an obligatory wave to the mums nattering at the side of the oval as he carried the large kit bag towards the cricket pitch in the middle of the grass. As he directed the children to put the little yellow cones out on the ground to mark the different skills stations, a couple more cars arrived and more kids spilled out. Most of them were large, dirt-covered four-wheel drives—Prados or Patrols with the odd crew-cab ute thrown in for good measure, so he looked twice when an old-fashioned ice-cream truck drove in.

'Ice-cream!' shouted the kids, abandoning the tasks he'd given them and rushing towards the van.

He watched as Ned leapt out the passenger seat and his aunty emerged from the driver's side. While the kids were obviously more excited at the prospect of a frozen treat, Ferg's mouth went dry at the sight of Tabitha Cooper-Jones in sporty black shorts and a tank top that accentuated her lovely curves. His gaze was drawn unwittingly to her legs, which were lightly tanned and the most perfectly shaped pins he'd ever laid eyes on. How had he not noticed how attractive she was before?

Their first meeting he'd been too busy staring at her half-missing arm to notice and on Tuesday he'd been focused on his apology, but right now ...

He shook his head and dragged his eyes up as she strode towards him, a flock of junior cricketers at her heels.

'No ice-cream until after training,' he heard her say and tried to focus on the thought of the cool delight himself in an aim to stop his body making a fool of him.

'Hey Mr McWilliams,' she said as she hit him with a killer smile. Her dark bob was contained under a cap with a WA MILK logo on it, and her eyes sparkled with warmth, giving her a girl-next-door kind of beauty.

She looked both sweet and pure, exactly the opposite of his thoughts.

'Hello, Tabitha,' he managed, 'and please, call me Fergus, or even Ferg.'

'In that case, feel free to call me Tab.'

Doing his best to tame his carnal thoughts, he nodded to Ned. 'Hey kiddo.' And then looked back at Tab. 'Well, guess I'd better try and herd these cats,' he gestured to the kids all running amok, 'into some kind of order and get training started.'

She chuckled. 'Good idea. How do you want to do this? Last year Terry and I got everyone warmed up together and then we split the group in two—I took the new, younger players and Terry took the ones who'd already been playing a year or so. But you're the coach, so I'm at your service.'

Ferg frowned. '*You're* one of the helpers?'

Had Joanne mentioned Tabitha would be assisting him? He thought he'd have remembered such pertinent information, but was rapidly beginning to learn that a lot of assumptions were made in the country. The grapevine wasn't merely an expression, it was a real live thing, so everyone just expected that everyone knew what everyone else was doing.

Tab's smile wavered a little. 'Yes. I've been assistant coach for a few years.'

'Assistant coach?' He didn't mean to sound so sceptical as his gaze once again dropped to her arm, or rather her stump. Was that what you'd call it? He wondered why she didn't have a prosthetic attachment.

'Do you have a problem with that?' she asked, her tone suddenly frosty.

He snapped his eyes back up to her face, but hesitated a moment before replying. She might be able to throw okay but how could someone with only one functioning arm bat properly, never mind direct the kids how to?

'You don't think I can play or coach cricket with only one arm?' Her voice rose and he was aware of the fact that not only had the kids stopped dashing madly about, but their parents at the edge of the field were watching him and Tab with bated breath.

'I didn't say that.'

'You didn't have to. And didn't your mother ever teach you not to stare?'

Ferg couldn't help prickling at the mention of his mother.

'I'll have you know,' Tab went on, 'I can coach cricket just as well with one arm, if not better, than you can with two. In fact, you'd be surprised what I can do with one arm.'

He heard laughter from the parents, but there wasn't any such amusement in Tab's eyes. She looked as if she was about to raise her good fist and slam it into his face.

'Sorry, I didn't mean to—'

'No, no one ever does. They're just ignorant and so are you. But don't worry, I don't give a damn what you think anyway. I'm here for the kids, so let's not waste any more time debating my credentials.'

She turned away and he blinked, totally discombobulated. Feeling the watchful eyes of the parents on him, he resisted the urge to try to talk to Tabitha further, turning to address the kids instead.

'Alright everyone,' he shouted and clapped his hands together to get their attention, 'come on in close so we can get started.'

The sound of Mr McWilliams' voice was akin to nails down the blackboard. Tab fought the urge to leave him to it, to stalk back to her van and go fume quietly somewhere else, but she wasn't about to abandon Ned or the rest of the team to such an ignoramus.

It would be much better to stick around, show him just how capable she was and have him eat his shitty words. It wasn't like he was the first person to make a judgement about her because of her little arm. These days she barely even registered such comments, so she couldn't believe she'd gone at him like that.

It wasn't that he didn't deserve it, but she shouldn't have yelled at him in front of the kids. Honestly, if it weren't for them she might just have hit him. Tab was usually a much bigger person than that and the violent streak was definitely new, but something about the new teacher had gotten under her skin. She was surprised by her burning desire to show Fergus that he was not only an arsehole but completely wrong. His opinion shouldn't matter—*didn't* matter—but she owed it to all amputees to show him just how capable she was.

So, when he instructed the kids to do a half-lap of the oval to warm up, she launched into a run after them, channelling all her angry energy into the activity.

'Now,' Fergus said, when they were back in a group. 'We're going to start with some skills practice—a little bowling and batting—and then we'll split into two groups based on your ages and play a couple of friendly matches. How does that sound?'

Usually at this stage the kids would groan about having to do anything like actual proper practice but they all nodded enthusiastically. They were obviously all as in love with him as Ned appeared to be.

'Good.' Ferg looked to her. 'Tab? Do you want to take the bowlers or the batters? We'll do about fifteen minutes each and then swap the groups over.'

She glared back at him, not giving the bastard an inch. 'Either's fine with me.'

'Okay then. I'll take the batters.' He divided the group into two, quicker than either she or Terry had ever managed, not that she'd ever admit that to him.

'Come on, guys.' Tab directed her group to one side of the oval where there were already some cones set up and the bag of balls. She picked one up. 'Does everyone remember how we bowl in cricket?'

There was a chant of 'yes' in reply, but Victoria Wellington shoved her hand up in the air. 'This is my first season of cricket. Do you use two hands?'

The others laughed at her and Tab quickly shushed them. 'No, sweetheart. Here—I'll show you and then you can have a go. Ned,' she called and pointed to one of the yellow cones, 'you stand over there and I'll throw to you.'

Eager as ever to help, he jogged across to the cone. 'Ready, Aunty Tab.'

'Okay. Come close, Victoria, and you can see how I hold the ball. First, you make sure your thumb is on the seam, like this, and then you line up your index finger on the seam opposite your thumb. Got it?' Victoria nodded and Tab continued. 'Once you've got a firm grip, you lift the ball close to your chin with your elbow bent. Bowling in cricket is a whole body experience, you're not just throwing with your arm. Take a run up, plant your lead foot on the ground so it's pointing towards the batter, and then shift all your weight to that leg as you thrust your bowling shoulder forward and swing your arm like a windmill. Snap your wrist forward just before you release the ball.'

Tab enacted each step as she spoke, very aware that Fergus appeared to be watching her rather than getting his group started. So she had to bite down on a very bad word when the ball plummeted to the ground a few feet away, rather than hurling through the air to Ned as she'd intended.

A few of the kids laughed.

'Bad luck, Aunty Tab,' Ned called, running to pick up the ball and throw it back to her. 'Try again.'

'Thanks.' She shot her arm out to catch it but missed by a mile, heat sweeping across her cheeks as she went to pick it up. The next bowl was equally as bad, flying wide of Ned, so it would be impossible for him to catch it. Ned frowned and Tab felt her heart race.

'How about we just get started,' she said, flustered, as she ordered her group into pairs. 'One of you start bowling and then swap over when I blow my whistle.'

As she watched the kids, Tab focused on her breathing, trying to centre herself again, but her skills didn't improve as they went on. Normally when the kids played the friendly game she'd join in, but today it was like someone else had taken over her body. She was a complete and utter klutz—dropping balls left, right and centre, bowling so badly the poor kids had no hope of hitting the ball, and missing entirely when she tried to bat herself.

So much for showing Fergus what she was made of.

About halfway through the game, Adeline arrived with her camera and began taking shots for the paper, which only made Tab worse, and that was saying something considering how bad she'd been so far.

When the training session finally ended, she could have sung hallelujah to the heavens, but before she could escape, the kids expected ice-cream. With not so much as a backward glance at her co-coach, she strode towards her van. The kids flocked, but even scooping ice-cream, which she could usually do in her sleep, proved difficult. Her arm kept wobbling unsteadily and it took her longer to serve everyone than it normally did.

'Are you okay?' asked Tennille, leaning against the window when the kids were finally done.

'Fine,' she snapped. 'Just tired.'

'Pregnancy will do that to you.' Tennille chuckled. 'But I also couldn't help but hear what Mr McWilliams said about your arm earlier. I'm sure he didn't mean any harm.'

'I know. But meaning harm and causing harm are two different things.'

She pulled the service window shut and exhaled deeply in the quiet safety of her van. Tears rushed to her eyes and she swiped them away. She wasn't sure whether she was angrier at Fergus or herself for letting him get to her.

Chapter Nine

On Saturday morning, Ferg was woken just before the crack of dawn by a loud scratching nose. *Damn cat.* Somewhere in the distance a rooster welcomed the day. He wanted to roll over and pull the sheet over his head, but knew that Mrs Norris wouldn't stop until he got up and let her in. She'd been out pretty much every night since they arrived, preferring the insects and mice she caught, tortured and then devoured, than his company indoors.

So much for cats being good companions. That was only the case if they liked you, whereas Mrs Norris hissed if he got too close, even when he was trying to feed her. He had scratch marks up both his arms and had told his students he'd been attacked by a tiger, which didn't feel far from the truth. More than once he'd asked himself why he'd agreed to keep her.

'Morning,' he grumped as she sashayed into the laundry, her tail high in the air. He dished some disgusting looking fishy stuff into her bowl. 'There you are, breakfast is served.'

Mrs Norris didn't even acknowledge him so he made himself some coffee and toast, which he took out onto the back verandah to eat. It really was peaceful here, nothing but blue skies and paddocks as far as the eye could see. So different to the city where there was always some kind of background noise—kids playing in the garden next door, planes flying overhead, rubbish trucks on their collection, folks mowing lawns. He'd welcomed the quiet initially, but it felt almost eerie this morning when he knew it was all he had to look forward to for the next two days.

Why couldn't school be seven days a week?

He smiled wryly at the thought. While he guessed many parents would applaud this idea, he had to be the only teacher who would. But the kids made him laugh and teaching gave him a sense of meaning and purpose, which currently lacked in every other area of his life.

At least from next weekend he'd have junior cricket on Saturday mornings and he supposed he could always go to church on Sundays. *Yeah, right.*

Ferg shoved the last bit of toast into his mouth and went back inside, pausing when he saw the envelopes he'd dumped on the hall table. His mail was being forwarded to school, but he wasn't expecting anything special, so hadn't bothered with it last night, opting instead for a couple of beers and a night in front of the TV.

He put the windowed envelopes aside to deal with later and then frowned at the purple envelope on the bottom of the pile. There was no return address, but he'd recognise the scrawl on the front anywhere. It was Eider's, and he couldn't care less about what was inside. She must have discovered he'd had his old phone number changed so had resorted to an old-fashioned approach.

Why couldn't she and Jools just leave him the hell alone?

Annoyed, he ripped the envelope into tiny pieces, dropped them into the bin and then went to take a shower. When he emerged, Mrs Norris was on the middle of his bed, sleeping off her night's adventures. Ferg dressed, put on a load of washing and then sat down to work on some lesson plans. He paused only to hang out his clothes.

After what felt like hours, he glanced at his watch thinking it must be time for lunch and was dismayed to discover it was barely past ten o'clock.

How the hell was he going to get through the next twenty-four hours without going insane?

Searching for another distraction, he went to check out his landlord's bookshelf. Even without running a finger along the spines, the dust was obvious. Layers of the same were to be found on the old lady's ornaments and he could only imagine how Mrs Lord herself would feel if she could see the state of her things, never mind what she'd think about a stranger living in her homely little cottage, having access to them all.

He felt a gut-wrenching sadness for someone he didn't even know, or maybe it was the realisation that this could be him one day. A sad old man with no family and a whole load of possessions left to rot.

Now that was a sobering thought.

Maybe if Mrs Norris was more of a companion he wouldn't be feeling like this. Weren't pets supposed to be good for the soul? Adeline Walsh and her dogs landed in his head—perhaps he should take her up on that offer of a puppy. Yet even as he contemplated the idea, he rejected it, not only because Mrs Norris would torment it, but because he also knew that any cute little white ball of fluff would come with very tight strings attached.

His gaze drifted out the window towards the weeds sprouting in the rose garden. It wasn't only the inside of Mrs Lord's house that needed a little TLC. Ferg had never had the time nor interest in gardening before, but wasn't it supposed to be therapeutic? Doing something physical and getting some fresh air had to be better than staying inside feeling sorry for himself.

But the weeding only kept him occupied for so long before the darkness started to creep in again. Flashes of that awful day a few months ago when his world had been shattered kept barging into his head, filling him with a dangerous cocktail of anger, disappointment and bitter sadness. He wondered if it was too early for a beer?

Would drinking alone before noon on a Saturday make him an alcoholic? Did he even care? He abandoned the weeds and trekked inside to the fridge, only to remember he'd finished his beers last night.

'Dammit!' As he slammed the fridge shut, he remembered Ned's dad—what was his name? Lawson?—had given him an open invitation to drop around any time for a chat. Perhaps a short fix of conversation would drag him out of his funk and then he could get on with the weekend, do a bit more gardening, maybe watch a couple of movies.

Ferg grabbed his keys and wallet and only hesitated a few moments at the front door—it still felt strange and against the grain not to lock it—then headed for his car. He was halfway down the long gravel drive when a thought struck.

What if Tabitha was there?

Ned said she lived in a haunted house, but it could quite easily be another house on the same farm. Or even if she lived in town, she might be visiting. Two out of the three times he'd seen her she'd been with family. The idea of another run-in with her didn't appeal; he seemed to have a habit of putting his foot in it whenever she was around. He'd tried to apologise again at the end of cricket but she'd brushed him off, making it clear she didn't want to talk about it and wasn't in the mood for forgiveness.

Ferg tossed his keys in his hand. Maybe he'd just go for a drive instead.

* * *

Twenty minutes later after cruising through Walsh, where all the shops had been shutting down already at midday, Ferg found himself driving into an even smaller town not too far away. The sign on the outskirts said Rose Hill, but there was no population listed like on the 'Welcome to Walsh' sign, nor could he see any hill or roses. There was a petrol station, but that looked closed. If he'd blinked he'd have missed the only sign of a life—a few cars parked outside a small cluster of shops, which looked as if they were the only buildings here that had received any attention in decades.

'Eliza's Tea Rooms' was painted in a fancy vintage font on a sign above the corrugated verandah, the bright white print standing out against the rustic red background. There were also window baskets overflowing with pink, white and purple everlasting flowers and a chalkboard sign by the entrance of the middle shop.

He slowed a little and squinted to read the specials: 'Sweet Potato and Pumpkin Frittata', 'Sausage Rolls & Meat Pies like Granny Made' and 'Classic High Tea'. Ferg's stomach rumbled, reminding him he hadn't eaten anything since his toast early that morning, so he pulled over.

Even before he stepped inside the tea rooms, the smells that wafted at him were mouth-watering. They reminded him of one of his many foster homes, where his foster mum had been constantly baking. The few weeks he and Eider had spent in her care were some of the best weeks of their childhood. They'd both put on weight, devouring the home-cooked goodies at every opportunity because, like everything else in their lives, they'd known it wouldn't last.

Ferg pushed open the fly-screen door and then paused just inside as it clunked shut behind him. There were two big ceiling fans whirling above and everyone sitting at the tables appeared to be enjoying themselves, their cutlery clinking against their plates as they ate and chatted.

Off to one side of the main café area, there was some kind of craft shop and gallery. It was the type of thing Jools would have adored. He pushed that thought aside and stepped up to the counter to order. He could hear chatter coming from the kitchen behind and was about to press the bell for service when his gaze fell upon a glass cabinet full of different flavours of ice-cream.

'Tabitha's Ice-Creamery' he read on a little sign above the cabinet, the dots connecting in his head at the exact moment a figure appeared behind the counter. He looked up and came face to face with Tabitha herself.

She exhaled loudly. 'Oh, it's you.'

'Is that really the way to greet potential customers, Tab?'

'It's Tabitha to you.' She held her chin high and Ferg suspected if she'd had two arms, she'd be crossing them right now. 'Are you going to place an order or are you just going to stand there drooling over my counter?'

He took a moment to consider his reply. She obviously hadn't forgiven him for the cricket episode and although he felt a weird compulsion to attempt another apology, he had a feeling that wouldn't go down well. 'That looks good,' he said, glancing at a nearby table, where a three-tiered plate thing was piled high with treats.

'The high tea is usually for two people.'

He contemplated suggesting she take a break and share it with him, but didn't think that would go down too well either. 'Lucky I'm hungry then,' he said as he dug his wallet out of his pocket.

She shook her head, but took his money before storming off out the back. Forgetting about Jools, he wandered into the gallery and admired some of the stunning landscape oil paintings hanging on the walls. They were obviously local settings—he even recognised the tea rooms in one but didn't recognise the name of the artist, Archie Weaver. There were lots of knitted soft toys, along with some handmade candles and other things he had no desire for but imagined sold well to tourists.

Even though Rose Hill was pretty much a ghost town, the tea rooms seemed to have a steady traffic. He heard the bell on the screen door go again and looked back into the café area to see a young couple come in. Tabitha was far more civil than she had been to him. He'd obviously really hurt her. Maybe if he hung around, he'd get the opportunity to try to make amends again— it would be good to do so before the next cricket training as the kids deserved better than coaches who could barely stand to look at each other.

Although if he was honest with himself, he was quite happy looking at Tabitha. She was easy on the eye, even when she was glaring at him.

He went back to the table, scooping an old copy of the *Walsh Whisperer* off the counter to read.

'Here you are.'

Ferg looked up as Ned's mum delivered a china cup and a tea-pot in a knitted tea-cosy that looked like a hive with tiny woollen bees scattered over it. 'Thank you.'

Although she smiled it was clearly forced, which he guessed meant Tab had told her what a jerk he was.

'Do you and Tabitha own this place?' He wasn't usually one for small talk, but perhaps the isolation had gone to his head.

'I own the building, but Tab and I are partners in the business and she lives here now. Anyway, I'll be back in a moment with your meal.'

'Wow, this looks wonderful,' he said when she returned with food enough for ten people. Perhaps he should have just ordered a pie, but he wasn't about to let this beat him. 'Do you guys make everything yourself?'

'Yep.' Meg nodded proudly. 'Right down to Tab's ice-cream. If you've still got space after all that, you really should try some. She won Champion Ice-Cream Award at the Perth Royal Show these past holidays.'

'Impressive. And does she live here alone?'

'Well, yes, but we've also got a B&B now, which means there are often others on the premises.' Meg looked at him suspiciously as if she wasn't sure he was trying to find out if Tabitha was single or if he was a serial killer looking for his next vulnerable victim. The truth was way off the mark—he was simply curious as to who the father of her baby was.

Why? He didn't know. Even if he were looking for a relationship, it would never be with someone pregnant with someone else's child. If his childhood had taught him anything, it was that loving a child who wasn't your own was pretty much impossible. Sure, you could take care of them—as many of his foster parents had—but love was something else entirely. And children needed love. If it hadn't been for his sister growing up, he may not have known the meaning of it.

'Do many people stay here?' he asked, not wanting to dwell on the past.

'It's becoming quite popular actually—the quiet and the historic buildings attract people, I guess. They like the idea of staying in a ghost town, and we're not too far from Bunbury.'

'Ned mentioned there's actually a ghost here?' Ferg tried not to show his scepticism.

'Oh yes.' Meg gestured to an empty table by the window. 'Eliza. She's been here a long time—the tea rooms were actually her idea and she's happy as long as we run any new ideas by her. That's her table over there.'

'Is anyone allowed to sit with her?'

'I often sit down for a chat. And Tab sometimes will. Eliza's hit and miss with the customers, but if someone sits there and spills their drink or breaks a glass, we know to keep an eye on them.'

Ferg was happy he hadn't chosen that table—knowing his luck, he'd have spilt his drink *and* broken something, not that he actually believed in ghosts. 'Fascinating.'

'You should hear her whole story.'

He waited, hoping Meg might tell him, but she changed the subject.

'Anyway, Ned's enjoyed his first week at school. Hope you've been settling in well.'

'Thank you. I have.'

'Great.' She nodded. 'Enjoy.' And she hurried back to the kitchen, no doubt to warn Tabitha what a weirdo he was.

He sighed and picked up a delicate chicken salad sandwich, reminding himself it didn't matter what people thought of him. He hadn't moved here to make connections, he'd moved here to sever them.

Chapter Ten

Tab yawned as she emerged from the local hospital's A&E on Monday afternoon. To say the last few hours had been exhausting would be a gross understatement. So much for a relaxing day off. She'd just sat down on the couch to binge the next few episodes of the Netflix series she was watching when her phone buzzed with a call from Triple Zero.

There'd been a head-on collision on the highway two kilometres out of Walsh, both cars carrying multiple passengers. The last thing Tab had felt like doing was throwing on her green St Johns' uniform and wading into the carnage, but they were short on volunteers at the moment and she wouldn't be able to relax knowing others were under the pump. With her little arm, she was only trained as a lowest level volunteer and mostly just drove the van to allow the more qualified people to focus on first aid, but with so many casualties today she'd been forced to do what she could.

'You coming to the pub for a drink?' asked Boots, one of the other volunteers.

They'd lost two kids and one adult today, two families shattered because one man had made an error of judgement when overtaking a road-train. The hospital had been crazy; their two ambulances had to go back and forth from the crash site, delivering patients and then bodies. They'd had to take a couple of the critical but stable passengers out to the airstrip to wait for the Flying Doctors, and, because the two nurses on duty, the local doctor and the few other hospital staff were busy with the emergency, Tab and a couple of the other volunteers had sat with the two surviving kids, who had already lost their father and still might lose their mother. Although they didn't have the same level of training as the city paramedics, she'd seen some pretty horrific things in her time as a volley—drug overdoses, suicides, anaphylactic shocks, even a crop-duster crash—but it never got any easier to lose a patient, and the terror and heartbreak of those poor kids would forever be imprinted in her mind. She'd never felt more in need of a drink.

'Nah, thanks, but I think I'll go see Gran and then head home for an early night.'

'No worries.' Boots gave her a quick hug. 'Do you want one of us to grab your van from the sub-centre and bring it here when we drop the ambulances back?'

'It's okay. I can walk.' It wasn't far and the fresh air would do her good.

As Tab's fellow volunteers went one way, she headed in the other direction towards the aged-care arm of the hospital. Unlike most city facilities, Walsh's nursing home was directly attached to their hospital and staffed by the same nurses. Today things were a bit crazy, but the small nature of the facility meant usually the nurses could spend quality time with the six elderly residents who they treated more like family than patients. Tab hated that her grandmother needed to be in a home, but it was comforting to know that this one was a lot better than most.

'Well, isn't this a lovely surprise.' Although her words were slightly slurred, Gran's face lit up when Tab entered her bedroom.

'Hello, Granny.' She leaned down and kissed her cheek. Usually at this time of the day, the eighty-four-year-old would be sitting in the communal living area watching TV, but as she had severe Parkinson's, she required the assistance of a nurse or orderly to get there.

'Have you been on a callout?' Gran said, lifting a shaky hand to indicate Tab's uniform.

She nodded. 'Terrible, terrible car accident.'

'I thought something was going on. Kelly just brought afternoon tea to my room; I haven't seen the nurses since lunchtime. Are you okay? You need to look after that great-grandbaby of mine.'

Tab perched on the edge of her recliner and squeezed her hand. 'We'll be fine. I'm just knackered. Can I get you anything? Do you want me to help you out into the living room?'

'Thank you, that would be lovely.'

She pretty much lifted her gran to her feet and into her wheelchair, and then helped her to the toilet. When they emerged into the communal living area ten minutes later, the only male resident looked up from where he sat at the kitchen table, a knife and fork clutched tightly in each hand.

'What in heaven's name is going on around here?' Len muttered, glaring at them. 'Where's my dinner?'

Tab and Gran exchanged a bemused look. Gran still had her full wits about her, but some of the other patients who were stronger physically were fading mentally. Len Walker, once a local dairy farmer, could no longer read the time on the gold watch that had been in his family for generations, but his stomach was almost as good for keeping the time.

'I'm sure it'll be here soon,' Tab said, securing her grandmother's wheelchair and wondering if she should offer Len some biscuits or something to tide him over.

Before she could, Kelly the cook bustled down the corridor with a trolley full of food.

'About bloody time,' said Len.

Things were obviously still crazy if Kelly was hand-delivering the meals. Usually that was an orderly's job and they and the nurses would sit down and feed the patients who needed assistance.

'Do you want me to help gather everyone?' Tab asked.

'Oh, would you mind?' Kelly sounded as flustered as she looked. 'Everyone else is still dealing with the car accident.'

'No worries.'

Tab had barely stepped inside Penelope Walsh's room when she heard Kelly shout from the room next door. They met each other in the corridor and spoke at once.

'What is it?'

'Have you seen Mrs Lord? She isn't in her room!'

'I haven't. I went straight to see Gran. But maybe she's outside?' Tabitha said, trying to calm the other woman.

Kelly shook her head frantically. 'The doors to the courtyard are locked when we're not around.'

She pushed past Tabitha and the two of them quickly searched the rest of the facility, including the courtyard just in case, but Mrs Lord was nowhere to be found.

'I'm going to have to tell Donna,' Kelly said, her complexion pale as she referred to the nurse in charge.

Tab nodded. 'You do that. I'll get the others to the table and start giving them their dinner.' That was probably against code, but this wasn't the city; country folk did what needed to be done, and right now the most important thing was finding dear Mrs Lord.

Tabitha had always liked her elderly neighbour, who'd been a member of Stitch'n'Bitch until a couple of years ago when it became clear she'd misplaced her marbles. When her mum died, Mrs Lord would pop around every couple of days with a big delivery of cookies and cakes for Dad's smoko and her and Lawson's school lunches. Whenever Tab came to visit Gran, she made a point of going and sitting a few minutes with Mrs Lord as well. The old woman never showed any recognition, which was probably a blessing because being in residential care would be so depressing if you didn't have visits from family and friends to look forward to.

Tab had just finished delivering Penelope Walsh to the table when Donna came running down the corridor with Kelly. 'And you're sure you've looked everywhere?'

'Yes.' Kelly was almost sobbing by now.

'I don't know how she could have got out. We're going to have to call the police,' Donna said tersely as if they were referring to an escaped jailbird.

Within half an hour, the hospital was swarming with local cops, fire and ambulance volunteers, and others who'd heard about Mrs Lord's disappearance and were ready and willing to join the search. It always happened like this. They could go days, sometimes weeks, without an emergency and then one came after another with barely time to catch their breath between.

'Vera can't have got too far,' Sergeant Skinner said, his expression grave, 'so we're going to focus our search on the couple of kilometres surrounding the hospital. She could have been missing up to five hours, so it's likely she's very disorientated and possibly dehydrated by now.'

'Do you think she could be trying to get home?' asked Funky, dressed in the local volunteer firefighter uniform. Lawson, having left the evening milking to Meg and Ethan, stood between him and Tab.

Sergeant Skinner looked to Donna.

'It's possible that's where she had in mind when she left—if she actually had anywhere in mind—but that's what?' Donna looked to Tab and Lawson. 'Twelve Ks out of town?'

'About ten,' Lawson replied. 'The Lord's farm is a little closer than ours.'

'Do we even know she left here on her own?' asked Boots.

Again, the sergeant and Donna exchanged anxious looks. 'The hospital security camera that covers the exit appears to have stopped working recently, but we hadn't noticed. We've been so under the pump.'

'It's alright,' Sergeant said. 'It is unfortunate, but right now, we have no reason to believe there's anything sinister behind Vera's disappearance and our priority has to be on finding her, not coming up with possible conspiracy theories. I've put out a description with the state police and a media release, so people will be looking for her further out as well. Right now, we need to get searching before it gets too dark.'

Tab glanced out the window—they'd almost missed that boat—and her heart squeezed with anxiety as she thought about poor Mrs Lord. Wherever she was, she had to be confused at best; the worst wasn't worth thinking about.

The sergeant started explaining the plan of attack and allocating the search volunteers to specific areas of town.

'Shouldn't someone at least check her old place?' suggested Kelly. 'Maybe someone gave her a lift?'

The sergeant nodded. 'The new teacher is living there now, so I'll need a volunteer to go and bring him up to speed. I'll be sending a group of you out to search her farm as well. Lawson and Tabitha, are you still leasing that land?'

They nodded in unison.

'Good. You probably know the area better than anyone, so do you guys want to lead up that search team? And pop in to the teacher and let him know what's going on.'

Tab's hackles rose at the mention of Fergus McWilliams but she wasn't going to let her personal gripe with him stop her searching for Mrs Lord.

A few more instructions from the sergeant and the groups were on their way. Lawson dropped Tab off at the sub-centre to collect her van, while Funky and his younger sister Carrie went ahead to talk to Fergus. Dodged a bullet there, she thought as she climbed into her van and followed Lawson out to Mrs Lord's place.

Although still physically exhausted, worry for their elderly neighbour and adrenaline at the situation had revived her mentally. Before she started her car, she crammed a muesli bar she had in her bag into her mouth and drank almost a whole bottle of water, so that by the time she parked her van alongside Lawson's and Funky's utes, she was ready to go. She threw her torch into a backpack with her phone and another bottle of water, then went to meet the others who were gathered on Fergus's porch, talking to the man himself.

'Hi Tabitha.' He inclined his head slightly as she joined them, but she ignored him.

'We've searched the house,' Carrie said. 'She's definitely not there and Fergus said he hasn't seen any sign of her.'

Lawson nodded. 'Let's check the buildings, paddocks and dams, just in case.'

'Fergus has offered to help too,' Funky said, giving him a warm smile.

'Great.'

That was not the word that initially came into Tab's head, but she guessed the more eyes, the better. 'What are we waiting for?'

'Let's split into two groups,' Lawson said. 'Tab and I will take one each since we know the area best.'

'Why don't you take Fergus with you and I'll take Funky and Carrie,' Tab suggested, in a tone that told her brother there'd be no arguments.

'Can I go with Lawson instead?'

Tab did not miss the way Carrie's gaze flickered to Fergus. At twenty-three, she'd just moved back to live with her folks after breaking up with her city boyfriend—she'd been heartbroken according to Funky, but it looked as if she might be ready to move on now.

'Whatever,' Tab said, ignoring the irritation that sparked inside her. 'Let's just go.'

Leaving the others still working out logistics, she strode off in the direction of the milking sheds, no longer in use because she and Lawson leased this land for their crop and did all their milking on their own farm.

Funky jogged to catch up with her. 'What's the rush?'

'Um … Mrs Lord is missing,' she snapped.

'I know. Sorry. It was just a figure of speech.'

Suitably chastised, Funky was uncharacteristically quiet as they looked in every nook and cranny in the sheds and then did a wide sweep of the paddocks on their side of the designated search. Two hours later it was pitch black and all Tab had to show for their efforts were blisters on her toes and mosquito bites. They'd touched base on the radio with Lawson a couple of times, but they hadn't found anything and there'd been no reports of good news from town either.

'Where the hell could she be?' Tab was close to tears when they returned to the house just before nine o'clock. 'Do you think they should get divers out to the dams?'

Lawson shook his head. 'We checked around all of them. There's no sign of any human activity at all. It was a long shot anyway. She's got to be closer to town.'

'So why haven't they found her? She can't have just vanished.'

Funky squeezed her arm. 'Hopefully she's found a quiet place and fallen asleep or something.'

But the grim expressions on all of their faces said none of them had high hopes of this.

'Would anyone like something to eat?' Fergus asked. 'I don't have anything fancy, but I could whip up some toasted sandwiches?'

'Oh, that would be lovely. I'm starving,' Carrie exclaimed, reaching out to briefly touch his arm.

Lawson tossed his ute keys in his hand. 'Thanks for the offer, but I think I'll head back into town and see if I can be of use there.'

'Me too,' Tab and Funky spoke at once.

Lawson frowned at her. 'You should go home to bed. You look exhausted, and the last thing Mrs Lord would want is you sacrificing you or your baby's health to look for her. There are plenty of people on the ground. We'll find her.'

Tab wanted to argue—she'd never been good at resting on her laurels when there was an emergency—but her eyelids felt ridiculously heavy. She was struggling to keep them open and wasn't sure she'd even manage the drive to Rose Hill.

'Okay,' she relented, 'but call me the minute you hear anything, and do you mind if I stay at your place tonight? That way if you're still looking in the morning, or have a really late night, I can help Meg and Ethan with the milking.'

'Of course you can stay but you don't have to lift a finger. You're allowed a sleep-in every once in a while as well, you know?'

'I know.' Tab gave Lawson a hug goodnight, but only because she wanted him to stop worrying about her and concentrate on finding Mrs Lord.

'If the search is still going,' Fergus began as Tab turned to head to her van, 'I'm happy to come in and help too.'

'Don't you have to work tomorrow?' she heard Funky ask. 'How the hell will you face a class of kids with next to no sleep?'

Tab slowed a little to hear Fergus's chuckled reply. 'I can survive on coffee for a day.'

'In that case, that'd be great,' Lawson said. 'The more hands on deck, the better.'

'I'll drive with you into town,' Carrie offered. 'The roads round here can be a little disorientating in the dark.'

Tab snorted as she opened her van—if Fergus had half a brain and a GPS he wouldn't need Carrie's help. Not with the roads anyway.

Chapter Eleven

Seven o'clock Tuesday morning, Ferg's phone buzzed on his bedside table. Not ready to face the day when he'd only had a few hours' sleep, he flung his arm out to silence the alarm. Only a few seconds after the ear-piercing beeping had stopped and he was blinking himself awake, did the peculiarity of the situation strike him.

He sat bolt upright in bed.

Where the hell was Mrs Norris?

Although he set it out of habit, not once since he'd been the sole owner of the cat had he actually needed his alarm. Without fail she'd woken him well before he needed to get up—either by jumping on his chest and swishing her tail in his face or scratching on the screen door and meowing so loudly he couldn't go back to sleep.

He tried to recall if she'd been inside or out when he'd arrived home just after 2 am, but he'd been so dog tired after searching through scrubland at the edge of town that he'd just fallen into bed, clothes and all. What if something had happened to Mrs Norris? Jools would kill him. He immediately pushed that thought aside—she wouldn't kill him because he wouldn't tell her—but it didn't stop him from feeling anxious. The cat was such a damn pain in the arse but the thought of not having it around …

He flung back the covers and strode across the room to open the door. He'd barely registered the fact that it was closed, and he didn't remember shutting it, when the smell of bacon wafted towards him. His mouth and stomach groaned but his spine prickled with unease as he slowly walked down the hallway, glancing around for something he could use as a weapon. The best he could find was an ornate glass vase, but surely a burglar wouldn't be cooking breakfast?

And then it hit him.

Mrs Lord! It seemed implausible that she could have made it this far out of town, never mind actually found her way home without any of them catching sight of her, but miracles did happen, and he couldn't think of any other likely explanation. Unless one of the single women had decided to surprise him with breakfast?

No, surely even Adeline Walsh wouldn't go to that extent.

He loosened his grip on the vase and crept closer to the kitchen as quietly as he possibly could. If it was Mrs Lord, she'd probably think *he* was the intruder and he didn't want to scare her.

'Is that you, Harold?'

Ferg almost jumped out of his skin at the sound of the decidedly elderly voice. Before he had the chance to work out how to reply, an old woman appeared in the doorway. She was wearing loose grey pants, a floral blouse, a red apron, which he knew came from one of the kitchen drawers, and some slippers, which looked as if they'd seen better days. Her white hair was cut short in standard elderly woman fashion and there were a few strands of hay or something scattered through it. He braced himself for her shock and fear at seeing a stranger, but instead her whole face lit up, smile lines crinkling at the edges of her eyes.

'Hello, love, ready for some breakfast?'

'Um …' He guessed Harold had to have been her husband.

'Cat got your tongue?' She chuckled as she stepped forward and took a hold of his arm. Her paper-thin skin felt soft against his and when he glanced down, something inside him squeezed a little at the almost bluish tinge and the veins clearly visible.

'Sorry, still half-asleep,' he said as he let her lead him into the kitchen.

'That's my Harold, always busy busy busy. Take a seat and I'll get you a cup of tea.'

As he lowered himself into a chair, Mrs Norris waltzed into the kitchen and straight over to Mrs Lord.

'Hello, dear little thing.' She wobbled slightly as she stooped to stroke Mrs Norris's head and Fergus tensed, ready to intervene if the cat took a swipe, but breathed a sigh of relief as she purred loudly and weaved herself in and out of the old woman's legs instead.

What the?

'I know you don't like cats in the house, love,' said Mrs Lord, 'but this poor little thing was scratching at the door this morning.'

Poor little thing? Ferg struggled to contain a snort.

'Absolutely starving,' she continued. 'I gave her some milk but couldn't find it in me to throw her back out. Maybe she could stay and catch mice for us?'

'Sure,' Ferg didn't know what else to say at the pleading expression in her soft brown eyes.

'Oh, thank you!' She threw her arms around him. 'You act like such a grumpy goose but you've got a heart of gold really. Now, let me get your breakfast.'

Ferg watched as Mrs Lord turned back to the stove and poured eggs she'd obviously already whisked into a saucepan. Behind it, bacon sizzled in a frying pan, little droplets of fat spitting up into the air. He glanced at the clock on the wall. He needed to notify the authorities that she was okay.

'I'm just popping to the loo. Back in a moment.'

'Don't be too long, or your tea will get cold,' she scolded, her tone good-natured.

'I won't,' he promised as he ambled out of the kitchen then made a mad dash down the hallway and into the bedroom. He closed the door quietly behind him and snatched his mobile off the bed-side table. He was searching for the number of the Walsh Police Station when he heard a clatter and a shriek from the kitchen.

Still gripping his phone, Ferg hurried back to find the frying pan on the floor, bacon scattered everywhere and Mrs Lord clutching her hand against her chest.

'Fuck. Have you burned yourself?' As he spoke he rushed across and turned off the stove before anything else got burned.

'No need for language like that, Har … Har …' Her eyes widened and suddenly filled with fear. 'You're not Harold.' She backed away slightly as if he were an angry bull. 'Who are you? What are you doing in my house? Harold! Harold!' Her gaze darted around the room and Ferg was unsure whether she was wondering why Harold wasn't coming to her rescue or looking for something to use against him in self-defence.

He needed to calm her, but he also needed to see her hand, assess how bad the burn was and treat it asap. 'It's okay, Mrs Lord,' he said, holding up his hands as he took a tentative step towards her. 'I'm a friend. My name's Fergus and I'm not going to hurt you.'

'Do you know Harold?' she asked, her voice still wobbly and her face contorted in distrust.

He decided a white lie was forgivable in the circumstances. 'Yeah, he's a top bloke. And very lucky to have such a gem like you for a wife.'

As her lips twisted ever so slightly at the edges, he took another step.

'Could you let me have a look at your hand?'

She hesitated a moment and then slowly reached out, turning her palm up to show him. Her skin was already red raw and beginning to bubble. It was a massive effort not to wince but he didn't want to make her any more anxious.

'Let's get that under some water.' He led her across to the sink, turning the cold tap on full bore and then gently guiding her upturned hand under it.

'I'm such a silly duck,' she said as water streamed over her red raw skin and tears trickled down her cheeks. 'Harold always calls me his clumsy chicken. Do you think he'll be back soon?'

Ferg glanced at his phone, which he'd tossed onto the table when he'd seen her hand. 'I'd say so, but maybe we should take you to the hospital to get that checked out.'

'No.' She all but shrieked and yanked her hand from under the tap. 'I'm not going to the hospital! I'm staying right here in my house. You can't make me go!'

'Okay,' he said, adopting the calm but firm voice he usually reserved for difficult or distressed children. 'Okay, but you need to put your hand back under the water and I'm going to find something to treat your burn.'

Reluctant to leave her but not seeing he had any choice—she'd freak if she heard him calling an ambulance—he headed into the bathroom, closed the door behind him and called triple zero.

Chapter Twelve

Tab had a heavy heart as she came in from the milking and yanked her dirty old gumboots off. Ever since moving to Rose Hill, she'd done a lot less farm work and she missed it. But today the quirky personalities of the cows and the monotonous work of getting them on and off the milking machine didn't bring her peace the way it usually did.

She couldn't stop thinking about Mrs Lord being out there somewhere, alone. Anything could have happened to her. She could have fallen and broken something. She could have been bitten by a snake. She could have stumbled into a dam. Some sicko could have picked her up and be doing who knows what with her. The more time passed, the more likely the possibility that the old dear had met some kind of unfortunate end. Despite broken sleep due to worry, Tab planned on having a quick shower, borrowing a change of clothes from Meg and then heading into town to join the search again. But as she pulled her phone out of her pocket to undress, it started ringing.

Her heart leapt as she saw Triple Zero on the screen and when she punched in her code to access the conference call, many of her fellow volunteers were already on the line. They let out a collective sigh of relief when the operator told them that Mrs Lord had been found at her old house, but that she'd suffered a bad burn from a frying pan and as a result had become a little agitated.

No wonder, Tab thought, being alone with Fergus was enough to agitate anyone and the poor woman must have been terrified to find a strange man in her cottage. Once the operator had relayed all the information, the volunteers talked among themselves, determining who was available to attend the callout. Boots and Funky volunteered and although the prospect of seeing Mr Mc-Rude-and-Grumpy didn't fill Tab with warm fuzzies, she couldn't do nothing when she was so close.

'I'll head there now,' she offered, 'and see if I can put her a bit at ease before you guys arrive.'

'Thanks, Tab, you're a star,' Funky said before they disconnected the call.

She grabbed the farm first-aid kit, said a quick goodbye to Meg and Ned and was on her way. As she drove the short distance to the Lord's farm, she fumed at the thought of the old woman's injury. Where was Fergus when she'd been cooking up a storm? Surely he couldn't be *that* deep a sleeper that he hadn't heard someone break and enter his house.

And how the hell had she even got there? Someone must have given her a lift. No way she could have walked twelve kilometres without becoming dehydrated, and surely someone out of the hundreds who were looking would have seen her. So where had she spent the night? Why hadn't they seen any sign of her when they'd been searching the farm yesterday evening? It was a mystery and one she wasn't sure they'd ever find the answer to.

She turned at the now faded sign that read HM and VE Lord and drove as fast as was safe on the gravel drive, parking under a jacaranda tree by the cottage a mere five minutes after she got the call.

'What are you doing here?' Fergus said as they met each other on the front porch. All he wore was a pair of black shorts and a white chesty singlet and it was hard not to stare at his bare legs and arms.

Tab forced herself to be civil. 'I'm a local St John's volunteer.' She held her chin high as she spoke, bracing herself for his surprise that they'd let someone with only one functional arm sign up. He probably thought they'd done so out of pity. But he nodded, and the expression in his eyes looked more like relief than scepticism.

'The ambulance is on its way, but I stayed at Lawson and Meg's last night, so it made sense for me to come straight here and see what I could do first.' Tab went to step past him, but Fergus blocked her way and held the door handle firmly.

'She's okay.' His voice was low, almost a whisper, and annoyingly it sent a pleasurable shiver down her spine. 'I've had her hand under cold water for the last ten minutes and I found some burn gel pads in the bathroom cabinet, which I've just applied. They're a little out of date but I figured they were better than nothing. She doesn't seem to be in too much pain but she's very adamant that she doesn't want to go to the hospital, so …'

Tab sighed. It wasn't surprising, but it could make getting her into the ambulance difficult. 'Okay. Thanks for the heads-up.'

Fergus stepped aside and held the door open for her. It led straight into the living room and for a second, she startled. She'd just assumed he'd have put his own mark on the cottage, but it still looked as if an elderly couple lived there.

Mrs Lord was sitting on the floral sofa, a crocheted rug and a rather large, semi-long-haired cat on her knee. One of her hands was resting on a cushion, the palm upturned sporting a burn pad, the other gently smoothing the cat's fur. That was until she noticed Tabitha.

'Who are you?' Her voice was shaky, her eyes wide.

Tab summoned her warmest smile. 'I'm Tabitha Cooper-Jones from next door.'

Mrs Lord frowned and shook her head. 'Tabby is only a little girl.' She looked to Fergus. 'What's going on?'

He crossed the room in two strides, lowered himself onto the sofa beside her and put a reassuring arm around her shoulder. The cat swiped out its paw and scratched his leg, its fur standing up, but Fergus ignored the blood it had drawn on his leg. 'It's alright, love,' he said in the gentlest voice she'd ever heard. 'You just haven't seen Tabby for a few years, but hasn't she grown into a lovely young lady?'

Tab averted her gaze from Fergus's bare skin—she wasn't here to apply first aid to a cat scratch—as slowly a smile appeared on Mrs Lord's face. 'Oh yes, I see the resemblance to your mother now. How is she? I haven't seen her in a while, I don't think.'

A lump welled in Tab's throat. Although her mum had passed away well over a decade ago, the pain never really went away. 'She's ... She's fine.' Tab decided a white lie was kindest. 'She's just really busy at the moment.'

Fergus looked straight into Mrs Lord's pale blue eyes. 'Tabitha would like to take a look at your hand. Do you think that would be okay?'

'I'm not going to the hospital.'

He nodded. 'Let's not worry about that right now.'

'Okay.' Mrs Lord glanced down at her hand and then smiled tenderly at Fergus. 'Whatever you think is best.'

Tab took that as an invitation to get closer. Carrying her first-aid kit, she went to kneel in front of the sofa, so she could get the best access.

'Careful,' Fergus warned. 'Mrs Norris isn't the friendliest of felines.'

Mrs Lord frowned. The two women replied at the same time.

'We're not calling her Mrs Norris and what do you mean she's not friendly?'

'Mrs Norris from *Harry Potter*?' Tab vaguely remembered Ned saying something about a class theme. If Fergus was that much of a HP fan that he named his cat after a character, it would be very hard to continue to disapprove of him.

'Who is Harry Potter?' added Mrs Lord, once again looking anxious and confused.

'Sorry.' Fergus cleared his throat and smiled again. 'What do you want to call her?'

'I think Buttons is a lovely name for a cat, and this one is cute as a button.'

Personally, Tab had never understood that phrase—what was so cute about buttons?

But Fergus nodded. 'Great name. Buttons it is.' He looked to her and mouthed, 'Be careful.'

'Hello, Buttons,' Tab said, reaching out to scratch the cat under its chin. Although she'd witnessed its earlier swipe, it looked so content sitting on Mrs Lord's lap that it didn't seem much of a threat. A loud purr immediately emanated from the fur ball.

'She likes you,' said Mrs Lord, visibly relaxing.

'Wonders never cease,' Fergus muttered. 'Must just be me.'

Tab looked up and met his gaze, wanting to convey that if he treated the cat like he treated her, no wonder it didn't adore him, but something inside her jolted as she looked into his warm caramel eyes. It was impossible to ignore the sadness she saw there.

She immediately looked back to Mrs Lord. 'Let's take a look at that hand.'

The old woman winced as Tab gently lifted the burn gel pad so she could take a peek. *Youch.* She tried not to wince at the red raw skin beneath, already boasting some vicious-looking blisters.

'I'm going to replace this pad with a new one,' she said, knowing Mrs Lord would be less likely to panic if she was kept informed, 'and then I'm going to wrap it with a bandage, which will make it easier to keep it there.'

'Want some …' Fergus began but then snapped his mouth shut as Tab reached down to open the first-aid kit.

It was obvious he was going to ask if she needed help, and while she conceded he might do that with anyone, she had a burning urge to prove herself to him. Still, holding the gel pad in place while keeping an elderly arm from shaking, and also wrapping a hand gently but firmly enough to do its job, was tricky even for those with two functioning hands.

She grabbed the bandage from the kit and handed it to him. 'If you could open that for me, that would be great.'

He did as she asked and then she got him to open the gel pad as well. Surprisingly, the cat stayed on Mrs Lord's lap as Tab removed the old pad and discarded it on the floor. The old woman's hand shook, and Fergus reached out and held it as Tab lowered the pad onto what she guessed were second-degree burns.

'Thanks.' She held out her hand for the bandage and as he gave it to her, she kept Mrs Lord informed. 'Now I'm going to wrap your hand, okay?'

Her patient was thankfully distracted by the cat and didn't seem to notice how awful her burn was. Tab's hand shook a little as she carefully wound the bandage, Fergus shifting his hand as necessary. Part of her wished she could have done it herself, but there were more important things than pride. And she'd never admit it, but they actually made quite a good team.

'Thank you, Tabby,' Mrs Lord said when she was finished. 'I'm sorry to have wasted your time. I feel so very foolish. Now, can I get you a cup of tea?'

Tab and Fergus exchanged looks.

'Thanks, but I'm fine.' Tab smiled.

At the same moment, Fergus said, 'How about I make the tea?'

She nodded. It was probably a good idea to keep Mrs Lord as calm as possible while they waited for the others to arrive with the ambulance.

While Fergus headed into the kitchen, Tab reached out again to stroke the cat. It had the softest fur—no wonder Mrs Lord found it calming.

'Harold doesn't really like cats,' she said, 'but I'm going to convince him to keep this one.'

Content to admire the cat, who was clearly adoring the attention, Mrs Lord didn't require much conversation, and so Tab took the opportunity to surreptitiously look over her for any signs of other injuries. Although she couldn't see any scratches or bruising, there were a few tiny tears in her trousers, dried mud on her shoes and hay in her hair. She wished she could ask her where she'd been the last twenty hours, but that would only confuse her and it was unlikely she would remember anyway.

'Here we are,' Fergus said when he returned a couple of minutes later, carrying a tray with a teapot, a jug of milk and three cups on it.

He placed the tray down on the coffee table but just as he began to pour, they heard cars on the gravel drive. All three of them looked out the window and saw the ambulance approaching. A police car followed immediately behind.

'What's going on?' Mrs Lord's voice was high-pitched and she jumped in her seat, startling the cat, who sprang off her lap and darted off down the hallway. 'Why are the police here?'

'Your hand is pretty bad,' Tab said, ignoring her last question. 'I've done what I can but we really do need the doctor to check you out.'

'No. No. No.' Mrs Lord shook her head and started rocking back and forth. 'I'm not going to hospital. No hospital. No. Don't let them take me back.' It was the first indication that she had any idea she'd ever lived anywhere but here. She looked pleadingly to Fergus as the doors of the emergency vehicles slammed and Sergeant Skinner, Constable Morris, Boots and another St Johns' volunteer, Steve, approached the cottage.

It broke Tab's heart to see her old neighbour so distressed. 'I'll go talk to them,' she told Fergus as she got to her feet.

He nodded and reached out to take the old woman's good hand. As Tab went out onto the porch, she heard him talking softly to her but couldn't make out the words. He seemed to have developed a rapport with his landlord.

'Hey, Tab.' The sergeant nodded towards inside. 'So, it's really her?'

'Yep.'

The three men shook their heads and Constable Morris asked, 'How on earth did she get here?'

Tab shrugged. 'That's your job to work out, but aside from the burn, which she only got once she came here, she seems physically fine. Mentally is another issue. She was quite calm until she saw you guys arrive and now she's in a bit of a state. I'm not sure it's going to work trying to sweet-talk her into coming with us.'

'I don't want to manhandle an old woman,' said the sergeant, running a hand through his thick grey hair. 'Maybe we should call Dr Palmer to come out and give her a sedative or something?'

'We could try the green whistle,' Boots suggested. 'Tell her it's for the pain. It sometimes has a calming effect.'

'It might,' Tab said—methoxyflurane was a wonderful pain relief, 'but I think calling Dr Palmer and asking her to come out might be a good idea. I honestly don't think Mrs Lord is going to get in the ambulance willingly, and …'

Before she could finish her sentence, the screen door opened and they turned to see Fergus ushering the elderly woman out, one arm wrapped around her shoulder. She held her bandaged hand out in front of her like a gift as she looked warily from face to face.

'Mrs Lord doesn't want to go in the ambulance,' Fergus said, his tone telling them not to argue with him, 'but she's agreed to come into town and get checked out if I take her.'

Tab noticed he didn't mention the word hospital at all.

The others exchanged looks.

'And you're okay with that?' the sergeant asked.

'Yep. If someone could just let the school know I might be a little late?'

Constable Morris held up her phone. 'On it.'

'Okay, then.' Sergeant Skinner nodded. 'Thank you. That sounds like a good plan. We'll follow you in.'

'Is there anything I can get for you?' Tab asked.

Fergus looked down at his shorts and singlet and almost smiled. 'Do you think you could grab me a pair of jeans and a shirt from the wardrobe in the bedroom? Also the black shoes by the door and a pair of socks?'

'Of course,' Tab said, as Fergus slipped his bare feet into a pair of thongs on the verandah. Against her better judgement, she found herself warming to him slightly—it was hard to hate someone while they were being so sweet to an elderly woman.

They all hung back as Fergus ushered Mrs Lord over to his car and helped her into the front seat, clicking her seatbelt into place with tenderness and patience. Tab watched as he started down the driveway, the ambulance and police car following closely behind, and then she turned and went back inside, feeling only slightly awkward about being in his house alone.

The awkwardness went up a notch as she trekked down the short hallway and found his bedroom. Although Mrs Lord's touch was still very evident on the walls, the bed was rumpled and unmade with brown sheets and the aroma in the room was decidedly masculine. Mixed with a not at all unpleasant smell of sweat was a rich earthy scent, and on the dresser she found a small bottle of cologne. Without thinking, she sprayed a little into the air and inhaled deeply. Overtones of what she thought were patchouli and rosewood tickled her nose hairs and her eyes closed as a shiver of pleasure shot through her.

What was it about certain scents that had such power?

'*Meow!*'

Tab almost jumped out of her skin, her eyes flashing open and the bottle slipping from her grasp as Fergus's cat wound its way around her legs. Her hand to her chest, she bent and picked up the bottle, put it back on the dresser, and then reached down again to rub the cat.

'Oh my goodness, girl, you scared me half to death.'

The cat nuzzled against her hand and purred. Tab gave her a few more moments of attention—the poor thing was obviously starved of affection—and then marched over to the wardrobe and flung it open. Surprised to find all the clothes neatly arranged—trousers on one side and shirts on another—she grabbed the first pair of jeans she came across and a classic navy-blue gingham shirt that seemed smart enough for work but casual enough for a classroom.

Ignoring the instinct to snoop a little more, she folded the clothes neatly, grabbed the shoes and socks, and went back through the house. Out of the corner of her eye she saw the kitchen was still in a state, with strips of bacon on the floor and milk and eggs out on the bench. If Fergus didn't return home until after school, ants would likely have found the bacon, and the milk would be off. It would only take her a few moments to clean up the mess. Whatever her feelings regarding the man himself, Tab had too much respect for milk to let it go to waste like that.

As she opened the fridge to return the few items, she couldn't help shaking her head. Aside from the eggs, bacon and a stale loaf of bread, there was very little else. Her heart squeezed at the sight. This was exactly what Lawson's fridge would have been like in the days following Leah's death if Tab hadn't intervened.

In her books, an empty fridge was a sure sign of someone not in a good mental state. Despite their unfortunate beginnings, Tab felt a ridiculous urge to do something about it.

Chapter Thirteen

Fergus was surprised to see Tabitha's ice-cream van outside the house when he arrived home just before five on Tuesday afternoon. He got out of his car just as the door opened on the front porch and Tabitha herself stepped out of his cottage.

Their eyes met. She looked like she'd been caught in the middle of a crime. In theory she *was* trespassing, as he hadn't invited her in, but he wasn't about to call her on it after what they'd gone through together this morning.

'Good afternoon,' he said.

'Hey, I know this looks suspicious but I have a very good explanation.'

He cocked his head to one side as he joined her on the porch. 'I'm listening.'

'I thought you might be too exhausted to cook after being out half the night searching for Mrs Lord, then having to go into work after this morning's dramas, so I made you some dinner. I assumed you'd be home by now and that I could give it to you in person, but I didn't want to just leave it on the step in case—'

'An animal got it,' he finished the sentence for her, smiling.

Tab held up her hand as if he were holding a gun at her. 'I do not want you getting the wrong idea. I promise I'm not cracking onto you. The food means *nothing*. I would do this for anyone who had gone out of their way like you did this morning to help Mrs Lord.'

And although she protested a hell of lot, he believed her.

'Anyone would have done what I did this morning,' he said. 'The poor woman broke my heart, but the food does mean something. After the day I've had the last thing I feel like doing is slaving over a hot stove. I considered going to the pub for a meal but …'

'The kitchen isn't open on Monday and Tuesday nights.'

'Exactly. So thank you.'

'And, I'm not sure they do much in the way of vegan cuisine at the pub anyway.'

'Vegan?' He couldn't help but screw up his nose.

'Aren't you a vegan?' she asked. 'That's the talk around town.'

'What? No!' He couldn't hide his horror; then it clicked. 'Ah, I know where that came from. I went to a barbecue with the teachers at Joanne's and this woman dropped by—she has three single daughters or something—and when she asked if I wanted to come around for a roast Joanne told her I was a vegan. Not that there's anything wrong with being a vegan, but me? I love my meat.'

'Right.' Tabitha nodded slowly. 'That must have been Eileen Bennett—Joanne did you a massive favour. And now that I think about it, the food you ate at the tea rooms wasn't vegan.' She sighed. 'I should have realised, but … I'm afraid it means you might be a little disappointed with the dinner I made you.'

'What is it?' he asked warily, his mind conjuring all sorts of tofu and mung bean concoctions.

'Lasagne. Obviously I've never made vegan lasagne before, so I had to find a recipe. And then it was hard to find some of the ingredients at IGA, so I improvised. Promise it's all still vegan … not that it really matters, I guess.'

He laughed, but inside he couldn't help feeling chuffed at the effort she'd gone to. The urge to apologise again almost overwhelmed him, but at the same time he didn't want to bring it up and possibly ruin what felt like a tentative truce.

'Would you like to come in for a drink?' Sometimes actions spoke louder than words.

She shook her head. 'I'm pregnant, remember.'

'It doesn't have to be an alcoholic one, but after you've gone to all this trouble, it's the least I can do. What about coffee?'

Her lips twisted up slightly and her shorter arm shifted at her side. 'Coffee? Now, do you really mean coffee or should I be worried that *you're* trying to crack onto *me*?'

He laughed loudly. 'Touché.'

'I'm not really drinking coffee either,' Tabitha admitted. 'But I could go an orange juice, and I happen to know you now have some in your fridge.'

'I thought you just brought me dinner?'

She winked. 'You should know, Fergus McWilliams, that I never do anything by halves.'

'In that case,' he gestured to the door behind her, 'let's go have an OJ.'

The moment he stepped inside, he was hit by an aroma like he'd noticed at her café and once again his stomach rumbled accordingly. He held the door open for her and led her into the kitchen where they found Mrs Norris, standing on the table, pawing at the alfoil on top of a rectangular casserole dish.

'Get down,' he shouted as he launched himself at the cat. Of course, the horrible feline stood her ground, hissing and swiping out to scratch him as he tried to shoo her off.

Tabitha cackled. 'She really doesn't like you, does she?'

'Not at the best of times,' he said, looking around for something to throw at Mrs Norris.

'Here, kitty cat.' Tabitha stepped towards the table and held out her hand. It was like watching a magician. Immediately the cat's fur smoothed again and he heard her purring as she allowed Tabitha to scoop her up. 'So what did you do to her?'

'I did nothing.' Ferg picked up the casserole dish and transferred it safely to the oven. 'I've been nothing but a gentleman to her, I promise, but she's actually not mine. I recently broke up with my girlfriend; the cat used to be hers.'

Tab frowned. 'Did you keep her to be vindictive?'

'What? No!' He chuckled as he shook his head slightly. 'You don't have a very good opinion of me, do you?'

'I don't know what to think of you, to be honest. One minute I think you're an arsehole, the next minute I think maybe you've got a few redeeming qualities. Then again …' she stroked Mrs Norris, 'animals are usually very perceptive.'

He snorted, loving the way she didn't hold back. 'Not this one.'

'So how did you end up with the cat then?'

He didn't know what possessed him to tell her. 'A couple of months ago, my fiancée called off our wedding.'

'Oh shit. I'm so sorry.'

He shrugged as if the betrayal hadn't nearly killed him—she didn't know the half of it, but he didn't want her pity any more than he wanted the mortification of admitting the whole sorry story. 'Better to find out before we tied the knot or had kids, I guess. Anyway, she had the cat when we met and it never took a liking to me.'

Tabitha continued to bestow affection upon the psychopathic beast, or maybe she was simply a misandrist.

'My ex's new partner is allergic to cats, so she begged me to keep Mrs Norris. I was stupid enough to think that when it was just the two of us, she'd come round. But so far, despite me spoiling her rotten with expensive cat food and letting her sleep on my bed, she can still barely bring herself to look at me,' he said as he opened the fridge to grab the juice. 'Holy shit!'

Tabitha laughed as he stared into the fridge.

'You weren't joking when you said you didn't do anything by halves.' In addition to the lasagne and a freshly baked loaf of bread he'd noticed on the bench, his fridge was full of fresh fruit, vegetables, and of course the promised orange juice. 'How much do I owe you for all of this?'

'Nothing. Most of it's from my garden anyway and it's just my way of saying thanks for taking care of my old friend. I guess I should have realised you weren't vegan when you had eggs and bacon here this morning.'

'Never mind.' He grabbed a glass, poured two orange juices, handed one to her and then gestured she take a seat at the table.

'Thanks,' she said as she lowered the cat to the floor and then sat.

He sat too and held out his glass to chink hers. 'Did you know Mrs Lord well before she went into care?'

Tab took a drink, then, 'Yes, she was very good to my family after my mother died.'

So he hadn't been the only one telling the old dear porkies. Now that he thought about it, he recalled his colleagues talking about the cancer that had taken Tabitha's mother. 'Sorry to hear that.'

'It was a long time ago now, but Mrs Lord was always very kind, bringing us food and treats and helping Dad take care of us when our own grandma was busy. They were friends too—my gran is now in the hospital full-time as well, but Mrs Lord can't really be much of a friend these days.'

'Does your grandmother have dementia too?'

Tab shook her head. 'Parkinson's. I'm honestly not sure what's worse—being mentally alert and stuck in a body that no longer works or being fairly physically fit like Mrs Lord but not remembering anyone, anything or even how to take care of yourself.'

'Old age really sucks, doesn't it?'

'Yes, but the alternative isn't so appealing either. You were great with Mrs Lord though. I'm so glad we didn't have to use force to get her back.'

He sighed, because although that was the case getting her out of the house and into the hospital, once she realised she wasn't going home again, she'd acted exactly as they suspected she would. The local doctor had no choice but to sedate her and Fergus had left to go to school with a heavy heart.

As if she sensed the need for a change of subject, Tab said, 'So, how is school anyway? Ned has nothing but praise for you. Honestly, I'm considering paying him money *not* to talk about you.'

That made Fergus laugh. 'School's great. The kids are awesome.'

Tab raised an eyebrow. 'You've got some difficult cases in that class.'

He smirked, guessing she was talking about the Walsh twins, who could be a little domineering, and Mason O'Reilly, who hadn't yet learnt how to channel his excess energy into good. 'I didn't go into teaching because I thought it'd be a walk in the park. I wasn't the easiest of kids myself, and without the interest of a few good teachers, my life could have been very different. Those teachers made me believe I was worth something and that I could rise against my not so great start.'

'You didn't have the best home situation?'

'I didn't even *have* a home for most of my childhood. My mum had bipolar. She overdosed when my twin sister and I were seven, but even before she died, she didn't have her act together enough to pay regular rent. We lived on the couches of her so-called friends, sometimes her dealer. We were in and out of foster care long before we lost her for good.'

'Oh God.' Tabitha pressed her hand against her heart. She looked as if she was about to cry. 'Where was your father?'

'Your guess is as good as mine,' Fergus said. 'Mum met him at a B&S ball and didn't even know his name or where he came from. She always used to say, "one night of hot sex and a lifetime of penance" referring to us kids.'

'That's an awful thing to say to children.'

Ferg nodded. 'She was awful—half the time. The rest of the time she treated us like a little king and queen, but those times never made up for the bad.'

'Have you ever thought about looking for your father?'

'Wouldn't know where to start. He literally could be any-one, and there's a good chance he's as much of a deadbeat as our mother.' Why the hell was he telling her all this? He was usually a closed book. It had taken months of dating for him to tell Jools even a fraction of what he'd just blurted to this near stranger. 'Some things are better left alone.'

'What happened to your sister? Is she still …'

Her voice drifted off but he knew what she was asking. 'Yes, she's fine. She's a social worker, but we're … not close like you and Lawson seem to be.'

Tabitha smiled. 'Yes, he's my rock. I don't know what I'd do without him and Meg. And Ned. They're my life.'

'Ned's a cool kid,' Fergus said, glad for the change of subject. The mention of his family—of his *sister*, who was his only family—had him clenching his fingers around his glass.

'He is.' Tabitha smiled in way that made his stomach tighten, which also reminded him how hungry he was. Once again, his nose caught the scent of the lasagne.

'Would you like to stay for dinner? It's the least I could offer considering you cooked it.'

She rubbed her lips together, hesitating a moment—probably trying to come up with an excuse to turn him down without being rude.

'Forget it.' He stood quickly. 'I've already kept you long enough. You've probably got better things to do.'

'I wouldn't say better things,' she said, not making a move to stand. 'But I'm on the committee for the agricultural show. We've got a meeting tonight.' She glanced at her watch. 'Starts in half an hour and since the show is just over a month away, it'll be frowned upon if I skive off.'

Was there anything she didn't have a finger in? Still, he felt relieved at her genuine excuse. Despite his verbal diarrhoea about things he'd meant to keep to himself, he'd enjoyed her company.

'But ...' she added, 'maybe a quick bite? After all, I am eating for two and if I have to subject you to vegan cuisine, it's really only fair I try it too.'

'Yes. Definitely.' He nodded, already crossing to the cupboards to grab plates. 'When are you due?'

'Fifteenth of April.'

'That's my birthday,' he exclaimed, pausing a moment.

'No way?'

'Yep. Has been for thirty years.'

Tab laughed and got to her feet to help him. While he got the lasagne out of the oven and onto plates, she set the table. 'So, you're an Aries. That makes a lot of sense.'

'It does?'

'Yes, Aries are arrogant, self-absorbed and confrontational.'

'I'm not arrogant, definitely not self-absorbed, and—'

'You're arguing with me.' She smirked. 'Very confrontational behaviour.'

Fergus shook his head, but he was smiling too. 'I can't believe you buy into that bullshit.'

'Sometimes I do, sometimes I don't.' She picked up a plate. 'Shall we?'

'We shall.' He grabbed the other plate and sat across from her at the table. 'This smells absolutely delicious.'

'Let's hope it tastes as good.' Tabitha tore off a bit with her fork and popped it in her mouth.

Trying not to stare at how seemingly easily she managed one-handed, Ferg turned to his own dinner and tentatively took the first mouthful. 'Wow, this is … amazing.'

She grimaced, then cracked a laugh and put her fork down. 'And you are a big fat liar. It's awful. I won't be offended if you don't eat it.'

'It's not *that* bad,' he said and then to prove his point, scooped another chunk into his mouth.

She shook her head with a smile. 'You're crazy.'

'Nah, I just learnt growing up never to waste food as the next meal wasn't always guaranteed.'

She frowned and Ferg realised he'd said more than he meant to. 'So, what star sign are you?'

Tab hesitated a moment. 'Virgo. Born September first, which makes me intelligent, practical and reliable.'

He raised an eyebrow. 'Modest too.'

'Actually, yes.' She grinned. 'That is one of Virgo's positive traits.'

'Ah hah.' He stabbed a finger towards her. 'And let me guess, you listed all Aries' negative traits? What are my positive ones?'

She gave a coy smile. 'You'll have to do some research and find out for yourself.'

'I might just do that.'

Slightly awkward silence descended upon them and Ferg wracked his brain for something to talk about as he managed to force a few more forkfuls into his mouth.

'Tell me about the ice-cream,' he said eventually, when what he really wanted to ask was who her baby's father was. It shouldn't be any skin off his nose but he couldn't help wondering if she'd left him or the other way around. Her ex would not only have to be an idiot to dump someone as warm and vivacious as her, but also a jerk to leave someone who'd just become pregnant with his child. Maybe that was the reason? Maybe the jerk didn't want kids?

'You mean how I got into making it?' Tab asked, and for a second he forgot what he'd said.

Pulling himself together, he nodded. 'Meg said you've won some awards, so you must be pretty good.'

Her cheeks coloured slightly. 'Well, I'm not sure how much you know about the dairy crisis in WA, but not long ago things were pretty dire for a lot of dairy farmers. A number of local families, including us, were given notice that WA Country Milk would no longer be able to take as much milk as they once had. I've always been an ice-cream junkie and have been making it at home for as long as I can remember. When I began to make more than Lawson, Ned and I could eat, I bought the van and started taking it round to local shows and festivals. It all went better than I ever expected. Then, when we were faced with having to start culling our cattle and turfing perfectly good milk, Meg suggested I take the business to the next level. That's when I started using the space at the back of her tea rooms and upped my production. Now as well as the ice-cream we sell ourselves, I also distribute to a number of small cafés and some country stores.'

'That's impressive,' he said.

Her brow arched. 'You're wondering how I do it all with only one arm?'

'No, that's not what I was thinking, I promise. But must be hard to compete with the big brands.'

'I'm not trying to compete. I pride myself on offering something different and of a higher quality that you can get in the frozen section of Coles or Woolies, but the business has grown faster than I could ever have imagined. Thank God we only open the tea rooms four days a week or I wouldn't have time to actually make the ice-cream. Speaking of time …' She glanced at her watch and gave him a regretful smile. 'I better be off to my meeting.'

He tried not to show his disappointment. He'd been enjoying talking to her more than he'd imagined he would. Until the last twenty-four hours, where he'd had more to do with adults than children, he hadn't realised how much he'd missed grown-up conversation, and there were so many things he still wanted to know about Tabitha.

'Of course. Sorry I kept you so long.' He reached over to grab her plate, but she got in first, standing and taking it and her cutlery and glass to the sink. When she turned on the tap, he said, 'Leave that. I'll do it later.' It was the least he could do after she'd cooked. 'There's not much.'

'You sure?' she asked, already drying her hand against her T-shirt.

'Yes. And I'll clean the dish and get it back to you ASAP.'

'No hurry. Unlike arms, baking dishes are not something I'm lacking.'

He couldn't help but laugh.

She gave Mrs Norris a quick pat goodbye and then Ferg walked her to the door. 'Thanks for the food and the chat,' he said as they lingered a moment on the porch.

'You're welcome.' She grinned and tossed her keys in her hand. 'I have to admit I said yes because I felt sorry for you, but the conversation was almost pleasant.'

He laughed. 'Look, I know I've said it before but I really am sorry for the way I behaved when we first met, and then for my ignorant attitude at cricket. I know it's no excuse but … I wasn't in the best headspace when I arrived and it's clear to me—'

She cut him off before he could finish. 'I get it. You came to Walsh with a wounded heart and wary of all women. Believe me, I understand firsthand what hurt can do to you, so let's agree to call it a truce. Deal?'

She held out her hand and he reached out and shook it, all the while wondering if the hurt she referred to was associated with the father of her baby.

'But,' she added before he had the chance to decide whether or not to ask, 'if you *ever* cross me again, I promise you, I won't be so forgiving.'

'Noted,' he said, unable to contain his grin as she took the steps off the porch two at a time.

She waved as she walked. 'See you at cricket, Thursday!'

'See you then.' Now that they'd cleared the air, he couldn't wait.

Tabitha was almost at her van, when she turned. 'Pity I thought you were a vegan or I'd have brought you some ice-cream for dessert. Although maybe my next experiment should be vegan ice-cream. You can be my guinea pig!'

'Now, now, let's not get carried away,' he joked.

Yet he had a feeling that no matter the flavour, if Tabitha Cooper-Jones made it, he'd like it. His first impressions of her had been completely off the mark and he'd never been happier to have been wrong about someone in his life.

Chapter Fourteen

'Why are *you* so late?' Adeline glared at Tab as she entered the town hall five minutes after the show meeting was supposed to begin.

'Sorry.' Tab gave the rest of the committee an apologetic smile as she slid into a chair around the table. Then, because Adeline's eyes were still boring into her, she couldn't help herself. 'I was having dinner with Fergus and lost track of time.'

'The new teacher?' Eileen Bennett frowned in disapproval.

'*You* were *what*?' Adeline looked at Tab like she was cow shit on gumboots. '*Why*?'

Tab stifled a smile. 'He was up half the night searching for Mrs Lord, and then this morning, after helping us get her back to the hospital, he went to work. I simply did the neighbourly thing of making him a meal and when I delivered it, he asked me to join him.'

'That was lovely of you,' said Tennille, 'considering you've had a very stressful twenty-four hours yourself.'

Adeline snorted. 'You're not even neighbours anymore.' And although Carrie was more subtle, it was clear on both their faces that they didn't think there was anything altruistic about Tab's actions and that they wished they'd thought of using the excuse to pay him a visit.

'I must admit I've been a bit uncertain about him,' Tennille added. 'He came across as a little arrogant both times I've spoken to him, but Boots said he was very caring towards Mrs Lord.'

'Yes, he was,' Tab confirmed. Even if she hadn't just spent a lovely couple of hours in his company, his treatment of Vera Lord would have made it very difficult to hold onto her grudge. 'If you didn't know better, you'd have thought she was his grandmother. He definitely wanted the best for her and watching her in distress upset him.'

'Maybe he's got some sort of power issue going on,' Eileen said. 'He's obviously far more comfortable with the vulnerable, like kids and the elderly, than he is with his peers.'

'I don't know ...' said Beth, one of Tab's favourite old ladies, who also happened to be Beck's grandmother. 'Beck said the kids adore him. In general, kids and animals are very perceptive about people.'

Tennille chuckled. 'True. The girls think the sun shines out of his arse.'

Tab decided not to mention what his cat thought of him, although cats had complicated personalities and thus probably couldn't be trusted. Thinking about Mrs Norris made her remember what he'd told her about his ex. What kind of woman cheats on someone and then expects them to take custody of their cat? Hell, what kind of woman would cheat on a man like Fergus McWilliams full stop? Sure, he had his faults, but if the last twenty-four hours were anything to go by, his virtues far outweighed his flaws. He was not only easy on the eye, but he was smart, caring when it mattered and had the kind of dry sense of humour she related to. He definitely didn't deserve all this scuttlebutt about him.

She feigned a yawn. 'So what have I missed so far?'

'Yes, let's get back to business,' said Chloe Wellington, Tennille's mother-in-law, Boots and Carrie's mum and, most importantly in this scenario, the president of the Walsh Pastoral and Agricultural Society. 'With just under five weeks until show day and now no band for the evening entertainment, we really do need to focus.'

'No band?'

Chloe nodded at Tabitha's question.

'What happened to The Barefoot Cowgirls?'

'I was just saying before you arrived that we'd had a major setback. The girls are hugely apologetic but they've had an opportunity to tour with Keith Urban in America. They're going to be his ...' She made a clicking noise with her tongue. 'What do you call it?'

'Opening act,' Carrie informed her with a slight roll of her eyes.

'Wow, that's awesome for them,' Tab said genuinely, but also trying to ignore the tug of jealousy. Ryder hadn't been the only thing she lost when she lost her arm. If damn cancer hadn't paid her a visit, maybe she'd be touring with Keith.

'Yes, but not so great for us,' Adeline said, tapping her ridiculously long nails on the table. She was in charge of entertainment and had gloated for weeks when she'd first managed to book The Barefoot Cowgirls. 'And we had a contract.'

'There's no point dwelling on it,' Tennille said, reaching into the middle of the table to grab a Tim Tam, then dipping it into her tea. 'We need to channel our energy into finding another band, pronto.'

Chloe looked around the table. 'Anyone got any other ideas or contacts?'

'There's always the high school band,' Beth suggested. 'I know I might be biased because my grandson is the drummer, but they've got good rhythm.'

Adeline screwed up her nose.

As usual, Chloe tried to smooth over the tension. 'They are good,' she said, 'but they were going to be The Cowgirls opening act, and they're hardly the big name we wanted to put our hundredth anniversary show on the map.'

Sadly, everyone agreed. There was a lot riding on the annual show this year. Usually, it only drew attendees from Walsh and the surrounding few towns, but this year they had high hopes of drawing people from much further afield to showcase what their small but vibrant community had to offer.

'I know!' Carrie sat up straight, knocking the table in her haste and spilling her tea. As her mother handed her a serviette to mop up, she said, 'What about Ryder O'Connell? He's kind of a local.'

Tab's heart turned to ice, the cold rapidly filling every other part of her body as all eyes around the table snapped to her.

'Great idea,' someone said. Tab was too numb to register who.

'Maybe you could ask him?' This from Carrie, who looked proud of her suggestion.

Everyone nodded hopefully, their heads clearly in the clouds.

But even if Tabitha could, she wouldn't. The last thing she wanted was the guy who'd broken her heart and still haunted her dreams, strutting around town and ruining show weekend for her. Ever since she was a little girl it had been her favourite time of the year—the rides, the fairy-floss, the friendly competitions about who could bake the best scones or grow the best roses, the fireworks. Who wouldn't love it?

'I haven't spoken to him in almost ten years—I've got no more hope of getting through his "people" than any of you do. And quite frankly, I think you're dreaming.'

There was no way in hell Ryder would give a weekend of his time to come all the way just to help them out. Although they'd met in Perth, he had other tenuous links to Walsh besides her—his second cousins owned one of the local dairies—so the town claimed him as their own, but as far as Tab knew, he hadn't visited them since hitting the big time. Although he was a country music star who sang about droughts, floods and hooking up in outback pubs, she'd bet her ice-cream business that his fancy boots hadn't ever seen real dirt. He was a joke really, and anything the P&A Society could afford to pay him would be a pittance to him anyway.

'Well, we can only try,' Adeline said, with a sneering twist of her lips. 'You're not usually one to have such a defeatist attitude, Tabitha.'

'I'm also not one to waste my time. But,' she shrugged, pretending to be nonchalant when she felt anything but, 'by all means, go ahead and ask. I'm happy to be proven wrong.'

'Okay. I will.'

Although Tab was certain even Adeline wouldn't be able to twist Ryder's arm, the discussion of him had sent the good mood she'd arrived in out the window and all she wanted to do was flee with it.

Chapter Fifteen

'Fergus!' Joanne called to him as he headed to his car Thursday afternoon and he turned to see her waving something small above her head.

'What's up?' he said, glancing at his watch.

She caught her breath as she landed beside him. 'You heading off to cricket training?'

He nodded.

'I've been meaning to ask you how that's going?'

'So far so good. The kids are enthusiastic, I'll give them that.' He was pretty certain that unless they showed some miraculous improvement, they had Buckley's chance of winning their first game this weekend, but there was more to life than being the best.

'And have you got enough parent help?'

'Actually only Tabitha assisted last week, but we managed.' He didn't add that there'd been a number of women on the edge of the oval—some he suspected were not even parents—none of whom had offered a hand, but many of whom had been eager to get him talking afterwards.

Joanne beamed. 'Isn't Tab great? Anyway, I won't keep you, but you got a phone call today that I couldn't put through because you were on playground duty, and then it slipped my mind. I took a message though.'

'Oh?' Dread filled his lungs because even before she said anything more, he knew.

'Yes, lovely woman—said she's a friend of yours from Perth. Jools? She sounded really keen to talk to you. She said it was about your sister and really important. Said you should have her number but just in—'

'I don't need her number.' He grabbed the post-it note from Joanne's hand and screwed it into a ball. How on earth had Jools and Eider found out where he'd moved? He'd been careful not to broadcast his new location, so as far as he knew only the education department had that information.

Joanne blinked, clearly taken aback, and Ferg sucked in a breath.

'Sorry.' It wasn't Joanne's fault Jools wouldn't let things alone. Damn Jools. When they first met, he'd found her persistence in pursuing him so appealing. He'd loved that she was such a go-getter. But now that same trait aggravated him something chronic.

'She's my ex-fiancée,' he explained, shoving the scrunched-up note in his pocket, annoyed he needed to explain. 'We broke up a little before I came down here and—'

'She can't accept that it's over?' Joanne gave him an understanding smile. 'Say no more. Sometimes it's hard letting go, but there's no point forcing a relationship if you're not feeling it. Was that why you took the job?'

He nodded; her assumption less mortifying than the truth. 'I wanted to put some distance between us.' Unfortunately, it didn't seem three hours' south was distant enough. The jobs he'd applied for next year, up in the far north of Western Australia, were looking more and more appealing. 'Not that I'm not enthusiastic about the job and the kids here as well, it's just …'

She reached out and patted his arm. 'It's okay. I understand. And I have no complaints about your work ethic or your teaching. You've been a blessed addition to our school community.'

'Thanks.' He cleared his throat. 'Anyway, I'm sorry you've been unwittingly involved in my personal life, but if she calls again, can you please ask her not to contact me?'

Joanne nodded. 'Consider it done. Now, I best let you get off to cricket. Have a good afternoon.'

'Thanks. You too.' Ferg turned to go, then added as an afterthought, 'Could I ask you one more favour? If someone named Eider calls, please don't take a message or put her through either.'

He hated asking Joanne to do his dirty business, but he didn't want his ex and sister tag-teaming him.

The acting principal's eyes widened. 'Another ex?'

'No!' He forced a laugh. 'She's … she's a friend of Jools and …' How should he put it? He definitely didn't want to go into all the messy details.

'Enough said. No Jools and no Eider. I'll tell Beck as well. I'm sorry to have caused you any distress.'

'It's fine. Thanks.' Ferg strode off to his car, feeling anything but fine as anguish filled him from head to toe and had every muscle in his body tensing.

When he arrived at the oval, there were already a few cars parked on the edge and some children spinning around on the grass. He hauled the training equipment out of his car and headed over to them. One of the mums intercepted him on the way.

'Hi Fergus. It's great to see you again.' As she flashed him a wide toothy grin, he realised she wasn't a mum at all, but the young woman who'd been searching for Mrs Lord with him the other night.

'Hey.' He forced a polite nod. What was her name? Corrine or something? It was on the tip of his tongue. But why was she even here?

As if she could read his mind, she pointed over to the kids. 'I brought Victoria and Milly—I'm their aunty—and since I'm here, I'm happy to help. I was on the junior cricket team myself not too long ago.'

'Great. Thanks,' he said, conscious of the way she held his gaze and the way her tongue darted out to moisten her lips after she spoke.

At that moment the ice-cream van rolled into the car park and Ferg immediately felt some of the tension caused by Jools' message ease. Almost forgetting Karen or whatever her name was, he watched as Tabitha climbed out of her van. Once again, she was wearing those tiny black shorts and a T-shirt that left little to the imagination. He felt his breath quicken.

'Hey Mr McDuck,' Ned shouted as he joined the growing group of kids on the oval.

'Hey Ned.' Ferg waved and then turned to Carly. 'Do you want to start getting the kids warmed up—a few stretches, a quick run around the oval, that kinda thing—while I talk to Tabitha about the rest of the activities?'

She didn't look too pleased to be dismissed, but quickly covered over any disappointment with a smile as she twisted a few strands of her honey-blonde hair around her finger. 'Whatever you say. I'm at your service.' Then she turned and cupped her hands around her mouth as she hollered, 'Alright kids. Everyone over here.'

As the children gathered around his newest recruit, Tabitha approached, a bottle of water in one hand and another tucked under her arm.

'Good afternoon.' Grinning, she tipped her cap at him.

'Is it?' The words came out of their own accord.

She raised an eyebrow as she placed the bottles down on the ground near the equipment bag. 'Bad day?'

He swallowed the impulse to unload on her about Jools and Eider. Just because they'd shared one nice meal together didn't mean they were friends. 'Nah, not really. How was yours?'

'Yeah, good. Spent the day with Meg in the kitchen prepping food for the tea rooms. It's good to be outside for a break. So, coach,' she cleared her throat, 'what's the plan for this arvo?'

He kinda liked it when she called him coach. 'Well ...' He gestured to the kids who were dotted around the perimeter of the oval. 'Victoria and Milly's aunt is getting everyone warmed up and then I thought we could split into three skills stations since we have an extra pair of hands.'

Ferg cringed the moment the words were out of his mouth, but Tabitha didn't even flinch.

'Carrie's helping us?' she asked.

'Ah, Carrie, that's her name.'

Tabitha laughed and shook her head. 'So what are you thinking? Batting, bowling and ...?'

'I noticed last week and also during PE at school that many of the kids lack good hand-eye coordination. So I reckon we get them to do some simple throwing and catching practice. Which group do you want to take?'

'I'll take the bowlers,' Tab said as Carrie arrived back with the kids.

It took a few minutes to organise them into groups and then everything went smoothly for the next half an hour. The kids actually seemed to be making inroads on their skills, so Ferg decided it was time to put their practice into action and give another game a try. He wanted to be sure they all knew the rules before their first game this Saturday. Dividing them into two teams, he put Tabitha in charge of the batting team and Carrie in charge of the fielders.

'I'll umpire.' It would give him a chance to take stock of each player's strengths and weaknesses.

They were barely two minutes into the game when Ned—making a mad dash between the wickets after an awesome hit—tripped, thanks to his leg pads, and face-planted the ground. *Youch*, Fergus winced as the bat somehow collided with the boy's head; he could almost feel the crack himself.

'You alright, mate?' He rushed forward, Tabitha right behind him. 'That was a pretty nasty knock on the head.' They crouched low and Ned looked up, dirt and grass in his mouth and his eyes wide. He was clearly trying not to cry. 'My hand hurts.'

Ferg glanced down at the boy's arm as he helped him into a sitting position.

'Where exactly?' Tabitha asked.

'Here.' He pointed to his wrist and shrieked a little when she touched it.

Ferg and Tabitha exchanged a look. He'd seen his fair share of breaks in his time as a teacher and he guessed as an ambulance volunteer she probably had as well.

'Sorry, I'm going to have to bail and take him to the hospital,' she said.

He nodded, ignoring the tug of disappointment that hit him in the gut.

Carrie piped up, 'Don't worry, Fergus and I have everything under control. Hope you feel better soon, Ned.'

After they left, Ferg tried to get the kids to focus again but they were all unsettled over the incident. Half of them seemed genuinely worried about their friend, a few were anxious that some similar accident might befall them and the rest were simply upset that it meant they wouldn't be getting ice-cream today.

He couldn't blame them. He really couldn't concentrate either.

★ ★ ★

'My arm really hurts, Aunty Tab,' Ned said as she helped him into the van. 'Do you think I'm going to have to get it chopped off like you did?'

'No,' Tab soothed, trying not to chuckle. She strapped him in and then walked around to climb into the driver's side, glancing back to see a big grin on Carrie's face.

The younger woman had practically salivated when Tab said she'd have to leave. And *what* was she wearing? A short denim skirt and crop top were hardly appropriate attire for coaching a bunch of kids. Not to mention her hair flying around wildly in the wind because she hadn't tied it up. Tab probably looked like a middle-aged PE teacher in comparison, but that's because she'd chosen her clothes for practicality, not to impress the hot coach.

Carrie must have been taking lessons in seduction from Adeline, not that her techniques had got her very far. Tab might not be an expert in men but even she could see that throwing yourself at members of the opposite sex would more likely have the guy in question running for the hills. Carrie's behaviour was actually quite sad and embarrassing, and really none of Tab's business, but she still found herself irritated by it.

'I want Dad,' Ned sobbed as she sat in the van beside him. The bravado he'd been trying to display in front of his friends vanished as tears fell fast and furious down his cheeks.

'Oh, sweetie.' Pushing all thoughts of Carrie and Fergus out of her head, Tab reached out and gave Ned a hug, careful not to hurt his arm. 'We'll call your dad as we drive. I'm sure he'll meet us at the hospital.'

'Okay. And do you think whatever they're going to do will hurt?'

Tab smiled warmly at him. 'No more than what you're feeling now. They'll give you some nice painkillers, and then maybe you'll get a cool cast and all your friends can write their names on it.'

Ned cheered up a little at this prospect and Tab took the opportunity to call Lawson, using Bluetooth through her car stereo.

He answered after only a few rings. 'Hey, sis, what's up?'

'Look I don't want you to panic,' she rushed, 'but there's been a little accident at cricket. Ned tripped and landed awkwardly on his arm. We're on our way to the hospital to get him checked out.'

'Shit.'

'Don't swear, Dad.' Ned giggled, then, 'it really hurts.'

'I bet it does, little man. But be brave. I'm already on my way.'

Less than ten minutes after Tab called her brother, he and Meg rushed into the tiny emergency department at Walsh Regional Hospital. The nurses had already given Ned some painkillers and an icy-pole to keep his mind off his injury while they waited for Dr Palmer to arrive.

'And how are you going?' asked Jenny, a nurse who was a few years older than Tab at school. 'Past that awful nauseous stage yet?'

She nodded. 'Yes, thank God. And I've gained back a little more energy the last week or so, which is a godsend.' She'd been beginning to wonder how she'd keep going if her tiredness levels had stayed the same but didn't want anyone to think she was crazy for doing what she was doing.

'Hey Dad, hey Meg,' Ned said, lowering the icy-pole only momentarily as they rushed into the emergency room. 'Look what they gave me. Although, between you and me, it's nowhere near as good as Aunty Tab's ice-cream.' He said the last bit in a stage whisper and Jenny laughed.

'Nothing's as good as Tabitha's ice-cream,' she agreed. 'What's your latest flavour?'

'I've been testing a few new ones for the show—honey-rhubarb seems to work well.'

As Jenny made a mouth-watering sound, Ned said, 'And she also made a really cool glow-in-the-dark one.'

Five minutes later the doctor arrived and barely had to look at Ned's arm to confirm what Tab already suspected.

'My guess is a break in the lower radius or ulna. You'll need a cast, Ned, which we can do here, but I'd rather you get an X-ray first.'

'Cool,' he exclaimed. 'I've never had a photo of my bones before.'

Dr Palmer grinned. 'Your first break and your first X-ray are definitely a rite of passage, but I'm afraid you'll have to go to Bunbury as our X-ray machine is on the blink.'

Ned thought about this for a moment, then looked to Lawson. 'Can we get Maccas for dinner?'

Lawson laughed as he ruffled his son's hair. 'If this isn't a situation deserving takeaway for dinner, I don't know what is.'

While Dr Palmer wrote up a referral and called ahead to Bunbury to let the hospital know to expect them, Tab, Lawson and Meg talked logistics. The cows still needed to be milked, no matter what.

'I'll take Meg home,' Tab offered, 'and help her and Ethan with the milking.'

'Aw,' Ned whined. 'Can't Meg come too?'

Trying not to feel left out, Tab placed a hand on her belly and smiled. 'Go,' she urged Meg. 'Ethan and I can handle it on our own.'

'Are you sure?'

She nodded. Cricket practice would be almost over by now, so no point heading back there. She tried to stifle the disappointment at this thought as a flash of Carrie flirting with Ferg came into her head. 'Of course. You guys go and don't worry about the cows. Maybe bring me back a packet of those Ronald McDonald cookies. Do they still even have those?'

'Thanks, sis, you're the best. And,' Lawson chuckled, 'I'm not sure about the cookies but if they have them, they're all yours.'

'Thanks, bro.'

She walked Lawson, Meg and Ned to their four-wheel drive, waved them out of the car park and then headed to her van, where she called Ethan to fill him in as she drove out to the farm.

'Ned's broken his arm, so you and the girls are stuck with me tonight. I'm heading there now. I'll grab my boots and meet you at the sheds.'

'Poor little tacker, but his bad luck is my good fortune. You're a lot easier on the eye than Lawson.'

'And you are a terrible flirt,' Tab said grinning because she knew he was all talk and that, totally smitten with Kimmy, he probably wouldn't even notice if Tab turned up to the shed in a bikini and stiletto heels.

She laughed at the ridiculous image as she disconnected.

Chapter Sixteen

Carrie grinned at Ferg as the last of the parents drove away. 'Well, I'd call that a successful training session.'

He raised an eyebrow, wondering if she'd been in a different realm to him. Clumsy Ned appeared to be their best player—at least he'd managed to hit the ball before he'd tripped, whereas hardly anyone else on the team could make that claim. Although to be fair, their dismal batting skills were likely as much the fault of their dismal bowling skills.

'Yeah, thanks for helping,' he said, looking around as he put the training equipment into his boot, and suddenly realising he and Carrie were the only ones left. 'Where are the girls?'

'Oh.' Carrie waved her hand dismissively. 'My sister-in-law came to get them, which means I'm free for a post-training drink or even dinner. The pub does a great chicken parmi on Thursday nights. What do you say? You look like you could do with a beer, and the first one's on me.'

Ferg wasn't a fool—it was clear her offer would include a lot more than just food and drink if he wanted it to. Running around on the oval with the kids hadn't alleviated his tension in the way he'd hoped, but he reckoned a few hours with Carrie might put a dent in it. She was undeniably hot, and if the way she was looking at him now was anything to go by—as if *he* was the chicken parmigiana and *she* was ravenous—he guessed she'd be more than willing to let him lose himself between her legs.

When he took too long to reply, her tongue darted out to lick her lower lip and she said, 'What do you say Mr McWilliams? You hungry?'

Ferg shifted uncomfortably. It felt like forever since he'd had sex and the pull of temptation was strong. If he thought she'd be happy with a one-night stand, he might have succumbed to it, but he got the feeling that once he gave Carrie a little, she'd want a lot more.

He didn't have a lot more to give right now and even if he did, she wouldn't be his type, so it wouldn't be fair to lead her on. Not to mention the fact that he didn't want to become fodder for gossip, just when the town's interest in him finally appeared to be dying down.

'Thanks.' He closed the boot of his car and shot her an apologetic smile. 'But I think I'm going to go check on Ned.'

Carrie's shoulders sagged and the disappointment was clear on her face. 'Okay then. Well, maybe next time.'

'Maybe,' he said. 'Thanks again for your help.'

Ferg climbed in to his car before Carrie could try to change his mind and then high-tailed it out of town.

A kilometre or so past the turn-off to Mrs Lord's, he slowed as a sign loomed on the right-hand side of the road. 'Cooper-Jones Dairy' read the lettering, with 'L, M and T' above the Cooper-Jones in fancy font. He found it sweet that even though Tabitha no longer lived on the farm, they'd still included her in the sign. Once again, evidence of the sibling's closeness left him feeling a little empty.

He thought of his own sister—his best friend, confidante and lifeline as they were growing up. Even after everything, he still missed her.

Shaking his head free of that unhelpful thought, he turned into the gravel drive and followed it past a number of paddocks until he came to a cluster of buildings. What seemed to be hundreds of black and white cows were being herded towards the largest of the sheds by a big bloke Fergus didn't recognise, riding a motorbike. The man waved and kept going, ushering the cows with the help of a couple of dogs.

Ferg drove on towards a house in the not too far distance. The closer he got, the more it looked like something out of a TV farm drama—big limestone bricks, a shiny tin roof and verandahs all round. Two wicker rocking chairs sat on the verandah with large pot plants adding a lovely greenery and making the place look like a real home. A lump formed in Ferg's throat and he was seriously considering turning around when the front screen door opened and Tabitha stepped out of the house onto the verandah.

She lifted her good arm and waved, the wide smile on her face telling him she was happy to see him. He could hardly leave now, so he parked under a big gum tree not far from the house and got out.

He waved as he strode towards the house. 'Hey.'

'Long time no see,' Tabitha called back. She'd changed into baggy black work pants and an oversized blue shirt, but still looked hot.

'I came to check on Ned.'

'That's really sweet of you.' She bent down to shove her feet into a pair of gumboots and he couldn't help marvelling at how she managed with only one arm.

Luckily, he averted his gaze just as she looked up.

'Lawson and Meg have taken Ned to Bunbury for an X-ray and probably a cast, which means I'm on milking duty with Ethan.'

'Who's Ethan?'

'Our worker.' She chuckled as she started towards the sheds. 'He's really much more than just a worker now. Ethan's from Ireland but been with us a couple of years. Don't know what we'd do without him.'

She spoke so fondly that Ferg wondered if there was something going on between them. Tab had said she was single but *someone* had to be the father of her baby.

'Well then, I suppose I'd better go,' he said a little awkwardly.

She paused in her stride and turned back. 'You're not interested in meeting the girls?'

'The girls?'

She laughed. 'Our cows. I know they're a little smelly but most of them are such sweethearts.'

Ah, right. 'I wouldn't be in the way?'

'Not at all. I might just put you to work, but,' Tab glanced down at his clean white sneakers, 'we'll have to lend you a pair of boots. Come on.'

He laughed as he shoved his car keys in his pocket and fell into stride beside her. Not too far away he could see a horde of cows waiting in the pens on one side of the largest shed. They were what he guessed you'd call 'lowing' as if they were all in conversation about what they were about to do. The two dogs he'd seen earlier were running back and forth between the cattle, barking orders.

'That's Clyde and Cane,' Tab said, following his gaze. 'Clyde— the kelpie—is a fabulous worker, takes after his mother Bonnie, who sadly died last year, but Cane ... He still gets a bit excitable.'

Ferg guessed Cane was the large white dog, which looked a bit like a snowstorm churning up the dirt. 'Hang on ... is Cane a Maremma? Is he ...?'

Tab cracked a chuckle. 'Yep. One of Adeline's—she sold him to Lawson when she was trying to get into *his* pants. But we don't hold his origins against him.'

He laughed. 'So, have you lived here all your life?'

'Yep, all twenty-seven years of it, aside from three at boarding school for Years 10, 11 and 12.'

'What was that like?'

'Boarding school?' She shrugged. 'Some days it was like living at Malory Towers and other days it was hell on earth. Mostly the girls were nice though, they became a bit like sisters, and being in Perth let me pursue some passions that weren't possible down here.'

'Like?'

'Music.' The word sounded a little choked. 'I used to sing and play guitar.' She cleared her throat and gestured to the shed in front of them. 'Anyway, here we are.'

The noise and smell from inside hit Fergus in the face even before they entered so that he forgot all about her mention of music as he covered his nose. 'How do you handle that smell?'

It was a terrible combination of sour milk, manure and disinfectant or something.

'I'm so used to it, I don't even notice it. I only remember when we have a visitor who isn't from around here, but you'll get used to it quick enough.'

Ferg wasn't so sure but followed her nonetheless.

Tabitha stooped just inside the door to pick up a pair of black, well-used gumboots. 'Here, put these on. They're Lawson's—I think they'll fit.'

'Thanks.' He took them from her, their skin touching in the exchange and he couldn't help a quick intake of breath. It had been so long since he'd touched anyone that the feel of Tabitha's bare skin on his almost felt like an electric shot.

As he yanked off his sneakers, she walked around the mammoth milking platform-machine-thing to the other side of the shed. He shoved his feet into the boots and followed her, just as the machine started to turn.

'Well, well, well, who do we have here?' said the bloke he'd seen earlier as he joined them at what Fergus guessed was the start of the circular milking platform. 'G'day.'

The typically Aussie greeting sounded weird in such a strong Irish accent, but he nodded up at the guy and said, 'Hi.' He couldn't offer his hand as the man was standing up in the pens ushering cows one by one onto the milking platform.

Tabitha was already working hard on the ground level, spraying each cow's udders, then wedging the hose in her armpit as she used her hand to clip some kind of metal suction thing onto the udders as the animal passed her. She smiled and nodded between the two men. 'Ethan, meet Fergus—he's the new teacher in town and came to check up on Ned. Fergus, meet Ethan, he tells terrible jokes and has a penchant for quoting Aussie movies at us—you'll learn to ignore him.'

Ethan aimed his middle finger at Tabitha but his wide grin said he meant it in the most good-natured way.

'What's your favourite movie?' Ferg asked.

Ethan screwed up his face as if deep in thought as he nudged another animal onto the machine. 'Tough question—have to be a toss-up between *The Castle* and *The Dish*.' He rubbed another cow's behind in a very tender manner. 'What about you?'

'I'm more of a fantasy guy myself. *Avatar* is a bit of a fave, and I've lost track of the number of times I've watched the *Lord of the Rings* and *Harry Potter* movies.'

'*Harry Potter*, hey?' Ethan winked. 'Our Tabby's a bit of a fan of those.'

'The books are even better though. Anyway, enough of the chitchat, do you want to have a go?' She nodded to the bare bum of the cow nearest to them and Ferg's heart dropped.

'What if I get it wrong?'

'If a one-armed woman can do this, anyone can. Here, I'll show you how and then I'll do the spraying and you can attach.'

Taking a deep breath, he stepped up close, unsure who he was more terrified of—Tabitha or the bovines. Putting the hose spray under her arm again, she unhooked one of the suction things from where they were hooked on a bar that circled the machine and proffered it. As he took it, she sprayed the nearest udders. 'Right, now grab one udder with your other hand, then squeeze the suction cup and put it on. It's not rocket science.'

Feeling ridiculously nervous—he didn't want to make a fool of himself in front of Tabitha and Ethan—Ferg followed her simple instruction and was stupidly proud when it worked. He felt a massive smile grow on his face as Tabitha praised him with a simple 'Good'.

There wasn't time to celebrate his victory before she added, 'Quick, do her other one. The rotary may look like it's going slow, but we need to be quick or a cow won't get a full milking before it goes the whole way round.'

When the rotary was about two-thirds full, Tab gestured for him to follow her again. 'Ethan will keep things going here now and we'll start taking them off at the other side.'

Nodding, he went after her again. 'How long does it take to go round? And do all the cows only go through once?'

'This rotary holds fifty cows, one rotation is ten minutes and, yep, once round each.'

'How do you know they've all been through? They look pretty indistinguishable to me.'

'Shh. Cows have feelings too, you know.' There was teasing gleam in her eye as she pointed up at the nearest one. 'You see that tag on her ear?'

He nodded.

'They're part of our electronic tag-on system—it registers as they get on and off and helps us ensure the whole herd gets milked. Much, much easier than the old days.'

He paid close attention as she began the disembarking process, explaining exactly what she was doing as she unclipped the suction cups from the first cow, sprayed her udders with the disinfectant and then unclicked the little chain that was holding them into the rotary just as the machine delivered them to the exit gate. The cows backed out of the rotary and then ambled into the exit pens. He swore a few of them gave him a bemused look as they went their merry way, but Tabitha captivated him far more than the big black and white beasts.

She seemed more proficient at doing most things than anyone with two arms would be. He was so in awe that he didn't notice he was staring at her little arm again.

But she did.

His cheeks heated as she caught him looking and he was about to apologise when she said, 'Cancer.'

He blinked. 'Excuse me?'

'That's how I lost my arm.'

His stomach grew hard. 'You don't have to tell me.'

'It's not a big deal.' She shrugged one shoulder. 'Usually I tell people as soon as I meet them. It's easier once it's out in the open, but with you …'

'I was a jerk and so you changed your MO.'

Her lips quirked as if she was struggling not to laugh. 'Something like that. Anyway, not long after my sixteenth birthday,

I was home for the school holidays when I noticed I had a lump about the size of a golf ball on my arm. I just thought I'd knocked it on something and probably wouldn't have gone to the docs, except that it was affecting my guitar playing. Our local doc thought it was tennis elbow, so I got by on a lot of painkillers and pretty much forgot about it. When it was still there a year later, Gran made me go see a locum. He immediately sent me to Bunbury for scans, and it turned out I had a sarcoma.'

She kept working as she talked but Ferg was hanging on her every word, semi-shocked by the matter-of-fact way she spoke. He'd had girlfriends who'd wallowed more over the loss of a nail.

'Anyway, I was operated on, but,' she sighed loudly, 'another year later I got another birthday present. Just after I turned eighteen, we discovered the sarcoma had returned and the only option was to amputate.'

'Fuck. I hope that first doctor was held accountable for such a monumental stuff-up.'

'He retired not long after as the locals totally lost faith in him, and now we have Dr Palmer. She's brilliant, and had she been the doctor to see my arm the first time, I'm sure I'd still have it, but life's like that. I focus on what I have, not on what I've lost. I survived to tell the tale, thanks to my amazing family and friends. There are a few things that are tricky with only one full arm, but I don't let much get the better of me and I feel so very blessed with my life.'

He wanted to ask what she found difficult, but that felt wrong somehow—a bit like someone driving slowly past a car crash—so instead he said, 'Is there a reason you don't have a prosthetic?'

'What makes you think I don't?'

He didn't know what to say to that, but she just laughed.

'I do—it's hiding somewhere at the bottom of my wardrobe. When I moved to Rose Hill earlier in the year, I actually considered turfing it, but I figure sometimes I'm all alone out there and it might make a good weapon if I ever need to bong someone on the head.'

Now he laughed too as an image of Tabitha assaulting an intruder landed in his head. He reckoned she'd definitely give as good as she got.

'The truth is my plastic arm is pretty useless. The few things I struggle to do with one arm—opening cans, doing up buttons, putting on bras—weren't any easier when I was wearing my prosthetic, so I didn't really see the point. I actually feel less disabled without it, although I sometimes think other people would be more comfortable if I wore it.'

'Who gives a toss what other people think?'

'Not me.' Tabitha winked at him. 'Well, not usually. Anyway, I see what you're doing. Distracting me so I don't notice you slacking off. Don't just stand there, you can help at this end too, you know?'

'Dammit.' He made a show of clicking his fingers in disappointment, then stepped up close to her again so she could instruct him.

They chatted easily as they fell into a routine—Ferg unclipping the suction cups so she could spray the udders clean before he unclipped the chain. He even had to get up into the bed at one stage and try to 'encourage' a cow who'd decided to take a little nap to keep going. Tab cracked up as he tentatively pushed at the cow's behind and for his efforts was rewarded with an explosive spurt of poo that landed on his boots and splattered up his legs. Milking in shorts was proving a dangerous business.

'You've well and truly been initiated.' Tab was still laughing. 'And let me guess, you barely even notice the smell now?'

She was right. He didn't. In fact, there was something almost calming about being involved in this early stage of milk production, or maybe it was just being around Tabitha. The time went fast in her presence and he found everything she told him about dairy farming fascinating. It was so much more involved than he'd ever imagined. To think that they did this twice a day every day, yet despite the long hours and the seeming monotony of the work, it must be deeply satisfying, knowing you were feeding a nation. He got a similar satisfaction from teaching, knowing that he had a hand in shaping future generations.

Once the cows were heading back to pasture, Ferg helped Tabitha and Ethan hose down the shed and make sure everything was ready for them to do it all again tomorrow morning.

By the time they'd finished, the sun had almost set. The sky—all orange and deep purple—looked like a pretty painting and Ferg felt better than he had in weeks. He hadn't quite forgotten about the message from Jools, but it no longer bugged him as much.

'What you up to tonight?' Tabitha asked Ethan as they lingered just outside the shed.

Ferg didn't think it was possible for the man's smile to be any bigger, but it grew even more at her question. 'I'm going into town to see Kimmy.'

Tab grinned back. 'I certainly hope you're going to have a shower before you go visit lover-girl.'

Ah, so there was nothing going on between Tabitha and Ethan. Ferg felt ridiculously pleased by this knowledge but immediately pushed the thought away. It shouldn't matter if there was anything between Tab and the Irish larrikin.

Ethan wriggled his bushy eyebrows up and down. 'Kimmy prefers me when I'm dirty.'

Tab whacked him playfully. 'Too much information.'

'Anyway,' Ethan said, holding out his hand to Ferg, 'it was great to meet you. Thanks for your help.'

Ferg shook his hand. 'Likewise, and no worries. I had fun.'

'See you both later.' Ethan turned to go, whistling as he walked away.

'Does he live on the farm?'

'Yep. We've got a cottage—you'd have passed it on your way in but it's a bit hidden by trees. It was built for my grandparents when Mum and Dad got married and moved into the big house. When Granddad died and Gran moved into town, Lawson and Leah lived there as newlyweds. Then when Dad retired and moved to Bunbury with his new wife, Lawson and Leah moved into the big house and I went to the cottage. We've all lived there at some stage, but now it's for workers.'

'Hang on ... I thought Ned's mum was Meg?'

A sadness washed over Tabitha's usually cheerful expression. 'Meg is Ned's stepmum. She and Lawson only got married a year ago.' She hesitated a moment. 'Leah, Ned's mother, was killed in an armed robbery while she was working at the service station.'

'Jesus,' Ferg breathed, lost for any other words. That poor kid. That poor guy.

'She was pregnant with their second child. They both died at the scene.'

The hairs on the back of his neck stood up, although he'd never have guessed Meg wasn't Ned's biological mother, which surprised him. After years of foster care, he thought himself pretty good at picking the real parents from the temporary or replacement ones. 'I don't even know what to say to that.'

She reached out and touched his arm. 'You don't need to say anything.'

For a moment they stood like that—eyes searching each other's, his heart beating so hard he swore she could probably see it through his dirt-splattered T-shirt.

Ferg had an almost irrepressible urge to kiss her. But eventually kissing led to other things and sleeping with Tabitha would be an even bigger mistake than sleeping with Carrie. She was pregnant with someone else's child and he'd long ago made the decision that he'd never father a child that wasn't his own. There were too many ways to stuff it up. But even if she wasn't pregnant, he was only in town temporarily and he liked her. He could see a long-term friendship developing if he wasn't stupid enough to let lust stuff it up.

He cleared his throat. 'Well, I suppose I'd better be going, before this cow shit cakes itself onto my skin.'

She smiled as she snapped her arm back to her side. 'Yes, good idea.'

They started back towards the house, Ferg and the dogs following her lead. As they walked, he felt the need to fill the silence.

'Adventurous, courageous, versatile, positive, lively and passionate.'

'What?' She looked at him as if he'd just spoken in a foreign language.

'They are the positive traits, or virtues if you like, for those of us born under the Aries star sign.'

Tab glanced at him as she walked, her eyebrows slightly raised. 'I thought you didn't buy into that bullshit.'

'I don't—none of those words are ones I'd use to describe myself, which proves it's all bollocks, but … I like to be informed.'

'I don't know,' Tab mused, looking at him in a way that made him feel as if she could see deep into his soul—also bullshit and something he didn't believe possible. 'Moving from the city to a little country town could be considered adventurous, you'd have to be a little versatile to work with primary school kids, and I've seen how passionate you are about them.'

He couldn't help grinning. 'I reckon you could twist things any way you wanted, couldn't you?'

She grinned back as they approached the house. Thankfully the 'moment' between them earlier appeared to have been forgotten.

He dug his keys out of his pocket. 'Thanks for this evening's adventure. Hope Ned's break isn't too bad.'

'You're welcome, but ...' She pointed to his feet. 'Haven't you forgotten something?'

He glanced down to see the filthy gumboots. They were so comfortable, he *had* almost forgotten he was wearing them.

'As attractive as they look on you, I thought you might want to take your sneakers.'

Attractive? A warm buzz shot through his body.

'Definitely,' he agreed as he followed her up onto the verandah and started yanking off the boots.

'I'll be right back. Don't go anywhere,' Tab ordered, rubbing her feet on the heavy-duty doormat before disappearing inside.

Ferg could hardly ignore her request, however much his head was telling him to get away from her. He was tying up the shoelaces on his sneakers when she returned, carrying a plastic bag.

'Here.' She thrust it towards him.

He took the bag from her, ignoring the touch of her silky skin as their hands brushed once again. Oh Lord, he really needed to get laid. 'What is it?'

'Ice-cream.'

'Not vegan?' He feigned horror.

'No.' She laughed. 'But it is something new I've been testing. I hope you like it, and I want your honest feedback. Okay?'

'Okay,' he promised. 'What flavour is it?'

Tab shook her head. 'Not telling. That would ruin the fun. I want you to guess.'

And then she turned and headed into the house, leaving nothing for him but to go home and enjoy his dessert.

Chapter Seventeen

When Tab walked into the hospital late Sunday afternoon to visit her grandmother, she did a double-take at the sight of Fergus sitting on a plastic chair in the residents' lounge, holding court with four elderly women.

He looked up and smiled. 'Good afternoon, Tabitha.'

She blinked as his smile sent a jolt to her nether regions. *Oh no!*

Ever since milking together on Thursday night and the moment they'd shared outside the shed, she hadn't been able to get him out of her head. And unfortunately, it wasn't in the rage-filled way he'd filled it a couple of weeks back.

She blamed pregnancy hormones and the fact that all the gossip around town about how dreamy Fergus was had planted that seed in her head. Everything she'd read about the second trimester said that some women experienced an increase in libido, which was all very well when you had a boyfriend or husband to help scratch the itch. But none of the brochures the clinic had given her about doing pregnancy alone had mentioned anything about how to deal with *that* alone!

'Hi.' She managed a reply and some sort of a smile, before trekking over to kiss her grandmother on the cheek.

'Hello, sweetheart.' Gran frowned as she looked up at her. 'You're looking very tired. Are you looking after yourself properly?'

'I'm fine, really.'

'You shouldn't have bothered coming in to see me. Sit down and have a rest.'

Tiredness wasn't Tab's issue right now, but she pulled up another plastic chair and lowered herself into it. 'How are you?'

Yet although she was genuinely interested in the question, she barely heard Gran's answer as she was too distracted wondering why Fergus was here. Whatever the answer, he'd certainly presented himself better than she had. Her hair was flat and oily from being in the kitchen all weekend and she was still wearing the tea rooms' uniform of a black polo shirt and smart black shorts. Sadly, after a day preparing and serving food, they were looking anything but smart. In comparison, Fergus was wearing nice, slightly faded jeans and a red polo T-shirt, the colour perfectly accentuating his dark skin and eyes.

Tab couldn't help noticing how good he looked and smelled; even from across the room she could make out the scent of that lovely cologne she'd discovered on his dressing table. And it wasn't helping any with her pesky feelings.

Maybe she should get a vibrator? She knew many of her friends had them—some of her married ones even swore it was how they kept the spice in their long-term relationships—but the thought had always seemed a little desperate to her.

'Can I get you a cup of tea, Tabitha?'

Fergus's voice jolted her from her thoughts. Her cheeks heated, terrified that everyone could guess what she'd been thinking.

'That would be lovely. Thanks,' she said as he got up and went into the small kitchen off to one side of the communal area.

'How long's he been here?' Tab whispered, leaning in close to her grandmother.

'Half an hour or so. He came the other day as well, to check that Vera was okay after her episode. He says he's living in her old house. Next door to the farm?'

'Yes, he is.' She nodded, still feeling off-kilter.

'Seems a lovely man and he's very good-looking, isn't he?'

Tab swallowed. 'He's not bad—if tall, dark and handsome floats your boat.'

Gran snorted. 'You'd have to be dead for *that* not to float your boat, as you call it.'

'I'm going to help him with the tea.' Best thing to do would be to talk to him and get over the awkwardness of the moment they'd shared the other night. There probably hadn't even been a moment. Maybe it had all been in her head—her crazed pregnancy libido messing with her by concocting things that weren't even there. If Fergus acted normal when she spoke to him, she could assume that to be the case.

As the kettle started whistling, Tab sidled up beside him. 'Want a hand? I have one that's happy to help.'

He laughed, and some of the tension that had been building within her eased. 'I think I've got it under control, but you *can* tell me when I can get more of that ice-cream.'

'You tasted it?'

'Tasted it?' He grinned. 'Hell, I devoured the whole tub that night, but I couldn't quite work out what it was. It was like nothing I'd ever had before.'

Tab felt immensely pleased by his description. 'I'm not sure if I should tell you. You'll probably change your mind.'

Ferg raised an eyebrow. 'Don't tell me the colour came from something like broccoli or Brussel sprouts?'

She laughed at the almost green colour his face turned as he spoke, then announced, 'Coconut Avocado.'

'No way.' His grimace told her he thought that was almost as bad.

'Good thing I didn't tell you before you tasted it, hey?' she said as he dumped tea bags into mugs of boiling water. 'Wait till you try my cheese flavour.'

'Cheese?' His scepticism was written all over his face.

'It tastes way better than it sounds,' she said as he handed her one of the mugs and then took a sip of his own.

'I might have to take your word for that. By the way, how's Ned? We missed him at school on Friday.'

'Yeah, he was gutted not to be able to show off his cast to his friends, but apparently the pain had him up half the night, so Lawson and Meg thought it better to keep him home.'

'Makes sense ... although his break is such a shame. I'm pretty sure he's the best player on our cricket team.'

Tab laughed, then remembered that their first proper game had been yesterday. 'How'd they go against Brunswick?'

He gave her a wry smile as they started back to the lounge area, cups of tea in hand. 'The other team kicked our arses. At least we didn't have to travel far, but the next game is an hour away.'

'Sorry I can't come to the games, but Saturdays are our busiest day in the tea rooms.'

'Don't be silly. You don't even have a kid on the team.'

'I know ... but I feel like I do. Before Meg came along, I was kinda Ned's surrogate mum and helping with stuff like this came with the territory.'

'Sounds like Lawson and Ned were lucky to have you.'

'I was lucky to have them. I am lucky. Speaking of which,' she said, nodding towards the four old dears and lowering her voice as they approached. 'It's nice of you to come and visit Mrs Lord.'

He shrugged one lovely muscular shoulder. 'I don't like the thought of her having no family to visit. I know she doesn't know or remember me from visit to visit, but she seems to like me well enough.'

Tab couldn't blame her—once you got to know him a bit he was indeed very likeable.

They sat back in their plastic chairs and Tab's grandmother spoke up again.

'Fergus has been telling us about how he plays the piano accordion. I think he should bring it in and play it for us.'

'Great idea,' Tab said. 'How did you learn?'

'I kinda taught myself. There was one at one of my foster homes and I just picked it up one day and started to fiddle. It was my carer's ex-husband's and she said I could have it. It's old and a bit knocked about, but the kids love it.'

The conversation went from music to milking when Fergus mentioned he'd been out to the farm the other day and Gran shared some stories of how farming had changed in her lifetime. Mrs Lord interjected with a comment totally off-topic every now and then, which Len Walker countered with an equally ridiculous reply, and although Penelope Walsh—Adeline's grandmother—seemed to be listening, she'd been stuck in her own body, unable to speak properly since her stroke a couple of years back.

When Tab's phone started ringing, she reluctantly dug it out of her pocket in case it was important. A quick glance at the screen told her it was Chloe Wellington and she couldn't think of any reason why the Ag Society's president would be calling her this late on a Sunday.

'I'll be right back,' she told her grandmother as she went out into the courtyard to take the call. 'Hey Chloe. What's up?'

'Hi Tab, dear, how's your Sunday been?'

'Great but exhausting. The tea rooms were busy and now I'm visiting Gran before heading out to the farm for a roast dinner.'

'That's nice.' But Chloe's tone made Tab think she hadn't even registered what she'd said.

'Is something wrong?'

'I'm afraid I've got some news you might not welcome, but I wanted to let you know before our next meeting, or more likely before you heard it on the grapevine.'

'Oh?' Tab's stomach's squeezed tight and even before Chloe delivered the news she guessed what it was.

'Adeline has managed to convince Ryder O'Connell to come sing at the show for a very reasonable fee.'

Oh God. She almost dropped the phone as her hand instinctively fell to her belly.

'Tab? Are you okay?' Chloe's anxious voice burst from the phone as Tab lifted it back to her ear.

'Of course I am,' she said, hoping the other woman didn't hear the near hysteria in her voice. 'No skin off my nose. We broke up years ago. We were barely really even together. Great that he can come at such short notice. It'll be great for the show. We should definitely get some media attention now.'

Aware that she seemed to have contracted a terrible case of verbal diarrhoea, Tab forced herself to stop and take a breath.

'Yes, that is a bonus,' Chloe conceded, still sounding apologetic. 'Are you sure you're okay with it?'

'Yes, of course,' she lied, because really what would be the point in confessing the truth—that the thought of seeing Ryder O'Connell after all these years had every bone in her body quivering. It wasn't like the committee would *un*-invite him for her! 'But I've got to get back to Gran.'

'Yes, of course. I'll see you Wednesday.'

'Yes. Sure.' And if Adeline was there, Tab might just stab her in the eye with a knitting needle.

When she disconnected the call, she realised it wasn't only that her heart was quaking, her hand was trembling too. She took deep breaths in and out, trying to calm herself. Really, what was the problem if Ryder did come and strut his stuff on the makeshift stage at the showgrounds? She probably wouldn't even get to see him—she'd be too busy in her ice-cream van and he'd be mobbed by all the teenage girls in a five hundred kilometre radius.

The place would be so crowded, she probably wouldn't be able to get close to him even if she wanted to. Which she most certainly did not. But she had to wonder if Chloe and Adeline had really thought this through. Even with his recent misdemeanours, Ryder was a massive drawcard—his concerts usually sold out months in advance. They would need to up security, maybe even think about bringing in more portable loos.

Not that Tab was going to worry herself about any of this—*she* wasn't the one who'd invited him.

Oh God.

What if their paths did cross? Her stomach cramped at the thought and she dropped her head into her hand. Why did his opinion still matter so much to her after all these years?

'Tabitha. What is it? Are you okay?'

She cringed at the sound of Fergus's deep voice as the door banged shut behind him.

He rushed over to her. 'Have you had bad news, or … is it the … baby?'

At his kind tone, a lump swelled in her throat and tears rushed to her eyes. As if this day could get any worse, now she was going to fall apart in front of someone who wasn't much more than a stranger. Taking a moment, she willed the lump to dissolve and the tears to back the hell away.

'Tabitha?'

She made the mistake of looking up into his face. His eyes were so warm and filled with concern that any hope she had of reining in her tears evaporated.

'I'm fine,' she said through guttural sobs as the tears that fell freely down her face made her out to be a liar.

'You don't look fine.' Fergus wrapped an arm around her and ushered her over to a wooden bench. He dug a tissue out of his pocket and handed it to her. 'It's clean, I promise. Someone's always got a snotty nose at school, so having back-up has become a bit of a habit. Do you need a drink of water? Should I call one of the nurses?'

'No!' The last thing she needed was a local getting wind of the fact she was falling apart over Ryder O'Connell. It was bad enough Fergus had stumbled upon her. Oh Lord, she felt herself starting to hyperventilate again. This was freaking ridiculous.

She buried her nose in the tissue and gave her tear ducts a good talking to. *You're just in shock. Pull yourself together.*

'Thank you,' she said, after taking another deep breath. 'I'm okay. I just … It's stupid really.'

'It didn't look stupid.' He stared at her with those beautiful big caramel eyes. She could see the stubble on his jawline and that cologne she loved was stronger now he was so close.

Tab swallowed. She had to tell him something after he'd found her in such a state. 'I just found out that my ex-boyfriend is going to perform at … at the show in a few weeks and it's …' She sighed. She really didn't want his pity but nothing she could possibly say was going to put her in a non-pathetic light. 'It's unnerved me.'

'Your ex-boyfriend is in a band?'

'Nope. Well, he's got musicians I suppose that back him up, but he's a sole performer really. The name Ryder O'Connell ring a bell?'

'*Ryder O'Connell?*' His eyes bulged. 'Can't say I'm a fan, sorry. I'm more of a rock kinda guy, but of course I know him.'

'You don't need to apologise for not being a fan,' she said wryly. 'If you were, we might not be able to be friends anymore.'

'Are you still in love with him?'

Tab didn't know how to answer that question. The time in her life when she'd been singing with Ryder had been so blissful and carefree—they'd been so in tune with each other. When they were writing songs, it was almost like they were in the same head. And when they sang together, people said it was magic. Probably because it was—they were so in love, in the way that only teenagers could be. So consumed with each other. Tab had ate, slept and breathed Ryder and believed he felt the same way about her. But, when push came to shove, he chose the lure of fame over them and in the process shattered her heart and soul into a million pieces.

She'd done a good job of pretending she'd recovered, but he'd broken her in more ways than one.

'No,' she said eventually, 'I don't think so. I don't really even know him and I'm not sure I ever did but … I don't like the way he makes me feel.'

Ferg nodded. 'Is he the father of your baby?'

'What? No!' Tab couldn't help laughing.

'Sorry. I just … He's the first I've heard of you being romantically involved with anyone.'

'Geez, the bush telegraph must be faulty,' she said, still amused—which had at least succeeded in distracting her from the issue at hand. 'I used a sperm donor to get pregnant.'

She hadn't thought it was possible for him to look more shocked. 'Really? Why?'

Tab didn't know whether to laugh or feel affronted by his question.

He quickly backtracked. 'I'm sorry. That's totally none of my business.'

'It's fine.' She sighed. Usually she was an open book, yet although she'd proudly told her friends and family why she'd made her decision, it felt slightly mortifying admitting the truth to him. But what else but the truth could she say? 'I wanted to have a baby—it's as simple as that. And my track record with relationships is pretty dismal, so I got sick of waiting for true love to come along and I took things into my own hands. You probably think I'm crazy.'

'I think you're brave and your baby is very lucky to have you as its mum.'

How could she not smile a little at that? 'Thanks.'

'How long ago did you and Ryder break up?'

'Just over ten years ago.' At the expression on his face, she added, 'Told you it was silly. I doubt he's given me a thought in all that time. I shouldn't even care about seeing him again, never mind what he thinks of me.'

'But you do.'

Tab wasn't sure if it was a question or a statement but she nodded, irritated with herself. 'It's just … we weren't only dating, we also played together. We had big dreams and seemed to be going places—everyone said we sounded unreal together. And then I got sick. When I lost my arm, I could no longer play the guitar and Ryder said that's what we were. Two guitarists who also sang. He said he thought it would make sense if we went our separate ways—professionally *and* personally.'

'He broke up with you when you lost your *arm*? What a bastard.'

'Part of me didn't blame him, but another part of me hated him so bad. The only good thing was that I came back home to the farm and he moved east to pursue a solo career, so although we'd run in similar circles in Perth, I didn't have to see him again. And now he's got all these hit songs behind him, girls hanging off his every word, and I've barely even had another boyfriend since him and I look so desperate that I had to …'

Again, her voice drifted off. Her feelings were so stupid she couldn't even put them into words.

'You know, ignore me if this is a stupid idea, but …' He stalled then shook his head. 'Nah, forget it.'

'Tell me,' she urged, nudging him in the side with her little arm. 'You can't begin a sentence like that and then leave a girl hanging.'

'Okay.' He took a quick breath. 'Why don't we pretend to be together, so that when he's here …' Ferg flushed a little as he tried to explain. It was super cute. 'I just thought maybe if you have someone at your side, you'd feel … I dunno, less vulnerable.'

'You mean like a fake boyfriend?' She was about to laugh, then realised he was serious.

'I'm not offering for entirely selfless reasons,' he admitted. 'You'd be doing me a favour as well. Carrie is getting pretty persistent in her advances, and she's not the only one. Maybe if people thought you and I were together, they'd leave me the hell alone.'

For a moment, Tab was almost tempted, but, 'No one would ever believe that.'

He blinked. 'Why not?'

Now she did laugh.

'Um … have you *seen* yourself in the mirror lately?' It was a rhetorical question but she took the opportunity to run her eyes slowly down his body as she listed his credentials. 'You have the most startling eyes I've ever seen, you have a great body and a lovely smile, when you care to share it. Hell, even your grimace is more attractive than some people's grins. My grandmother thinks the phrase tall, dark and handsome was created for you.'

A corner of a smile appeared on his face.

'But it's not just your looks. You're great with the kids in your class, and the way you pitched in to help search for Mrs Lord, the way you help with the cricket after school hours … all these things are noted and appreciated in the country. You are about as eligible as it's possibly eligible to be, whereas *me*?' She shrugged. 'I'm just a pregnant, plain Jane with no arm.'

He raised his eyebrows but didn't shy away from her gaze as he said, 'From where I'm looking, you have an arm and a half and can do more with what you've got than most people I know. But even if you had no arms, so what? There's absolutely nothing plain about you, Tabitha Cooper-Jones. If I wasn't sworn off women …'

Tab tried to laugh, but that damn lump in her throat returned. She wasn't used to people bathing her in compliments, even if she knew his compliments were as fake as his proposition.

'So what do you say? Will you be my pseudo girlfriend?'

Part of her was hugely tempted—how wonderful would it feel to have a guy like Fergus McWilliams at her side over the next month or so? How much more confident would she feel about facing Ryder again if she were in a relationship? Maybe people might even believe it if they held hands and stuff like that? Her insides twisted a little at the thought. But even if it did get her through seeing Ryder again, inevitably it would have to end, and then everyone in town would feel sorry for her.

She could already imagine what people would say behind closed doors and whispered hands, and she didn't want that mortification and pity for the few minutes of security it would give her to be able to introduce Fergus as her boyfriend to Ryder.

'No,' she whispered, taking Fergus's warm hand in hers. 'I don't play games, and I might have had a few wobbly moments, but I don't need a man to feel good about myself. But thank you, for listening and for your offer. It was a very sweet one.'

And to show her appreciation she leaned in to kiss his cheek. But, not expecting her to lay one on him, he moved his head at the last moment and she ended up kissing him on the mouth instead.

Chapter Eighteen

It felt like ages since he'd kissed a woman and maybe that's why such a chaste kiss had every muscle in Fergus's body contracting. Tab's lips were as soft as fairy floss and just as tasty. Who was he trying to kid? They were better than any cotton candy could ever be. The kiss itself—if you could call it that—must have lasted only a second before they both pulled away, but it felt like an eternity and sparked a hunger in him he didn't want to feel.

He had to use every ounce of willpower he possessed not to put his hands on her face and drag her lips back to his. She'd just spent the last fifteen minutes pouring out her heart—it was clear she had unfinished business where Ryder bloody O'Connell was concerned, no matter how much she denied it.

If that didn't tell him she didn't want to be kissed, he didn't know what did, and that was a good thing. He'd meant it when he'd told her he was sworn off women—they brought way more pain than pleasure.

If the way he was feeling after that brief brush with her lips meant anything, it was probably a good thing she'd turned down his ridiculous offer. Imagine how hard it would be to control himself if he had to hold her hand, even kiss her occasionally, to keep up a pretence.

Should he apologise for the accidental smooch or pretend it didn't happen?

As Ferg was deliberating this, Tabitha let go of his hand and made a joke. 'Well, I clearly need to work on my aim. That was …'

Unexpected. Amazing. Something I'd like to repeat this instant. 'My fault,' he assured her. 'I'm sorry. But I promise I didn't move my head on purpose.'

'Of course you didn't.' She laughed nervously and her cheeks took on a soft pink tinge that stood out against her pale skin and dark cropped hair. Her lips were the same colour, only a few shades darker but … man, he needed to stop staring at her lips.

'Will you be okay?'

She nodded. 'I'm always okay. I just had a moment, but thanks.'

'No worries. We should probably go back in. Your grandmother will be wondering where we've got to.'

Inside, the nurses were busy assisting the residents to the table ready for dinner. Tabitha said goodbye to her grandmother and Ferg did the same to Mrs Lord.

'You heading back to Rose Hill now?' he asked as they walked out to the car park.

'Nope. I'm going to the farm. We usually have Sunday dinner together—it's been a tradition since we were kids. Mum always made up a big roast for Sunday lunch and I kept it up when she died, but then when Meg and I opened the tea rooms, Lawson took over because Sundays are one of our busiest days. You should come.'

'I wasn't angling for an invitation.'

'I know, but I'm offering. Lawson isn't the greatest cook, but he tries his best and he and Ned always make way too much. You'd be doing us a favour.'

Happy family dinners weren't really his thing—not anymore—but his stomach rumbled. 'I wouldn't want to encroach on family time.'

'Oh, don't worry about that. We often have extras—I'm pretty sure Ethan's bringing Kimmy tonight.'

Well, that killed that excuse and he didn't really want to come up with any others for fear Tabitha would assume it was because of their not-quite kiss. 'Okay then, if you're absolutely sure.'

'I wouldn't have asked if I wasn't.' She nodded towards her van that happened to be parked next to his car. 'I'll see you out there.'

He stopped by the pub, bought a six-pack of Crownies and a bottle of Margaret River wine, then headed out to the farm. Hopefully the dinner would stop things getting weird between them.

Maybe if he stopped thinking about that kiss it would be a start. *Focus on the baby*, he told himself as he pulled up out the front of Lawson's house for the second time in a matter of days. Tab's van was already parked under the eucalypt tree.

She's pregnant. You're done with relationships. You're only here temporarily. She's still raw from her ex.

Did he need any more reasons why harbouring lustful thoughts about her was a bad idea?

Ferg grabbed the wine and beer from the passenger seat and, as he opened the car door, Ned erupted from the house.

'Mr McDuck,' he yelled, loud enough that the cows in the furthest paddock probably heard.

'Hey.' Ferg slammed the door behind him and lifted the wine bottle in a wave. 'How's that arm?'

Ned screwed up his face. 'It's a pain. But I got a cool cast. Can I get everyone at school to sign it tomorrow?'

'Sure,' Ferg said as he and Ned headed towards the house.

'Can you sign it first? Well, not first, Dad, Meg, Aunty Tab and Ethan already have.'

Ned angled the arm covered in bright blue plaster to show him and Ferg couldn't help noticing the big heart next to Tab's name. Yep, that pretty much summed her up—only a few weeks in her acquaintance and he knew she had a big heart, but he didn't think she liked wearing it on her sleeve. He had a feeling she'd never have volunteered all that information about her ex if he hadn't found her in such a state.

'Well, hello, hello, hello. Long time no see,' Tab welcomed them from the front door as they came onto the porch. Her chirpiness sounded forced. Her gaze went to the alcohol in his hands and she shook her head. 'You didn't have to bring anything.'

'Wouldn't have felt right turning up with nothing,' he said, toeing off his shoes alongside the row of boots before following her inside and down the hallway into the kitchen.

Meg and a redhead he didn't recognise, but guessed must be Ethan's girlfriend, were sitting at the table in a dining room just off to one side of the kitchen.

'Hi.' He nodded to them as he breathed in the aroma of roasted meat and veggies. Tab may have said Lawson wasn't a great cook, but it smelled damn fine. 'Thanks so much for letting me crash your dinner,' he said as he offered Meg the drinks.

'You're welcome.' She put the wine and beer on the table, gave him a quick hug, then gestured to the other woman. 'This is Kimmy, the local vet. And this is Fergus, Ned's teacher.'

'Hello.' Ferg smiled and shook her hand. With her hair tied back in a no-nonsense ponytail she looked like a vet somehow. 'Where are Lawson and Ethan?'

'Still milking, but they shouldn't be long now. Why don't you crack a beer? Kimmy, glass of wine?'

The vet's eyes twinkled. 'Someone has to keep Fergus company.'

Tabitha got Kimmy a glass, let him take one of the beers and then put the rest in the fridge, while Meg poured what looked like homemade lemonade for herself and Tabitha.

They were all migrating to the table when Ned flew into the room, waving a black marker in his hand. 'I got it,' he shrieked as he thrust the pen at Ferg. 'Here you go.'

As he scribbled on the blue cast, Kimmy hit him with a question. 'What do you think of Walsh so far?'

He put the lid back on Ned's pen as he thought about how to answer. Walsh was fine, but adjusting to life on his own, not being able to call his sister and tell her about his day, that was not so easy. 'It's great. Busier than I imagined.'

'I know. I thought small towns were quiet until I moved here. My friends in the city were worried I wouldn't have a social life, but there's always something going on. I'm looking forward to the show, are you?'

He glanced at Tab and saw her smile fade and her knuckles whiten around her glass.

'Yeah, I suppose.' He shifted uncomfortably in his seat. 'The kids at school are excited. We're starting on our entries for the contests this week.'

'I won the junior photography contest last year,' Ned piped up, pride in his voice. 'Do you want to see my winning entries?' He'd pushed back his seat and shot to a stand even before Ferg could reply.

Meg chuckled as he dashed from the room. 'He's so passionate about everything. I worry he'll trip and break his other arm, but there's no keeping that boy calm, hey Tab?'

'Huh?' She blinked, then nodded quickly. 'Right. No.'

Ferg looked between the two women— although Tab was distracted, it was clear they both adored the kid. Ned was lucky to have someone like Meg for a stepmum.

'Are you okay?' Meg looked at Tab with concern.

She exhaled loudly, then dumped her glass on the table with a bit of a bang. 'The big news around town tomorrow will be that Ryder is going to play at the show.'

Meg's eyes widened but Kimmy looked confused as she glanced between the other women. 'Who's Ryder?'

'Ryder O'Connell,' Meg supplied.

Kimmy's recognition came within seconds. 'Oh my God! Are you serious? I'm his biggest fan.'

'Well, I'd offer to introduce you,' Tab said, her tone bitter, 'but he hasn't spoken to me in almost ten years.'

Kimmy blinked a few times in quick succession, clearly confused.

'He's Tab's ex-boyfriend,' Meg explained, her gaze flicking to her sister-in-law in concern. 'You okay?'

'I've already had my moment. Poor Fergus had to witness it. But I've got another few weeks to prepare myself and Ryder will likely be mobbed, so I might not even have to see him.'

'I'm sorry, I … I didn't know.' Kimmy looked slightly abashed but before anyone could say anything else, Ned bounced back into the room, his arms laden with photo frames.

'Check these out,' he said, clearly oblivious to the tension around him as he dumped the photos on the table.

Ferg looked through the images, which were mostly of calves, the milking shed and sunsets. 'These are awesome. You've definitely got a talent.'

They spoke a few moments about where said talent came from—apparently Tabitha's dad, Ned's grandfather, was a keen photographer.

'He did our wedding photos,' Meg said, and for a second Ferg thought maybe she was going to ask if he wanted to see them. Thankfully, there was a loud scratching on the front door, distracting them all. The last thing he wanted to look at was happy wedding snaps, so close to the time he should have been smiling for his own.

'That'll be the dogs,' Tabitha shot up and Ned followed after her.

Meg leant across the table and whispered to Ferg. 'Is she really okay? Ryder was long before my time, but I've heard enough to know she was heartbroken when they split.'

He didn't want to betray Tabitha's confidence, but neither did he want to tell Meg she was fine when she clearly wasn't. 'She seemed pretty shaken, to be honest.'

'Thank you for being there for her.'

He nodded, unsure whether he was happy to have been in the right place at the right time or not.

'I ... I didn't meant to upset her.' Kimmy looked genuinely stricken. 'I didn't know.'

At that moment, Cane and Ned barrelled into the room, followed closely behind by Tabitha and the older dog. The massive white ball of fluff made a beeline for Ferg and as he ruffled the dog's fur, he hoped Tabitha didn't guess that they'd been talking about her.

'I thought farm dogs usually stayed outside?' he said, trying to create a diversion.

Tabitha laughed, but it wasn't as natural and carefree as she usually sounded. 'That was always the case round here too,' she volunteered as she flopped back down into her seat, 'but Cane was Meg's dog first—Lawson bought him for her—and so he got used to her spoiling him and living in the lap of luxury over at Rose Hill.'

'We couldn't very well make him stay outside here,' Meg added, 'but then the other dogs wanted in as well.'

'I like having them inside,' Ned said, laying down on the floor and leaning into the kelpie.

'Careful with your arm,' Meg said, as the front door opened and more voices and footsteps approached.

Lawson and Ethan strode into the room.

'Look, Mr McDuck signed my cast.' Ned leapt up off the floor and rushed over to his dad as Ethan crossed the kitchen, yanked Kimmy out of her chair and pulled her into his arms.

'Hello, gorgeous!'

She laughed as wine splashed up out of the glass still in her hand and then screwed up her nose as she palmed her other one against Ethan's chest. 'Ew, you stink.'

'He told us you like that.' Tab winked at Ferg as if they shared an in-joke and he ignored the squeeze in his chest.

'What have you been saying?' Kim hit her boyfriend playfully on the arm. 'I like you much better when you don't smell of cow shit. I have enough bad smells at work.'

As everyone laughed, Ethan pouted at her. 'Sorry, babe, but I just couldn't bear to wait a second longer before seeing you again. I'll go clean up now.'

He retreated, but not before he gave her another big smooch on the lips. It was clear they couldn't get enough of each other, and although Lawson and Meg were more subtle, the way he looked at her when he greeted her with a quick kiss on the cheek made it obvious they were also mad for each other. Watching these two couples was enough to make Ferg believe in love. Almost. But the fact Tabitha was still so shaken up about Ryder after almost ten years was a helpful reminder just how much of a risk it could be.

Ferg looked away as once again he remembered how her mouth had felt against his. His tongue darted out to lick his lips of his own accord and dammit, he could still taste her. How could his mind and body be in such opposition?

As Lawson went off to shower, Ned looked to Meg, 'Can I show Mr McDuck my new PlayStation game?'

She hesitated a moment. 'Go on. But only till your dad and Ethan are ready and only if Fergus doesn't mind.'

'I'd love to see your game.' Ferg couldn't jump up fast enough and followed Ned into the lounge room, welcoming the opportunity to lose himself in something as simple as a video game. Hopefully racing around a cyber track in a bright green sports car would keep his thoughts from wandering down such unhelpful paths.

* * *

Right at this moment Tabitha was glad of Ned's obsession with video games. It gave her a few minutes reprieve from Fergus.

Oh Lord, she couldn't believe she'd kissed him.

What on *earth* had possessed her to *kiss* him? It was only meant to be a friendly peck on the cheek, but he'd moved his head at the last moment, making it lip action instead. She'd felt sparks crashing into each other from the tip of her toes to the end of her nose, but they were obviously one-sided. She'd just bared her soul to him and he'd only offered to be her fake boyfriend because he'd felt sorry for her. He'd made it more than clear he wasn't in the market for a relationship and couldn't have pulled away fast enough. She'd never wished more in her life for a UFO to beam her up far, far away.

And *then* she'd prolonged the agony by going and asking him to dinner. The poor guy was likely here against his will and there had to be rocks in her head.

She eyed the glass of wine in Kimmy's hand, wishing like hell she could just have a little sip, but no way was she doing anything to jeopardise the precious life growing inside her. She needed to remember that her baby was the most important thing in the world and she didn't need anything or any*body* else. If she focused on her child and their future together, maybe she could manage to maintain some semblance of normal around Fergus, maybe she could ignore the stupid pregnancy hormones that were obviously wreaking havoc with her normally unflappable common sense.

It was probably a good thing she hadn't accepted his well-meaning offer—she didn't need to add any more complications to her life.

'You and the spunky hunk of teacher seem to be getting along well,' Meg said, jolting Tab from her thoughts.

She willed her cheeks not to heat. 'He was visiting Mrs Lord at the hospital. It just felt right to ask him for dinner.'

Meg and Kimmy exchanged knowing smirks, but she ignored them, stood and went to check on the food. They could think what they liked, but if they thought anything was going to happen between her and Fergus, they'd be disappointed. Thankfully, Meg dropped the subject and the three of them got things ready for the return of the boys instead. Tab made gravy, while Meg carved the joint and Kimmy set the table.

When they all sat down to eat, Tab once again thanked the Lord for Ned. Without him, this would feel far too much like a couples dinner. Dishes were piled high with roast beef, crispy potatoes and steamed veggies, and then drowned in gravy. As everyone began to eat, the conversation flowed easily.

'Will you go back to Perth at the end of your contract here?' Lawson asked after they'd grilled Fergus on where he'd lived and worked in the city.

'Hopefully not. I've applied for a few more country jobs—one up north in the Pilbara in a remote Aboriginal community.'

The Pilbara? But that was so far away. Tab immediately berated herself for this stupid thought. What would it matter if it were Alaska or Antarctica?

'Wow, I imagine that will be quite a lifestyle change. Have you always wanted to teach country?' Kimmy wanted to know.

'It wasn't ever anything I put a great deal of thought into, because ...' He hesitated a moment. 'Well, my life was in Perth, but a few things changed recently and I thought maybe it was a sign to step out of my comfort zone and put myself where I can really make a difference.'

Tab guessed his move had something to do with his ex, but the takeaway from his statement was that he wasn't staying in Walsh, so she'd be stupid to let her pesky pregnancy hormones latch onto the idea that there could ever be anything between them. Those hormones were turning her brain to mush—if she hadn't managed to score a guy before now, her luck was hardly going to turn around in her current state.

'Surely there are children and schools in Perth where you could make a difference too,' Kimmy argued.

'Yes.' Tab saw Fergus's grip tighten almost imperceptibly around his beer bottle. 'Of course there are, but it's slightly easier to fill those teaching positions. What made *you* decide to go country?'

Kimmy glanced at Ethan. 'I heard there were a bunch of hot single farmers down here ...' His grin spread wide across his face, then she added, 'Sadly, I found this one instead.'

Everyone laughed as Ethan pressed a hand to his heart pretending to be wounded, but Tab felt a yearning deep within her. She was usually okay with other people's public displays of affection and she didn't begrudge her closest friends and family love, but today, watching Ethan and Kimmy and Lawson and Meg, only reminded her of what she didn't have.

Of what she'd *never* have.

Conversation turned to Ethan's reasons for coming down under and he explained to Fergus how his year backpacking around Australia had turned into almost four and that, although he missed certain things about home, he wasn't sure he'd ever go back for good.

'What about you? Are your family all in Perth?'

Tab squirmed a little in her seat, knowing that Fergus didn't have much family. She'd practically forced him to come to dinner and now everyone was giving him the Spanish Inquisition.

'There's only me and my twin sister left,' he said, then took a long swig of his beer. 'She's in Perth.'

Ned had been listening intently while stuffing his face with roast potatoes, but his head snapped up at this statement. 'You said you didn't have a sister.'

'Huh?' Fergus frowned as all eyes turned to him.

'When we were all telling each other three things,' Ned said, sounding more than a little affronted. '*Remember?* Victoria asked you if you had brothers or sisters and you said you had none.'

Fergus lowered his fork to his plate. 'I … I'm sorry, Ned. Things aren't great between my sister and me, and I don't like to talk about her.'

'Why not? What happened?'

'Ned, that's none of your business,' Lawson chastised, glancing apologetically at Fergus.

'It's fine.' He smiled at Ned but his smile didn't quite reach his eyes. 'We had a disagreement and we haven't spoken to each other since.'

Ned looked like he had more questions, but another sharp look from Lawson had him shutting his mouth again. Tab couldn't help wondering what could possibly have been so bad as to cause such a rift between Fergus and his only sister. Sure, she and Lawson had the odd disagreement—mostly over stupid stuff like TV shows and whose turn it was to do a chore—but she couldn't comprehend either of them doing anything that would cause estrangement. And if that ever happened, it would break her heart even more than Ryder O'Connell had.

She had an intense urge to reach across the table and squeeze Fergus's hand.

'Would anyone like a second helping?' she asked, pushing to a stand. Her plate was still half-full but she had to do something to rescue him.

'Can I have some more potatoes, Aunty Tab?' Ned asked.

Ethan glanced down at his empty plate. 'I've always got room for seconds.'

'None for me, thanks.' Kimmy patted her stomach. 'I'm saving room for dessert. Is your ice-cream on the menu, again?'

'Of course.'

The food distraction worked—everyone seemed to get the message that they'd grilled Fergus enough. While they ate far too much ice-cream, they kept to safe topics of conversation such as Carline's treatment progress, the mural Fergus was painting with the kids at school and possible names for Tab's baby.

There were all sorts of suggestions—some lovely traditional ones and some so outlandishly ridiculous that they all couldn't help laughing. It became a bit of a contest as to who could come up with the most bizarre option. As a teacher, Fergus had a number of terrible ones to throw in the mix: Darth, Dorcus, Moonbeam, Cobra and Abcde were just a few of the kids he'd apparently taught.

'At my last school there was a girl in kindy called Candida.'

'No way.' All the adults gasped in unison and Ned wanted to know what was so bad about it.

'It's a nasty infection,' Lawson told him with a smirk as he ruffled his hair. 'A bit like naming your kid Chicken Pox.'

Ned thought this hilarious and Tab smiled at her brother's quick thinking. She felt a bit awkward talking baby stuff considering what he and Meg were currently going through, but they seemed as invested in the contest as anyone, and focusing on the baby helped keep her mind off Ryder and her hormones off Fergus.

'Are you planning on finding out the baby's gender?' he asked.

'I don't think so.' She'd given this quite a lot of thought. 'I like surprises.'

'Can I play some more PlayStation with Mr McDuck,' Ned asked, interrupting the conversation, which he was clearly bored with.

'I don't think so,' Lawson said. 'It's a school night and past your bed time already.'

'Aw.'

As Ned groaned, Fergus glanced at his watch. 'Sorry, mate, I should be getting home anyway, but let me help with the dishes first.'

'No way.' Meg would hear of no such thing. 'You're a guest in our house, and besides, we have a dishwasher.'

'It was great to have your company tonight,' Lawson added as everyone began to stand.

Despite Meg's objection, Fergus helped carry all the dishes over to the bench, as did Ethan and Kimmy as Lawson took Ned off to bed. Together, the remaining adults cleared the table, loaded the dishwasher and wiped down the surfaces so that Meg and Lawson wouldn't be left with much to do. Then Kimmy and Ethan, hand in hand, bid everyone goodnight and made a hurried escape to his cottage.

It was no mystery what they were off to do and Tab felt an annoying flush of jealousy. Not of Kimmy getting to be with Ethan, but anyone getting to be with anyone. These pesky pregnancy hormones were really becoming a problem.

'Thanks again,' Fergus said to Meg, jolting Tab from her thoughts. 'Dinner was delicious and I had a great night. The company sure beat that of my cranky feline.'

Meg laughed. 'This cat sounds like a character, but you're welcome anytime.'

Tab wasn't sure whether to linger and make an excuse about waiting to say goodnight to Lawson to avoid the possible awkwardness of going outside alone with Fergus, but in the end Meg made the decision for her.

'You'll see Fergus out, won't you, Tab?' she said with a devious smile.

Tab hoped Fergus didn't notice and made a mental note to speak to her sister-in-law later about her misguided matchmaking. Then she pasted a carefree grin on her face as she and the teacher bid a final farewell to Meg and walked out into the night.

'I'm sorry for all those questions,' Tab said, feeling the need to say something as they headed to their cars. Her arm swung alongside his, her hand so aware of his only inches away.

'It's okay. Your family, Ethan and Kimmy—they're all impossible not to like. I had a good night. Thanks for inviting me.'

'No worries,' she swallowed, her mouth suddenly dry as they stopped in front of her van. 'As I said, we always have way too much food anyway.'

Ferg nodded as the moon went behind a cloud and light flickered briefly across his face. He looked pensively down at her and the air suddenly felt stifling.

'What is it?' she whispered.

His answer, or rather his lips, caught her by surprise. One minute she was berating herself for the stupid fantasy that he might want to kiss her and the next minute he actually was. His hands landed either side of her face, his palms deliciously warm against her skin as his tongue ran along the seam of her lips, nudging her mouth open.

Not that there was much nudging required.

Her mind might have been in shock but her body was on fire. She dropped her bag and reached her hand into his hair, running her fingers through his thick dark locks, anchoring his mouth to hers. He tasted of beer and roast beef and despite the late hour, she could smell a hint of the deodorant he must have sprayed on that morning.

Her senses were in overdrive, every nerve ending in her body buzzing as she kissed him as if her life depended on it. And if the hardness pressing into her belly was anything to go by, it wasn't just *her* body affected. The knowledge she'd made him hard had her head spinning and made her want to taste him—not just his mouth, but all over.

Forgetting where they were, Tab slid her hand down his back, loving the feel of his hard muscles beneath his soft T-shirt. He groaned into her mouth as she cupped his butt, pressing him against her and the sound was sweeter than anything she'd ever heard. He was sweeter than anything she'd ever tasted.

And then suddenly it was over.

His hands fell from her face and he stepped back, putting distance between them. 'I'm sorry, Tabitha.'

Before she could ask what exactly he was apologising for, he yanked his keys out of his pocket, unlocked his car and climbed inside. She jumped at the sound of the door closing, and her heart was still racing, her lips still buzzing, as he drove away.

What the hell?! Tab stood there like a stunned mullet as Fergus's headlights faded into the distance. Rage filled her body.

'Oh no you don't, mister,' she muttered as she scooped her handbag off the dirt and fished for her keys. He couldn't just drive off and leave her like that. He didn't get to kiss her like she'd never been kissed before and then leave her standing alone in the dark, wanting and wondering. That might be how people did things in the city, but country folks were upfront with each other, at least she was.

She might have been able to continue as normal if they'd left things at the almost-kiss they'd shared in the hospital, but he'd just made that impossible.

Chapter Nineteen

Fergus didn't look back as he hooned down the gravel driveway towards the road that would lead him home. His hands were clenching the steering wheel so tightly his knuckles hurt.

He deserved a bloody medal.

It had taken every ounce of self-control he possessed to break that kiss and walk away when his instincts were screaming at him to yank them both down onto the ground and have his wicked way with her right there in the dirt, only fifty or so metres from her brother's house. He was still hot and hard and doubted he'd get any sleep that night but he'd done the right thing. Hadn't he?

This question weighed on his mind as he swerved onto the road. After only a few metres, a light flickered in his rear-view mirror. He knew it would be Tabitha heading back to Rose Hill. Perhaps he should pull over, signal her to stop and try to apologise properly for his monumental stuff-up.

Perhaps he was a coward for deciding not to, but he didn't trust himself in the dark with her and he got the feeling she wouldn't appreciate his efforts anyway.

The sign to Mrs Lord's farm loomed close and with a heavy sigh, he slowed his car and turned in. Mrs Norris better not rile him tonight because he wasn't in the mood.

But the car behind him didn't continue on.

It turned in right after him—its headlights getting dangerously closer, its driver clearly in a rage. If he didn't know who was behind the wheel, he'd be freaking out; as it was, he didn't know whether to slow down or speed up. Tabitha was so close that if he stopped she'd probably ram right into him.

Dread tightened his chest—what the hell was she doing?

His heart pounding, he tried to drive steadily on towards the rickety old carport at the side of the house. The van came to a stop right behind him and as he tentatively climbed out, its door flung open and Tabitha emerged.

The moon gave enough light that he could see her expression as she slammed the door and stormed towards him. Her nostrils flared, her eyes were cold and her lips as flat as a ruler. Every feature on her face radiated fury, and crazily, she looked even more gorgeous than usual.

'What the hell was that about, Fergus McWilliams?' The words fired out like gunshots and her chest heaved.

He opened his mouth but didn't know what to say.

Tabitha had enough words for them both. 'I'll tell you what that was, or at least what it felt like. A kiss between two people who are clearly hot for each other. But maybe I'm wrong. Maybe I felt things that you didn't. Was it a pity kiss? Is that it? You feel *sorry* for the poor disabled girl and were trying to make her feel better? Well, you failed at that, because I—'

'You know it wasn't that,' he growled, taking a step towards her. How could she even say such a thing? Couldn't she feel the heat still emanating off him? 'Being around you was driving me crazy. I'd been fantasising about kissing you all evening. I just couldn't help myself.'

'Then *why*?' she yelled, before deflating slightly. 'Why did you apologise and then run the hell away?'

She looked as if she might be close to tears and that would unravel him, but he couldn't mess her about. 'Because this isn't right.' He shoved his hands into his pockets to stop from reaching for her. 'Kissing you was a selfish move. I'm not in the zone for a relationship. I'm only here temporarily, and even if I wasn't—'

Fergus was about to explain why nothing serious could ever happen between them, but she interrupted.

'That's very presumptuous of you.'

'What?' He blinked, confused.

'Thinking that *I* want a relationship,' she said. 'Thinking that one kiss from you would have me falling in love, fantasising about the future. I'm not that kind of girl, Fergus. The day we met I told you I was quite happily single and I meant it. I've got my life mapped out for me and my baby; just because I'm attracted to you doesn't change any of that. But it does frustrate the hell out of me.'

And with those words, she closed the gap between them, pushed up on her toes and crushed her mouth against his. The force of her lips almost unbalanced him and he held onto her hips to save himself. As her tongue snuck into his mouth, his stomach muscles squeezed and he felt his resolve wavering. She tasted so damn good he wanted to eat her all up. But alarm bells clanged inside his head.

How would they ever look each other in the eye if he let this go on?

Once again, he somehow found it within himself to pull back.

Tabitha let out a frustrated breath. 'What now?'

'I don't want to do this and ruin our friendship,' he said, thinking that the hard-on she must have felt against her belly probably called him out as a liar. He wanted to do this more than he wanted to do anything, he just wasn't sure he should.

'What friendship?' she sneered, and he felt a prickle of hurt at her words. 'We haven't even known each other a month. Besides, you don't think things aren't going to be awkward between us after this anyway? We may as well ruin them entirely.'

He cocked his head to one side. She had a point. And maybe if they succumbed to this chemistry between them they would get it out of their systems.

'Stop thinking so much, Fergus,' Tabitha said, her tone frustrated as she reached out and placed her hand on his crazily beating heart. 'We're both adults. We both want this, so let's scratch the itch and move on.'

'So just one time?' he clarified.

'What makes you think I'll want any more?'

He chuckled at that, but had to be absolutely sure she knew what she was doing. He didn't want to get started and have her change her mind, or worse, feel remorse tomorrow morning. 'You sure this isn't just a reaction to the news about Ryder co—'

She pulled his face down towards hers. 'Would you just shut up and put your mouth back on mine?'

And seriously, what court of law could say he hadn't tried to offer her an out? So he did as she asked—he put his mouth back on hers as he scooped her up into his arms and carried her into the house, kicking the door shut behind them. Mrs Norris greeted them loudly and ferociously. Cursing the stupid cat, he reluctantly set Tabitha down as he switched on a light.

'I'll be right back,' he said, and then went into the laundry to sprinkle biscuits into the cat's bowl.

But when he returned to the living room, Tabitha was nowhere to be found. His heart sank. For a second he thought she'd had second thoughts and left, but then he heard her calling from his bedroom. 'How long does it take to feed a feline? I don't have all night you know.'

In a mere four strides he was in his room, swallowing at the sight of Tabitha completely naked on the bed, a soft glow from the bedside lamp spilling over her delicious body. His mouth went dry and his body hardened again as he looked his fill. Her skin was glowing, her hair tousled around her face, her breasts beautifully round and her belly slightly curved. *With child.*

'This isn't an art exhibition,' she said as she stretched her arm out and ran it up and down the edge of the bed. 'You can look with your hands as well as your eyes.'

Her seductive tone sent shivers down his spine. He didn't need to be asked twice. After toeing off his shoes and pushing the thought of the child from his mind, he stalked to the bed and lowered himself down beside her.

She rolled towards him and smiled. 'What took you so long?'

In reply, he pulled her towards him and kissed her hard. He groaned as her breasts pressed against his chest. His jeans suddenly felt tight and he struggled to breathe as his erection pressed against the denim. He couldn't wait to be inside her, but didn't want to rush.

Summoning all his self-control, he deepened the kiss. Tab groaned into his mouth as he moved his hand down over the curve of her breasts and then scraped his thumb over her already hard nipples.

He pulled back to gaze at her. 'You're so damn beautiful.'

Her cheeks flushed deliciously and she snuck her hand between them, cursing as she fumbled with the button on his jeans. 'I want to touch you,' she whispered.

He remembered her mentioning that buttons were one of the few things she found difficult with only one hand. And he *could* have helped her. But once he was naked as well, he wouldn't be able to control himself and he didn't want this to be over barely before it had begun. If they were only going to do this once, he was going to take his time and make damn sure it was worth it.

For both of them.

'Soon.' He grabbed her hand and lifted it to his mouth, sucking one finger into it. She shuddered and let out the sweetest sound he'd ever heard. If she reacted like that for a finger, he could only imagine the sounds she might make if he put his mouth elsewhere. And he wanted to. He wanted to taste every last inch of her.

Placing a quick kiss on her lips, he pulled back, gazed down at her a moment and then dipped his head and sucked one nipple into his mouth.

Man, she felt good, she tasted *so good*.

'Oh Fergus.' Her body bucked beneath him and he smiled around her nipple as he swirled his tongue, driving them both to insanity. 'Please.'

He lifted his lips again and grinned down at her. 'You like that?'

Already breathless, she simply nodded.

'Then what about this?' He licked under her breast, his hand cupping the other, before he moved his mouth lower, teasing her belly button before venturing even lower and puffing hot breath onto the apex of her thighs. Her legs fell apart and he put his mouth to her, pushing his tongue inside, tasting the very flavour of her. She was already so slippery and wet for him that it was all he could do not to yank his jeans down and surge into her.

But this would be over in a matter of seconds if he did, so instead, he focused on the task at hand, licking and nibbling and touching and taunting until she was a writhing mess beneath him. He felt the pleasure shudder through her and lifted his head to meet her gaze.

'Wow,' she whispered, which only made him grin and grow harder. 'Now I need to repay the favour.'

'That was no favour,' he growled, brushing his fingertips against her breasts before stooping to brush his lips across her mouth again. 'That was pure selfishness. And so is this.'

He rolled off her and, in record time, yanked his shirt over his head, ripped at the button of his jeans and shucked them down his legs. She gasped as he turned back to her; the way her eyes widened as she gazed at his erection was very good for his ego.

'You're pretty ... *big*.'

Fergus chuckled. 'I could take that as a compliment, but *this* is all because of you.'

Then, crawling back on top of her, he smashed his mouth to hers, positioned himself and ... 'Shit.'

She stilled beneath him. 'What is it?'

'I don't have any condoms.' *This* wasn't on his agenda.

A little puff of amusement escaped her lips. 'Well, I'm safe, are you? Because you're too late to get me pregnant.'

And, not wanting to dwell on the fact, he covered her mouth with his again and thrust into her.

As Fergus filled her so deliciously, Tabitha ran her hand down his back and then gripped his butt, wanting to drive him deeper and deeper, wanting the sensations flooding her body to never ever end.

She couldn't believe this was actually happening.

She was having sex—*real* sex with a *real* man. And it was freaking fantastic. Her pregnancy hormones were very pleased with her indeed. Without them, she doubted she would have had the guts to follow this through, but lying beneath him now she was very glad she had.

Tonight, she'd been more daring than she'd ever been before where men were concerned. Her fury had spurred her on to follow and confront him. Her bravado had surprised her but it had been worth it. She'd never felt so much like a woman than in that moment when he'd carried her into the house. And then the cat had interrupted them and the hiatus had given her a few moments to think.

She'd glanced around the old woman's house and fear had filled her body.

What am I doing?

She had no idea how to seduce a grown man, no idea how to have sex. It had been so long since the last time that she was practically a virgin again.

What if I do it wrong? What if I'm not any good?

There'd been two opposing forces in her head—the pregnancy hormones telling her to take what she wanted and to hell with the consequences, and the voice of reason telling her to snap out of this silliness and retreat.

But she recognised the voice of reason as nerves and she'd be damned if she was going to let a little anxiety rob her of this experience. So, she'd hurried into the bedroom and stripped right out of her clothes before the voice of reason could grow stronger. It would be harder to run for the hills if she were naked. Lying spread-eagled on the bed, she'd called to him, telling herself if she feigned bravado, maybe she could do this without making a fool of herself.

Her heart had nearly leapt out of her chest it was beating so fast as she heard Fergus's footsteps coming towards her, but the jitters had evaporated the moment he entered the room and she realised that she was responsible for the hot look of lust in his eyes. It sent a shiver down her spine and her bravado had taken on a life of its own.

She didn't know where the flirtatious come-on—*You can look with your hands as well as your eyes*—had come from but she was definitely enjoying the results.

As Fergus pounded into her and the ripples of pleasure built stronger within, they both opened their eyes and their gazes met.

She saw fire in his eyes. He looked like a man possessed, and the knowledge she had the power to make him react so strongly sent an orgasm like nothing she'd ever felt before crashing through her.

He let out a guttural groan as his release came only a second later.

Together, the aftershocks of their frenzied union still rocking through them, they lay there trying to catch their breath and all Tab could think about was what she'd been missing all these years. It was a travesty.

Sex with Ryder had never been like that. Maybe because there'd been so much more of a build-up with Ryder. They'd been two timid teens who'd talked about doing the deed for so long that it had been a bit of a let-down when they actually did. Maybe this had been so good because there'd been no time for building it up into something unrealistic. Some things were better if you didn't think about them too much. Or maybe it was because Fergus was more experienced than Ryder had been. Maybe her senses were heightened by pregnancy. Or maybe … it didn't matter.

Whatever this was, it would be an experience she'd treasure always, even if it had probably ruined any friendship that might have been developing between herself and Fergus.

That thought brought her crashing back to reality.

She was lying here naked underneath a man she barely knew, he was still *inside* her, and she had no idea what she was supposed to do next. The urge to snuggle into him was strong, but that wasn't part of the deal, so she palmed her hand on his chest and pushed upwards.

'I need to …' Her cheeks flamed as the words died on her tongue. Talking about cleaning herself up wasn't sexy but the sooner she did, the sooner she could leave, which was what she was supposed to be doing. *Wasn't it?*

He nodded and rolled off her. 'Do you know where the bathroom is?'

'Yes.' She couldn't bring herself to look at him as she stooped to gather her clothes from the floor. Her shorts fell as she hurried across the room and, as she bent to pick them up again, she silently cursed her little arm. If she had two, this might be a whole lot easier and a whole lot less mortifying.

'Do you want some help?'

'No.' She practically shouted the word, feeling his gaze boring into the back of her naked body. Why couldn't he be a gentleman, ignore her mishap and look away?

She made it to the bathroom—still stuck in the 1950s with lime-green tiles on the walls and a brown mosaic on the floor—and shut the door, her heart stammering as she leant against it. A shower would probably be a good idea, but part of her didn't want to wash the scent of him from her skin just yet, and also it would take too long. After a quick clean up, she dressed and ventured out into the corridor.

Fergus was standing there. He'd put his jeans back on but was still shirtless. Still gorgeous. 'You okay?'

'Yes.' She summoned a smile for him. 'Are *you*?'

He nodded. 'Are things going to be weird between us now?'

The question made her smile real, but she wasn't a liar, so she nodded. 'Probably. But I don't regret this. Do you?'

He shook his head.

'I guess I'll be going then.' She was already turning towards the front of the house.

He followed her out onto the porch and part of her stupidly hoped he'd ask if they could see each other again, maybe even do *it* again, but all he did was kiss her on the cheek.

'Goodbye, Tabitha. Drive safely.'

Perhaps he hadn't found it as mind-blowing as she had.

Trying not to show her disappointment, she retreated to the van and, like the gentleman he was, he waited until she was safely inside before he went back into the house. Glancing in the rear-view mirror, she saw the porch light go off, and shook her head slightly as she focused back on the long driveway.

What the hell had she just done?

Chapter Twenty

Tab didn't sleep well that night and woke the following morning with her heart racing and her sheets wet and tangled. She hadn't had an accident and her waters hadn't broken early—*thank God*—it's just that whenever she'd closed her eyes, her head had filled with images of Fergus and what they'd done together. So much for forgetting about her moment of reckless lust and moving on. At least he'd succeeded in taking her mind off Ryder, but now she felt like a beast who'd had the taste of blood and wanted more. Only she didn't even have Fergus's number, he was probably almost on his way to school *and* that hadn't been what they agreed to.

Maybe she would have to get a vibrator. But even as she thought this, she knew an inanimate object would never be able to make her feel, make her scream, *satisfy* her the way he had. Dammit, she'd have to find another way to take her mind of their X-rated liaison because *somehow* she had to get it out of her head.

After throwing back the bedcovers and having an *actual* cold shower, Tab made herself some breakfast and then sat on the back step talking to Eliza as she ate. As much as she adored Meg, no way she'd be confessing to her sister-in-law, or anyone else, what she and Fergus had done, but she needed to talk about it with someone.

However, Eliza found the whole situation amusing—her laughter echoing in the house behind them.

'You're as bad as Meg,' Tab scolded as she stormed back inside, dumped her empty dishes in the sink and wondered what to do today.

Mondays were usually her relaxing day—no housework, pure chilling, either with a book or in front of the TV with her knitting needles. But today she knew that lazing around wasn't going to relax her. She needed to do something to keep busy, to keep her mind from wandering.

Perhaps it was time to make a start on the nursery. And focusing on her baby would help keep her focused on her priorities. Hot sex was all very well but it wouldn't bring her the kind of love her baby would. The kind of unconditional, long-lasting love of family she craved.

Some of her tension began to give way to excitement as she wandered upstairs and into the little room next to her bedroom, which she'd earmarked for the baby. It was pretty much empty as Meg had never used it, so Tab had a blank slate to do with it as she pleased. The first thing would be a coat of paint, but she wasn't sure what colour. Even if she knew what she was having, she didn't want to go the traditional pink or blue. Maybe a soft lemon would be nice. Yellow always made her feel chirpy, but then again, it would depend on what furniture she bought and what theme she went for.

At this thought Tab had a sudden uncharacteristic urge to go shopping.

She wasn't a girly girl and didn't usually find much joy in shopping for the sake of shopping, but today she had the best purpose of all. Decision made, she called her dad, in Bunbury, to see if he and her stepmum were up for lunch and a little retail therapy.

They were delighted—Dad by the prospect of food and Sandra to have been asked to be involved in the baby shopping.

Tab had been in Bunbury by 10 am and couldn't remember having so much fun shopping in her life. She chose not to think about the tally on her Visa and only stopped when her van was full of flat-pack furniture, baby clothes, toys and some things she hadn't even known existed until now. She'd spent way more money than she'd meant to, and half the stuff she probably could have got in good condition second-hand or borrowed from friends in Walsh. But she didn't care, because her baby deserved the best and the shopping had well and truly succeeded in drawing her out of her funk.

'Will you be okay with all of this at the other end, sweetheart?' her dad asked as he clunked the back of the van shut on all her purchases.

'I'll get Lawson to help me,' she lied. 'Thanks for spending the day with me at such short notice.'

Sandra beamed as she put her hand on Tab's stomach. 'It was our absolute pleasure. I hope we can do it again sometime.'

Tab chuckled. 'I think I'll need to give my Visa time to recover first but I'll let you know when I'm here for my next ultrasound and maybe we can do lunch again.'

'It's a date,' said her dad, leaning in to give her a hug. 'Text me when you get back to Rose Hill to let me know you got home safely. I do worry about you all alone out there.'

'I'm fine,' she said, 'but I'll text, I promise.'

The drive home was carefree. Tab listened to an audio book rather than risk hearing Ryder's voice on the radio, and managed to only think about Fergus a couple of times.

When she arrived back at the tea rooms there was a car parked on the street.

'I'm sorry, we're closed today,' she said, pulling up on the side of the road to talk to the couple in their early sixties standing out the front of the building.

'Oh.' The woman blinked. 'We have a booking to stay here for the night.'

Shoot! In the aftermath of her evening shenanigans, she'd completely forgotten she was expecting guests this afternoon, or was this the infamous pregnancy brain kicking in? Thank God the beds were always clean and the rooms ready in case of last-minute bookings.

'I'm so sorry, of course. I …' She shook her head. 'Let me just park around the back and I'll come let you in.'

The man lifted a hand. 'No worries. Take your time.'

Despite his words, Tab hurried to park and then hurried inside and through the building, grabbing the keys to the guest suites on her way to the front door.

'Welcome to Rose Hill,' she said as she stepped out onto the verandah. 'I hope you weren't waiting too long.'

'No, not at all,' said the woman with a warm smile.

Thank God they didn't seem the type to complain, Tab thought as she showed the couple, Shirley and Fred King, through to their rooms.

'This is so quaint,' Shirley said, looking around the bedsit, which was decorated like something from early nineteenth-century Australia, in keeping with the age of the building.

'Thanks.' Tab smiled. 'The credit has to go to my sister-in-law Meg; she's got a knack for design. Now, are you okay for dinner?' Occasionally she offered to cook for her guests but tonight she just wanted to get stuck into building furniture. 'There's not much open in Walsh on Monday nights, but the IGA is open till six and as there are no other guests, the kitchen in here is all yours. I can do breakfast for you any time between seven and ten o'clock, and can either bring it in here or you can come across to the tea rooms.'

They agreed to come to her just after eight, then Tabitha left them to settle in. Surprisingly, despite the drive and the full day shopping, she wasn't feeling too tired and was itching to get started on all the furniture, so she headed back to the van to start bringing it all inside.

The smaller items were easy—she was used to carrying things with only one arm—but the flat-pack cot, rocking chair and change table proved more of a challenge. Tab cursed and wiped sweat off her brow with the back of her hand as she stared into the van at the three large boxes remaining. Frustrated, she went inside to grab a Stanley knife and returned to slip open the first box.

'Hello!' Fred's voice startled her as he appeared at the back gate.

One side of a cot under her arm, she looked up at him. 'Do you need something?'

'I was actually coming to ask you the same.' He nodded towards the back of the van, full of open cardboard boxes with wooden parts spilling out. 'Want a hand getting this lot inside?'

Tab knew he meant well but she bristled as she always did at the offer of help. She hated admitting defeat but she also didn't want to be rude.

At her hestitation, he added, 'Someone in your condition shouldn't be carrying all this heavy stuff on their own. Let me help, love.'

It took her a second to realise he was looking at her stomach, not her little arm, and she glowed, overjoyed she now looked pregnant enough for people to tell. And he was right—even if she did have two functional hands, carrying such heavy boxes probably wouldn't be a smart move in her current state. 'Thank you, that would be wonderful.'

Together, they carried everything upstairs into the baby's room, Fred asking questions about the building and Rose Hill as they went. He was fascinated by the history of the town and wanted to know if it really was haunted as he'd heard. Tab enjoyed telling him the story of Eliza.

'You should get a ghost expert down here. There's some paranormal investigators in Perth who've made a TV show; they might be interested in taking a look.'

'I'll give it some thought,' Tab promised, knowing she and Meg would never invite any such people to disturb Eliza's peace.

When they were done, she offered him a drink but Fred said he'd better be getting back to Shirley, who was making them bangers and mash for dinner. 'Would you like to join us, love? I'm sure there's plenty.'

'Thanks,' she said, glancing around the nursery, 'but I'm going to get stuck in here.'

'Okay then, see you in the morning.'

Tab walked Fred to the door and then made herself a cheese sandwich, which she ate quickly before heading back upstairs. Although starting to tire, she was eager to assemble everything and see her baby's room begin to take shape. Hopefully if she kept busy until she was absolutely exhausted, she'd not only make good progress, but be too tired for a certain man to haunt her dreams tonight.

The instructions were easy enough—she'd built enough flat packs in her time with her dad and Lawson—but it soon became apparent that putting everything together one-handed was not.

She startled as two pieces of the cot, which she thought she'd just managed to put together, fell apart, thumping loudly against the carpet. *Dammit*. She curled her fingers into a fist as tears sprung into her eyes. She was going to have to ask Lawson or Meg to help her, and there was nothing she hated more than having to ask for help.

* * *

Thursday afternoon when Fergus drove into the sporting grounds for cricket training, his heart jolted at the sight of Tabitha's ice-cream van parked on the edge of the oval. He hadn't seen her since she'd walked out of his house Sunday night, but that didn't mean she'd been far from his mind. He'd thought of her *way* more than he should—every day when he drove into town past their farm sign, whenever he helped Ned with something in class, at night when he was by himself with nothing but the company of a cat that hated him, *and* he thought of her when he finally fell into bed because his sheets still smelled of her sweetness.

He should probably change said sheets but he hadn't been able to bring himself to do so. He'd been half-hoping to run into her this week and half-fearing it—not knowing how he could ever act normal again now they'd done what they'd done. But he'd assumed Ned wouldn't be playing cricket for a while because of his arm, and therefore Tab wouldn't have any reason to help. He'd been wrong on both accounts, and confronting her again now, in front of most of his class and half of their parents, gave him heart palpitations.

Taking a deep breath, Fergus got out of his car and walked around the back to grab the training kit. His hands were suddenly slippery with sweat and it took him two attempts to open the boot, and then he grabbed the bag so awkwardly he almost dropped it on the ground. *Shit*, he needed to pull himself together or he'd never get through the next hour.

Shoving his keys in his pocket, he carried the gear across to the kids and the women who were gathered on the grass. The mums turned to look at him and he felt certain each and every one of them knew exactly what he and Tabitha had done. But that was unlikely. He didn't think she'd kiss and tell; she had, after all, been the one to try to warn him about the nature of other women in town—how ironic was that?

'G'day,' he said to the group and then cringed. Who actually said '*g'day*'?

Thankfully, no one appeared to think this odd, all replying with variations of hello, including Tabitha who said, 'Hi Fergus.'

His name had never sounded so appealing. He'd not met her gaze until now but, at her words, he forced himself to. Perhaps it was like ripping off a bandaid, better to get it over and done with fast.

'Hello, Tabitha.'

Nope. None of the tension flooding his body evaporated as their eyes met. Did she get more gorgeous every time he saw her? He hoped his words didn't sound choked because one look at her and every muscle in his body tightened. It was like the past few days were stripped away and once again they were alone in his house on Sunday night.

His cheeks burned at the thought and hers flushed a lovely soft pink as if she too were thinking along the same torrid lines. *Dear God*. It was all he could do not to storm across the grass and take her into his arms.

He forced himself to break their gaze, looking to Ned instead. 'You come to cheer on the team?'

The boy gave him a what-kind-of-question-is-that look. 'No, I've come to train. I heard Brunswick kicked your butts last week and we can't let that happen again. Right, guys?'

Ferg couldn't help laughing at the determination in Ned's voice and the faces of his little mates as they roared in agreement. 'But what about your arm?'

'If Aunty Tab can play cricket with only one full arm, I'll be fine with a broken one. *Please*, let me play?'

At this request, Fergus chanced a glance at Tabitha again. 'Are Lawson and Meg okay with this?'

She nodded and smiled. 'He wouldn't be here if they weren't. And what's the worst thing that can happen? He breaks his other arm, but if we don't let him do this, we'll never hear the end of it.'

'Okay.' He looked down at Ned, thinking that this was one amazing family or maybe it was just that country folks were indeed tougher than their city counterparts. 'Let's do this. Give me one lap round the oval to warm up, everyone.'

As the kids shot off, the mums moved to the edge of the oval, leaving he and Tabitha alone. He wondered if he should mention the other night or completely ignore it. What would make things less awkward between them?

Up close, she was still gorgeous, but he couldn't help notice she also looked exhausted, pale, but with dark circles under her eyes. He wondered if the pregnancy was taking its toll, or if it was the stress of the upcoming show, or if, like him, she hadn't been able to sleep properly the last few nights. Possibly a combination of all three. Whatever the reason, she looked like she needed a rest far more than she needed to be here helping him, but he dared not suggest this for fear she'd think he didn't believe her capable again, or worse, that he didn't want her here.

Neither was anywhere close to the truth. He wanted her here— he wanted her full stop, more than he cared to admit.

So, he chose not to acknowledge what had gone between them. 'You do realise that we'll need a miracle for this lot to even come close to winning.'

She rewarded him with one of her bewitching smiles. 'Oh ye of little faith. They might not have a heap of skill or talent, but what they lack in that department, they sure as hell make up for in enthusiasm. Determination can go a long way, and they have us.'

Ferg chuckled, pretending he wasn't at all affected by the way this glorious woman said 'us'. 'I guess you're right. How's your week been anyway?'

She sighed. 'Busy.'

'You do look tired.'

She raised her eyebrows. 'That's really just a polite way of saying I look crap, right? I'm beginning to think this whole pregnancy-glow thing is an urban myth.'

'No. I …' Damn, why did he have such a habit of putting his foot in his mouth around her? 'You never look crap, I promise.'

Her cheeks flushed at his words.

'We should set up the drills,' Tabitha said, dropping her gaze. Was he imagining the breathlessness in her voice?

He nodded. 'Yeah, good idea.' Then he turned to the bag to grab the marker cones. As he handed them to her, their hands brushed in the exchange and the hairs rose on the back of his neck. How the hell was he supposed to get through an hour in her company without succumbing to the urge to touch her again?

'Thanks,' she replied, quickly turning away and beginning to set out her cones on the ground. This was the third time they'd done this now, so they didn't need to discuss anything, which was probably a good thing. The less he had to look at her right now, the better.

Thankfully, just as they were finishing, Victoria arrived beside them, so they didn't have to make further attempts at conversation.

'I won,' she shrieked, barely puffing. Just because she couldn't bat or throw a ball to save her life, didn't mean she wasn't a good runner.

Ferg looked at Tabitha and could tell she was also stifling a laugh. He looked back to the little girl. 'Well, it wasn't a competition but if you run that fast on Saturday, maybe we will win. We're certainly going to give it our best shot, aren't we, gang?' he said as the rest of the kids gathered back around them.

They all erupted into cheers, jumping up and down in excitement—Tabitha wasn't wrong about their enthusiasm.

'Okay,' he shouted, trying to get their attention again. 'If we're going to do this, I need you all to listen really hard today; we need to work together as a team. Every one of you has strengths and we're going to play to them. Understand?'

The expressions on their faces turned serious as they nodded solemnly. Once again, he and Tabitha split the groups in two and he concentrated on the kids, making a concerted effort not to glance too often at Tabitha.

At half time they took a quick break for oranges. Ferg devoured a few slices, relishing the juicy sweetness and not thinking at all about how much he'd rather be tasting his assistant coach. Then they played a game, splitting up the kids randomly: Tabitha in charge of one group and he the other.

'May the best team win,' she said, tipping her cap to him and winking mischievously. The effect of this small gesture travelled straight to his groin.

'Oh, we will,' he managed. Then, trying not to stare at her butt as she led her lot over to the sidelines, he turned to his team. 'Right, spread out. Positions everyone. Jimmy, you're bowling first.'

Although it was only a scratch match, the kids gave one hundred and ten per cent. Even Milly Wellington, who couldn't seem to understand one end of the bat from the other, managed to hit the ball far enough to score a few runs. You had to laugh watching them play, talking tactics with each other like they were playing for their country. His and Tabitha's eyes met across the top of the little heads on more than one occasion, and each time he felt more than just the jolt of amusement between them.

'Team, you were amazing,' Ferg addressed the kids as they came together at the end, and he meant it. Under his and Tabitha's careful instruction and encouragement, both sides had scored a number of runs and the kids all appeared to have improved over the hour. It would still take a miracle for them to win, but maybe they wouldn't lose as dismally as they had the previous week. He finished his pep talk and turned to Tabitha standing beside him, close enough that he could feel the heat radiating off her. Or maybe the heat was all him. 'You got anything to add, assistant coach?'

She held up a finger. 'Just one thing … who wants ice-cream?'

'Me!' the kids squealed in unison, already rushing over to the van to line up.

Ferg chuckled. 'Want some help?' He wasn't exactly sure what he could do, but the question had just rolled off his tongue. Maybe doing something mundane would help cool him down a little. Failing that, he could always eat some ice-cream.

'Sure.' Tabitha smiled and they started off after the kids. 'We make a good team,' she added as they approached the van.

He felt ridiculously pleased by her words.

'Don't tell Terry, but I think the kids have already improved under your coaching. I'm disappointed I won't be able to see the match on Saturday.'

'I'll take lots of photos,' he promised.

'Do you call this an orderly line?' Tab scolded the kids and they all immediately formed one. She'd make a good teacher, he thought.

She opened the back of her van and Ferg held the door, then climbed up inside after her, closing it behind them. There wasn't a whole lot of room for two of them in there and it was pitch black.

'I'll just open the hatch,' she said, but as she went to do so their bodies collided.

Tabitha stilled. 'Sorry,' she whispered, her breath warm against his cheeks.

His eyes were beginning to acclimatise to the darkness. 'Are you really?'

A second later they were kissing; all the heat that had been building up between them over the last hour expelled into each other's mouths as he slid his hands into her hair and drew her close. Their bodies moulded together and Tabitha let out a little whimper of pleasure that turned him on like nothing ever had before.

He pulled back slightly, still clasping her face as he looked her straight in the eye. 'I don't think one time was enough.'

She nodded. 'But we can't do it *here*.'

At her breathy declaration, he glanced around. Sure the space was tiny, but the way he was feeling right now, he reckoned he could manage anywhere.

As if she could read his mind, she laughed softly. 'I meant because of the kids.'

'Shit, right.' He let out a sigh, having almost forgotten where they were—despite the faint noise of excitable children just outside.

'But,' she brushed her lips lightly across his, 'this won't take long, then I'll drop Ned home and head round to yours.'

It wasn't a question but he nodded anyway, then took another quick breath, trying to cool himself as she finally opened the hatch. Light spilled into the small space and Ferg barely had a chance to take in the inside of the van before Ned's little face appeared.

'Why were you guys taking so long?'

'The lock was stuck.'

He was impressed with Tabitha's quick thinking. Thank God she didn't wear lipstick, otherwise he'd probably have it smeared across his face.

As she reminded the kids about the orderly line, Ferg took a proper look around, amazed at what could fit in such a compact space. A smaller version of the ice-cream display cabinet at the tea rooms ran along the side opposite the window, and on the other side were cones, a row of ice-cream scoops, paper cups and waffle cones.

Following his gaze, Tabitha said, 'I keep things simple—no toppings to detract from the ice-cream flavours, although this lot really only like vanilla, chocolate or rainbow anyway. No imagination.'

He laughed as she shook her head and reached for one of the scoops. 'What can I do?'

'You hold the cones while I scoop.'

He knew that usually she popped the cone in a little holder while she scooped and was happy that this time she let him assist. Soon all the kids were happily slurping ice-cream as their parents bundled them into cars.

'Thanks Tab, thanks Mr McWilliams,' said Victoria and Milly's mum—he'd forgotten her name—as she waved through the open hatch. 'See you Saturday.'

'Will do.' Ferg waved back.

Alone again, Tab turned to face him. 'So what flavour do you want? Are you game to try my cheese one?'

'I thought you only brought the kiddie flavours?'

She winked. 'I brought some just for you.'

His chest squeezed at the idea she'd been thinking of him. 'In that case …'

He picked up a cone and held it out to her. She scooped, and once again their hands touched in the exchange. He flicked out his fingers, closing them around hers to prolong the connection. Sparks erupting inside him, he snatched his hand back and lifted the ice-cream to his mouth.

The cold had barely touched his tongue before Tabitha closed the hatch, swamping them in darkness again. 'You can give me your opinion in fifteen minutes but it better not be a long one because talking isn't what I have in mind,' she said, then stepped past him and opened the back door.

'Are we going home now?' Ned was standing at the back of the van, chocolate staining the corners of his mouth and an impatient expression on his face. 'Everyone else has gone and I'm *bored*.'

'I'll be fifteen minutes, max,' she promised Fergus and then climbed into the driver's seat beside her nephew.

Those fifteen minutes felt like the longest of Fergus's life. He drove home, fed Mrs Norris and then made sure his bedroom was presentable. Tabitha likely didn't give a damn about his house-keeping skills and he didn't plan on giving her the time to think about such things anyway, but it kept him busy until he heard her van pull up outside.

He met her as she was climbing the porch steps and yanked her into his arms, resuming the kiss they'd started just half an hour ago. They stumbled into his house, and in a matter of moments they were tearing at each other's clothes. This time they were so hot for each other that they didn't even make it to his bed. There wasn't much need for foreplay; the last three days of fantasising about this was enough for the both of them.

They collapsed onto the couch like a couple of randy teens, hands and mouths sliding against each other as Fergus drove into Tabitha. Even with her legs clamped around him, he wanted to go deeper, wanted to feel the very essence of her as he took them both where they wanted to be.

Afterwards, they simply lay there, slippery with sweat and panting. The worrying fact of the matter was that Fergus knew this mad coupling, although incredibly satisfying, hadn't sated his need for her nearly enough. A few more minutes to recover and he reckoned he could quite easily go for it all over again, but would that be giving her the wrong idea? Just because the two of them had out-of-the-planet sex, didn't change how he felt about relationships. Didn't change the fact she was pregnant and he was only here temporarily.

As if Tabitha could read his mind, she reached up her hand and smoothed her fingers over his furrowed brow. 'How long till you leave?'

He did a quick calculation in his head—term four was always a short one. 'Six weeks.'

'Okay,' she whispered, 'then stop thinking so much. Don't make this into more than it is. We're two grown adults enjoying each other's bodies—I don't see why we shouldn't continue doing so until you leave.'

He blinked. 'Really? You'd be okay with that?'

'I thought by now you'd have realised I don't say or do anything I don't want to, but if you'd rather just be friends …' She ran her hand down his bare back, her nails leaving a trail of goose bumps in their wake.

Like hell he would, he thought as he rose from the couch, scooped her into his arms and carried her into his bedroom. If they were going to be friends with benefits, or fuck buddies, or whatever the hell it was people called it these days, then he was damn well sure gunna make the most of it.

Chapter Twenty-one

Just as Tabitha thought the lunch rush was dying down, the bell above the door dinged and she looked up to see Fergus entering. Her heart did a little flip. Instinctively, she lifted her hand to check her hair and almost dropped the tray she was carrying.

'Hi.' She smiled as he strode across to where she was standing next to one of the now empty tables, resisting the urge to throw herself into his arms.

'We won!' His face exploded into a grin.

'No way,' she exclaimed, putting the tray down on the table. 'Are you freaking serious?' She'd have thought Lawson would have messaged her and Meg with the news, but then again, they'd been busy today. This was the first moment's reprieve they'd had, so neither of them had had the chance to check their phones.

Fergus nodded, his thick dark hair bouncing on his forehead. Tab resisted the urge to reach up and push it back.

'You should have seen them. And Ned was a superstar. The other team underestimated him because of his arm. Granted, they were nowhere near as good as Brunswick last week, but our little cricketers were on fire. Maybe it's all that ice-cream you've been feeding them.'

'I wish I'd been there. Did you get some photos?'

'Tonnes, and some videos.' He handed her his phone and she scrolled through the images, delighted at the action shots and the beaming faces in the team photo at the end.

She handed him back the phone. 'This is so great. Have you had lunch? Can I get you anything to eat or drink?'

He screwed up his face slightly. 'I had a sausage roll but it wasn't good.'

She screwed hers right back—there was nothing worse than bad pastries. 'I'm sure we can do better than that. Take a seat and I'll see what we have left.'

'Sounds good.' He got out his wallet, but Tab waved her hand.

'This one's on the house, in celebration,' she added, before he could read anything into it. Then she went out back where Meg and their junior kitchen hands, Lucy and Bonnie, were starting to put the kitchen back together.

'They won!' Tab and Meg announced to each other at the same time.

Meg frowned, her phone in her hand—she'd obviously just checked her messages. 'How do *you* know?'

'Fergus is here. He came to tell me the good news.'

'*Fergus?*' Meg raised an eyebrow. 'That was nice of him. Rose Hill is not exactly on the way back.'

'He's excited and he knew I would be too, don't go getting any silly ideas.' Tab felt her cheeks heat but she held her chin high, determined not to give anything away.

Ever since dinner last Sunday, Meg had been in her ear about the supposed chemistry she'd seen between them. At first Tab thought she might have witnessed the kiss by their cars, but it soon become clear Meg was just engaging in some wishful thinking.

She'd be delighted if she knew the truth but Tab wasn't going to tell. However close they'd become over the past couple of years, she wasn't sure Meg would understand they were both just in it for a bit of fun.

Keeping their 'affair' private felt vital to keeping it light and uncomplicated.

'I'm going to take him a plate of leftovers,' she told her sister-in-law firmly, 'and then I'll finish helping with the clean-up.'

'Good idea. After all, the way to a man's heart *is* through his stomach.'

'I'm not trying to get to his heart,' she said. *Into his pants?* Now that was something else entirely. He was making her into a very naughty girl but she deserved a last hurrah before she had the baby and became a sensible single mother, didn't she?

'Pity,' Meg said. 'Either way, Bonnie, Lucy and I are fine here. Why don't you take him a big slice of chocolate cake and share it with him?'

Tab gave her a warning look. 'Why don't you take your head out of the clouds and stop meddling?'

Meg sighed and held up a hand. 'I'm sorry. But the least you could do is keep the poor man company while he eats. No one likes to dine alone, do they, Lucy? Bonnie?'

The teenagers looked from Meg to Tab as if they weren't really sure what was going on. 'I guess not,' Bonnie said eventually.

Tab's feet were aching from being on them for hours, and she did want a blow-by-blow account of the match, but she wasn't sure she could trust herself out there alone with Fergus. Besides, the sooner they finished cleaning up, the sooner she could get rid of the others and have her way with him again. A thrill skittered through her at the thought.

'Here you are. Enjoy,' she said to Fergus as she delivered a plate of leftovers to him.

'This looks amazing,' he said, but he was looking up into her eyes as he spoke. 'It's good to see you.'

'Same.' She leaned in a little closer and lowered her voice. 'Do you want to hang out when we close up here?'

'You not too tired?' he whispered back.

Twenty minutes ago she'd been ready to fall into bed and sleep the rest of the afternoon away, but one look at him and she'd found a second wind. They only had six weeks—it wouldn't be smart to waste too much of it.

'I'm fine.' She glanced back into the kitchen, where thankfully Meg didn't appear to be snooping but wiping the counters down furiously as if her life depended on it. 'I'll get rid of them as soon as I can, but maybe when you've finished that, pretend to leave. You can drive down the road to the service station and park around the back. They won't see you when they drive out of town that way.'

He grinned deliciously at her. 'This sneaking around business could be quite fun. I always wanted to be a spy when I was little.'

Tab laughed and straightened again. She'd been so worried when she turned up at cricket that things might have been uncomfortable between them, but that wasn't the problem at all. If they kept on having sex until he left, maybe they could avoid the awkwardness all together.

'Eat up. You'll need your strength,' she said with a wink as she headed back into the kitchen.

It seemed she wasn't the only one eager to get everything done. Meg was cleaning almost manically. 'You okay?' Tab asked.

Meg glanced at Lucy and Bonnie, and seeing they were busy chatting as they put the clean plates back into cupboards, she whispered, 'I've been charting my ovulation via my temperature. I just popped to the loo to check and I'm in prime ovulation time right this second. I need to get home, put a movie on for Ned and take advantage of my husband.'

Even though Meg was talking about her brother, Tab couldn't help but smile. 'What are you waiting for? I can finish off here. You need to get on home and make me another niece or nephew.'

Meg half-chuckled but there was a sadness in her eyes. 'Don't get your hopes up. The amount we've been bonking lately, we should have spawned a whole football team by now. If it doesn't happen this month we're biting the bullet and starting IVF.'

Tab pulled her into a hug. 'It'll happen. Now go. I'll see you tomorrow.'

'You sure you'll be okay? What about our last customer?'

'Fergus?' Tab pretended to dismiss him with a shake of her head. 'I'll kick him out soon, and you can turn the sign on the door to closed when you leave so we don't have any latecomers.'

'You're the best. Thank you,' Meg said, grabbing her handbag and calling to Bonnie and Lucy, who she always drove back to Walsh after a shift. 'We're knocking off early.'

They didn't have to be told twice; their phones were out of their pockets and they were following Meg out of the kitchen without even closing the cupboards behind them. Normally Tab didn't like a half-finished job but she couldn't bring herself to care today.

'They left in a hurry,' Ferg said, wiping his mouth with a serviette, and then shifting his seat back and tapping his knee. 'Did you scare them off?'

'Something like that,' she said as she all but fell into his lap and then did what she'd wanted to do since he first walked in. And *oh sweetness*, he tasted so delicious. Even better than she remembered. They kissed for what felt like hours and although she was hungry for more of him, this was good too. Kissing, she decided, was underrated and he was very, very good at it. His tongue danced with hers and occasionally he nibbled gently on her lower lip as his fingers massaged the back of her neck. Their previous couplings had been urgent and electric, but neither of them appeared in a particular rush today.

Eventually, however, kissing was not enough. Tab felt the heat rising between them and knew neither of them would be able to hold out much longer. She pulled back. 'I think I should give you the grand tour of this wonderful historic building.'

He nodded, his expression serious. 'That sounds good. I'm *very* interested in history. Perhaps we should start with your bedroom?'

'That's as good a place as any,' she said as she pushed off his lap, grabbed his hand and led him through the kitchen to the stairs at the back.

Tabitha was pretty certain Fergus didn't take in any of the high ceilings with their decorative plaster that Meg had lovingly restored or the beautiful hundred-year-old woodwork on the stairs. And she didn't care because he only had eyes for her. There'd be plenty of time to wow him with history and give him a proper tour later. That's if he wanted to stick around a bit. This no-strings sex thing was completely new for her and she wasn't a hundred per cent sure of the boundaries. Were they allowed to hang out and have fun together as well or was it *purely* a sex thing?

The answer would have to wait because they'd arrived at her bedroom. A cold draft wafted past them as Tab pulled him inside and she hoped that was Eliza making an exit, but not even the thought of a ghost spectating was going to stop her now. She kissed Fergus into the room until he fell back onto the bed, then laughed as she climbed on top of him and picked up where they'd left off downstairs.

Previously he'd been so attentive to her needs, but this time she wanted to make sure she was attentive to his as well. With only a little assistance from the man himself, she unbuckled his jeans and freed the very thing she'd been dreaming about since she'd first laid eyes on it. She stooped her head and kissed it.

Fergus felt his eyes roll back in his head as Tabitha's mouth closed around his erection. He groaned as he lost the ability to think and gave himself over to the sensations. It didn't take long before he was on the edge, but he didn't want to be the only one getting his rocks off today.

'If you don't ... stop that ... now ... this is going to be over before it's begun. Come here,' he said, dragging her up and putting his mouth on hers, before seeking the waistband of her shorts.

It didn't take long to get her where he was and, after removing the rest of their clothing, he was inside her again. Only this time she was up top and he got to touch and taste and gaze at her breasts as, once again, they flew over the edge together. He'd never managed to be so in sync with a woman before.

'Wow,' they whispered in unison as she collapsed onto him. He could feel her heart thumping against his chest and his working just as hard.

Fergus knew that according to the rules of a 'fling,' he was supposed to give her a quick kiss goodbye, yank his jeans back on and leave. But he didn't want to go back to his boring house and another lonely evening with Mrs Norris, cheap beer and bad TV. Not just yet anyway.

'Did you mean it about giving me the grand tour?' he asked.

She smiled. 'Course I did. Just give me a few moments to catch my breath.'

'Take as long as you need,' he said, planting a kiss on her forehead.

After another few moments, they climbed out of bed and Tabitha went down the hallway to the bathroom while he put on his clothes. It was the first time he'd had a chance to take stock of his surroundings. The walls were almost the same white as the ceiling, which had that intricate plaster art popular in the early 1900s, but the big prints that hung on the walls added colour. The room felt bright and cheery, just like Tabitha, and he imagined it would be hard to wake up in a bad mood in here.

Fully dressed again, he ventured out onto the landing, which was darker and much less modern than the décor in the bedroom. There was an antique hall table and a mirror of similar vintage along one wall, and gold-framed paintings of rural Australian landscapes, like the ones he'd seen in the gallery downstairs. No sign of Tabitha, he wandered on to the next room and pushed the door open a fraction.

He gasped at the sight of what looked to be hundreds of pieces of wood scattered across the floor. What the hell had happened here? Some kind of furniture explosion? He narrowed his eyes as he tried to make head or tail of the mess, and had just made out what he thought was the side of a cot when Tabitha appeared.

'What are you doing?' Her voice was sharp and he spun around and almost into her.

'Sorry, I just …'

'Started the tour without me?'

He couldn't tell by her tone whether she was angry or amused. 'What's all this?' he asked, as he nodded into the room.

She sighed. 'I started putting together my baby furniture, but …'

She didn't need to finish the sentence for him to understand. Putting flat packs together could be a nightmare with two hands, so he could imagine the challenge with only one. 'Surely Lawson or someone would help you?'

'I didn't want to ask him.'

Fergus knew Tabitha didn't like to admit any kind of weakness but sometimes she was too stubborn for her own good. 'That's ridiculous. You don't have to try and prove yourself by doing everything on your own, you know.'

'That's not why.' She paused. 'Meg and Lawson are struggling to get pregnant, so shoving all this in their faces just doesn't feel right, but if I asked anyone else it would probably get back to them and then they'd get angry that I didn't ask them in the first place.'

'Oh Tabitha.' He shook his head and took a step into the room. 'Where are the Allen keys?'

'What are you doing?'

'I'm helping you make some damn baby furniture,' he said, in a tone that dared her to argue with him.

'You don't have to do that.'

'I know I don't. But I want to. I actually quite like making things. Besides, we're friends, aren't we?'

When she nodded, he added, 'Well, friends help each other out, but if you can't accept that then consider this as repaying the favour you did me when you brought me dinner.'

'That wasn't a favour,' she objected. 'That was just to show my appreciation for what you did and how you were with Mrs Lord.'

He hit her with his most seductive smile. 'And this is to show my appreciation for you making my stay in Walsh way more exciting than I originally imagined.'

Her cheeks flushed and she bit her lower lip as if trying not to smile. She was damn cute when trying to put up a fight but she wasn't the only stubborn one in the room.

'Look we could stand here all afternoon arguing about this, or we could actually build you a nursery.'

'But what about the tour I promised?'

He shrugged. 'I'm here six more weeks. We've got plenty of time.'

'Okay, then. If you're sure.'

'I'm sure, Tabitha.'

Finally, she stepped into the room and started through the disarray, stopping to bend and pick up an Allen key. 'I think this is what you need?'

He took it from her, ignoring the usual thunderbolt that shot through him as their fingers touched. If he succumbed to that, they'd never get anything done here. But working on the baby furniture would be a good reminder that however strong the chemistry between them, sex and friendship were all that could ever be on the table.

'Thanks.' He dropped to his knees and assessed the pieces. 'Cot first?'

She nodded and kneeled down beside him. 'By the way, please call me Tab. Tabitha reminds me of when my grandmother is angry at me.'

'Tab it is. I definitely don't want you to be thinking about your grandmother every time you look at me.'

She whacked him playfully on the arm. 'Do not even go there.'

Chuckling, he picked up one end of the cot. 'Do you want to hold this steady and I'll attach the side?'

As she did so, she said, 'I probably shouldn't have told you that about Meg and Lawson before, but something about you has me speaking before thinking. I need to learn to keep my big mouth shut.'

He smiled at that—turned on by the thought that he flustered her enough to forget propriety. 'I promise I won't say a word to anyone. I guess that's why she wasn't drinking at dinner?'

'Actually …' Tab hesitated a moment. 'I suppose it's okay to tell you because Meg's history is now common knowledge.'

'What history?'

'When Meg came to Rose Hill she was trying to start fresh after a difficult time in her life. She'd struggled with various addictions and although recovered now, she didn't drink even before she was trying to get pregnant.'

Tab went on, and the story she told him of what her sister-in-law had been through totally surprised him. Not that he'd led any kind of a sheltered life himself, but Meg simply didn't seem the type to get herself caught up in such troubles. It just went to show, you could never truly know anyone and almost everyone was capable of hitting rock bottom if pushed far enough.

'I'd wondered what brought her to Rose Hill, ' he said, as he secured the other end of the cot. It was finally starting to take shape. 'So, is this place really haunted? Ned told the class you lived in a haunted house and Meg mentioned the ghost when I first came here. What was her name? Eleanor?'

Right there, right then, the last piece of the cot, which had been leaning against the wall behind him, crashed onto the floor, only narrowly missing his leg. He startled, dropping the Allen key. Tab laughed long and hard. 'You should see the look on your face. Like you've seen a ghost.'

'Hah hah.' Although a shiver scuttled down Ferg's spine leaving goose bumps in its wake.

'Eliza is her name and I think she just gave you her answer. She likes to be taken seriously.'

At what had to be a disbelieving expression on his face, she said, 'I know, I know. I wasn't a believer until I heard some of Meg's stories and even then I wasn't completely convinced, but when I moved here myself … Well, it's impossible to live here and not feel Eliza's presence. Sometimes I even *hear* her.'

'How do you know she's called Eliza, or did you give her that name?'

Tab shook her head and offered him a pitying expression. 'Fergus, Fergus, Fergus, do you know nothing about the paranormal? You don't *make up* the name of a ghost, you do your research. You find out what you're dealing with, why the spirit is still lingering between this world and the next and then, if you can, you help them find peace. Some ghosts will finally move on after that but Eliza seems pretty happy where she is.'

Ferg shivered as he reached for the final side of the cot—the piece Eliza had tried to give him a heart attack with. It would be pretty brave living out here alone, but living out here with an actual ghost … He had a newfound respect for Tab. 'What research did you do?'

'Not me, Meg,' she said and then told him how her sister-in-law had started to do research in the old historical society across the road after she could no longer write off her encounters with the ghost as faulty wiring, creaky floorboards or strong drafts getting through gaps in the old doors and windows.

'She wasn't exactly scared but she wanted to get to the bottom of it. She found some old newspaper articles about the building and some photos, and worked out that a woman called Eliza had supposedly thrown herself over the balustrade upstairs because her lover had chosen someone else.'

Ferg shook his head. 'Love makes people do crazy things.'

Tab snorted. 'Love makes people do murderous things.'

He frowned. 'What do you mean?'

'We're pretty sure Eliza didn't kill herself.'

'She was murdered?'

Tab nodded.

'Any idea who did it? Was that why she didn't pass on? Because she wanted to seek revenge for her death?'

They finished the cot almost on autopilot and barely commented on the achievement as they flipped it over; Fergus was far too riveted as she told him the whole story. He'd never been one for ghost stories but he found he believed this one and that only made what Tab told him more outrageous.

'And Penelope Walsh got away with it? Her family just kept on living in and ruling over the district for all these years?'

Tab nodded sadly. 'No court would ever touch the case. You can't exactly summon a ghost to the witness box.'

'Geez. And there I was feeling sorry for the old duck every time I go to visit Mrs Lord. Seems wrong that she's the one that has a loving family and a stream of visitors.'

'Right? Makes it hard to believe in karma, but, since her stroke, Penelope's been trapped inside her own body and I guess that's a kind of prison in itself.'

'So, maybe karma just takes its time.'

Ferg chuckled as they moved onto the change table and as they worked, Tab entertained him with more stories of Rose Hill and nearby Walsh. She told him that the landscapes in the gallery downstairs had been painted by a hermit who'd lived in the service station when Meg first arrived, how they'd become friends and that the chickens out back had belonged to him. She told him about how Meg and Lawson met, and the divided opinions among the people of Walsh when the truth about her past finally came out. She talked about all this and much more.

Putting together baby furniture was the last thing he'd expected to be doing on his Saturday afternoon, but it was the most fun he'd had in weeks. Except for his interactions with Tabitha between the sheets, of course.

'Wow. Thanks so much for this,' she said, when they'd finished the change table. 'I can't thank you enough. Do you want me to get you a drink? Or maybe you're hungry? I could make some dinner?'

He was beginning to hunger—not just for food either—but he wanted to put the rocking chair together before he stopped. 'A little, but let's finish here first.'

Chapter Twenty-two

Tab's routine changed over the next week or so. While previously her life had revolved around her ice-cream business, the tea rooms, her various committees and clubs, coaching cricket and spending time with her family, now a great chunk of her time was spent with Ferg. They stole almost every night together, and the days between those nights dragged as she counted down the hours to when she could be in his arms again. With the amount of sex they'd had, she'd thought her pregnancy hormones might have been sated, but so far there was no sign of that happening. She couldn't get enough of him and luckily, the feeling seemed to be mutual.

Meg and Lawson had both commented that there was something different about her, but thankfully they bought the story that her second trimester had given her a fresh burst of energy.

This was backed up when they'd driven out yesterday to collect something Meg had left at the tea rooms and Tab proudly showed them the progress on the nursery. They couldn't believe she'd managed to make all the furniture and paint the room a lovely soft lemon all by herself. She hadn't exactly lied, but had failed to mention that Fergus had helped her with the furniture, and had turned out to be a dab hand with a paintbrush. When she'd told him her plans to paint the room yellow, he'd not only insisted on helping but had shown up the following evening with tins, brushes and drop sheets.

'Pregnant women should not be painting walls on their own,' he'd insisted when she tried to put up an argument.

She liked these times almost as much as she enjoyed being in bed with him. It was during these breaks between shagging each other silly that they talked. Okay, mostly she did the talking, but sometimes Fergus let down his guard. He loved hearing her tales of growing up on the farm because it was so far removed from his own childhood. By piecing together snippets of things he dropped in conversation, she'd worked out that the longest he'd spent in any one house growing up was twelve months—and this hadn't been with his own mother, but with a foster mum who'd taken both he and his sister into her care.

There'd even been talk of this carer trying to adopt them, but sadly she'd remarried and her new husband wasn't as keen. He wanted to travel and didn't want them to be tied down or paying for children that weren't their own, at least that was the impression Fergus had got. Occasionally he'd tell her a horror story from his time in foster care, which would make her blood boil and him inevitably retreat for a little while. She usually managed to draw him out of his shell again with sex.

She wanted to know more about his sister. They'd obviously been close as children—having only had each other to rely on—but whenever they got close to discussing them as adults, he changed the subject again. Fergus definitely preferred it when they were talking fun and light stuff—like movies, favourite foods, books they'd loved, places they'd been and places on their bucket lists—so Tab tried to resist grilling him on the tough subjects. She'd tried not to get frustrated when she'd suggested he do a DNA test to try to track down the missing side of his family—*Aren't you curious about your father? You could give him the surprise of your life if you found him and told him you were his son.* But he'd brushed her off. *Surprises aren't always a good thing, Tabitha.*

He only very rarely called her Tabitha now and when he did, she knew not to push him any further. But overall, the last two weeks had been euphoric, and Meg and Lawson weren't the only ones to notice the change in her.

'Earth to Tabitha!'

'I'm sorry.' She roused at the sound of Chloe Wellington calling her name. They were in the middle of a show committee meeting, but Tab had no idea what they'd been discussing. 'What were you saying?'

Tennille chuckled as she picked up a homemade choc-chip cookie. 'Looks like pregnancy brain has struck. That's it for you now, Tab. Once it strikes you're stuck with it—pregnancy brain gives way to baby brain, which never seems to go away.'

'Maybe if you stopped having babies it would,' Carrie said with a good-natured wink.

'You're probably just tired,' said dear old Beth, giving Tabitha a sympathetic grin. 'I don't know how you manage to do all you do, and then here we are making you come all the way back into town for a late night meeting.'

'It's hardly late,' Adeline snapped, tossing an aggravated glance at her watch, 'but we should be focusing on the agenda.'

'You don't actually look that tired,' Eileen Bennett mused, ignoring Adeline as she scrutinised Tabitha.

Chloe agreed. 'You really are glowing. Pregnancy was never so kind to me.'

And although the thought of her baby made her heart sing, Tab had a feeling her pregnancy wasn't solely responsible for her current supposed glow. 'Anyway, what were you saying?' she asked, before her mind slipped away again.

Chloe cleared her throat and glanced at her iPad, which held the meeting agenda. 'I just asked if the food trucks map you sent me is final?'

Tab nodded. 'Yep. Everyone's locked in and excited about the show.'

'I hope you've informed them that our numbers are likely to be a lot more than we initially estimated,' Adeline said, then added unnecessarily, 'now we've got *Ryder*.' Her smile at having secured such a big name was enough to rival the one Tabitha had been wearing permanently the last two weeks.

Tab shot her a synthetic grin. 'Oh, don't you worry, I have.'

Everything came back to Ryder. First item on tonight's agenda had been the extra security they'd hired to handle the crowds and the added portaloos that had been booked. Some committee members were anxious about the extra costs but Chloe and Adeline ensured everyone that presold tickets had already more than paid for the added expenses. This had been the first time in the hundred-year history of the Walsh Agricultural Show that they'd opened tickets sales before the actual day—the last few years they'd almost had to give away tickets to get people to come.

This had been Beth's genius idea to ensure that locals didn't miss out on the show to people who were prepared to travel from further afield simply to see Ryder. Her whiz-kid grandson Jake, who was studying 'something about computers' at uni, had whipped them up a booking system for their previously archaic website.

They'd also given locals a two-day head start to buy tickets before out-of-towners were able to. And, if the fact the caravan park, the motel, the pub and all nearby B&Bs (including Tabitha's) were booked out for the weekend within half a day of announcing

Ryder's performance was any indication, then plenty of people were prepared to travel. Tab thought the show was in danger of becoming more about Ryder than their centenary celebrations, but dared not raise this for fear everyone would think she was simply upset at the prospect of seeing him again. Thankfully, some of the older members of the committee shared her worries. So to ensure the non-local ticket holders didn't only come for the evening concert, but also patronised the stalls, rides, displays and other offerings, they'd decided gates would close at 2 pm and anyone who hadn't arrived by then would miss out. Lastly, they'd put a cap on tickets—sales on the day would only be permitted for anyone who lived in the Shire of Walsh and for some reason hadn't already secured tickets.

The excitement was buzzing around town at the prospect of such a famous singer coming to *their* show and Adeline was basking in the glory of securing him. The way she spoke, you'd have thought she'd managed to bring Elvis Presley back from the dead and lure him to Walsh.

Nobody seemed too concerned about Ryder's recent indiscretions, and the media had already run a story about his community spirit and the fact he was forgoing payment to support country folks. Only a few people had stopped Tab in the street or in the supermarket and expressed concern over how she might be feeling about the situation, but she'd told them it didn't bother her at all. And this was actually true. She found she didn't really care what he thought of her and no longer even bristled when she heard his name. In fact, it was getting a little boring the way everyone was frothing at the mouth over him. So he had a good voice and knew how to use it? He wasn't the only one.

'I was just thinking that we might need to move the food trucks a little further away from the stage, that's all,' said Chloe.

They debated this issue for a while, then moved on to the last item on the list—the busy bee at the showgrounds scheduled for the weekend. Tab felt guilty about not being able to help, but she and Meg were already closing the tea rooms for show day so they didn't want to lose another day's trade.

'I can spend some time there during the week though,' she offered. 'Clean the toilet blocks or something?'

'Don't be ridiculous,' Chloe tsked. 'You've done more than enough, and we've got plenty of volunteers for the busy bee. Right, I think that ticks everything off my list; has anyone got any further business?'

When nobody came forward, Chloe officially announced the meeting closed and Beth went to put the kettle on. No one ever missed an opportunity for a bit of a chat and although Tab usually hung around for a cuppa, tonight she was out of there so fast she could have given Cathy Freeman a run for her money.

'Where are you off to in such a rush?' Adeline called .

'To bed. I'm stuffed.'

That wasn't a lie—she *was* heading for bed, just not her own, at least not straightaway. There was a spring in her step as she walked to her van and a massive grin on her face as she climbed into the driver's seat. Hopefully everyone was too busy nattering to notice that when she drove out of the town hall car park, she didn't turn in the direction of Rose Hill.

* * *

'Finally,' Ferg exclaimed as he heard the sound of Tab's van on the gravel. It felt like hours since he'd finished school and since then he'd been counting down the minutes until their tryst. With a grin, he pushed up from the couch where he'd been watching some stupid reality show, switched off the TV and went to greet her.

'What time do you call this?' He pretended to be cross, tapping his finger on his watch as she jogged up the few steps onto the porch, her hair swishing about.

'I got away as quick as I could,' she said breathlessly.

'Well, you're here now, that's what matters.' With these words, he pulled her inside. Their mouths sought each other even before the door had banged shut behind him and his hands grasped at her clothes as they feasted on each other.

A little voice in his head told him he should pause and ask her how her day was, maybe offer her a drink or something to eat, but his physical urges were far stronger than the voice of reason. And if the way her hand snuck under his shirt and slid over his skin was anything to go by, she didn't give a damn about niceties either.

'Man, you taste so good,' he whispered, breaking their kiss so he could whip her T-shirt over her head.

'You don't taste so bad yourself,' she replied as she moved her hand lower.

He sucked in a breath as she slipped her fingers past the waistband of his jeans and felt how hard he was for her. She smiled against his mouth. He'd never been so hot for anyone and he kept waiting for their chemistry to fade, but so far there was no sign of that happening. If anything, the more he had her, the more he wanted, but he pushed that thought aside, not willing to give it the attention it probably deserved and ruin the moment.

Right now, the moment was all that mattered. He reached around and unhooked her black bra, replacing the material with his bare hands. Her breasts fit so perfectly in his palms, her skin so soft, her nipples so hard. She groaned at his touch and it was the most magical sound in the world.

'Shall we take this to the bedroom?' He barely managed to get the words out as he gazed down at her perfect breasts.

'What's wrong with right here?'

He chuckled—'What indeed?'—and then made quick work of removing the rest of Tab's clothing. When she was beautifully naked in front of him, he shucked his own jeans and jocks so there was only his T-shirt between them. She yanked it off over his head just before they fell onto the carpet, then she climbed on top of him and he thrust up into her.

Magic. It was like when they came together they went somewhere else entirely. He couldn't think. He didn't want to. He only wanted to feel. And the feelings just got better and better every time.

A few minutes later, when his breathing had almost returned to normal, the little voice returned and somehow he found the wherewithal to speak. 'Are you hungry?'

Tab smiled at him. 'Not as much as I was when I got here.' Then she kissed his bare skin just below the shoulder.

He chuckled. 'That's not what I meant. Have you had dinner?'

'I had a cookie at the meeting.'

He frowned. 'That's not enough.' *Especially in her condition*, added that pesky little voice. It was easy to forget when they were in the throes of passion that Tabitha was pregnant. But he shouldn't forget. That information was exactly what he needed to keep the boundaries between them.

She hit him with a look. 'We make big cookies in the country, you know, but if you've got something else on offer, you might be able to twist my arm.'

'How about I make you an omelette?'

'Is that all you've got the ingredients for?' Tab tsked. 'Do I have to restock your fridge again?'

'To be fair, I haven't had that much time to shop.' During the days he was at school and lately most nights belonged to her. Not that he was complaining. Time down here was going much quicker now he had her keeping him busy. 'But I promise you, it'll be the best omelette you've ever tasted.'

'Is that right? How can I resist then?'

'You sit.' He pointed to the 1970s era bar stools on one side of the bench as they entered the kitchen. 'Tonight it's my turn to wow you with my culinary skills.'

'I can hardly wait.' Tab settled onto one of the stools as he started to get the eggs, cheese and bacon out of the fridge.

He poured her a juice. 'How was the meeting tonight? Things must be ramping up now the show's so close.'

She nodded and filled him in on what they'd discussed.

'I can't believe all that goes into the organisation of a small country show,' he said as he poured the egg mixture into the hot pan.

'The show is our biggest day of the year and this is our hundred-year anniversary, so it was always going to be huge, but now that Ryder's singing it's become mammoth.' She barely batted an eyelid as she mentioned her ex-boyfriend and, not wanting to upset her, he decided not to ask her how she was feeling about him.

'Shall we eat these in the lounge room or out on the back verandah?' he asked, as he slid two pretty good-looking omelettes, even if he did say so himself, onto two plates.

'Let's go outside,' she said, picking up her glass. 'It's a beautiful night.'

As they sat out on the porch in two ancient rocking chairs, Ferg had to admit she was right. He couldn't recall a more perfect night and it wasn't simply that the sky was so clear you could see thousands more stars than he'd ever seen in the city. It was also so quiet; in the far distance he could only just make out the soft lowing of cattle—probably from her family's farm. But the peace wasn't what made it perfect either. Tab was so easy to be with, so easy to talk to, that sometimes he felt himself letting down his guard, almost telling her things he'd rather not share. Other times they sat in comfortable silence and that was good too.

They were in the middle of one of those silences now when Tab said, 'I've just realised something.'

'What?' He stilled, fearful she might say something that would break this carefree ease between them. 'That I was right and I do make the best damn omelettes in the world?'

She laughed. 'No, that wasn't it, although I do concede that omelette was up there in my Top Ten.'

'Only Top Ten? I'll have to try harder next time.'

'Anyway,' she said emphatically, 'what I was trying to say is that I just realised you haven't played your accordion for me yet.'

'Oh.' He relaxed a little. 'I guess we've been busy with other more pressing things.'

Her cheeks flushed, which only made him want to do something to make them flush more, but she was persistent. 'Can you play it for me now?'

'Well, I would, but it's at school.'

Tab snapped to her feet. 'Come on then.' She picked up her plate and glass and started inside.

Maybe she didn't hear him correctly, he thought, as he followed her inside. She was already at the sink rinsing her dishes.

'You're not suggesting we go to school now so I can play for you?'

'That's exactly what I'm suggesting.'

He chuckled and shook his head—it was almost ten o'clock. 'How about I bring it over to your place tomorrow night?'

'I don't want to wait until tomorrow,' she said, taking his plate and dumping it in the sink. 'I'm in the mood for some accordion-playing now.'

'What if someone sees us?'

She turned slowly from the sink to look up at him. 'We'll be stealthy. But anyway, they won't. This is dairy country, folks have long been in bed by now. Come on … live a little dangerously with me.'

And how could he ever say no when she batted those eyelashes at him?

He couldn't, which is why Ferg found himself following Tab's van to the school, parking beside it, holding her hand as they crept through the yard like burglars, and then letting them both into his classroom in what felt like the middle of the night. The good thing about this plan was that it would eliminate the awkward parting at the end of the evening. This way they'd both just go their separate ways. He always felt a little guilty about sending a pregnant woman out into the night whenever she visited him, but asking her to stay wasn't the right thing to do either. Actually sleeping the night together would blur the lines of what this was supposed to be, and for this to work, they had to keep those boundaries firmly in place.

'Stay here,' he told her, 'while I turn off the alarm.' The last thing they needed was security being alerted to a break-in and Joanne woken up in the middle of the night to find he and Tabitha in the middle of a jam session.

'Okay, all good.' Ferg held the door open and ushered her into his classroom.

'Isn't this fun?' Tab said with a big grin as she turned slowly and glanced around. 'This was my classroom for a number of years, you know? Sadly, I never had any teachers quite as cute as you.'

With that, she closed the distance between them and kissed him on the lips. For a second he thought she'd lured him here under false pretences and maybe now she wanted to fulfil some weird fantasy about doing it in her old classroom, but she pulled back before the kiss could take off. 'Where's this accordion then?'

He couldn't deny the tug of disappointment. 'Here it is,' he said, crossing the room to where he kept his shiny red pride and joy on a shelf just out of reach of little hands.

Tab watched as he picked up the instrument and strapped it to himself.

'So it's like a cross between a piano and bagpipes?' she asked as he pointed out all the bits to her—the treble keyboard, the bellows and the bass buttons.

He gave a simple explanation of how it all worked, then sat down on a chair to play a song. 'Any requests?'

'Play me your favourite,' she said as she perched herself on the edge of his desk, swinging her legs as he began.

'Okay.' With a deep breath, he pressed on the bellows with his left arm, put his right fingers on the keys and started to play 'Hotel California'—a song he hated almost as much as he loved because of the memories it evoked. Usually he sang along as he played, but he'd never really performed for anyone aside from the kids in his classes. Jools and Eider had often heard him play, but they were just around, neither of them particularly interested in music. So he felt a little self-conscious and couldn't even bring himself to look at Tabitha as he played.

After a while her voice broke through the music. 'It's such a beautiful instrument.'

He looked up to see her crying. 'What's wrong?' he said, breaking off mid song.

'Nothing.' She sniffed and gave him one of her full-faced smiles. 'I'm fine. It's just … that was my mum's favourite song. She'd always have it on repeat in the car.'

He didn't have time to tell her it was his mum's favourite too, because Tab nodded towards the accordion. 'Please … keep going.'

Within a few minutes, her tears dried up and she started singing along, bopping in time and belting out the words. It was all he could do to keep on playing, knowing that if he stopped she probably would too, but *wow. Just wow.* He knew she'd been very dedicated to her music as a teen, but he had no idea she had this much talent.

When he came to the end of the song, he couldn't hold back anymore. 'Why aren't you singing for a living?'

'What?' She blinked and semi-laughed.

'You. Your voice. It's like nothing I've ever heard.'

Tab's cheeks tinged red. 'I'm not sure about that, but I do enjoy a good sing-a-long. What else is in your repertoire?'

But he wasn't letting her get off that easily. He'd play another song for her but first he wanted some answers. 'Why did you stop?'

She exhaled loudly, clearly annoyed. 'I didn't stop. I still sing in the shower and I'm singing now, aren't I?'

'But didn't you want to sing for a living?'

'I wanted to play the guitar *and* sing, but … well, dreams don't always come true. I accepted my life had a different path. Now, can you please play something else?'

Not wanting to push her and ruin this night, he nodded. 'You like Paul Kelly?'

Her lips twisted into a smile again. 'Who doesn't like Paul Kelly?'

So he played 'To Her Door' and 'Before Too Long' and she started singing again, and Ferg felt he could play all night if it meant he could keep listening to her.

'I can't believe you taught yourself,' she said between songs, 'and before the era of YouTube tutorials.'

He laughed, secretly chuffed. 'It wasn't that hard. And it gave me something to do as a kid. I never stayed anywhere long enough to make real friends or join a club or a sporting team.'

'Do you reckon I could have a go?' she asked.

Ferg didn't mean to, but he frowned. He reckoned Tabitha Cooper-Jones could do almost anything she set her mind to, but the accordion required the use of two hands—for the piano keys and the bass buttons. But they were having such a nice night and he didn't know how to say that without upsetting her.

She chuckled. 'Just let me do the keyboard—I used to play a little piano as a kid—and try the bellows. You can push the buttons for me.'

'Okay.' Relieved and also excited at the prospect of sharing his passion, he stood and started unbuckling the instrument.

Tab slid off the desk and stepped towards him. He lowered the accordion into her lap, positioning the bottom of the keyboard just between her legs, before awkwardly trying to secure the straps. Tab giggled as he slipped his hands between her body and the accordion to tighten them.

'I didn't know you were ticklish,' he said, his face close.

'Only in certain places,' she replied with a cheeky wink. 'But don't go getting any ideas right now. I want to play this thing.'

The wink and the determination in her eyes were attractive, but he pushed aside the urge to kiss her and focused on the task. 'Do you remember any of the songs you learned as a kid?' he asked as he dropped to his knees, positioning himself next to her so he could press the bass buttons and help with the bellows if need be.

'"Hot Cross Buns".'

He laughed. 'Let's give that a go then. This is middle C,' he said, pointing to a key. 'As you press down on the keys, gently press the bellows in and then out again.'

She stuck her tongue out slightly as she followed his instructions and her face exploded into joy as sound came from the accordion. 'Oh my God! I did it. This is so cool.'

'Yes.' He beamed at her excitement.

She tried again, and they'd almost got through the whole song when the classroom door flew open, Fergus sprung back, and they both shrieked at the sight of two cops standing in the doorway.

'What the hell is going on in here?' demanded Sergeant Skinner, who Ferg remembered from their interactions regarding Mrs Lord. Beside Skinner stood the young female constable—Morris, if Ferg recalled correctly—and both of them looked half-asleep as if they'd been yanked from bed for this. *Shit*.

Thank God he hadn't succumbed to the impulse to kiss Tabitha because their track record of pulling back wasn't that great. He shuddered to think what the local constabulary might have encountered.

Pulling himself together, Ferg strode across to offer Skinner his hand as if this type of thing happened all the time. 'Evening, sergeant, constable. I've just been teaching Tabitha to play the accordion.'

'Really?' Skinner's monotone voice and the way his bushy grey eyebrows almost met his hairline said he didn't quite buy this story. 'Bit late for a music lesson, isn't it?'

And really, what could Ferg say to that?

'We got a call from Mrs Rodgers next door,' Skinner continued, 'saying she'd heard unusual noises coming from a classroom.'

'I'd hardly call the accordion unusual; rare maybe, but …' Ferg's voice drifted off at the expression on the old sergeant's face. Constable Morris looked to be stifling a smile, but her superior was clearly *not* amused.

Tab, accordion still attached to her—how was that for evidence?—came across to join them. 'I'm sorry, sergeant,' she said, flashing him a smile. Surely no man could resist that. 'Don't be angry at Fergus, this is entirely my fault. I practically forced him to bring me here.'

'Is that right?' He turned to look at Ferg, although he still didn't sound convinced.

Fergus wanted to argue the point as it didn't feel very gentlemanlike to let Tab take the blame, but as he opened his mouth, Skinner shook his head and continued. 'I can't believe I left my warm bed for this.' He let out a heavy sigh and then tried to cover a yawn with his hand. 'If you two insist in continuing these late-night music lessons, can I suggest you do it in Rose Hill where you won't disturb the neighbours?'

'Yes.' Tab nodded, a solemn expression on her face, despite the twinkle in her eyes. 'I promise we'll do that, won't we, Ferg?'

'Yes, so sorry to have ruined your evening. It won't happen again.'

'We'd better go next door and tell Mrs Rodgers it was a false alarm,' Skinner grumbled, already starting towards the door.

Constable Morris leaned in close to Tabitha, 'Go Tab, you dark horse,' before hurrying after her boss.

Tab exploded into laughter. 'Oh my God.'

Ferg himself wasn't sure whether to laugh or cry. What would Joanne say when she heard about this? He didn't think he'd technically done anything wrong, but still. Either way, music lessons were over for tonight and they both needed to head home and get some sleep.

'Thanks for a fun night,' she said as they stood beside their cars to say goodnight.

'No, thank you,' he said, then brushed his mouth quickly against hers. Despite the embarrassing way it had ended, he had to concede it had been a very fun night indeed. 'Drive safely home. And say goodnight to Eliza for me.'

Chapter Twenty-three

By the following morning everyone in town had heard about Tabitha and Fergus's late night shenanigans in his classroom, and as the story passed from person to person it flourished and bloomed. By the time Tab arrived at Stitch'n'Bitch, she had some serious explaining to do. Having already fielded phone calls from Meg and some of her other friends, she'd contemplated giving knitting circle a miss this week—especially since she had a B&B guest arriving later—but a no-show would likely only make things worse.

'Afternoon, Tabitha,' sang those women already there when she arrived. The blessing was there was only a skeleton crew at knitting as half the usuals were busy with show business.

'What's this I hear about you and the teacher being caught late last night at the school?' Eileen demanded. 'Are you two an item now?'

'I hear they were having *sex* on his desk,' Adeline said with clear repulsion, or was it envy? 'Sergeant Skinner should have arrested them!'

Oh my God. Part of Tab wanted to tell them it was true for shock value, but she didn't want Fergus to get in to trouble.

'And a lovely afternoon to all of you,' Tabitha said as she sat down in one of the chairs and pulled her knitting from its bag. 'Not that it's any of anyone's business, but Fergus is teaching me to play his accordion and we simply lost track of time. We're sorry to have disturbed the police, but I'm afraid it isn't anything more exciting than that. We're friends and share a passion for music, that's all. If there *was* something going on between us, we certainly wouldn't conduct it at the school.'

Tab refused to meet Meg's gaze as she delivered this little speech, because against her better judgement, she'd admitted to her sister-in-law earlier on the phone that she and Fergus may have slept with each other once or twice. Meg had gone crazy on the other end of the line and Lawson had come running from the other end of the house wanting to know what on earth was going on. So much for keeping things secret. At least she trusted them not to tell anyone.

They'd been so excited about the idea of a romance for Tabitha that she'd had to set them straight, tell them it was just a fling.

'Are you sure you know what you're doing?' Meg had asked.

They were worried about her heart, about her feelings … *yadda yadda yadda*. She appreciated their concern, really she did, but it was her heart and therefore hers to risk. Tab was having far too much fun with Fergus to worry about how she might feel when he left. As long as she kept reminding herself that this was simply an affair, she'd be fine. At least his departure wasn't going to be a surprise—not like Ryder's rejection. And, once Ferg had left, she'd have her pregnancy and the upcoming birth to focus on. Once she'd had the baby, she wouldn't have time to pine after him.

'Yes,' she'd reassured Meg and her brother, 'I'm a big girl. I know what I'm doing, and weren't you the one who told me to have a little fun?' Before Meg could answer, Tab added, 'Seriously, you don't need to worry about me.'

They had their own problems to worry about.

'How can you play the accordion with only one arm?' asked Eileen Bennett, her brow creasing even more than normal.

It got so tiring having to explain to people how she used her arm, but in this case Tab was happy for the change of focus. She admitted that she wasn't able to play it completely by herself, but that she'd managed the bellows and the keys and Fergus had operated the buttons.

'I've always loved the piano accordion,' Kathy mused with a smile. 'My grandfather used to play it. They're extremely underrated.'

'I couldn't agree more,' Tabitha said, starting to knit. 'Did your grandfather have an accordion? Is it still in your family?'

A few moments later Tab breathed a sigh of relief as the conversation continued around special instruments that had been handed down in families through generations. It appeared most of the knitting circle had bought Tabitha's story that she and Fergus were not together and she was happy to have the heat off her once again.

But later, when everyone was packing up the chairs, Adeline sidled over to her and whispered, 'I know you can do a lot with one arm, Tabitha, but I'm not as stupid as this lot. You need *two* hands to play the accordion.'

'Is that right?' Tab replied, refusing to take Adeline's bait.

'Yes. Personally I'd never go out with a school teacher. They get paid a pittance, and most men that teach only do it because they didn't get the grades to do anything better. But I guess you take what you can get.'

Tab glared at the other woman. Her instinct was to retort, *I don't see you getting anything at all*, but she swallowed it. She was furious at her insinuation about Fergus—he was *way* too good for her—but beneath the anger was pity. Adeline was such a sad, sour person, there was no way she could be happy. '*What* is your problem?'

Adeline blinked and shook her head in clear irritation. 'What do you mean?'

'Why are you so horrible to everyone? You're a beautiful woman, Adeline, and you've got a lot going for you, but the way you treat people is awful. Perhaps stop worrying about what me and Meg and other women are doing and start looking at yourself! If you're not happy here, then do something about it, but stop taking your disappointment out on the people around you.'

With that, Tab turned and stormed out of the hall. She'd had enough of people for one day. The only person she really wanted to see right now was Fergus. She couldn't help worrying about what kind of day he'd had—no doubt he'd been cross-examined by his colleagues at school, or worse, the parents.

The kids were pouring out of school as she drove out of town and every bone in her body wanted to pull into the car park and go check on him, but being seen together wouldn't help the rumours any and also she had a guest arriving soon. Tab didn't want to make a habit of leaving her guests waiting or their current good rating on TripAdvisor would plummet. So she resisted the urge to see him and settled on a quick text when she got home.

Hey there—hope your day wasn't too stressful. I got interrogated at Stitch'n'Bitch by Adeline but I think everyone else bought the story that we're just friends.

Stitch'n'Bitch? Came his almost immediate reply.

She smiled down at the screen. *I'll explain later. Will I see you tonight?*

A debrief after last night would do them good but they were going to have to be a little more cloak and dagger about their liaisons now that the town had reason to be suspicious.

I'd like that. Your place or mine?'

Tab contemplated a moment, trying to work out which would be safer.

I've got a guest arriving soon, but as long as I'm home by morning, I could come to you. Saying that, my van is more recognisable than your car, so maybe you should come to me?

Good plan. I'll go home, feed Mrs Norris and then come under the cover of darkness.

See you then.

She was just putting her phone on charge when the bell rang at the front of the tea rooms.

'Coming!' Tab grabbed the B&B key from the hook and hurried to greet her guest.

Moments later, she opened the door to reveal a very tall and pretty woman. She had the body of a supermodel but her face was far more natural and friendly than most supermodels Tab knew of.

'Hi.' The woman offered her a warm, wide smile and glanced briefly at her little arm, before snapping her head back to Tab's face. 'I'm Julia. Hope I'm in the right place. I called yesterday to make a booking.'

'Yes, welcome to Rose Hill. I'll show you through to your room.' As they walked next door, Tab said, 'So what brings you to the area?'

The woman hesitated a moment. 'I've come down to hopefully talk to someone.'

'Oh?' As Tab was the lone resident in Rose Hill, Julia must be after someone in Walsh or one of the other nearby towns.

Julia frowned as they stopped in front of the B&B building. 'Do you know many people in Walsh?'

Tab slipped the key in the lock and pushed open the door. 'Yeah,' she said warily as they ventured inside. There was suddenly something about this woman that made her uneasy. She'd said she was 'hoping' to talk to someone, which sounded like they weren't expecting her or might not want to chat at all. 'I'm from Walsh. I've only lived here a few months.'

'Great.' The woman's face lit up. 'My friend is a teacher and he transferred down here not long ago. His name's Fergus McWilliams. Do you know him? I'm not sure I should just turn up at the school, but I seem to have misplaced his forwarding address.'

Tab's stomach twisted into the kind of knot only an expert could make. There was something fishy about that story. Who *was* this woman and what did she want with Ferg? Why hadn't she called ahead to notify of her visit? Obviously whoever she was, she didn't know much about living in a town the size of Walsh, or she'd realise that when a new, sexy, single teacher arrived, everyone knew about it. But Tab wasn't about to hand over his address to a stranger.

Could this be his estranged sister? She disregarded this possibility almost immediately—he and his sister were twins and this woman was his opposite in almost every way. She had pale skin, pale hair, an almost Scandinavian look compared to Ferg's more Mediterranean one. A clammy heat washed over Tab's skin— perhaps it was his ex? Mrs Norris's owner? The woman who'd ditched Fergus for someone else? Maybe she'd changed her mind and wanted to get back together!

'I've met him,' she said after a long period of hesitation. 'We actually coach the junior cricket team together.'

'Do you know where he lives? It's really important I talk to him.'

'Who are you?' Tab asked, deciding on the straightforward approach. 'If you're friends, don't you have his phone number?'

Julia's eyes dropped to floor, but not before Tab saw sadness flash across them. 'We used to be together. Things ended a little messily, but it's paramount that I talk to him. It's about his sister. She's sick.'

The relief Tab felt that Julia wasn't here to try to win Ferg back was short-lived, replaced by a sudden tightness in her gut. 'What kind of sick?'

Julia rubbed her lips together. 'I'd really rather talk to him about this.'

'Okay,' Tab said. Annoyed at her tone, she marched briskly into the bedroom. 'This is your room, bathroom's in there and there's a communal kitchen with tea- and coffee-making facilities. If it gets too hot you can open the window, but the fan above the bed works really well.' She started her spiel about breakfast, but Julia interrupted.

'Thanks. Looks perfect. I'm not a big breakfast person, and if I manage to talk to Fergus tonight then I might not even stay, so don't worry about feeding me. I'm just going to have a shower and then head into Walsh. Do you know where he lives?'

'I think he's staying on a farm somewhere,' Tab said, before making a hasty retreat back to her place to grab her phone.

Fergus answered after the second ring. It sounded like he was in his car. 'Well, hello there. Couldn't wait till tonight to hear my voice?'

'What's your ex-girlfriend's name?'

'What? Why do you want to know that?'

'Because I think she's here. Someone called Julia Loder just booked into the B&B and said she's come to talk to you.'

'Fuck. What the hell is she playing at?'

Tab guessed that confirmed it. What on earth did he see in *her* when the last woman he'd been with had practically been a supermodel? 'I didn't tell her where you live but she's heading into town soon. I don't need to tell you that someone will tell her.'

Ferg swore again. 'Sorry, I don't mean to take this out on you, but I transferred down here to get away from them. You know how I said Jools left me for someone else?'

'Yes.'

'She left me for Eider, my sister. Two months before our wedding they came to me and told me they were sorry but they were in love.'

Tab gasped. 'Oh my God. I'm—'

'Don't say you're sorry. I don't need your pity,' Ferg growled. 'But I also don't need *this*. Ever since I've been down here they've been trying to call me, send letters; they just won't get the message that I don't want them in my life anymore.'

She thought of what Julia had said about Eider being sick. It had to be pretty serious for her to have gone to all this effort. 'Maybe you should talk to her. It doesn't sound like she's going to leave you alone until you do.'

'Don't worry, I've just turned around. I'll be there as soon as I can. I hate to drag you into this, but do you think you could tell Jools to stay there? The sooner I have this out with her, the sooner she can leave again.'

'Of course. Drive safely.'

After disconnecting the call, Tab took a moment to let everything he'd said sink in. Her heart went out to him. Being cheated on and having a broken engagement was bad enough, but she could only imagine the betrayal he must have felt losing his fiancée to his sister. No wonder it hurt him too much to talk about her.

Feeling very overprotective towards him, she went back next door, hoping she'd be able to deliver the message without unleashing the anger she suddenly felt towards this woman.

'Did you forget something?' Julia asked, her tone friendly enough but a little distracted when she answered Tab's knock a few moments later. She had a fresh face of make-up and a new outfit of capri jeans and a pink floral top, making her look even more glamorous than she had before. 'I was just heading into Walsh.'

'I just spoke to Fergus,' Tab said, unable to keep the coolness out of her voice. 'I told him you were here and he's on his way to speak to you.'

'Really?' Julia's eyes widened. 'Wow. Thanks.' She laughed nervously. 'That was easier than I thought. How long will it take him to get here?'

'Not long.' Tab wondered if she should offer to make them some tea, cut a few slices of the banana bread she'd baked that morning, but decided it was better to make herself scarce instead. 'Let me know if you need anything.' This was a weird situation because although her loyalties lay firmly with Ferg, Julia was her guest.

'Thanks, I will.'

Tab retreated back to her place, then paced the building until, about ten minutes later, she heard Fergus's car pull up outside.

Should she go out and meet him? Or let him go straight over to the B&B?

The car door slammed and before she could decide on her next move, she heard raised voices outside. Part of her desperately wanted to listen, but if she crept up close to the windows they'd see her, and besides, eavesdropping simply didn't sit right with her. If Fergus wanted to tell her later, he would.

Chapter Twenty-four

Jools emerged from the B&B before Ferg had even climbed out of his car. Once upon a time the sight of her took his breath away, now it only made his blood boil.

'Can't you take a hint?' he shouted as he stormed towards her.

'Please!' She held up her hands. 'This is important. Hear me out.'

'I already heard you both out two months ago, but maybe you didn't hear me,' he said, getting right up close in her space. He couldn't help but notice her eyes were a little bloodshot and had bags under them, as if she hadn't slept well in weeks. 'I don't want anything to do with either of you ever again. I thought moving here would make that even clearer to you, but—'

'Eider has breast cancer, Fergus! I'm sorry we hurt you. I wish like hell there was another way, but not everything is about you. The woman I love is sick and—'

Fergus recoiled, his chest deflating like a balloon. 'Is this some kind of joke? A trick to get me to talk to you guys?' Eider was too young to have breast cancer!

'Surely you know me better than to believe this is something I would ever joke about.'

He shook his head, unable to believe this. It was a warm spring afternoon, but he felt a chill on his skin. 'How long?'

Jools' shoulders sagged. 'We found out at the end of September, not long after ... She tried to call you, but you didn't return her calls. You made it clear you didn't want to talk to her. Did you even open the letter she sent you? She's heartbroken, Fergus. She misses you so much and she's scared and the treatment is awful, and it's breaking my heart. I'm supporting her as best I can but she needs *you*.'

So that's why Jools and Eider had been trying to get in contact with him. And here he was thinking they felt guilty about what they'd done!

'Is she going to die?'

Jools visibly flinched. 'Hopefully not. The doctor is fairly confident they caught the lump in time, but she's scared. She needs you. She needs her brother's support.'

Thank God. He wasn't sure what he'd have done if she'd said Eider's condition was terminal. 'Maybe she should have thought about that before she stole the woman I was about to marry.'

'She didn't *steal* me. Neither of us planned this, it just happened. I loved you as best I could, Fergus, but I didn't feel like myself until I let myself feel for Eider. If I'm honest, I've always been attracted to women, but due to my family upbringing I guess I tried to repress my true sexuality. But with Eider—'

He snorted. 'I don't need to hear all this again. Once was more than enough. I'm glad you've sorted your feelings now, I just wish I never got caught up in the process.'

'I'm sorry,' Jools said, her lower lip wobbling. 'But don't take your anger at me out on Eider. You two are too close to let that happen.'

He knew that look—she was close to tears. Maybe she thought if she turned on the waterworks, his anger would melt away and he'd feel bad enough to forgive them.

'Correction, we *were* close, but Eider can't have her cake and eat it too. She's got you. I'm sure you'll support her through her illness. But please don't waste your time, or mine, trying to contact me again.'

And with that, he strode back to his car, climbed inside and sped off down the road out of Rose Hill. As he headed towards Walsh, his breath came in short fast bursts; he felt like he was having a bloody heart attack. The thought of Tab back there, of her likely having overheard that excruciating conversation with Jools, made him feel sick. Despite being teased a little in the staffroom about being caught with Tab last night and the few raised eyebrows he'd got from parents, he'd had a great day at school and had been looking forward to seeing her that evening. But right now he needed to calm the hell down and get his head straight before he spoke to anyone again.

He didn't want to take his anger out on Tab, so he'd take it out on a few beers instead. Thankfully, the attendant at the drive-in bottle shop was a gangly, pimply guy he hadn't met before, who looked barely legal to serve and didn't try to engage him in any conversation, so Ferg bought a six-pack and headed back to the farm.

As he drove down Mrs Lord's long gravel driveway, Ethan rode past on a quad bike in one of the paddocks and waved; Fergus forced himself to lift his own hand in reply and noticed it was shaking. Damn Jools. And damn Eider. Just when he'd been starting to really get used to life without them, they'd gone and dropped this bombshell.

He wouldn't wish cancer on his worst enemy and he hoped Eider did recover, but he couldn't be a part of that process. Watching her and Jools together hurt too damn much.

* * *

The shouting stopped as quickly as it had begun, and a few moments later, Tab heard Ferg's car tear off down the road. She winced as brakes screeched at the corner near the roadhouse and then silence descended on Rose Hill once again. But it didn't feel like the peaceful quiet that usually surrounded her.

And where on earth was he going? Although he hadn't planned to come over until later in the evening, she'd assumed that now he was here, he'd stay. Maybe he was going home to feed Mrs Norris first, or maybe he simply didn't want Julia to see him here, to know there was something going on between them. This squeezed her heart more than it should, but she pushed the feeling aside—this wasn't about her.

Should she ask her guest to leave? Fergus might not return if he thought she was still there and Tab very much wanted him to return. Or should she go after *him* instead?

She was still deliberating when the bell on the door downstairs echoed through the old building. Tab froze a moment, wondering what Ferg's ex might want with her, and then jolted to action, hurrying down the stairs and to the front door.

'Hi,' she said when she peeled it back and tried not to recoil at the sight of her guest. Supermodel was no longer a term that came to mind. Her make-up was smudged around her eyes and her nose was running. When she spoke it sounded like she might start crying again at any moment.

'I'm really sorry, but I'm going to head back to Perth. I've done what I came for and …' Her voice trailed off, then she thrust the guest key at Tab. 'Anyway, thanks for your hospitality. I'm still happy to pay for the night and I'm sorry for any inconvenience I've caused you.'

'It's okay,' Tab said, not sure what to feel for this clearly broken woman as she took back the key. She knew Julia had hurt Fergus beyond repair, but if the shouting had been anything to go by, he'd clearly attempted to give as good as he got.

Julia turned to go but then hesitated. 'Do you know Fergus well?' she asked.

Tab swallowed—it was a difficult question for someone terrible at lying.

'Not really,' she said eventually. In a few short weeks, she'd grown to care about him and come to know his body like the back of her hand, but she wasn't delusional enough to think she really *knew* him. She'd known he was estranged from his sister and that he had a broken engagement but she didn't know any of the crucial details; he hadn't trusted her enough to ever properly open up. 'We've hung out a bit because we coach cricket together but—'

That seemed to be enough for Julia. 'Do you think you could try and talk to him for me? I thought telling him about Eider's cancer in person would—'

'His sister has cancer?' Tab interrupted. Of course it made sense—it was the most common serious illness and touched such a large portion of the population—but it also made this feel more personal. She'd been there herself and her family had been her lifeline while she was going through treatment and surgery and then recovering from the loss of her arm. Without Lawson, Dad and Granny, she reckoned she'd have fallen into a deep black hole during that time, and who knows if she'd have managed to climb out?

'Yes. And I can't believe Fergus won't talk to her.' Julia sniffed again and this time a tear snuck down her cheek; she absentmindedly swiped it with the back of her hand. 'He never used to be so cold. I know inside his heart he cares, we just hurt him so bad and I feel so responsible and so helpless. Eider needs him right now more than she's ever needed him in her life, and considering all they went through as kids, that's saying a lot. But I don't know what else I can say, or do, to make him see sense. Maybe you'll have better luck?'

Tab wasn't sure that was the case or that it was her place to meddle in Fergus's business, but at Julia's desperate tone and the pleading expression on her face, she agreed to at least try. She was also doing it for him—if he didn't go and see his sister and she lost her battle with cancer, he'd have to live with guilt and remorse for the rest of his life. How could he ever recover from that?

'Thank you,' Julia gushed, surprising Tab as she threw her arms around her. 'Can I give you my mobile number so you can let me know how you go?'

'Sure.' Tab went into the building and returned a few moments later with her phone.

Julia tapped her details into Tabitha's mobile and thanked her again but didn't dilly-dally any longer—she was eager to get back to Eider.

Once Tab was alone again, she stared at her phone, suddenly doubting what she'd just agreed to. But whether or not she followed through on her promise to Julia, she wanted to check on Fergus.

You okay? She shot off a quick text, then went to double-check that Julia had locked up the B&B properly—not that it would really matter; thanks to the population of zero (only more if you included the ghosts), the crime rate here was non-existent.

When Fergus hadn't responded five minutes later, Tab didn't know whether to be annoyed or worried. He'd driven off angry and that was dangerous, but as an ambulance volunteer she would hear if there'd been an accident. The sad, more likely truth, was that he wasn't in the mood to talk to her. It was his right to shut her out—he didn't owe her any kind of explanation—but she'd never been good at letting things lie, so when he still hadn't messaged or reappeared a couple of hours later, she grabbed a tub of choc-coconut ice-cream and climbed into the van. She kept thinking of the pain and anguish in Julia's eyes, remembering her own battle with cancer and imagining how devastated she'd be if Lawson was gravely ill.

It was dark by the time she slowed her van in front of the cottage and the absence of lights on inside made her uneasy, but his car was parked in the carport, so he had to be here.

'What are you doing here?' came his slurred voice from the shadows on the porch as she climbed out of her van. She hadn't seen him sitting in the rocking chair but she heard the creaks as he rocked back and forth. Was he drunk?

'I got sick of waiting for you to come to my place. Did you forget we had an arrangment? I was hoping to learn a few more keys on the accordion.'

'You should go home. I'm not good company tonight.'

Okay, so he wasn't in the mood for their usual banter, but if he thought she was that easy to push away, he had another thing coming.

'You weren't good company when we first met either, but I haven't let that scare me off,' she said, marching up the stairs and dumping her bag and the ice-cream by the door before going over to him to assess the damage. Thanks to the moonlight, she could see four empty beer bottles at his feet. He'd obviously chosen to retreat into the bottle over her and that pricked a little, but she wanted to support him through this. 'You had anything to eat with these?'

'Stop fussing,' he groaned, reaching out and tugging her hand so she fell onto his lap. 'Hello.' He grinned a silly, sad smile and her stomach flipped over. Even drunk and with beer-scented breath, this man did terrible, *wonderful* things to her insides.

'Hi.' She smiled resignedly back at him as she cupped his cheek with her hand. 'Do you want to talk about this afternoon? Julia's gone now, but she told me why she came.'

Darkness fell across his face like a thunderstorm sweeping across the sky. 'No. I don't want to talk about her. Or *them*. I don't even want to *think* about them.'

Tab managed to hold back a sigh as her chest tightened. Why were men so damn infuriating? Why would they rather drink their feelings away than discuss them?

'Besides,' Fergus leaned close to her ear, 'I can think of better things to do with our time than talk.'

Before she could respond, his hand snuck up to cup her breast and she sucked in a breath as he squeezed it, a little rougher than usual but still in a way that set her on fire. A way that made it almost impossible to think. She moaned as his finger circled her nipple through her bra—this was *not* what she'd come here to do but her objection hadn't even made it out of her mouth before he smothered it with his.

With his tongue in her mouth, his hand moved lower, sliding—*ooh*—inside the waistband of her jeans. She squirmed in his lap as she lost herself to the sensations already rippling through her.

'Man, you are so hot. So gorgeous,' he breathed as he worked his finger at her core. She was shuddering on top of him in seconds, her head flopping back as he sucked her nipple through her bra as she came. There were no words necessary; within moments, they were both naked from the waist down.

Tab climbed back on top of him, and yelped, gripping the back of the rocking chair as he thrust up into her. *Oh. My. God.* Maybe Ferg wasn't that drunk after all as his performance wasn't substandard in the least. It was definitely different though—he wasn't as tender as usual. He kissed her hard as he pumped into her and she felt his hands almost digging into her backside. His fervour only made her more aroused and she came harder than she'd ever come before.

'There now,' he whispered into her ear as she flopped against his heaving chest, 'wasn't that better than talking?'

With the aftershocks still pulsing through her body she had to agree, but she felt frustrated at herself for letting him distract her so easily. Although perhaps now she'd put him in a better mood it would be easier to have the conversation she needed to have with him.

'Oh shit, the ice-cream' she said, suddenly remembering it sitting by the front door. And it was a warm night so if they didn't eat it or put it in the freezer, it would melt.

Ferg grinned. 'What flavour did you bring?'

'Why don't we go inside and you can find out for yourself?' She stood, yanked up her jeans, then walked over to rescue the ice-cream. Ferg followed her into the house and into the kitchen, where she put it in the freezer. 'Do you mind if I just freshen up?' she asked.

'Sure. Do you want something more to eat than ice-cream? I could make you a cheese toastie.'

'Your culinary skills astound me,' Tab replied with a smile, 'but that sounds wonderful.' In all the drama of the afternoon, she'd only managed to scoff a couple of biscuits, so a toasted sandwich would fill the hole in her stomach nicely. And while they ate, they could talk.

Tab returned to the kitchen a few minutes later to find Ferg sucking on another bottle of beer, a plate full of toasted sandwich triangles on the bench. 'What can I get you to drink?' he asked.

'Just a glass of water will be fine.'

He filled a glass from the tap at the kitchen sink and then handed it to her. 'Thanks,' she said, wondering if she was imagining the awkwardness in the air that felt as if something had shifted between them. She took a long sip, then, 'Where should we eat?'

'In front of the TV?'

She nodded, but the problem with this scenario was that talking seriously with an old episode of *Seinfeld* on in the background was almost impossible.

Or maybe Tab was just chickening out. She wanted *him* to raise the issue of what had happened with Jools this arvo first, but he was clearly trying to pretend it never did. After two sandwiches and ten minutes of casual commentary about what was happening on the screen in front of them, she tried for an equally casual, 'So, how long were you and Jools together?'

She felt Ferg's body tense beside her, but he took a gulp of his beer and then said, 'Just under two years. You'd think she might have realised she was in love with my sister sooner, since she met her almost as soon as we started going out.'

His voice dripped with hostility and Tab didn't blame him, but she knew that holding on to such feelings would slowly destroy him, eating him up from the inside, and that was even without the added complication of his sister's illness.

'How'd you meet?'

'At a friend's fancy dress birthday party—Jools was the sister of one of my colleagues. We both were single at the time and we both arrived dressed as characters from *Harry Potter*. We hit it off, or so I thought.' There was that bitterness again. 'Eider and I were living together, we had been ever since we stopped being wards of the state, and so she and Jools ended up spending a fair bit of time together. I loved that they got on so well because I couldn't imagine ever having anything serious or long term with someone my sister didn't approve of. We'd always been very protective of each other—in my mind, no girl was good enough for her—but I stupidly had no idea that Jools was that way inclined as well.'

He downed the last of his beer. 'Do you mind if I have another one of these? It feels wrong drinking when you can't, but …'

But he was drowning his sorrows, Tab finished Ferg's sentence in her head when his voice drifted off. She didn't think that was the best way, but maybe if he was relaxed from the beer, he'd keep talking. 'It's fine. Can you get me another glass of water?'

He nodded, left the room and returned with both drinks, her tub of ice-cream and two spoons. 'I just remembered about this.' His eyes sparkled as he passed her the water, then he put everything down on the coffee table and flopped back into the couch.

'What did you say Eider did?' Tab ventured as Fergus peeled back the lid of the ice-cream. She remembered perfectly him telling her that his sister was a social worker, but simply wanted a way to start the conversation.

'Do you mind if we talk about something else?' He asked, staring down into the tub of ice-cream. 'I'd really rather we forgot about this arvo.'

You can't just forget about your sister was what Tab *wanted* to say, but at the warning look in his eyes, she nodded instead and forced a smile. 'Sure.' Perhaps it would be better to let him cool down a bit first.

They ate the ice-cream together, occasionally feeding the other, and Ferg deserted the last beer as he finished off almost the entire tub instead. 'I thought your avocado and coconut ice-cream was pretty good, but this is amazing. *You* are amazing.'

She couldn't help but glow at his words. 'Thanks.' But it was getting late and she was tired. The long, energetic nights of the last couple of weeks were finally catching up with her and maybe the emotion of the day also had something to do with it. She stifled a yawn, then glanced at her watch. 'Perhaps you can bring your accordion over tomorrow night after cricket and I'll let you try a new flavour I've been experimenting with.'

Perhaps then she'd be able to keep her promise to Jools.

Tab stood. 'I'm gunna call it a night. See you tomorrow.'

But as she leaned down to kiss his forehead, he reached out to take her hand and whispered, 'Stay.'

'I'm tired,' she replied, her exhaustion finally ruling over her libido.

'I know.' His grip tightened. 'That's why you shouldn't have to drive home. Stay with me. I promise I'll be on my best behaviour and let you sleep.'

Tab couldn't believe what he was suggesting. While part of her longed to accept—and not just the part of her that wanted to collapse into a comfy bed and sleep for a week—would it be something he'd offer if he was stone cold sober?

'Aren't you always the one telling me not to think so hard?' he said, looking up at her. 'Come on, let's go to bed.'

And, despite the warning voice inside her head, Tab wasn't woman enough to resist those words uttered in his sexy drawl, so she let Ferg lead her into his bedroom.

Two hours later, having used a new toothbrush he hadn't yet opened and borrowed a T-shirt and boxer shorts, she was lying in *his* clothes, in *his* bed staring at the ceiling while he snored softly beside her. As promised, he'd been on his best behaviour and hadn't tried anything. Instead, he'd pulled her into his side after switching off his bedside light and they'd snuggled together, his arms around her, her head resting on his shoulder, and it was the most comfortable she'd ever been in her life.

They didn't talk and within minutes he'd drifted off to sleep, but this sleeping in someone's arms was something she could definitely get used to. The warmth of his body against hers, the sound of his breathing, the musky smell of his skin that tickled her nostrils, she'd never felt so intimate with someone in her life.

It was maybe even better than sex.

Which wasn't good.

This wasn't something she could allow herself to get used to. Or was it? Fergus wasn't *that* drunk, she was certain. Someone completely plastered would not have been able to do the things he'd done to her out on the verandah. A pleasurable heat pulsed through her at the thought. Could she dare to hope that maybe this wasn't a one-off? That maybe the boundaries they'd put in place were starting to crumble?

She understood he'd been hurting when he arrived in Walsh and that he'd be wary of rushing into another relationship after what had happened with his fiancée and his sister, but sometimes things happened when you least expected them. Things so powerful that in the end it was futile to try to fight them. That's what this thing between her and Fergus felt like. It felt too damn powerful, too damn right for it to be over in a matter of weeks.

The thought of not seeing him again after the end of the term left her feeling utterly cold and bereft. She could no longer lie to herself that she didn't want more from him. From *them*.

But maybe, just maybe, Fergus asking her to stay meant that he felt the same. Even if he wasn't quite ready to admit it yet, he'd wanted her to be here with him tonight when he was feeling vulnerable. He may not have been ready to talk about his sister and his ex-fiancée and all the hurt inside him, but he'd wanted Tab to be with him.

That thought gave her a hope she hadn't dared harbour before, a hope that maybe they could break the terms of their fling and extend them indefinitely. And he was such a good teacher, that he'd clearly be an amazing dad—she didn't just want him for herself, she wanted him for her baby too.

Her imagination running away with her, Tab closed her eyes and finally fell asleep with images of Fergus and their baby filling her head.

Chapter Twenty-five

The next morning Ferg woke with Tabitha lying peacefully beside him. Still a little sleepy, he instinctively shuffled closer and put his arm over her. The T-shirt he'd loaned her had crept up and as his fingers touched her bare skin, his erection grew harder. She whimpered in her sleep and he smiled.

The morning sun sneaking in through the gap in the curtains fell across her face, highlighting her long dark eyelashes and the soft flush of her cheeks. She was gorgeous, and being this close to her made him hot as hell. He glanced at the alarm clock. As there was still a while before he needed to get up and go to work, Ferg was contemplating waking Tab up in the most delightful way when his hand registered the gentle curve of her stomach and he froze.

Reality crashed down upon him.

Tab was pregnant with some random stranger's child and *this* wasn't part of their deal. Why was she still here?

Suddenly the events of the previous afternoon came flooding back and, at the thought of Jools' visit, Ferg's good mood evaporated. He remembered fleeing in anger from Rose Hill and Tabitha coming over to check on him. He remembered how what they'd done on the verandah had lifted his mood in a way six beers in quick succession hadn't. He remembered how he hadn't wanted her to leave.

Although he did worry about her heading home late at night tired, asking her to stay had been as much about his needs as it was about her safety. The last couple of weeks sneaking around with Tab had made him feel happier than he'd been in months. They'd had a lot of fun together and she'd helped him forget his pain, but now he realised just how dangerous that could be.

The lines were blurring. Sex was now only part of what they shared; there was also companionship. They were getting to know each other better, coming to rely on each other, and that wasn't good. He couldn't afford to get emotionally involved. For his sanity, but also for hers and her baby's.

'Good morning.'

Ferg jolted at the sound of Tab's voice.

She smiled drowsily up at him. 'Sorry, did I give you a fright?'

'I …' Half of him wanted to spring from the bed and run, but the other half wanted to push all rational thought out of his head and just *feel*. Feel her bare skin against his and her inner muscles clenching around him as he drove into her. Maybe instead of a conversation about her staying the night and how it couldn't mean anything, he should succumb to the urge.

The damage was done now anyway—she'd stayed the night. Perhaps sex would cover over any awkwardness and remind them exactly what they were about. From now on he'd be on guard, careful to not allow a repeat of last night. He'd go to her place instead of letting her come here and make sure that, like Cinderella, he always went home before midnight.

So, instead of finishing his sentence, he bent his head and kissed her. Within seconds Tabitha was as awake as him, her hand flying over his skin and her legs wrapping around him. When he slid into her, she was already wet and ready for him and they moved together as if they were born to do this. *No.* Fergus banished that thought as he thrust, harder and faster, till they were both flying over the edge.

'I better get ready for work,' he said, seconds after they finished. He could barely bring himself to look at her as he climbed out of bed. He was almost at the bedroom door when he forced himself to turn back. Offering Tabitha breakfast went against his better judgement, but he'd be a jerk if he didn't.

'I've got to get to school soon, but feel free to take your time and get yourself some toast or eggs or something.'

With that he hurried down the hallway, retreating into a hot shower for a few moments' reprieve from her intoxicating presence. Whenever he was in it, he couldn't think straight.

The smell of bacon cooking hit him a few moments later when he opened the bathroom door. He got a sense of déjà-vu but this time he knew who he'd find at the stove.

After throwing on classroom-suitable clothes, he ventured into the kitchen to find the table set for two and Tab singing softly, wearing his T-shirt, as she fried bacon and eggs. One of Mrs Lord's aprons over the top did nothing to hide her long, smooth, slender legs and despite the fact he'd just got his rocks off, desire rose within him once again.

Was his libido insatiable where she was concerned?

'Hello, sexy. You hungry?'

It was her last two words and the way they reminded him exactly what she was doing that calmed his raging need a little. Her standing in his kitchen half-naked and cooking, the morning after she'd spent the night, screamed relationship at him, but this was his fault. He'd been the one who'd practically begged her to stay so he couldn't take it out on her.

'I don't have long,' he said, glancing at his watch. 'I've got to get to school.'

'Don't forget I've seen you eat before. You don't *need* long. Now sit, this is almost ready.'

He did as he was told, while Tab piled scrambled eggs and bacon onto a plate. 'Sorry, no toast,' she said as she laid it in front of him. 'I guess we used up all your bread last night.'

'It's fine,' he said and then remembered his manners as he picked up his fork. 'Thanks.'

'You're welcome.' Tab brought her plate to the table. 'Isn't this nice?'

Nice? It was too damn cosy, that's what it was. Too much like a real relationship. How many times had he and Jools enjoyed breakfast together before heading off to work? The thought made his heart beat too fast so he let out some kind of semi-agreeable grunt.

Tab ate a few more mouthfuls before breaking the silence again. 'How are you feeling after yesterday?'

Guessing she wasn't referring to their energetic coupling on the front porch, his hand froze halfway to his mouth. 'Fine.'

Tab put down her fork. 'I know you're hurting, and I know your sister betrayed you, but is holding onto your anger really making you feel better?'

His fingers tightened around his cutlery. 'I don't know about *better* but I sure as hell know seeing Jools again didn't lift my spirits. And seeing them together again would definitely make me feel worse.'

'What if you try and forget about Jools for now? Forget about Jools and Eider together and think about your sister. Think about that relationship and how much it means to you—she's your flesh and blood. And she needs you.'

Her words were remarkably similar to his ex-girlfriend's. 'Jesus. Did Jools ask you to talk to me?'

She rubbed her lips together but didn't deny it. 'This isn't about Jools. This is about you. I care about you and it's clear you're hurting. Last night you almost drank yourself silly trying to avoid the pain.'

Ferg wasn't sure who he was angrier with—Tab for interfering in something that wasn't at all her business or Jools for once again meddling in his life, coming between him and happiness. If it wasn't bad enough she'd stolen Eider from him, now she was putting a dampener on the fun he and Tab had been having together.

'I *drank*,' he told her, 'because I was annoyed. I came down here to get away from them and she found me. I don't need her trying to manipulate me or making me feel guilty, when they're the ones in the wrong. Eider made her decision—she chose Jools over me and now Jools can take care of her while she's sick. Isn't that what true love is about?'

'Maybe, but you also can't help who you fall in love with. They're obviously devastated and terribly guilty about what they did, or they wouldn't care so much about your feelings or want you back in their lives. You have a chance here to do something good, to be the bigger person, rather than hold onto your anger and your fear.'

'My fear?' Ferg pushed back his chair. There was still food on his plate, but his appetite had evaporated alongside his desire to discuss this any longer. 'Don't you worry your pretty little head about my "fear", okay? You've got enough on your own plate without worrying about this and we're supposed to be about fun, remember? Don't forget our boundaries.'

'Boundaries?' Tab stared at him as if he were high. 'What exactly *are* our boundaries? It seems to me you shift them whenever they suit you. You're allowed to help me make baby furniture and paint my nursery, you're allowed to ask me to stay the night, but I'm not allowed to offer a little friendly advice?'

'You can offer but it doesn't mean I have to listen. And right now, I've got to get to school anyway.'

'She has cancer, for crying out loud,' Tab wailed. 'What if she dies? You'll regret it if you don't see her. Trust me as someone who's been—'

He cut her off, not needing to hear any more of her lecture. 'You don't get to tell me what I will or won't regret. How would you feel if Lawson betrayed you? What if it wasn't your arm that broke you and Ryder up, but him? Is that something you'd ever forgive?'

Tab opened her mouth, but he didn't wait for her answer. 'You can't know because, lucky for you, you haven't been in that situation. And anyway, Eider's not going to die. Didn't Jools tell you that bit? What's my relationship with my sister got to do with you anyway? You don't even know her!'

Sadness filled Tab's usually sunny face. 'But I know you. I care about you. I thought we were friends.'

He didn't hear past 'I care about you', which made his whole chest cramp. *No*, that wasn't what this was supposed to be about. He didn't want her to care about him and he certainly didn't want to care about her. He couldn't. Not only did he never again want his happiness to be dependent on someone else, but he couldn't risk Tabitha's baby's happiness on him.

'We're supposed to be having fun together, and this isn't fun,' he said through gritted teeth as he stood.

'You're right.' Her voice wavered and her pupils suddenly looked shiny as if she were close to tears. 'This is no longer fun. This is torture. I can't bear to see you so angry and upset because I've fallen in love with you.'

'What?' Caring was one thing, but love? He sucked in a breath. 'Don't say that. We haven't even known each other two months.'

'Time has no bearing on matters of the heart. From the moment I met you, there was something about you. You unbalanced me, you made me angry when the same words said by someone else would be water off a duck's back. And I may be stupid,' she said, 'but I'm also brave. I'm not going to shy away from the truth because deep down I think you feel it too. I think there's more between us than you want to admit. I know what Eider and Jools did to you was unforgiveable, but should you really let it ruin the rest of your life? Just because Jools betrayed you, doesn't mean all women would. It doesn't mean I would.'

She looked up at him with raw, pleading eyes and his heart shifted. This amazing woman was absolutely right—he did feel it too. If he was honest with himself, he felt things for her he'd never felt for anyone before, not even Jools, and he'd been about to marry her. He knew in his bones that Tabitha was as good and true as they came, and he wanted to believe they could be the real deal.

Perhaps if she wasn't pregnant he could allow himself to risk it. But she was. And he couldn't.

'I'm sorry, Tabitha,' he said, lingering in the doorway, his heart breaking as he uttered the words that would break hers. 'But even if I felt the same way you do, we could never be together, because I never plan to raise another man's child.'

And then, because he couldn't bear to witness her pain, he turned, left the house and headed off to work, telling himself as he drove into town that he'd done the right thing. They'd agreed to be honest and he had been.

Chapter Twenty-six

'What time do you call this?' Meg called from the kitchen as Tab entered the tea rooms. 'Did you and lover boy oversleep?'

'Sorry,' Tab called back, hoping her sister-in-law couldn't detect the anguish in her voice as she bypassed the kitchen and headed for the stairs. 'I'm just having a quick shower and then I'll be down.'

'Okay!'

Tab had cried non-stop on the way back to Rose Hill and had only just managed to halt her tears. Meg wasn't usually here this early, so Tab had hoped she'd have time to have a shower and pull herself together before she arrived, but just her luck today was the day Meg chose to buck the trend. Tab didn't want to face her sister-in-law until her puffy eyes had the chance to go down and her flushed cheeks had returned to a more normal colour.

In her current state, Meg would immediately know something was wrong and Tab wasn't ready to admit her stupidity. Because that's exactly what it was. What other word was there for thinking she could give her body so freely to someone and not put her heart on the line as well? She wasn't a man like Fergus, who was clearly able to keep body and heart two separate entities. He'd just been biding his time until he could move on again, having a bit of fun.

Well, as he'd said, the fun was well and truly over—no one was laughing now.

The times they'd shared—the sex, but also the other less carnal moments—had meant something to her, but she could have been anyone to him. He'd needed someone to scratch an itch and she'd pretty much thrown herself at him in much the same way she'd thrown the plate of food at him that very first day.

Many times he'd tried to pull away, to warn her, but she'd just kept on at him. Chasing him home in her car like some kind of desperado.

She cringed at the thought as she stripped naked and stepped into the shower. How had she ever thought that someone like him would ever feel anything real for someone like her? An image of Jools landed in her head. Once Ferg had recovered from the pain of that break-up, he could have any woman he wanted, and Tab hated how jealous that thought made her.

She wasn't usually a jealous person. She wasn't usually so many things that being around Fergus had caused her to be. As she closed her eyes and let the warm water cascade over her, she hoped it would wash away the memories, not only of today, but also of the last few weeks. However pleasurable they'd been, this morning had well and truly erased all of that.

Why on earth had she meddled in his business? She didn't owe anything to Jools. Maybe if she hadn't pushed him on the issue of his sister, they could have continued as they were until he'd left. Maybe she wouldn't have been so stupid as to blurt her feelings in the middle of a heated discussion.

Then again, maybe this had just brought forward the inevitable. Their feelings were never going to match, so no matter how great the sex had been, eventually this heartbreak would have been hers. At least this way she'd have longer to get over him before she met her baby, and that was a good thing because she didn't want her sadness to take away from her miracle.

With that thought, Tab switched off the water and forced herself to get dressed. She'd had a little cry—okay a big one—and now it was time to move on. Never one for much make-up, today when she looked in the mirror, she had to admit she needed some. After applying hopefully enough to make her look a little less like a lovesick cliché, she picked up her mobile to tie up a loose end.

As much as she wished she hadn't meddled, the least she could do was tell Jools she'd tried.

Hi Julia. I tried to talk to Fergus about Eider but it didn't work. I wish you both the best and maybe in time he'll come around. Really sorry, Tabitha.

That job ticked off her mental list, she went to face the day.

As she headed downstairs, she heard Meg singing loudly as she clattered about in the kitchen. It was that Justin Timberlake song from the movie *Trolls*, and although Tab was neither a fan of the singer nor the film, usually she liked it. Today, however, both the lyrics and the upbeat tune were about as far from her mood as anything could get.

Taking a deep breath, she turned the corner into the kitchen and spoke as chirpily as she possibly could. 'Morning. How's things?'

Meg froze, her hand midair as she poured flour into a big mixing bowl. On her face was the biggest smile Tab had ever seen and the second she registered it, she knew.

'Oh my God. You're pregnant!'

'How'd you know?' Meg dropped the bag of flour and it spilled all over the countertop as she laughed.

Tab squealed as she rushed over and threw her arms around her sister-in-law. 'This is the best news ever.'

'I know.' Meg was half-jumping, half-laughing, half-crying, and Tab joined in. At least now she'd have an excuse for looking like she was crying.

'When are you due?'

Meg pulled back and bit her lip. 'End of July, but oh my God, Lawson is going to kill me. He wanted us to tell you together. We haven't even told Ned yet.'

Tab forced a laugh. 'I promise I'll act surprised.'

'It's still early days,' Meg said, her tone slightly anxious now. 'I literally just got the positive result this morning. I'm barely even a month. I probably shouldn't be getting so excited just yet.'

'Don't be silly. Everything's going to be okay. I have a good feeling in my waters—this baby is meant to be.'

'Thanks, Tab.' Meg sniffed. 'Sometimes I have to pinch myself when I think about how good my life has got since coming to Rose Hill. After my family died, I honestly never thought I'd ever find any kind of happiness again. I thought I was locking myself here away from the world, but Lawson didn't let me do that. I still don't feel like I deserve his love, or yours and Ned's, but I'm so damn glad I've got it.'

'You do deserve it. Don't let me ever hear you say otherwise,' Tab said firmly. 'It wasn't only that Lawson rescued you, remember? You brought him back to life as well, you gave Ned a mother again and I got not only a sister but a best friend. We're the lucky ones.'

'Okay, okay, enough of this before we both turn into a sobbing mess, are useless to cook and don't have anything to serve for lunch tomorrow.'

'Hey, we've always got plenty of ice-cream.' Tab shrugged and tried to keep her voice light. She was seriously happy for Meg and Lawson but the part of her that secretly longed for a strong family unit herself felt positively green as well. Why couldn't *she* have love *and* a baby? Was that too much to ask?

Meg smiled as she started to clean up the flour mess. 'As good as your ice-cream is, not everyone wants it as their main meal. And don't think you've got off scot-free. I haven't forgotten about your night with hot stuff. While we cook I want to hear all the sordid details. Is this the first time you've stayed over?'

Tab hesitated, unsure how to answer this question. She didn't really want to rehash the last twenty-four hours, but she couldn't lie to Meg either. 'Actually things aren't ...'

Oh Lord, even before she realised what was happening, tears were streaming down her cheeks and her throat was filling with snot.

'Oh my goodness, Tabby.' Meg abandoned the flour once more and rushed to her side. 'What happened?'

'It's ... we're ... we had a ...' She couldn't manage to get the words out.

'It's alright,' Meg said, ushering her out of the kitchen and leading her to a chair in the tea rooms. 'Sit down and breathe.' Then she rushed to grab some serviettes in lieu of tissues. As she handed them to Tab, she muttered, 'What the hell has he done to you? Have you guys broken up?'

Tab scoffed—you couldn't break up when you weren't even together in the first place. Still, she was pretty sure there wouldn't be any more late night accordion lessons or anything else between them, but she couldn't say any of this through the hysterical crying.

'If he's hurt you, I swear I'll kill him.'

The ferocity in Meg's words only had Tabitha sobbing harder. She couldn't believe this was the second time in a matter of months someone had witnessed her crying over a man and she didn't like it. It made her feel vulnerable, like a failure.

'It's not his fault,' she said after a number of nose blows. 'He never led me to believe we could have anything long-term. I've been such an idiot.'

Somehow, she managed to tell Meg the whole story, from Jools' visit, to Eider's cancer, Fergus's bitter anger and Tab's attempt to soften him. She couldn't bring herself to mention what he'd said about the baby, because that made her feel conflicted in a way she didn't want to feel. She wanted to be angry at his blatant rejection of her child, his inability to even consider helping her raise it, but she was angrier at herself. She couldn't help wondering if things might have been different if she wasn't pregnant.

And *that* made her angry at him. How dare he make her question her decision! How dare he make her think anything but wonderful, glowing, excited thoughts about her baby.

'You did the right thing,' Meg said, rubbing her back as though she were a little child. 'I understand why he's upset but holding onto that kind of anger, living in the past like that, is toxic. And if Fergus can't see you're only trying to help, then that's his problem.'

'Then why do I feel so bad?'

Meg cocked her head to one side and gave Tab a stern look. 'Because you fell in love with him, didn't you?'

Tab nodded and hung her head. There was no point denying it. Meg wasn't the type to say 'I told you so' but it was written all over her face. 'What's even worse, though, is that I told him how I felt.'

She still couldn't believe she'd done that, but Fergus had a habit of making her do and say things she probably wouldn't if she had time to think them through. In this case, the words had been as much a surprise to her as they were to him. She hadn't realised they were the truth until they'd tumbled from her lips. Probably because now she'd felt it, she realised she'd never actually felt it before.

But the knowledge that you weren't going to have sex with someone again didn't make not only your heart contract, but every bone, muscle and nerve-ending in your body ache. Only love could wreck you so physically and emotionally at once. They say you can't choose who you fall in love with, but you can choose to be smart about it, you can choose to protect yourself, and Tab had done no such thing. She had no one to blame but herself.

'You should have seen the look of horror on his face. He couldn't leave the house fast enough!'

'Oh, Tabby.' Meg held her close again. 'There's no shame in telling someone you love them. And it's his loss; he's the idiot if he can't see how wonderful you are. There's no way he'll ever find anyone better.'

'Thank you.' Tab squeezed Meg's hand but there was nothing anyone could say that would make her feel better right now. Usually baking helped lift her spirits—today, she didn't even think that would work. But prepping the food for the next few days needed to be done, and surely keeping busy would be better than sitting around dwelling on things.

Wiping her nose one last time, Tab said, 'Do you want me to start on the sausage rolls?'

'That would be great,' Meg replied, standing and starting back towards the kitchen.

When Tab joined her a few moments later, she said, 'Look, I know you don't want to talk about Fergus anymore and I respect that. Know I'm here if you change your mind, but just one last thing before we get stuck into baking.'

'Yes?' Tab's heart quaked.

'Would you like Lawson to go to cricket for you this arvo?'

Shit. Despite the fact they were about to start their weekly cook-up, Tab had completely forgotten today was Thursday, which also meant junior cricket training. As much as she didn't want to let Ned and his little teammates down, the thought of seeing Fergus again so soon left her cold. How would they face each other in front of an audience? He'd probably be over-the-top polite, treating her like a stranger and pretending nothing had happened between them, and that would be unbearable. Or maybe he'd try to talk to her, apologise for hurting her and … She shook her head. *No.* That would be even worse—she'd probably burst into tears again in front of everyone.

'But then we'll have to tell Lawson what's happened.' The thought of her brother knowing how stupid she'd been had her stomach churning.

'Tab, he's going to know something's up soon anyway—he's not stupid and he cares about you. He's also less likely to fly off the handle at Fergus, whereas if I see the jerk now, I might end up in jail again.'

This almost brought a smile to Tab's lips. 'Do you think he'd mind? I'm happy to do the milking instead.' Being with Ethan and the girls would be a zillion times more preferable to hanging on the oval with the man she'd naively fallen in love with.

'Of course he won't, but you don't need to worry about the milking—Ethan and I can handle it. You just take care of yourself and your baby.' She offered a sympathetic smile and placed a hand on Tab's stomach. 'I'm so glad our kids are going to be close in age. Are you going to find out the sex? I'm kinda hoping for a girl, so we have a pigeon pair. You?'

Tab welcomed the change of topic. 'I honestly don't mind, although if you guys have a girl, it would be cool if my baby was a girl too because then they could be cousins and best friends.'

'That would be perfect,' Meg said, and Tab smiled, because although her heart still ached, she had a lot to look forward to. Two months ago she didn't even know Fergus's name and she'd been excited about her future. Perhaps if she worked very hard at it, in another two months she'd have forgotten she ever did.

Chapter Twenty-seven

Just as Fergus was turning off his computer, it pinged, alerting him to a new email. Not in a hurry to get to the oval for cricket training after what had already been a long and trying day, he opened it.

Dear Mr McWilliams

We are writing to inform you that your application for teacher at …

He let out a sigh of relief as he read the letter from the Department of Education telling him he had a one year position at one of the Aboriginal community schools way up north, starting term one next year. If only he could start earlier, but as much as he didn't want to linger in Walsh now that he and Tabitha were through—for her benefit as much as his—he didn't want to desert the kids in his class either. They'd already had enough disturbance this year with Carline having to leave in a hurry, and they deserved better than that.

They deserved better than the kind of teacher he'd been today. Usually he managed to keep his personal and professional lives separate; even when he'd found out about Jools and Eider, he'd kept it together at school. But today everyone, even usually goodie-two-shoes Lisl, had been playing up and pushing his buttons. It felt like kids had a radar for when you weren't feeling great and he'd yelled and snapped at them more than once.

On reflection though, it hadn't been their fault. He couldn't focus on maths or spelling or anything he was supposed to be teaching because all he could think about was the look on Tabitha's face this morning when he'd walked out. How had things gone from blissful to dire so quickly? One minute they were laughing and sleeping together, and the next they were arguing like an old married couple. Her hurt and disappointment could have so easily been prevented if he'd just stuck to his guns and not let anything happen between them.

He'd kicked himself metaphorically a hundred times through the day and also found himself wishing and hoping that things could be different.

If only Jools hadn't come down and interfered. If she hadn't asked Tabitha to try to talk to him, they'd never have got into a fight.

If only he hadn't had a few too many drinks last night and asked her to stay.

If only she wasn't pregnant. He admired her independence and the way she'd taken her dreams of a baby into her own hands—it was all part of her incredible package—but he couldn't help wishing she'd waited just that little bit longer, because then … maybe …

No. He shook his head as he switched off his computer and stood. There was no point thinking 'if onlys' and 'maybes'. She *was* pregnant and no matter how she felt about him or he her, that was a deal-breaker. The only thing for him now was to try to get through the next few weeks in Walsh without hurting her any further.

His heart hammered as he drove to the oval. Should he apologise or try to act normal? They'd have to be careful, not only because of the kids, but also due to the eager ears of the parents. He didn't care what they thought about him—he'd be gone soon—but Tab had to live here and he didn't want them gossiping about her.

As he drove into the sportsground it quickly became obvious that Tabitha had decided to avoid him. Usually her ice-cream van stood out among the four-wheel drives and utes like a lamb in a pack of wolves, so today its absence was obvious.

Maybe she was simply running late?

This possibility was quickly eliminated when he climbed out of his car and saw Ned kicking the ball back and forth with his dad on the dry grass. Ferg wasn't sure whether he was relieved about not having to face Tabitha, but part of him was surprised at her no show. In the short time they'd known each other she'd never been one to shy away from anything, least of all confrontation, and her absence today spoke volumes about how badly he'd hurt her.

He'd never felt more like a jerk in his life.

'Oh look, here comes McGrumpy,' he heard Levi Walsh say. As the other kids giggled, Levi's mum scolded him but Fergus ignored him—after all, the kid was only speaking the truth.

Instead, he crossed over to Lawson and Ned. The boy's eyes lit up when he saw him, a testament to how great a kid he was that he wasn't holding one bad day against him.

'Hey, Mr McDuck.'

'Hey, Ned.' Ferg smiled at him and then offered his hand to his father. 'Hi Lawson.'

The other man didn't accept the handshake. 'Afternoon.' His cool tone and expression confirmed Fergus's suspicions that him being here instead of Tabitha wasn't some weird coincidence. No words were necessary to understand that Lawson knew what had happened with Ferg and his sister and that he wasn't happy about it either. Lawson seemed like a decent bloke, but Ferg got the impression if they didn't have an audience, he might have a few choice words to say or even a couple of physical blows to land.

He would have deserved either and he didn't blame Tabitha's brother for being angry at him. Right now he might even welcome a bit of physical pain to deflect from his internal anguish. Ferg knew the over-protective big brother role all too well as he'd played it himself on more than one occasion. The only times he'd ever got into physical fights growing up had been when other kids had done wrong by Eider. Where she was concerned, impulse had always overridden common sense. It was why her betrayal hurt just as much, if not more than Jools'.

But right now, it was the fight with Tab—the pain on her face and the reminder of it as he looked at Lawson's—that was forefront in his mind. He fought the impulse to try to explain himself, but now wasn't the time or place and even if it was, Lawson probably wouldn't understand or care. His primary concern was Tabitha and this thought consoled Fergus slightly—at least she had a supportive family; they'd help her get over him.

With a quick nod towards Lawson, Ferg called the kids into a group. They groaned as usual as he sent them off on a lap around the oval and then he and Lawson set up the drills, barely saying a word to each other. Without Tabitha here, cricket training dragged and wasn't nearly as fun. Ferg made a big effort to keep his own issues off the pitch but was overjoyed when the hour was up.

Without their usual post-cricket ice-cream, the kids were all eager to get home to dinner. As they shot off towards their parents, Lawson started to walk away, one hand on Ned's shoulder, leaving most of the final packing up to Fergus. He didn't care, there really wasn't much to collect, but just when he thought he'd avoided a confrontation, Tabitha's brother halted. Ferg saw him utter a few words to his son. Ned nodded and then Lawson turned and strode towards him.

Ferg braced himself for impact, but it was only words of warning Lawson hit him with.

'I don't know what you think you were playing at, getting involved with my sister in her current condition, but if you know what's good for you, you'll stay the hell away from her. Are we clear?'

Ferg nodded. 'I'm sorry. I—'

But even if he did have a good excuse, Lawson didn't hang around to hear it.

'Come on, Ned,' he shouted as he strode away from Fergus. The boy looked back and the confusion in his little face broke Ferg's heart all over again. The kid had the same big, bold, brown eyes as Tabitha and he knew that over the last few weeks of term, every time he looked at Ned he'd think of her and wish things could have been different.

With this thought, he heaved the heavy cricket bag over to his car, threw it in the boot and drove out of the sports ground. He was two kilometres out of town before he realised he wasn't heading home but in the direction of Rose Hill. Shit. Despite Lawson's warning still ringing loud and clear in his head, every instinct in his body wanted to go to Tabitha, to check she was okay and to say how sorry he was. But nothing had changed, and he didn't trust himself to be near her.

He slammed his foot on the brakes and did a three-point turn, making one of the hardest decisions of his life.

As Ferg drove back through Walsh on his way to the farm, he almost turned into the pub to grab himself another six-pack of beer. The urge to drown his sorrows was strong, but at the last moment common sense prevailed. Beer wasn't always the answer—just look at the trouble it had got him into last night.

So instead, he went home, ate the leftover ice-cream Tabitha had brought over and tried to distract himself with a little lesson planning. When that didn't work, he sat down on the couch next to Mrs Norris to watch some TV.

'Looks like it's just you and me again,' he told her.

She offered him her signature look of disdain, then jumped off the couch and stalked out the room, her tail and nose straight up in the air. It was the loneliest evening he'd spent in a long time.

Chapter Twenty-eight

'Do you want to come over for dinner?' Meg asked Tabitha on Saturday afternoon. The tea rooms had closed, and they'd just finished cleaning up for the day. Lucy and Bonnie stood by the door, already lost in their phones, thumbs flying over the screens as they waited to leave.

'Thanks, but I think I'm going to have an early night.'

This probably wasn't true as she likely wouldn't be able to sleep any better than she had the past two nights, but she didn't feel as if she'd be very good company this evening. As much as she adored Meg and Lawson, being around a couple so in love wasn't going to be any better for her mental health than hanging out alone. And also, she didn't trust herself not to pester Ned with questions about Fergus.

What had he been like at school on Friday? Had he acted any differently?

Even though it was only two days since they'd parted ways, it felt much longer. Life, she'd discovered, continued as normal after heartbreak. The sun still rose and set, her rooster still crowed at

283

dawn, her chickens still laid eggs and she went about business as usual, but everything felt different.

She hadn't heard a peep from him—not even a text message telling her how the cricket team had gone this morning—and this only rammed home how little he thought of her. Surely a decent person would have tried to call her, or at least sent a message to check she was okay? Then again, a decent person wouldn't turn his back on his family when they were sick and in need, so maybe he really had done her and her baby a favour. Yet no matter how much she told herself that they'd be better off without him, it still hurt like hell. No matter how much she told herself he was a jerk, there'd been times she'd seen otherwise.

During the day as she'd been waiting tables, she'd kept an ear out for any mention of him, but all that was on anyone's minds was the upcoming show. They'd been quiet today because many of the residents of Walsh were at the showgrounds helping with the busy bee or at home putting the final touches on their competition entries. The only information she'd overheard that vaguely related to him had arrived on the grapevine with Mrs Walker as she'd stopped in for a takeaway coffee on her way to visit her sister in Kojonup. News just in was that Carline's treatment appeared to be working and it looked as if she'd be fine to come back to school next year. Tab guessed that meant that even if Ferg didn't get one of the jobs he'd applied for up north, he'd be moving on.

While she was happy for Carline and Terry, she felt annoyingly conflicted about this. Her brain was happy not to have to worry about running into him, but her heart didn't like the fact that once he was gone, she'd likely never see him again.

'You sure?' Meg asked, staring intently at her.

'What?' Lost in her own thoughts, Tab had no idea what her sister-in-law was talking about.

Meg gave her an endearing smile. 'If you're not up to coming to the farm for dinner, maybe I could come back here once I've dropped off the girls. We could have an old-fashioned slumber party?'

'I'm fine.' Tab forced a smile. As sweet as the idea was, if she couldn't be with Fergus she'd really rather be alone. Or at least alone with Eliza, who understood heartache better than most and wouldn't insist on conversation.

'Okay then. Well, call me if you change your mind,' Meg said, grabbing her bag from underneath the bench and gesturing to Lucy and Bonnie that she was ready to go.

'I will,' Tab promised as she ushered the three of them out the front door and locked up behind them.

She went upstairs and had a long soak in the bath, while listening to an audio book to distract her mind from unhelpful thoughts. Afterwards, she went downstairs and reheated some leftover pasta, which she ate for an early dinner. Although part of her just wanted to curl up in bed, pull the covers over her head and shut out reality, she doubted she'd be able to succumb to rest. Even though she'd washed her sheets, trying to rid the scent of Fergus, the memories of him being in her bed were too strong and it no longer felt like the refuge it once had.

For this reason, she turned her hand to making a few more batches of ice-cream. It never hurt to be over-prepared; better to have too much than to run out on the day. She already had way more in storage than she could carry in the van, but they'd decided that if they got low, Lawson could sneak back to the tea rooms with their transportable freezer and restock.

Tab had just placed a big batch of caramel-chunk into the storage freezer when she heard a car door slam outside. She glanced at the clock on the microwave to see it was almost 7 pm and a shiver of unease swept over her skin. She rarely had any unexpected visitors out here, and definitely not at this time of night on a Saturday. Could it be Fergus? Perhaps he'd had a change of heart. Her own traitorous heart leapt at the thought and she hurried to the front of the tea rooms so she could peer out the window.

All her hopes vanished as she registered the man who was swaggering around the front of a very flash-looking black sedan. She didn't know much about cars, but she could tell this wasn't your average run-of-the-mill hire car. And she wouldn't expect anything less from Ryder O'Connell. He wore dark sunglasses, despite the fact the sun had all but set, and faded jeans (likely expensive and bought that way) hugged his hips as he gazed up and down the street.

The sunglasses made her snort—did he think he might get mobbed by fans? And what the hell was he doing here anyway? Not only in Rose Hill, but back in WA so early? The show wasn't until next weekend and she'd assumed he'd arrive the night before at the earliest. She'd expected to feel a lot more anxious about seeing him again, but all she felt was disappointment that he wasn't Fergus.

She could easily drop the curtain back into place, retreat and pretend not to be here. Tab was still contemplating this possibility when Ryder turned towards the building and his eyes connected with hers. Dammit, she thought, as his face lit up with a smile and he started towards the front door.

Oh well, she was bound to run into him sooner or later. She may as well get the meeting over and done with.

As she let the curtain fall, her thoughts went briefly to her appearance but the most she did was wipe her brow with the back of her hand—what did she care what he thought of how she looked? And then with a quick breath, she went to open the door.

Chapter Twenty-nine

Ferg couldn't concentrate on the cricket game any more than he'd been able to concentrate on sleep the last couple of nights. Tabitha's words kept playing over in his head like a broken record.

I love you. Cancer can be fatal.

Cancer can be fatal. I love you.

Cancer. You. Love. Fatal.

After a while, anger and hurt started to make way for other feelings. What if Tabitha was right? How would he feel if Jools was wrong and Eider didn't go into remission? What if she died? Could he live with himself then?

At this thought an overwhelming heaviness descended upon his chest. He struggled to breathe; it felt as if he were lying on the ground and an elephant had him pinned.

'Mr McDuck? Mr McDuck? *Coach?!*'

The chorus of voices snapped him out of his reverie. He blinked at the crowd of little faces and the parents gathered around him. Victoria and Milly's mum stepped forward and put her hand on his arm. 'Are you okay, Fergus? You look like you're about to have a heart attack.'

'I'm …' Thinking about the possibility of his sister dying was not something he wanted to share right now. 'Fine. Sorry.' He blinked and summoned a smile as he addressed the kids. 'Well done, guys.'

'Well done?' Lisl spat, her disgust scrawled across her face. 'We just won our second game; don't you think that deserves more than a "well done"?'

She was right, it did, but truth be told, he hadn't been paying attention.

He couldn't go on like this, so distracted that he couldn't focus on any task. It was no way to live and definitely no way to teach. The kids deserved better.

As the parents chatted and the children crammed oranges and end-of-game lolly snacks into their mouths, Ferg made his decision. He would go see Eider. Didn't mean he was going to forgive her but maybe just seeing her and making sure she was indeed on her way to recovery would at least get that niggle out of his head and also get Jools off his back.

So many times during the two and a half hour journey he almost turned back, but something kept his foot on the pedal and his eye on the road as he got closer and closer to Perth. It had only been seven weeks since he'd left, but in some ways it felt like years.

As he hit the outskirts of the city, he was reminded of the differences between country and city driving. In Walsh, his commute to work was a mere ten minutes and everything he needed—coffee, beer, cat food—was within walking distance of his classroom. He found he didn't miss the impatient drivers or the traffic lights that had him stopping what felt like every five seconds.

These thoughts distracted him from the reason for his journey, but the car seemed to know where they were going, so he'd all but arrived before he realised how close he was. As he turned into the street lined with beige and red-brick houses built in the eighties, bottlebrush trees and other Aussie natives filling the gardens, his stomach churned.

It was only the thought of Tabitha that had him parking on the cracked cement driveway, climbing out and heading to the front door. Besides, he'd come all this way; it would be cowardly and a waste of good petrol to turn back. Never before had he knocked on the door before entering this house, but even if Eider still kept a spare key under a gnome in the garden, it wouldn't feel right to use it now. What if he walked in on her and Jools in a compromising position?

He shuddered at the thought as he pushed the doorbell and held his breath as its musical tune echoed through the house. Less than thirty seconds later, the door peeled back and Jools gasped as her hand rushed to her chest.

'Hello, Julia,' he said, not even trying to eliminate the coolness from his tone. 'Is Eider home?'

Jools took a moment to recover and then nodded. 'She's watching TV. I … I can't believe you came.' Then her expression grew hard. 'You're not here to upset her, are you? She couldn't handle more aggro right now.'

Ferg's jaw tensed but he managed to reign in his own anger. 'You wanted me to come. Well, here I am, so if you don't mind?' He gestured inside, but Jools didn't budge.

'Okay, you can see her, but first I need you to go wash up. There's hospital-grade soap and disinfectant in the bathroom. You haven't been sick lately, have you? What about the kids in your class? We can't afford for Eider to catch anything while she's in the middle of chemo as it weakens her immune system.'

She'd pretty much begged him to come, and now he was here it felt as if she was trying to find a reason to get rid of him again.

'I'm perfectly healthy,' Ferg said, striding past her and towards the bathroom. The whole house smelt of Glen 20, and as he scrubbed his arms from his hands right up to his elbows, he heard the volume being lowered on the television and hushed voices coming from the lounge room. He dried his hands with a clean towel from the cupboard and then strode out to face the music before he could change his mind and flee.

'Fergus!' Eider cried from her position on the couch.

Her appearance stopped him in his stride. He almost didn't recognise her and feared he failed in his effort to keep the horror from his face. Perhaps deep in his mind he'd hoped the cancer was some kind of elaborate scheme to get him to come visit, but one look at Eider told him that wasn't the case.

His eyes grew hot as he stared at her. She was all but bald. She'd always had such thick, healthy dark hair—the last time he'd seen her it was almost halfway down her back—but now there was only the odd, barely visible patch of stubble. And she looked gaunt and tired. Her clothes swam on her and her cheeks were sunken into her face. Her eyes were bloodshot, carrying dark bags beneath them.

Something clicked inside him and instinctively he stepped towards her as the last remnants of his anger crumbled. All he wanted to do was hug her and take away her suffering. If he could take her cancer into his body, he would.

'Oh, sis,' he said as he sank down onto the couch and drew her into his side. Eider leaned into his chest and cried big heaving sobs that shook her whole body.

'I'm sorry,' he whispered after a while, worried the exertion would exhaust her.

She pulled back and looked at him with tear-soaked eyes. 'You're sorry? I'm the one who should be saying sorry, but I know that no matter how many times I say it, it won't change things. I'll never forgive myself for hurting you, but I love you both. I can't choose between you and Jools.'

'You don't have to,' he said, the fight having completely left his body. Suddenly his actions seemed so petty. How could he ever have let anything come between them? Blood was thicker than water. He glanced up at Jools standing only a few feet away, biting her nails in the manic way she did when anything was stressing her, and he felt nothing. No longer love, but not hate either. If the love had faded so fast, was it ever really as strong as he'd thought?

He wasn't sure, but he did know that the bond he and Eider shared was stronger than anything he'd ever had with Jools. The pain he'd suffered the last few months was more because he missed his sister and because Jools had hurt his pride than anything else. He'd be a fool to let one mistake ruin what they had, and he only hoped the chemo did its trick and Eider recovered enough for them to have many, many more years together.

'Can I get you something to drink?' Jools asked when he and Eider finally broke apart. 'Coffee? A cup of tea? Juice? Coke?'

He could tell she was nervous, but if he wanted to maintain his relationship with his sister, he was going to have to try to create a new kind of one with Jools. So he spoke kindly, trying to put her at ease. 'A cup of coffee would be great, thanks. Do you want some help?'

She shook her head and offered a small smile. 'I think I can manage. You stay with Eider.'

While Jools went into the kitchen, Ferg took Eider's hand and held it gently in his lap.

'I'm so glad you're here, Fergie,' she said, calling him by the nickname she'd had for him as a child. If anyone else had ever dared call him that, he'd have decked them, but Eider had always been able to get away with murder where he was concerned.

'I'm sorry it took me so long,' he replied, unsure he'd ever forgive himself for his stupid pride.

She half-laughed. 'Anyone listening to us would think we were having a competition about who could say sorry the most. How about we agree to stop apologising and look to the future? I want to hear about what you've been up to. What's it like living in Woop Woop?'

'Walsh is hardly Woop Woop,' he said, wondering what she'd think when he told her he was going even further afield next year. 'But country living is definitely different to city living. Everyone knows everyone else, half the town seem to be related, and it runs a lot on volunteers.'

He was in the middle of telling her about his farmhouse, how the owner who lived in the nursing home went missing and how he'd been involved in the search, when Jools walked in with two mugs of steaming coffee and a plate of Tim Tams.

'You not having a drink?' he asked when she placed the mugs down on the coffee table in front of him and Eider.

'I've got to go to the supermarket and get some groceries. Maybe I'll see you when I get back?'

He nodded. Jools was obviously making herself scarce and for that he was grateful. He wanted to spend some time alone with his sister, but also wasn't sure he was quite ready for the feelings his sister and ex-fiancée had for each other to be paraded in front of him.

When she left, he picked up the plate of biscuits and offered it to Eider. She shook her head.

'What's wrong with you? I've never known my sister to turn down chocolate before.'

'Cancer.' The way she spoke so matter-of-factly reminded him a little of Tabitha. 'Sadly, a few days or so after chemo, I feel so nauseous that almost nothing tastes good.'

His heart hurt at her confession—the reality of her situation slamming down on him—and he put the plate back on the table.

'How long have you been having it? How often? How else does it affect you?'

'I've had three treatments so far, every two weeks. It's not a walk in the park, but I'm doing okay. Work's been great allowing me to have time off, and Jools has been working from home a lot. Aside from the nausea and the tiredness, I'm drinking bucketloads of water, but every time I feel like complaining, I remind myself it's all for the greater good.'

Again, he thought of Tabitha—Eider's attitude reminded him so much of her and he knew they'd hit it off immediately if they ever met. Not that they would.

'Don't look so glum, big brother. I'm going to beat this thing.'

'I know.' He squeezed her hand and managed a smile. 'And I'm going to support you through it as best I can. I know I'm not just around the corner anymore, but I'll call every day and visit every weekend.'

Eider laughed. 'I'll hold you to the phone calls, but as much as I love seeing you, I don't want you to feel like you have to spend all your non-teaching time coming to see me. Maybe when I'm better, I could come visit you?'

'That would be good, but,' he sighed, 'I should probably tell you that as of next year I'll be even further away. I've accepted a job up near Newman at a remote community school.'

'Newman?' Eider made a face. 'Where on earth is that?'

Ferg chuckled—geography had never been her strong point. 'It's up north, inland, on the edge of the Great Sandy Desert. About a fourteen-hour drive or just under two hours by plane.' As Eider's eyes widened, he said, 'But if you need me to be closer, I'll tell them I can't take it.'

She shook her head. 'Don't be silly. Your skills will be so well-received up there and I'll be finished chemo and in remission by then.'

Once again, he loved her positive outlook.

'So, what made you change your mind?' she asked.

When he frowned in confusion, she added, 'What made you suddenly decide to come visit?'

He glanced down as his stomach quivered at the thought of Tabitha. If she hadn't pressed him they'd likely still be sleeping together, but also, he probably wouldn't have come. 'Just something a … a friend said.'

The moment the word was out, he knew it was the wrong choice—he doubted Tab would call them friends anymore.

'A *friend*? Is this friend male or female?'

Ferg squirmed in his seat. 'What's that got to do with anything?'

She pinned him with her stare. 'I was simply curious, but your defensive reply has given me my answer. So, are you going to tell me about her?'

'There's not much to tell,' he said, feeling his cheeks heat. 'She's the aunt of one of my students, we've been training the junior cricket team together, but we barely know each other.'

'Cut the crap, Fergus.' Eider sounded much more like the little sister he remembered again. 'You've always been a shit liar and I can still see right through you. What's the name of this woman you apparently barely know?'

'Tabitha,' he admitted.

Eider smiled a victorious grin. 'Tabitha—nice old-fashioned name like ours. I approve. So why the glum face? Doesn't this Tabitha like you as much as you clearly like her?'

Ferg sighed, the last thing he'd wanted to do today was talk about Tab, but Eider was like a dog with a bone when she wanted to know things and he didn't want to get into a fight with her so soon after their reconciliation. 'She does actually. She told me she's in love with me.'

'Oh my God!' Eider squealed. An expression that was halfway between happiness and relief—perhaps that this might let her and Jools off the hook a bit—filled her face. 'That's wonderful. Tell me more about her. What does she do? When can we—'

Ferg held up a hand before Eider could get too carried away. 'We're not together. And you're not going to meet her.' Despite the fact they lived in a tiny town, the way she'd managed to stay out of his way the last few days, he wasn't even sure *he* was going to see her again.

Eider's excitement evaporated. 'Please, Ferg, I know I hurt you. I know we both hurt you, but don't exclude me from your life, and please, whatever you do, don't let your experience with Jools scare you off giving your heart to someone again.'

'That's not what this is about,' Ferg said, although he did prickle slightly. She was right that he'd decided love hurt more than it was worth, but Tab had gotten so far under his skin that if that was the only issue, he'd risk it.

'Then what?'

'Tabitha's pregnant.'

'Wow.' That struck Eider dumb a few moments. 'Not your baby, I'm guessing?'

'Nope.' But how badly did he wish it was?

'So …' She shook her head slightly as if trying to wrap it around everything. 'Is she already in a relationship? Did you guys have an affair or are you really *just friends*?'

Ferg sighed again, picked up a Tim Tam and bit it clear in half. The few moments he took to swallow it gave him time to psych himself up to explain the whole damn situation. When he'd finished telling her about Tab's little arm, her ice-cream business, her family, the farm, and of course the baby that didn't actually belong to any-one but her, Eider said, 'Tabitha sounds like an amazing woman.'

'She is.' His heart ached when he thought about just how much.

'So, what's the problem?' Eider asked. 'If there's no other guy in the picture and you're clearly as in love with this woman as she claims to be with you, why the hell aren't you guys together?'

'Because I can't risk putting Tab's child through the kind of emotional torture we went through at the hands of some of our foster parents.'

Eider took a moment. 'Are you kidding?'

'No. I wouldn't joke about something like this. You know what it's like to be raised by people who don't love you; even the better ones were only going through the motions to take care of us. If I learnt one thing growing up, it was that loving a child that isn't your own flesh and blood is near impossible. What if I couldn't love Tabitha's baby like it deserves? What if Tab could tell? Or worse, what if we went on to have kids of our own and I couldn't help loving them more?'

They both knew that was always the case—no matter how much they pretended otherwise, foster parents always loved their own more than they loved the wards of the state. He didn't think Eider would be able to argue with that, but she did.

'Fergus Titus McWilliams, that's the most ridiculous thing I've ever heard and I can't believe someone as smart as you could be so damn dumb.'

He blinked. Had her cancer or love for Jools turned her soft in the head?

Before he could ask what exactly was so ridiculous about the truth, she barrelled on. 'You show your love for kids that aren't your own every single day you go to work and even at night and on the weekends when you don't. I've seen how hard you work and I know it's because you believe in what you do, because you care about the kids in your class getting the best education and life experience they can. I know we had a few less than ideal foster parents—'

'A few?' he scoffed.

'But we also had some great ones. Remember Carol?' she said, referring to the woman who'd baked her way into their hearts. 'And I know that you're one of the good guys and would be a good parent whether a child was your biological offspring or not. If you love Tabitha, then you have to believe that you'd love her child just as much, that you'd love it as your own. I believe in you. Maybe it's time you start believing in yourself.'

Her passionate speech packed a punch; he felt it in his gut. But Jools chose that moment to return, making quite a noise as she stumbled through the front door, laden with shopping bags. Ferg shot up to help her, welcoming the opportunity to end this confronting discussion. Once they'd put all the groceries away, they went back into the lounge room.

'So, what have you guys been talking about?' Jools said as she lowered herself into an armchair, still sounding nervous.

Ferg looked at Eider but she had the good sense not to mention Tabitha. That was the last thing he wanted to be discussing with his ex-girlfriend, even if they had unofficially agreed to move on.

'Oh, this and that. Ferg's been telling me about how he has a new job up north next year.'

'Really?' Jools frowned a moment. 'Are you going to take Mrs Norris?'

'Yes. Unless you want her back?'

Her shoulders slumped and she glanced quickly at Eider. 'I can't, but how is she? Does she like the country?'

'She's still a proper little madam. Barely tolerates me and spends a lot of time outside chasing rodents and all the other wonderful creatures at her disposal. My guess is once she's completely sufficient at catching enough to live on, I won't see her again.'

Jools looked appalled. 'That's terrible. You know we used to keep her in at nights so she couldn't attack the native wildlife.'

'Don't worry,' Ferg reassured her. 'All I've seen her catch so far is mice, and trust me, there are plenty of them. From what I can tell, most of the farmers have cats around to keep the mice from eating their crops and feed. But she's only wild around me.'

He told her about how Mrs Lord had turned up and fallen in love with Mrs Norris. 'The feeling was mutual. I've decided she must prefer girls; like you two.'

They laughed and Ferg couldn't help joining in. A few months ago, he'd have hit anyone who dared to tell him that his fiancée leaving him for his sister was amusing, but now he found he could almost see the funny side of it himself.

'And what about Tabitha?' Eider asked, a cheeky twinkle in her eyes. 'Does Mrs Norris like Tabitha?'

'Isn't Tabitha the woman who owns the B&B?' Jools said, glancing between Ferg and Eider. 'Why's she met Mrs Norris?'

He froze and glared at his sister, but neither of them had to say anything.

'Oh!' Jools' eyes widened and then her face broke into a smile. 'Is something going on between you two?'

He glanced down at his watch. 'Is that the time? I really should be going before it gets too late. Everyone says that driving at dusk is dangerous as all the kangaroos are out on the road.'

'*Kangaroos*?' Jools said, thankfully distracted. 'Wow, it's like you're living in a different world. I thought kangaroos running across the road was merely a myth we let foreigners believe.'

'Apparently not.'

'Can't you stay a bit longer?' Eider said, seemingly not interested in the discussion of Australia's national animal.

He glanced at Jools, wondering what she thought of this suggestion, but not wanting to say no to his little sister, especially in her current state. She hit him with her full-faced smile, the one that had once made his heart burst, but now merely seemed to remind him that she wasn't the demon he'd tried to imagine her to be the last few months.

'That's a great idea,' Jools said. 'The spare room's all set up and I'm making a chicken pasta for dinner. There'll be more than enough for you as well.'

His mouth watered at the mention of her famous chicken pasta and he felt his resolve wavering. He hadn't planned to stay this long, but it wasn't like he had any reason to be back in Walsh tonight. Except for Mrs Norris, but he'd left her biscuits on the porch. And there was Tabitha.

Once again, his heart rattled at the thought of her. Could Eider possibly be right? Could he dare to tell her how he really felt and ask if she'd let him help raise her baby?

The idea terrified him more than anything he'd ever faced, but also electrified him. He thought about how he'd helped her set up the furniture and paint the nursery, and he felt suddenly breathless at the thought of bringing the baby home to sleep there. Of getting up in the middle of the night to help Tab settle it. Of singing lullabies and reading some of his favourite picture books. He knew kids should be read to as early as possible, even in the womb wasn't jumping the gun.

Of course, said a pesky little voice in his head, *you'll be in Newman by then.*

Chapter Thirty

'What are you doing here?' Tab spat, her heart pounding as she stepped out into warm evening air.

Ryder smiled and pushed his sunnies up onto his head. 'Hello, Tabby. Is that any way to greet an old friend?'

His voice sounded deeper than she remembered and up close he definitely looked older, as if all those late nights on the stage had taken their toll. Despite that, she had to admit he was still good-looking, but in a much more artificial way than she recalled. His golden man-bun looked slicked back with some kind of product and she'd bet his hipster beard had been trimmed by an actual barber.

Still, it was the friend thing that had her snorting—it was almost as funny as the notion that she and Fergus were friends. Pushing thoughts of him out of her head, she replied, 'I'm guessing if we looked it up in a dictionary, the definition of friends would involve talking to each other more than once every ten years.'

'Ah …' He scratched his jaw, clearly at a loss for words. If he was hoping for a more enthusiastic welcoming party, he'd chosen the wrong week to waltz back into her life.

'So, what can I do for you?' She really wished she had two arms right now so she could cross them. Instead, she held her chin high and kept her lips in a tight line.

The egotistical smile fell from his face. 'I heard about what you're doing out here and thought I'd come check it out, say hello. I'm sorry, I should have guessed you might not be as excited to see me as I was at the prospect of seeing you.'

Tab felt the straight line of her lips wobble a little. Was he for real?

She didn't know what to say. 'You're here early,' she decided on. 'The show's almost a week away.'

'I know, but I needed to get away. I needed a bit of a break from it all.'

She found her interest piqued. Did he mean a break from the music? The city? A love gone wrong? Her stupid heart thawed a little at the stricken look on his face.

'I see. Well, I'm not sure how much of a break this'll be. I'm surprised you haven't been mobbed yet. To say the town is excited about you coming is an understatement.'

'Well, I only arrived this afternoon and I went straight to my accommodation, so I'm yet to see anyone really, except you.'

The last thing she'd expected was for him to seek her out. 'Where are you staying?'

He named an upmarket B&B on the other side of Walsh, owned by a couple of retirees from Perth. 'My manager booked it—he's coming later in the week with my band. But I should have stayed out here.' He glanced down the deserted street and then up into a nearby tree where a pink and grey galah sat plucking its feathers. 'It's lovely, so peaceful and quiet.'

'Unfortunately we're fully booked next weekend.'

'That's great. You're obviously doing really well with your little business.'

She bristled at the word 'little' and wondered how much he actually knew, but decided not to waste her breath arguing it. 'We are, but everywhere is fully booked, thanks to you.'

He smiled a little again, clearly pleased by the notion. 'What about during the week? Do you have guests now? Maybe I could stay here a few days and move back to the other B&B when you need me to?'

Her stomach flipped—they didn't have guests until Wednesday, but she didn't want him staying under her feet and couldn't understand why he'd want to. 'I don't think so.'

He sighed. 'Fair enough. How about a drink then? I know you don't owe me anything, but I really would love to catch up.'

Tab's instinct was to turn him away—to reject, and possibly hurt him like he'd hurt her all those years ago—but she found herself relenting. Perhaps his company for an hour or so would distract her heart and mind from Fergus. A little reprieve appealed.

'Okay. But you can't stay long. I'm tired—I've had a long day and have another busy one tomorrow.'

He grinned. 'No worries. You just say the word and I'll leave.'

A little voice in Tab's head said she should probably say the word right now. But, against her better judgement, she welcomed him into her home instead. 'I've just got to clean up in the kitchen,' she said, 'but feel free to have a look around while I do.'

Ryder's gaze followed as she pointed to the gallery. 'I'll help you instead.'

'Suit yourself.'

So he followed her through the tea rooms into the kitchen and did exactly as he promised, asking her about how she got into ice-cream-making and how the tea rooms came about.

'So Meg is Lawson's new wife?' Ryder asked. When she nodded, he added, 'I heard about what happened to Leah. Just tragic.'

Tab wondered why he hadn't thought to send condolences but bit her tongue. This was a weird enough situation without making things even more awkward. 'Yeah, I never thought I'd see him so happy again, but Meg is great and Ned adores her.'

'Ned's Lawson and Leah's kid?'

Tab nodded as she wiped the last of her ice-cream mess off the benches. It had been easy enough talking to him while they'd had something else to occupy them but she wasn't so sure about sitting down face to face. Still, she could hardly send him on his way after he'd helped her clean up. 'Now, can I get you a drink?'

'That'd be great,' he said. 'You got a beer?'

'Sorry, this is currently an alcohol-free zone. The best I can do is a cup of tea, coffee, Milo, soft drink or juice.' She could also offer a milkshake, but that'd be pushing the so-called friendship, as would offering him anything to eat.

'No worries. I should have picked something up at the pub, but I went for a drive and kinda just ended up here. Coffee will be great.'

Tab made him a coffee and a Milo for herself and then they took them into the tea rooms. When they sat down at one of the tables, she wracked her mind for something to say.

In the end he spoke first, pinning her with an intense stare. 'You're looking really good, Tabby. Being a business woman must agree with you.'

Or it could be my pregnant glow? Either that or my cheeks are still flushed red from all the crying the last few days.

Actually, Ryder was probably lying—when she'd looked in the mirror that morning, she'd looked ghastly—but she couldn't see what benefit lying would bring him.

'Thanks,' was all she said in the end and they were both quiet a few moments.

'Look … I know it's long overdue, but I want to say sorry,' Ryder said eventually and Tab almost spilled the Milo that was halfway to her mouth.

'Sorry for what?'

'For the way I acted when … you know.' He nodded towards her arm, obviously still too cowardly to actually talk about her cancer and her amputation. 'I was an idiot.'

She raised her eyebrows, not about to let him off the hook.

He sighed loudly. 'Okay, idiot doesn't even come close. There are no words that can ever convey how deeply ashamed I am for the way I treated you, for walking away when you really needed me. For choosing a career over us.'

'You know, you could have had both. I lost my arm, not my voice.'

'I know, but I was scared. I didn't know how to support you through something so huge, so I ran instead.'

She shook her head. 'It was never about supporting *me*, it was about having a girlfriend with a disability not suiting the image you wanted to portray. Don't try to rewrite history, because I have a memory like an elephant.'

Ryder hung his head. 'You're right. And I might spend the rest of my life regretting that foolish and selfish behaviour. There's never been anyone that got me as well as you did, anyone I've had such a connection with since—on stage, but more importantly, off.'

These were words she'd always wanted to hear. She'd fantasised about them, and in the early years, listened to his songs to see if there was anything about her in them—but his apology didn't affect her in the way she'd always imagined it would.

'So all those girls you've been photographed with in magazines didn't mean anything?'

His lips quirked upwards a little. 'You been following my career?'

'No, but this is a small town. People talk, and for some reason they like talking to me about you.'

'I guess they all have memories like elephants as well.'

She almost laughed at that but managed to stop herself, waiting instead for a proper answer.

'The girls were just part of the lifestyle,' he finally admitted, with an almost imperceptible shrug. 'The magazines, the tweets, the selfies, they all make it look and sound much better than it is. But women only want me for one thing—they want the street cred that comes with being linked to a musician. The attention was great at first, but as I get older, I want more. I want something real and it's almost impossible to find that in my world. I haven't had a meaningful relationship since you.'

'We were just kids,' Tab said quietly, although until recently she would have said the same about him. She'd gone out with Ryder longer than she'd even known Fergus, but now, sitting here with him, she didn't feel any of the things she'd been worried about. He simply felt like an old friend. Fergus was now the one who filled her head every waking moment.

'Maybe,' Ryder admitted, 'but lots of people marry their first love. Many a high-school romance lasts a lifetime. And it's true when they say you never forget your first. I've certainly spent a lot of time wondering how different things could have been if I hadn't let you go. Maybe I wouldn't be so damn lonely. Maybe I wouldn't be trying to fill the void inside me with other things. I suppose you heard about my recent charge for drink driving?'

She nodded. 'It was big news when I picked up Ned from school one day. People weren't impressed, but then the moment you agreed to come back for the show, they seemed to forgive and forget.'

He smiled sadly. 'What about you, Tabby? I'm not sure I'm doing a very good job of it, but I'm trying to apologise. What do you say? Do you forgive me for the bastardly way I treated you? I really am sorry. If I could turn back time, I would.'

And it turned out an apology ten years late was better than no apology at all. She wondered whether he'd have bothered if he hadn't happened to be in the area, but really, what did it matter? Forgiveness was as much about the person doing the forgiving as it was about the person asking for it. Tab thought about Fergus—how bitter he was about his sister and ex and how he needed to forgive them if he wanted to be truly happy himself. She couldn't think one thing for him and something different for herself.

'Yes, I forgive you,' she said, feeling a sudden lightness at simply saying the words.

'Thank you.' He reached across the table and squeezed her hand. 'So many times over the years I've wanted to reach out to you, but I've always been too ashamed by my actions. I only said yes to playing at the show because it would give me an excuse to come see you. To finally try and make some kind of amends.'

Tab smiled back at him, happy to realise she felt no sparks whatsoever. Instead, a bubble of amusement rose up inside her at this whole situation. She couldn't believe how terrified she'd been of facing him again—it felt like a cat being scared of facing a mouse.

'What's so funny?' Ryder slowly withdrew his hand, slight discomfort in his expression.

'Sorry, it's not what you're saying, it's just that I was so nervous about you coming back here and pitying me, but I never imagined you making me pity you.'

He frowned. 'What's there to pity about your life? You have family that love you, a community, a great business and a place to call your own. I envy that. Fame, and even wealth, isn't all it's cracked up to be and I'd give it up in a second if there was a better offer on the table.'

'You'd give up singing and playing the guitar?'

'Well, I couldn't completely. Music's part of who I am, not to mention the fact I've got contracts with the record company and would owe a lot of money if I broke them. But I wouldn't mind slowing things a little. I'm ready to settle down, perhaps even start a family.'

Tab blinked, not completely sure she believed him.

'What about you?' he asked. 'I know you're pretty busy, but is there any time in your life for music anymore? Do you still sing?'

'Actually, I have been dabbling a little recently,' she admitted, her heart squeezing as she recalled that night singing along to the accordion in Fergus's classroom. That had been one of her happiest nights with him. The joy of singing and trying to play an instrument again, of sharing that passion with someone she cared about, gave her a buzz like nothing else. 'I never stopped singing for myself but recently I sang in front of someone else again and I loved it.'

Ryder grinned. 'That's fantastic.'

He didn't ask who, and for that she was part grateful, part annoyed, but both feelings were short-lived because suddenly she felt a rumble in her stomach. And it wasn't because she was hungry. Instinctively her hand rushed to her bump as she tried to feel the movement from the outside, but it was too early. Yet Tab knew what she'd felt—that tiny bubble of movement was her baby and actually feeling it squirm inside her was the most magical thing.

'What is it? Are you okay?' Ryder's eyebrows drew together as he leaned towards her.

'Okay? I'm more than okay. I just felt my baby move for the first time.'

He recoiled and his eyes bulged as he tried to get a look at her stomach. 'You're pregnant?'

'Yes. I'm almost eighteen weeks.' With the baggy T-shirt she wore she was definitely still at that ambiguous stage, where her bump could be mistaken for over-indulging at lunch.

He blinked. 'Whose is it?'

'Congratulations is usually the correct response when someone tells you they're expecting,' she said. However, feeling magnanimous, she told him anyway. 'But the baby's mine, just mine. I chose to have it via artificial insemination.'

He'd looked shocked by the pregnant part but the emotion that flashed across his face now was definitely relief, which amused her and, she wouldn't lie, made her feel smug. It was nice to think that maybe he could still get a little jealous over her.

'Wow,' he said eventually. 'Congratulations.'

'Thanks.' Tab beamed back, glad she didn't feel embarrassed at all telling him, but empowered. She was proud to be taking control of her own destiny, focusing on the future, not the past. 'Which is why I told you this couldn't be a late night. The baby and I need our rest.'

Ryder nodded, taking her cue. He stood and picked up both their empty mugs. 'No worries, I understand. I'm so grateful for you giving me any time at all.'

'Leave those,' she said, nodding towards the mugs. As she escorted him to the front door, she added, 'This has been good for me too. I'm glad we cleared the air. Thank you for coming.'

He smiled warmly at her. 'Look, you can tell me I'm crazy, but …'

'What is it?' she prodded.

'What would you say to doing a duet with me next weekend?'

'What?' That was the last thing she'd expected.

'I thought it might be cool if we do one of our old songs. Don't you remember all those years ago that one of our first ever gigs was at the Walsh show?'

Of course she remembered. Their performances were some of the happiest moments of her life, but she'd closed the door on ever expecting to perform—especially with him—again.

'I thought the locals might get a kick out of seeing us back on stage together, and that you might enjoy it as well. But,' Ryder shrugged, 'if you don't want to, I understand. It was just a thought.'

Her instinct was to refuse, but for some reason the words wouldn't form on her tongue. There wasn't much she'd experienced in her life that gave her more of a buzz than belting out songs in front of an audience. The only things that had ever come close were feeling her baby move for the first time just now, and being with Fergus. The possibility of doing something to take her mind off him appealed immensely.

But was she crazy for even contemplating it? Was she simply still on a high from feeling her child? Or was this exactly the type of closure she needed? Things had ended so abruptly between them, she'd never known the last time they sung together would actually be the last.

'I'm not sure, Ryder,' she said. 'I haven't performed for almost ten years.'

He looked down into her face and smiled. 'It's like riding a bike, especially for someone with your natural talent.'

She rubbed her lips together. 'Can I give it some thought?'

'Of course. But don't take too long, because we'd have to practice a bit. Of course I'd happily fit around your schedule—mine's a blank slate this week.'

'Okay. Is there a number I can contact you on when I've made my decision?'

He pulled out his wallet, retrieved a business card and handed it to her. 'That's my private mobile. You can call me on that, but don't give it to anyone else. I only hand out this card to very important people.'

Then, before she could say anything to that, he leant forward, kissed her on the cheek, then pushed open the door and strode out into the night.

Tab blinked as she heard his expensive car start up. Had that really just happened?

Chapter Thirty-one

'Dammit.' Ferg thumped his fist on the steering wheel as he slowed his car to a standstill and eyed the unexpected traffic jam ahead in disgust. He looked from side to side, behind him, and when he couldn't see any way of escape, he climbed out of the car to assess the situation.

'Think we'll be here for a while, mate,' came a voice from behind. Ferg turned to see it belonged to a scruffy-looking man in a navy singlet who'd climbed onto the roof of his ute to get a better view. 'Looks like a road train has gone over. It's taken up the whole damn road.'

Ferg sighed and flicked a fly from his face, resisting the urge to temper his frustration with a swift kick to his car tyre. He was only half an hour from Walsh on the one road that went in and out of town. Cars were already grid-locked for a couple of kilometres on either side of him and the last road off this one was at least five kilometres back. He was well and truly stuck, unless he wanted to abandon his car and walk.

'Hope you don't need to be anywhere in a hurry,' called the bloke on the roof. 'It'll be a couple of hours before they clean up this mess I reckon.'

The mood he was in right now, if he had to listen to this guy's commentary for said couple of hours, he was liable to kill someone.

'Hopefully no one's hurt, ay?'

Ferg forced a smile at roof-man and nodded.

He should have left Perth earlier. But Eider had slept late and neither he nor Jools had wanted to wake her. Now it was almost three o'clock in the afternoon and Tabitha would be wrapping up things at the tea rooms, but the way it looked here, he'd not be getting there any time soon. The two hours' drive with his own thoughts had been bad enough—he kept wondering if his sister really had any idea what she was talking about—but if he had to wait another couple of hours stuck in traffic, he'd go crazy.

He couldn't wait to see Tab—one look at her and he felt certain he'd know in his heart what he needed to do.

With another heavy sigh, Ferg was about to climb back into his car when a shadow came up behind him and he turned to see roof-man approaching with two cans of Coke.

He held one out to Ferg. 'You look like you could do with a cold one. Lucky I stopped at the last servo and stocked up. You far from home?'

Ferg thanked him and cracked open the can. 'Um … I'm living in Walsh at the moment.'

The man nodded. 'Great little town. I'm from Barker, but my ex-girlfriend's mum came from there and I drive through it a bit, to and from jobs.'

Not really in the mood for small talk, Ferg took a sip of his drink. The sugary hit was a welcome reprieve from the frustrating afternoon.

'You play cards?'

'Occasionally,' Ferg replied, and before he knew what was happening the guy had whipped a pack out of his back pocket and was lowering himself onto the bitumen.

He looked up at him. 'Well? You got a better way to pass the time?'

As Fergus did not, he lowered himself to the ground. Thank God it wasn't a hot afternoon. 'What are we playing?'

'Gin rummy. You any good?'

'Okay.' That was a stretch; he was much better at board games. Eider had always whipped his arse whenever they played cards.

'Excellent,' said roof-man, and started dealing out the cards.

Within five minutes another three people had joined them, so they swapped gin rummy for poker and got quite a game going in the middle of the road. They weren't playing for sheep stations—although Ferg reckoned a couple of these blokes might own one—and for this he was grateful because he was even worse at poker than he was at gin rummy. But it passed the time and kept his mind from going round in circles about Tabitha.

Or at least he thought it did.

'Penny for them,' asked a lanky bloke with a long beard who was almost as bad at cards as Ferg was.

'Huh?' He looked up from his dismal hand.

'You've got something other than cards on your mind.'

And the other blokes agreed with him.

'I reckon it's a lay-dee,' sang roof-man. 'I've been following you from the outskirts of Perth and you've had your foot to the metal the whole way and you looked mighty pissed at our delay.'

'I'm just eager to get home,' Ferg said. How had this stranger known the truth when he wasn't even sure how he felt himself?

The four men shook their heads at him.

'How long since you've seen her?' asked the oldest of the lot.

'Only a few days,' he admitted, 'but we had a big fight and didn't part on the best terms.'

The men nodded solemnly.

'What'd ya fight about?' asked roof-man.

And maybe it was the fumes from some of the surrounding cars that were still running, but Ferg found himself confessing his whirlwind relationship with Tabitha and the reason why he'd pulled away.

'But you love her?' The question was posed by the oldest guy and Fergus answered honestly.

'Yes, more than I ever thought I'd love anyone again.'

'Then trust me.' The old guy clapped him on the shoulder. 'You'll love her kid just as much.' He pulled his wallet out of his pocket and flicked it open to a photo. 'See these three?'

Ferg looked down at a photo of two women and one man.

'They're my kids. All grown up now, but still my pride and joy. I came into their lives when they were ten, twelve and fifteen. It wasn't always easy, but I wouldn't be without their mother or them and I'd do anything for them. The youngest is just about to make us grandparents and I couldn't be more excited. Sometimes water *can* be just as thick as blood.'

The love in the old man's voice had Ferg choking up a little, thinking about what Eider had said, but there was a shout from one of the nearby cars before he managed to reply.

'Get up, you lot. We're moving.'

As roof-man gathered up the cards, the other men jumped to their feet and all slapped Fergus on the back—'You go get your girl!'—before heading back to their respective cars.

And, he realised, that's exactly what he wanted to do.

Full of hope from the old guy's story, he helped roof-man to his feet and then leapt into his own car. As the traffic started moving in front of him, he could actually feel his blood pumping through his body. He suddenly felt alive again.

He was going to see Tabitha and he was going to tell her exactly how he felt.

As he drove the remaining distance to Walsh and then turned down the road that would take him to Rose Hill, he rehearsed in his head exactly what he would say. He wanted to get the words out, to explain everything to her before he took her into his arms and kissed her, because the way he felt right now, he simply couldn't wait to hold her again.

It was almost 5 pm by the time he finally pulled up in front of the tea rooms and as predicted, the place was deserted. He remembered that it was Sunday and Tabitha usually went to the farm for a roast dinner.

The idea of facing her in front of her family wasn't all that appealing, but neither was waiting any longer to see her. He turned towards his car and suddenly noticed another car parked on the road that he hadn't even registered before. It must belong to someone staying at the B&B because it certainly didn't look like it belonged to anyone who lived around here. Then he heard music drifting from around the back and his heart leapt—perhaps she was home after all but hadn't heard him knocking over the sound of her stereo. Without another thought, he shoved his keys in his pocket and followed the music down the side of the building and around to the back of the house.

He slowed as he approached, realising it wasn't recorded music at all, but actual people singing live along to a guitar. One female voice and one decidedly male. The song ended and he heard Tabitha's beautiful full laugh.

'That was great,' said a deep voice. 'You are one of a kind. It's just like we were never apart.'

Then there was silence. Against his better judgement, Ferg peered round the edge of the building and every bone in his body turned to ice at what he saw.

Tabitha with some blond dude's arms wrapped around her, her head resting against his shoulder and her arm clinging to his back. The whole situation screamed intimacy, almost worse than if he'd stumbled upon them in the bedroom. He retreated as quickly and quietly as he could, knowing this bleak image would be imprinted onto his corneas for the rest of his life.

How could Tabitha—who'd professed to love him only days ago—have fallen so happily into the arms of her ex-boyfriend? Because without a doubt, that's who this bloke was—the guitar, the flash car, the way he'd held Tab as if he owned her and the fact the show was less than a week away meant it had to be him.

Everything Ferg had started to believe over the last twenty-four hours disintegrated. How could he ever compete? Sure, their few weeks together had been intense, but Tabitha had spent ten years pining after this man and now that he was back, she'd obviously quickly forgotten her so-called feelings for Fergus. Seeing her with Ryder reminded him far too much of the day he'd found out about Jools and Eider's betrayal. It made him feel like such a loser. To think that he'd been about to open his heart again. Perhaps the traffic incident was a blessing after all. It might just have stopped him making the biggest mistake of his life.

Better he got out of there fast before he risked making a fool of himself.

Chapter Thirty-two

The town of Walsh couldn't have asked for a better day for the hundredth anniversary of their agricultural show. The sun rose early and shone brightly and there wasn't a cloud in the beautiful blue sky. As Tab climbed out of bed at dawn, she tried to summon some of the weather's enthusiasm. She and the committee had been working towards this day for months and all their hard work was about to pay off. Not only that, but she was going to surprise her friends and family by getting up on stage and singing with Ryder.

Yet, although she was excited by this, everything was overshadowed with the permanent presence of Fergus inside her head.

She missed him all the damn time. They'd really only seen each other at nights but she missed knowing she'd be able to talk to and touch him later. She missed their laughs and the conversations they'd shared while they consumed post-sex snacks. So many times over the last week she'd almost succumbed to the urge to message him and she'd nearly told Lawson she'd go to cricket training yesterday, but common sense always prevailed.

What would she say to him anyway? She wasn't the type to beg; besides, he'd made it more than clear he didn't want to be a part of her baby's life, and they were a package deal. Despite her head knowing that he was no longer part of her life, her heart was taking longer to get on board. She'd heard that Fergus had been offered a position in a school up north and couldn't wait for him to take it so life could return to normal. So she could pick Ned up from school or walk down the main street without being on tenterhooks, wondering if she might run into him.

At least having to rehearse with Ryder was keeping her even busier than normal, allowing her less time to wallow in self-pity. She probably wouldn't have said yes if she and Fergus were still … well, whatever they'd been. But Ryder had been persistent, turning up at the tea rooms the day after he'd propositioned her, before she'd had a chance to reply. And, although slightly nervous, part of her really wanted to do this.

She had to admit she'd enjoyed spending time with her old flame this last week and finally felt the closure she'd been craving all these years. They'd laughed lots and got to know each other again. Fame may have changed Ryder's looks—he certainly wore more designer labels than he had before—but it didn't appear to have changed who he was at his core. She'd lost count of the number of times he'd apologised for how he'd treated her and finally she'd had to forbid him from using the 'S' word again, saying that if he did, she wouldn't sing.

Now, as she emerged from the shower, butterflies churned her stomach and she sort of wished he had, but it was too late to chicken out.

The tea rooms were closed today due to the show, so instead of throwing on her uniform, Tab chose some maternity denim shorts and paired them with a short-sleeved cotton shirt with little ice-creams all over it. She guessed she'd spend most of her day in the van and didn't want to be uncomfortable but made sure to pack some make-up and a dressier outfit for when she sang.

'Morning, Tab,' said Chloe's long-suffering husband as he waved her through the entrance of the showgrounds.

She smiled at him. 'Hi Richard. Bet you'll be happy when today's over and you can get your wife back.'

It was early and the gates weren't officially opened yet but there were plenty of people already here, setting up stalls and delivering livestock to the sheds. Sideshow alley had been erected yesterday afternoon with the usual rip-off rides and other amusements, but the showies were nowhere to be seen yet. Past experience said they'd turn up just before the gates opened—or maybe even a little later—smelling of last night's booze and cigarette smoke. Tab didn't think it could be much of a life, always travelling from one country show to the next, but they had to make a pretty little packet, judging by the prices they charged.

Slowly, she negotiated the van around people, cars and stalls and parked in the spot she'd allocated for it when she'd organised the layout of the food stalls. Meg, Lawson and Ned would be in soon to help serve through the day, but she wanted to set up so she was available to direct the other food vendors into position as they arrived.

After securing a few signs and ribbons to the outside of the van, Tab barely had two minutes to catch her breath before said food vendors started arriving and things really began to get busy. The coffee van was swamped even before the gates opened and as everyone queued for their caffeine, she had a quick wander around, taking a look at the craft stalls, displays and competition entries while she could.

By the time her family arrived just before the gates opened, carnival music was drifting from sideshow alley, animal noises were coming from the sheds, the scents of popcorn, roast lamb and coffee mingled together, and the atmosphere was well and truly buzzing with the excitement of show day.

Tab tried to get into the spirit of it all—pasting a smile on her face as the gates officially opened for ticketholders. Although a lot of people were waiting to come till later in the day so they'd be there for the fireworks and Ryder's performance, ice-cream was in demand much earlier than she'd predicted. She and Meg were busy inside the van, Ned was off with his friends trying not to spend all his money at once and Lawson spent much of the morning with Ethan in the big livestock shed where they were showing some of their best heifers.

However, by eleven o'clock, they had to call him back and ask him to head to Rose Hill to restock their supplies. Tab was thankful for the steady stream of customers, but she scooped ice-cream into cones and chatted to them on autopilot, all the while scanning the area in front of her for Fergus.

However, he was nowhere to be seen. Maybe he'd gone to Perth to visit his sister. Although he'd vanished off the face of *her* reality, she'd received a surprising text message from Jools on Sunday night, thanking her for convincing him to come visit and guessed that meant he'd mended bridges with them. While she was happy for him, she couldn't help being sad that he hadn't been the one to tell her about it.

'If we keep selling like this, we're going to run out, even taking all that extra Tabitha made into account,' Meg joked, as she wiped sweat from her brow, waved Lawson off and then turned back to take another order.

The next hour or so flew by and Tab tried once again to push Fergus and her nerves about tonight out of her mind, but when Funky delivered them all hot lamb rolls for lunch and offered to man the van a few minutes with Carly so they could eat, she found herself unable to stomach more than a few bites, even though she'd been starving.

'You okay?' Meg asked as she wiped gravy off the side of her mouth with a serviette.

'Fine, just tired,' Tab replied.

'Why don't you take a break for a bit? Lawson can help me with the ice-cream.'

Although her brother nodded, Tab was about to object—the van was safe in a way—but Ned ran over at that moment, interrupting the conversation. 'Can I have some money for fairy floss?'

'Oh my God,' Meg shrieked, pretending to be horrified at the sight of her stepson with blood and scars painted all over his face. 'What happened to you?'

'I got my face painted,' Ned replied as if that was a stupid question. He looked to Lawson. 'Can I puh-lease have some more money?'

'Have you already spent what I gave you?'

He nodded. 'But the rides are expensive, and the clown game is a rip-off. I played three times and didn't win anything.'

Tab smirked, impressed when her brother resisted the urge to say 'I told you so'. She put her roll down and dug into her pocket to see if she could find any change. 'Here you go. Don't spend it all at once.'

'Thanks.' Ned threw his arms around her. 'And when can you come see my photos and the papier-mâché sculpture I made at school? Lisl reckons hers is the best, but hers is a boring old horse whereas mine is Dobby from *Harry Potter*.'

'I'll come now,' Tab said, pushing off her seat, picking up her leftover lunch and throwing it in a nearby bin.

'Thanks, Aunty Tab.' Ned grabbed her hand and started yanking her towards the big hall, getting frustrated each time they had to stop to speak to someone. Everyone appeared to be having a grand old time and agreed that the anniversary show was turning out to be a cracker.

Not feeling she could take much of the credit, Tab filed away all the feedback to give to Chloe and the committee later as her nephew finally dragged her into the hall. It wasn't quite as busy as everywhere else, so she made a fuss of Ned's sculpture and photos.

She was about to ask him why he'd taken a photo of the toilet, when he tugged on her arm and said, 'Look, Aunty Tab, it's Mr McDuck.'

Her heart froze as she slowly turned and, sure enough, mere metres away, Fergus stood re-pinning a kid's painting to the wall.

'Hello, Tabitha,' he said, making every bone in her body turn to jelly.

Somehow she managed to reply, but her words came out huskier than she intended. 'Hi Fergus.' As her starving eyes drank him in, it was all she could do not to grab hold of his T-shirt, yank him towards her and beg him to reconsider. How could he just turn his back on her so easily? She was certain she hadn't imagined the connection between them. How could he just blatantly refuse to accept her baby?

All these questions were on the tip of her tongue but she couldn't ask any of them in front of Ned, so instead she said, 'The kids' work looks really good. You've obviously been busy.'

'All I did was hang it all up. They were so excited to have stuff on display, they worked in their recess and lunch breaks to finish.'

'That's awesome.'

He nodded, his hands shoved in his pockets, and then they both stood there in silence—it seemed they'd exhausted the topic of conversation. The knowledge they were like strangers again hurt Tab's already shattered heart. She had to get out of there before she lost not only her dignity but also the unshed tears that were causing her eyes to prickle painfully.

'Sorry, Ned, but I've got to get back to the van.'

She turned before either of them had a chance to say anything, but was only halfway out of the hall when she felt a tap on her shoulder.

'Tab, you got a moment?'

She sucked in a breath and slowly turned around to face Fergus, her heart squeezing in hopeful anticipation. Their eyes met and the rest of the world melted away. She could no longer hear any of the chatter around them.

'What is it?' she whispered.

'I just wanted to say thanks.'

Her stomach quivered. 'What for?'

'I went to see my sister—we've cleared the air—and I wouldn't have done so if it wasn't for you. You were right, I was being stubborn, but not talking to Eider was punishing myself as much as punishing them. I owe you a lot for confronting me.'

'You're welcome. I'm glad you sorted things out. Family is important.'

'It is,' he agreed with a smile that set her insides alight. 'Anyway, I'd better let you get back—I saw you've been pretty busy. It's great your ice-cream is so popular.'

What? It was all Tab could do not to recoil. *That was it?* Where was his declaration that he'd also been wrong about them? That the week apart had made him see sense and he couldn't live without her?

But he volunteered no such confession, so she uttered a quick thanks and fled to the toilet block where she sobbed as quietly as she could inside a cubicle, hoping no one could hear her.

When would this pain stop? She'd thought she'd felt heartache all those years ago when Ryder dumped her, but it was nothing on how she felt now. If she could stay in here all day she absolutely would but she couldn't leave Lawson and Meg to take care of her business. Dragging air into her lungs and then wiping her nose and eyes on a bit of toilet paper, she forced herself to leave the solace of the toilet block.

'Are you okay?'

She almost jumped out of her skin as she walked out to find a man in dark sunglasses and a cowboy hat (the kind that nobody actually wore in the country), holding a mammoth bunch of flowers, standing right outside. Although disguised well, she recognised Ryder's voice almost immediately and she reckoned it wouldn't be long before others also cottoned on that he was already here.

'How did you know I was in there?' she asked.

'I saw you leave the hall and tried to call out, but you didn't hear me, so I've been waiting outside.'

Lord, he'd probably heard her sobbing like a baby. 'You're here early. I thought you wouldn't show until closer to your performance.'

'*Our* performance.' He grinned, then held out the flowers to her. 'These are for you, to say thanks for giving me another chance. I came early because I wanted to hang out with you for a bit, experience the whole shebang of the country show.'

There were so many thoughts going through Tab's head. Where on earth did he buy flowers like that around here? She was only supposed to be singing one song with him, so it was hardly *their* performance. And what did he mean by 'giving me another chance'? But she didn't get the opportunity to voice any of this before he turned and introduced her to a man standing beside him.

'Tabby, I want you to meet Shaun, my manager and right-hand man. He arrived early this morning and he's mad keen to hear you sing.'

Shaun—who was a good foot shorter than Ryder and had oily black hair slicked back in the kind of style that was popular in the seventies—offered Tab his hand but she couldn't take it due to the fact her arm was busy with the flowers.

'Sorry,' he said awkwardly, withdrawing his hand and blushing as he stared at her stump.

'It's fine. It's nice to meet you, but I really have to get back to my ice-cream van.'

Ryder actually pouted. 'I was hoping we could go on a ride together, share some popcorn, maybe lose money on some of the amusements.'

'As appealing as that sounds, I don't think pregnant women are supposed to go on rides.' And she was most definitely not in the mood anyway. What she really wanted was to go home and curl into a ball, but show day only happened once a year and she was determined not to let Fergus ruin it.

'Bugger. What on earth are we going to do to occupy the next few hours, then?' Ryder asked.

Tab wasn't sure if he was asking her or his manager or merely pondering the question himself, but at that moment, a shriek pierced the air. 'Oh my God, is that Ryder O'Connell?'

His period of anonymity was over and as a teenager girl hurried towards them—'Please, pretty please, can I have your autograph?'—and others followed after her, Ryder pasted a smile on his face and Tab took the opportunity to escape back to the van.

'Who are the flowers from?' Meg's eyes lit up. 'Fergus?'

Tab shook her head. She no longer believed in miracles. 'These are from Ryder.'

'Really? I guess he's the reason for the kerfuffle over there. Are you okay?'

Tab nodded. 'Yes, I really am.' She hadn't confided to Meg or Lawson that she'd already seen Ryder more than once because she wanted to surprise them tonight, but also didn't want them to worry about her. After all the fuss she'd made, they wouldn't believe her if she told them she really no longer felt anything more than friendship for him. 'Now, do you two want to take a break? Go spend some time with Ned. I'll be okay by myself here for a while.'

Putting the flowers down at the side of the van—they were so big there was no room for them inside—Tab glanced over again to where she'd come from to see that security were now there trying to get the fan situation under control. It wasn't only teenage girls that flocked to Ryder, but younger kids and older women too, all waving various things and items of clothing in his face, begging him to sign them. Alongside security, Adeline had appeared from nowhere, and looked to be barking orders among the chaos, clearly loving her close proximity to the star.

Tab, on the other hand, was grateful for a few moments' reprieve.

Chapter Thirty-three

Ferg hadn't wanted to come to the show and now he wished he'd gone to see his sister as he'd contemplated—with cricket cancelled due to the festivities he could have left yesterday afternoon and spent the whole weekend with her. Instead, he'd let Joanne convince him that the kids would be disappointed if he didn't at least make an appearance.

Well, he'd made his appearance—he'd even taken photos of each of his students in front of their work—and now he could make his escape. If only he'd managed to do so before running into Tabitha. Being so close to her had been torture. He'd had to shove his hands in his pockets to stop himself reaching out and touching her to check she was real, to remember what she felt like. If Ned hadn't been with her, he might have succumbed to the urge and he could only imagine how embarrassing that would have been. Instead they'd engaged in painful and awkward conversation and it was clear she didn't want to be in his presence any longer than necessary.

Or maybe it was simply that she'd wanted to be in somebody else's.

If he'd had any doubt she'd moved on, it evaporated when he finally left the hall to see her only a short distance away with the guy that was currently the name on everyone's lips. Seeing her standing close to Ryder O'Connell, all flush-cheeked and smiling as she held a massive bunch of flowers that were clearly a gift from the man himself, had felt like a knife to the heart and now he wanted to be anywhere but here.

He was halfway to the carpark when someone shouted his name.

'Where do you think you're going, Mr McWilliams?'

Ferg slowed his steps, closing his eyes as he contemplated pretending not to hear. In the end, common courtesy got the better of him and he turned to see his colleague Haylee and her husband. There was a flock of kids trailing behind her, but she didn't seem to mind.

'Hey Haylee, Brad,' Ferg said, hoping he'd got the bloke's name right.

Brad offered his hand as Haylee replied, 'Hello yourself. You're not leaving, are you? The day's barely kicked off. Most of the fun happens after dark, doesn't it, kids?'

Her fan club loudly chorused their agreement.

'You have to stay for the fireworks, Mr McDuck,' said a boy he thought belonged to the massive Wellington clan.

'Um.' He glanced longingly towards the makeshift car park that was now so jam-packed he wasn't even sure he'd be able to find his wagon, never mind escape in it.

'I've been trying to get to the hall to see all the kids' work,' Haylee said, 'but I keep getting stopped by someone or tempted by delicious smells.' She lifted an open paper bag and offered it to him. 'Caramelised cashews. Made locally. You won't get better anywhere else, I promise.'

He took a couple to appease her; teachers were always bossy—especially those who taught the early years as she did—and bad at taking no for an answer.

'Have you had lunch yet?' she asked and Ferg made the mistake of shaking his head. Call him a chicken, but all the food offerings were near Tabitha's van and he'd steered clear on purpose.

'Come with us,' Brad said thumping him on the back, 'and we'll get a meat pie or something. Everyone's distracted by Ryder O'Connell at the moment, so the food vans are practically deserted.'

'Okay,' he found himself saying. He was hungry, so he'd have a bite to eat with Haylee and Brad and then leave.

An hour later as he sat on hay bales alongside Brad and Haylee watching a hilarious cow-milking competition, he saw his chances of escape rapidly diminishing. It was clear these two had taken him under their wings, deciding it was their responsibility to educate him in the ways of a country ag show, and to his surprise, he found himself enjoying their company and the whole experience much more than he'd imagined possible.

A few months ago, he'd have laughed if someone told him he'd have liked looking at vintage farm machinery or strolling through a manure-smelling shed admiring cattle, but the town of Walsh had snuck under his skin and this show was a representation of everything it stood for. He loved the community spirit and the pride the locals had in their land, their livestock and their industry. He'd even grown accustomed to the fact that everyone seemed to know everything about everyone else.

If things had been different with Tabitha, he'd have considered putting down roots here, but no way that would ever be possible now. Even if he hadn't accepted the job up north, even if Carline wasn't coming back to school and there was a job going here,

Ferg couldn't stay after what had gone down between himself and Tabitha. It would be too painful.

Although maybe she wouldn't stay herself. Maybe Ryder planned to lure her to the big smoke. Ferg couldn't rid his head of the image of them embracing, and the size of those flowers spoke volumes about Ryder's intentions.

Ferg only hoped he'd treat Tab right and take care of her and her baby. As long as she was happy in her life, he would somehow manage to get on with his.

In addition to the milking contest and the vintage farm machinery, Brad and Haylee made it their mission to ensure he experienced everything the Walsh show had to offer. Whip-cracking and wood-chopping, dog trials, even sheaf-tossing—there was not a moment to get bored, and that was even without venturing into the CWA pavilion where apparently competition was rife over who'd made the best pavlovas, lamingtons and scones. The showgrounds were packed, but although Ferg ran into many people he knew, he didn't get even a glimpse of Tabitha again.

He guessed she was busy in the ice-cream van, or worse, somewhere with Ryder. He didn't know what he'd do if he saw her again—the previous time was awkward and painful enough—but, a sucker for punishment, he couldn't help looking out for her.

When the sun started to fade, he once again decided it was time to go, but this time it was kids in his class lingering nearby who objected.

Lisl gave him a stern look. 'You can't go *now*!'

'The fireworks are the best bit!' agreed Milly.

'Why don't we grab a beer?' Brad suggested, grinning at the girls.

'Just the one,' Ferg relented. That way as soon as the last firecracker exploded colour into the night sky, he could be out of there. No way was he hanging around to hear Ryder O'Connell sing—he now had an even greater aversion to country music than he did before.

Not wanting to lose their prime position on the edge of the oval, Brad said he'd go get the drinks and left Ferg and Haylee to keep his seat warm. He returned ten minutes later with two bottles of beer.

'You're not having one?' Ferg looked at Haylee.

She blushed and leaned in close so that only he could hear her say, 'We've just found out we're having a baby.'

'Wow. Congrats,' he said and they both beamed ridiculously as Brad put his arm around Haylee and kissed her cheek.

As the first firework shot up into the sky, Ferg couldn't help feeling a twinge—okay it was more like a painful spasm—at the thought that Haylee and Brad were about to have what he'd, albeit briefly, fantasised about having with Tabitha. He took a long sip of his beer and tried to focus on the sparkles and bursts of colour painting patterns in the darkness above. All around him, kids shrieked with glee and in the distance he heard dogs barking. In another reality it could have been the perfect ending to the perfect day, except there was one vital component missing.

He wanted to be experiencing all this with Tabitha.

As the last rocket soared upwards and shattered into a million tiny red and blue lights, Ferg stood. He thanked Haylee and Brad for hanging out with him and then made a mad dash through the crowd in the direction of the cars.

He'd almost made his escape when someone grabbed his arm. 'Fergus!'

'Joanne. Hi.' He halted in his tracks as she eased her grip.

'You made it. Can't believe I haven't run into you yet today. Have you had fun?'

'Ah huh.' He nodded, not wanting to be rude but not wanting to linger either.

She turned to the woman beside her who was wearing a beanie on her head despite the warm evening air. 'I don't think you two have met yet. Carline, this is Fergus McWilliams, the wonderful young man who has been taking care of my class.'

Carline gripped his hand in something that was halfway between a handshake and an embrace.

'It's so wonderful to meet you,' she said, as another woman stood up on the stage and her voice boomed out of the microphone.

He tried to focus on what Carline was saying, not on the cheers that were erupting around him for Ryder O'Connell, and his head started to throb with the struggle.

'I was so worried about having to desert my little school, but everyone's had nothing but praise for you. I'm so sorry I haven't been in to visit yet, but my doctors warned me to stay away due to the risk of germs. Still, I want to say thank you. Knowing her class was in your good hands has meant Joanne has been able to take on my role and focus on that. And that has left me able to focus on getting better.'

Finally, Fergus managed to get a word in. 'It's lovely to meet you too, Carline, and I'm glad you're able to come back next year. I've really enjoyed my time in Walsh. It's a wonderful school and a great community.'

She opened her mouth but her reply was lost as a fancy guitar riff filled the air.

Both Joanne and Carline forgot him as their heads snapped towards the stage where Ryder was now leaning into the microphone as if he were about to give it mouth to mouth.

'I'm stoked to be back here in Walsh, a town that will always hold a large part of my heart, probably because it's where a very special girl lives.'

Good God. Fergus felt sick. Every word the guy said made him want to punch him in the mouth, and he really wasn't a violent person.

'No other woman has ever come close to this one, and so tonight, I wanted to kick-start this very special show by asking her to come up here with me and sing one of our old songs together. Tabitha Cooper-Jones,' called Ryder, glancing off to the side of the stage, 'will you join me for old times' sake?'

The crowd gasped and Joanne grabbed hold of his arm as if to steady herself, as Tab stepped out onto the makeshift stage in a cute knee-length blue dress. It was the first one he'd ever seen her wear and the first time her bump had been clearly visible when she wasn't naked. He'd lust after her if she were wearing a garbage bag, but up there in front of the lights, she simply glowed as she crossed the stage and kissed Ryder.

Although she only grazed her lips against his cheek, Ferg's chest burned as he wished he could un-see it. What the hell was he still doing here? This was torture!

As Ryder's band kicked into gear, Tab picked up a microphone and smiled out at the crowd. Seconds later, her voice came through the speakers and everyone around Ferg was mesmerised. What she sang was definitely a love song—something about love's young dream and the sky being the limit—and when Ryder's voice joined hers and he gazed not at the crowd but at Tabitha, Fergus knew he had to get out of there.

He started again towards the car park and this time, nothing was going to get in his way of leaving. Not the kids in his class, not friendly locals, not even his boss. The way he was feeling right now, he wanted to drive out of town and never come back.

It wasn't long before the music grew quieter behind him. He was inhaling deeply, trying to regulate his breathing, when he rounded the corner of a building and heard a deep voice. It sounded somewhat sinister, and instinctively he slowed his steps as a shadow appeared not too far ahead.

Fergus didn't know what it was that made him eavesdrop, but something about this guy being out here when everyone else was back with the music made him uneasy. Was he planning on breaking into some of the cars? And then he heard the man mention Tabitha.

'Relax, she doesn't suspect a thing,' he said. 'This was a rock-solid plan of yours. Granted, the baby thing threw a bit of a spanner in the works, but as Ryder said, maybe this'll work out even better than we originally planned. He'll look like a saint hooking up with his one-armed ex anyway, but a one-armed ex who's pregnant with someone else's child? We couldn't have planned things better ourselves—his reputation will be more than restored. But listen, I've got to get back there. I think they've started playing and I want to take some photos while the disabled chick is on stage with him.'

The disabled chick?

Ferg's fingers curled into fists, his nails digging into his palm. How dare this conceited jerk speak about Tabitha like that.

'Look, I've got to go, but I'll be sure to send through some photos you can leak to the press later. People will be uploading all over Instagram and Twitter anyway, but …'

The man turned around and met Fergus's eye. A scowl filled his face as Ferg recognised him as the man who'd been with Ryder O'Connell earlier that day. He had to hold himself back from grabbing him and pummelling him to the ground. Tonight he'd had more violent thoughts in half an hour than he'd had in his whole life, but violence wouldn't solve anything. If he beat this guy to a pulp, he'd be the one in the wrong and likely nobody—least of all Tabitha—would listen to him when he tried to tell them what he'd heard, the words that would reveal Ryder as the scum he really was.

So instead he turned and strode back towards the music.

The last thing he wanted to do was hurt Tab, but neither could he walk away knowing that Ryder was only pretending to care about her. How long would the bastard keep up the facade? Was he planning on following it through until the baby was born? How long after that? What lengths exactly would he go to for his reputation and his career?

Ferg's heart pounded and heat flushed through his body at the thought of Tab and her baby being a pawn in his game. If the man could be so selfish and conniving, who knew how he would treat the poor baby when Tabitha wasn't around.

Tab might not thank him for what he was about to do, but at least he wouldn't have the guilt on his conscience. She may not even believe him, but if he planted seeds of doubt, she'd at least be aware and on the look-out. It was the least he could do.

Chapter Thirty-four

As the crowd in front of her gave a standing ovation, Tab's eyes filled with tears. She was shaking but she'd done it. She'd sung with Ryder one last time and proved to herself she still had it in her.

'Isn't she phenomenal, ladies and gents?' Ryder said as he closed the distance between them and pulled her to his side. 'Let's give Tabby another round of applause, and who knows, if we're lucky, maybe I'll even be able to convince her to do an encore later.'

He kissed her on the cheek and whispered that he'd see her soon.

High on the thrill of performance, Tab felt a little drunk as she walked off the stage. She wasn't surprised to see a little group waiting for her as she descended the stairs, but she almost tripped when she saw Fergus among them.

'Aunty Tab, you were so good!' Ned shrieked as he threw his arms around her waist.

Lawson, Meg, even Adeline, joined him in congratulations, but she barely registered any of them.

'What are you doing here?' she spat at Fergus. He'd already ruined show day for her, but singing had lifted her spirits and she wanted to hold onto the buzz a little longer.

'I really need to talk to you,' he said almost apologetically as Ryder's pesky manager grabbed hold of his arm.

'I'll get rid of him for you, Tabitha,' Shaun exclaimed, glancing around. 'Security?! We need your assistance over here.'

'Let him go,' Tab ordered. It wasn't that she was overjoyed by his presence but she could fight her own battles. She glared at Fergus as Shaun loosened his grip. 'Well? Out with it. What do you need to say?'

Fergus glanced around them, meeting Lawson's furious eyes, before he looked back to her. 'I think it would be better if I say this in private.'

Tab sighed. If it were just Lawson and Meg here, she'd have told him that anything he wanted to say he could say in front of them, but Adeline and Shaun's presence had her relenting. She didn't like or trust either of them.

'Fine. Come to my van. You've got two minutes.'

'Thank you,' Fergus breathed.

Her heart suddenly racing for entirely different reasons, Tab marched towards her van with Ferg striding beside her. She switched on the light as she let them inside and then pulled the door shut behind them. Ryder's voice faded and the air felt stifling as she realised how close she was to Fergus again. 'This better be good.'

'Good's not exactly the word I'd use,' he said, anguish squeezing his features. The miniscule hope she'd been harbouring that he was here to declare his love evaporated. 'I'm really sorry to be the bearer of bad news but I couldn't live with myself if I didn't say something.'

Tab threw her hand up in the air. 'Say something about *what*, Fergus? Stop beating around the bush.'

He cleared his throat. 'I just heard one of Ryder's blokes on the phone to some PR person or something. He was talking about you. I know how much Ryder means to you and I get why you're back together with him, but he's using you. He's using you and the baby as some kind of publicity stunt to try and restore his reputation.'

'What?' Tab took a step back trying to register what he was trying to say. If it were true, it would be a kick in the guts, but also the least of her concerns right now. 'Why on earth would you think I was back together with Ryder?'

'I saw you. I saw you hugging him at your place last Sunday afternoon.'

Tab could barely remember last Sunday afternoon, let alone hugging Ryder or seeing Fergus there.

'And then there's the flowers he gave you today, the way you guys looked at each other on the stage. I'm not an idiot, Tabitha.'

'Actually, I think you're the biggest idiot I've ever met. Because Ryder and I are not together and nothing he could say could ever change that, because as I told you last week, I'm in love with *you*. Lord knows I wish I wasn't, but it is what it is.'

Fergus blinked. 'You and Ryder? You're not together?'

She shook her head. 'No. I'm not that shallow. I'm offended that you think I could just switch my affections from one guy to the next, but I also wonder why you even care? You made it clear you don't want anything to do with me and my baby, so what's it to you if Ryder is trying to use me?'

'I care because I'm in love with you!'

The temperature around them suddenly dropped. 'What did you say?'

'I love you. I should have told you earlier but I was terrified. I still am.' He glanced down at her stomach and she placed a hand on it protectively. 'I came to Walsh fresh out of a relationship that I thought was going to last forever. I was hurting and I felt like a fool. I certainly didn't plan on putting my heart on the line again, but then I met you.'

'Except I'm pregnant and you don't want to father another man's child!'

'It's not that I don't want to ...' He paused a moment and she saw his Adam's apple slowly move up and down. 'It's that I'm terrified of stuffing it up. Growing up, I was under the care of so many adults I couldn't keep track, and barely any of them treated me or Eider like we meant anything to them. Parenting is hard, and I saw first-hand how hard, how impossible it was for some people to love a child that isn't their own flesh and blood. I—'

Tab cut him off. 'Oh my God! You're scared you wouldn't be able to love a baby that wasn't yours? *That's* why you pushed me away?'

He nodded. 'Didn't I say that?'

'You said you didn't want another man's baby, but you didn't tell me *why*!'

Yet now it seemed obvious. She was such an idiot. Blinded by her own pain, she'd taken his words at face value, hadn't once questioned if there was something deeper at play. And she should have, because she'd heard about his childhood, knew how crap it had been for him. She shouldn't have given up so easily.

Yet at the same time, she felt an overwhelming frustration. She'd seen him with the kids in the cricket team, how tenderly he spoke to them, how invested he was in building their confidence. How could he ever doubt his ability to love? And, in trying to protect her baby, he'd actually already proven how much he cared.

'I'm sorry,' he said, pushing a hand through his hair. 'I do want you. I want you and the baby, but I'm scared. I don't want to stuff it up.'

'You think I do? I'm terrified of becoming a mum—I think living in constant fear is part of parenting, part of loving someone. But that doesn't mean I don't want to try. I'll make mistakes. You'll make mistakes. But I can't think of any person I'd rather make them with.'

'Really?' He blinked. 'I haven't stuffed it up?'

'I'll never pretend to understand what you went through,' she said, reaching out and taking hold of his hand, 'but you can't possibly compare yourself to some of your less than ideal foster parents. Every day you go to work, you show your love for loads of children who aren't your own, and I have faith that you would love my baby even more than you love them.'

'I'm pretty sure I already do,' he said, placing his other hand on her belly. It fluttered beneath his touch. 'And I think you and my sister would get along well, because she said almost exactly the same thing. She told me how much of a cowardly idiot I am and made me see sense. I was coming to explain everything to you and to beg you to give me another chance, when I heard you singing with Ryder and then hugging him.'

Tears welled in her eyes. That hug had lasted less than ten seconds and Sod's law, those were the ten seconds he'd witnessed.

'That was a hug between friends,' she told him, blinking back the rush of tears that came with the realisation of what was actually happening here.

He loved her.

Fergus McWilliams, better known as Mr McDuck, loved her as much as she loved him. And, lord knew, that was a lot.

She lifted his hand to her lips and was about to kiss it when Shaun pounded on the door.

'Tabitha? Are you in there? We really need you back at the stage. I've got a journalist who wants to talk to you and ...'

Tab shoved open the door before he could finish his sentence, almost knocking him over in the process. She didn't apologise.

'How dare you and Ryder try and use me as a pawn in some publicity stunt.'

'I don't know what you're talking about,' Shaun replied, but the two seconds hesitation before he did called him out as a liar. And she would believe Fergus over him any day.

'Whatever.' She poked him in his chest. 'If you want me to talk to a journalist, I will. I think they'll be very interested to hear why exactly Ryder accepted this country gig so quickly. Don't you?'

This time Shaun opened his mouth but shut it again quickly.

'Now, if you don't mind,' Tabitha said, 'I'm a little bit busy right now. I trust you'll say goodbye—no, actually, good *riddance* to Ryder for me. And you can also tell him if he really wants to clean up his image, maybe he should try to clean up his act. Giving up the grog would be a good start.'

And with that, Tabitha stepped back up into the van and closed the door behind her.

Ferg stood there with a startled expression on his face. 'Wow. You're …'

'Yeah, yeah.' She waved her arm at him. 'Amazing, I know, people tell me that all the time, but right now, the only person I'm interested in is you. And by the way, your sister is right. You are a stupid idiot—for ever doubting yourself and *definitely* for doubting me. But you're *my* stupid idiot, which means I'm going to let you make it up to me for the rest of our lives.'

'Good.' Ferg grinned, a tear slipping down his cheek. 'Because there's nothing else I want more.'

And then he pulled her to him and kissed her like he never planned on doing anything else ever again, and she was just fine with that.

Epilogue

'Let's go in here!'

'What?' Meg halted in her tracks and stared at Tab like she was crazy as she gestured to a boutique that specialised in bridal fashion.

Tab couldn't help laughing at the expression on her sister-in-law's face. So she was thirty-seven weeks pregnant and would give their pregnant heifers a run for their money in terms of size. *So what?* She was also engaged to the most wonderful man on the planet and it seemed a missed opportunity to walk past such a shop and not at least take a look.

'I want to look at wedding dresses. Get a feel for the kind of gown I might like.'

Fergus had proposed on New Year's Eve and she'd said yes almost before he'd finished the question. But the last few months had been crazy busy—getting ready for the baby, making sure the tea rooms had enough staff to keep it going while she was on maternity leave, helping Ferg move up to Newman and then maintaining their long-distance relationship—that she hadn't had time to start planning any aspect of their wedding.

Now with a few weeks until the birth, she and Meg were in Perth for a couple of nights in a fancy hotel—a present from Ferg—for a last hurrah girls' shopping trip and this felt like the perfect opportunity to start getting organised for their big day.

When Meg still looked dubious, Tab added, 'They sell bridesmaid's dresses too, so we can look for you as well.'

Meg looked even more horrified as she stroked her own blossoming bump. 'But you guys aren't getting married until after I've popped. Are you?'

Tab shrugged; she liked to tease when she could. 'That was the plan but … who knows, maybe I'll just get it out of the way in a couple of weeks when Fergus comes down for the birth. I'm sick of waiting. I miss that guy and I want his ring on my finger asap.'

'You're crazy, you know that?' Meg said, but she pulled open the door of the bridal shop nevertheless.

They were greeted with a smile by a silver-haired woman as they stepped inside and for once the woman's gaze didn't go first to Tabitha's little arm, but rather to both their bellies. Meg was so petite that she looked a lot more pregnant than twenty weeks. 'Good morning ladies, the maternity shop is two doors along.'

Meg raised her eyebrows and gave Tab an I-told-you-so look.

Tab ignored her and grinned back at the sales lady. 'Thanks. We've got enough maternity clothes, but we are in the market for a wedding gown and a bridesmaid dress.'

'Oh.' The woman's eyes widened. 'In that case, which one of you is the bride?'

Tab pointed to herself. 'That'd be me.'

The woman looked as if she might faint. Maybe Tab had taken this prank a little too far. The last thing she wanted to be doing today was first aid.

'It's alright,' she said. 'The wedding isn't until December but we were passing by and I just thought I'd have a bit of a browse. If that's okay with you.'

'Yes, of course.' The woman's shoulders sagged in obvious relief, then she grinned, introduced herself as 'Melody' and couldn't have been more enthusiastic or helpful. She got Tab and Meg each a glass of orange juice in a champagne flute and settled them on a plush velvet couch before grilling Tabitha about her style and fashion preferences. When Tab admitted that dressing up wasn't usually her thing, Melody took things into her own hands and started bringing in various different gowns to ooh and ahh over.

Although Tab couldn't try any of them on, Melody held them up against her as she stood in front of a mirror, which gave her quite a good idea. She'd definitely be coming back here when she'd lost some baby fat and was ready to make a purchase. Melody was warm and chatty and as she showed them dress after dress, she also asked a zillion questions and practically learned both their life stories.

'So the baby isn't your fiancé's and he's currently living twelve hours away? Wow. I hear some interesting stuff here, but yours is up there. How long will you be apart?'

'Not much longer,' Tab replied, smiling as she caressed her bump. 'He's coming down for the birth, and then I'm going back up to Newman with him and staying there until he finishes his contract at the end of the year. We'll head back to my place in Rose Hill after that and hopefully he'll find a teaching position within—'

She was about to say 'driving distance' but the words died on her tongue as she felt a gush of water between her legs. *Oh no!*

'What is it?' Meg and Melody said in unison as Tab's hand rushed to her chest.

She'd either wet herself or her waters had broken, neither of which she wanted to admit when she was sitting on this very comfy but expensive-looking sofa. Then again, the little patch of water on her maternity trousers probably said it all. 'I think my waters have broken.'

'Oh my God!' Meg leapt to her feet faster than a pregnant woman should.

'I'm so sorry,' Tab gushed as she too tried to struggle to her feet.

'Don't be silly.' Melody rushed forward to help her into a standing position.

'We need to get to a hospital,' Meg shrieked. 'I'll go get the car.'

'There's no rush. I haven't had any contractions yet. I'm sure we can make it back home.'

'Don't be ridiculous,' Meg snapped, already digging the keys out of her bag. 'I'll be right back and the only place I'm taking you is the hospital.'

'Your friend's right, dear,' Melody said, as Meg rushed out the store. 'Trust me, I had my third child on the back seat of a taxi and a car is no place to have a baby.'

'But …' Tears rushed to Tab's eyes. This was not how it was supposed to happen. She was supposed to have their baby in the birthing suite in Bunbury with the midwife she'd picked herself and, most importantly, Fergus by her side. Now it looked like she might have to have it in Perth, without her midwife or Fergus.

★ ★ ★

'You're fully dilated and we're ready to start pushing,' said a lovely man called Dr Reeves eight hours later.

Tab shook her head furiously. 'No. I need Fergus. I can't do this without him. Can you delay things until tomorrow?'

Dr Reeves squeezed her hand. 'I'm sorry, Tabitha, but this baby is coming very soon and there's nothing you or I can do to stop it. You can do this.'

'But I don't want to.' She sobbed. 'Not without Fergus. Sorry, Meg, no offence, you know I love you but …' Another contraction stole the end of her sentence.

'How about we call him?' Meg said when the contraction had ended.

'Yes.' Tab nodded. 'If he can't be here, maybe he can be on speaker. Or even FaceTime.' Damn, she wanted to see his face.

As another contraction came fast and hard, Meg whipped her phone out of her handbag and called him. She stepped away and Tab couldn't hear exactly what she was saying. 'Put him on!'

Meg turned back and held the phone close to Tab. 'Really sorry, but we can't get FaceTime to work. He's on speaker instead.'

And then his voice filled the air. 'Hello, angel,' he said. 'I hear you're doing a great job.'

'It hurts. I'm scared.' Tab sniffed. 'I wish you were here'

'I know you do, sweetheart. I wish I was too. But you can do this. You're *amazing*. And I will get there as soon as I possibly can. You're in the best place you can be.'

She stared at the phone, tears pouring down her face as another contraction took hold. 'I love you,' she managed.

'I love you too,' he said, but weirdly, she heard it in the room as well as in her ear. Despite the pain, her head snapped to the door and the phone fell from her grasp as she registered Ferg striding towards her.

'Oh my God.' *Was this a dream?* She looked from him to Meg and back again. 'How?'

'I called him when I left the bridal shop to get the car,' Meg admitted.

'And luckily the next plane was in an hour,' he finished. 'It was touch and go and I may have broken a few road rules getting to the airport, but … here I am.'

'Yes, here you are.' Tab pressed a kiss against his mouth as he leaned in to hug her. The pain didn't matter anymore. He was here and they were about to have a baby.

The next twenty minutes was a blur of pain and pressure and then, with Fergus holding Tab's hand and pressing an icy-cold cloth against her forehead, she gave one massive push and seconds later the most amazing sound she'd ever heard pierced the air.

'It's a girl,' Dr Reeves pronounced. 'A beautiful, healthy baby girl.'

'Oh my goodness. A girl.' Tab looked at Ferg but his eyes were filled with tears and he was too choked up to speak as the doctor placed their squirming, red, slimy baby on her bare chest. It was the most beautiful thing she'd ever seen.

'Does she have a name?' asked Dr Reeves after a few long moments.

'Yes.' Tab and Ferg exchanged a look.

'Her name is Daphne,' Fergus announced.

'After my mum,' Tab said with both a sniff and a smile. 'She'd have been such a wonderful granny.'

Meg beamed as she reached out and squeezed Tab's shoulder. 'I love it.' She snapped a quick photo then made her excuses, promising to be back later in the evening with Lawson and Ned.

Under the direction of the doctor, a nervous Fergus cut the cord, and then although there were still medical professionals flitting around, they all faded into the background as Tab and Fergus marvelled at Daphne. Nine months ago, she'd gone into this pregnancy alone and never in her wildest thoughts had she imagined it would turn out like this.

Sometimes the things you least expected turned out to be the most wonderful, and Tabitha couldn't be happier with her little family.

Acknowledgements

Many people helped me (in both small and big ways) as I wrote *Something To Talk About* and I want to offer them all the biggest thanks!

First, to my friend and ex-boss Lorreen Greeuw, who was the inspiration for Tabitha. From the moment I met Lorry many years ago, I both adored and admired her. Thanks for being such an awesome, amazing person and also for giving me a sensitivity read for this book. I'm sure Lorry's and Tabitha's experiences of being an amputee will not be exactly the same as all amputees but I just hope that I have written this story in a manner sensitive to all.

Next, to another friend, farmer and teacher Peta Sattler, who I met sitting on the breastfeeding couch at playgroup over fifteen years ago and who also happened to beta read my very first rural romance, *Jilted*, before I submitted it to publishers. Not only has she been a big support to all my books in the years since, but at the launch of *Talk of the Town* she told me it was time I wrote a book about a teacher coming to a rural town. There's a bit of a running joke in the small towns that teachers and nurses come to town for a short contract but end up staying because they fall in love with a farmer. Thanks for the idea, Peta, I hope you like what I've done with Fergus!

As always massive thanks must go to my fabulous publisher, Sue Brockhoff, who always goes above and beyond to support my work and help me make the book the best I can. And also to Sue's wonderful team: Annabel Blay, Jo Mackay, Johanna Baker, Adam Van Rooijen, Natika Palka and Sarana Behan.

To the HarperCollins design team who continue to create stunning covers for me, I think you all must actually be fairies and thanks for letting me judge the chocolate contest last time I was in the office. I'm available whenever you need such important decisions to be made again.

I write the book, but Dianne Blacklock helps me make it sparkle. Thank you so much for your wisdom on characters and, as usual, for helping me cut all my waffle. I hope we get to work together on many more books together. And also thank you to proofreader Julie Wicks for your eagle eye.

Big thanks to my agent, Helen Breitwieser. Thanks for being such a great sounding board and champion!

And to my close writing friends, who have become family – Bec, Anthea, Emily, Amanda, Lisa, Sally, Tess, Alissa, Leah, Bree, Cathryn, Susan, Fee and Fiona. What would I do without you all? Thanks for putting up with all my anxiety and paranoia – at least you all understand, cos basically you're all the same!

To my 'normal' friends – sorry for forgetting birthdays, not sending Christmas cards and begging you all to come up with ideas for future books. I'm surprised you're still hanging around, but I appreciate you all for supporting my career by buying my books and spruiking them to your other 'normal' friends!

To the awesome readers of my stories – you are my heroes. Thank you for buying my books, posting them on social media, writing reviews and sending me such lovely messages. You guys keep me glued to the keyboard when I really want to run away and join a circus.

Last, but never least, to my family – Mum, Craig and the boys – for putting up with easy dinners, distracted conversations, and so much more, especially when I'm on a deadline. You guys are the best!! xx

Love reading and talking about books? In addition to following Rachael Johns on Facebook and Instagram, you're invited to join her online book club. Simply search 'Rachael Johns Online Book Club' on Facebook and come join in the fun!

Other books by

RACHAEL
JOHNS

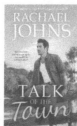 

  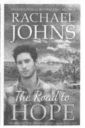

rachaeljohns.com

Don't miss these books by
Rachael
Johns

rachaeljohns.com